A Refuge *at* Highland Hall

Center Point
Large Print

Also by Carrie Turansky and available from
Center Point Large Print:

The Daughter of Highland Hall
The Governess of Highland Hall

This Large Print Book carries the
Seal of Approval of N.A.V.H.

EDWARDIAN BRIDES • BOOK THREE

A REFUGE *at* HIGHLAND HALL

Carrie Turansky

CENTER POINT LARGE PRINT
THORNDIKE, MAINE

This Center Point Large Print edition is published in the year 2015 by arrangement with Multnomah Books, an imprint of the Crown Publishing Group, a division of Penguin Random House LLC, New York.

All Scripture quotations are taken from the King James Version.

The characters and events in this book are fictional, and any resemblance to actual persons or events is coincidental.

The text of this Large Print edition is unabridged. In other aspects, this book may vary from the original edition. Printed in the United States of America on permanent paper. Set in 16-point Times New Roman type.

ISBN: 978-1-62899-794-1

Library of Congress Cataloging-in-Publication Data
Turansky, Carrie.
A refuge at Highland Hall / Carrie Turansky. —
    Center Point Large Print edition.
      pages cm
    ISBN 978-1-62899-794-1
    1. Large type books. I. Title.
PS3620.U7457R44 2015b
813′.6—dc23
                                          2015032951

This book is dedicated to my dear friend
and fellow author Cathy Gohlke,
who has challenged and encouraged me
on my writing journey,
always shown me Christ-like love,
and been a powerful example
of placing her faith and hope in God.

Cast of Characters

Sir William Ramsey—master and baronet of Highland Hall; husband of Julia; father of Andrew and Millicent (Millie); brother of Sarah (Ramsey) Dalton

Julia (Foster) Ramsey—wife of Sir William and former governess at Highland Hall; stepmother to Andrew and Millie

Katherine (Kate Ramsey) Foster—cousin of William; wife of Jonathan Foster; sister of Penny; born and raised at Highland

Dr. Jonathan (Jon) Foster—husband of Kate; brother of Julia; doctor at St. George's Hospital, London

Penelope (Penny) Rose Ramsey—cousin of William; sister of Kate; born and raised at Highland

Alexander (Alex) Goodwin—childhood friend of Jonathan and Julia; Englishman born in India; RNAS pilot

Andrew Ramsey—son of William and future heir of Highland Hall; fourteen years old

Millicent (Millie) Ramsey—daughter of William; ten years old

Sarah (Ramsey) Dalton—sister of William; wife of Clark

Agatha Dalton—Clark's aunt

Clark Dalton—head gardener at Highland; husband of Sarah

Mrs. Miranda Dalton—housekeeper at Highland; Clark Dalton's mother; grandmother of Abigail

Abigail Murray—Mrs. Dalton's granddaughter; Clark's niece; ten years old

Dr. Phillip Foster—husband of Mary; father of Jon and Julia; former missionary to India; Ramsey family physician

Mrs. Mary Foster—wife of Phillip; mother of Jon and Julia; former missionary to India

Lydia Chambers—lady's maid to Kate and Penny; sister of Helen; aunt of Emily

Helen Chambers—maid; sister of Lydia; mother of Emily

Mrs. Hester Murdock—cook from London who joins Highland staff

Mr. George Lawrence—butler at Highland; head of the male staff

Patrick Lambert—footman at Highland

Chef Lagarde—head chef at Highland; in charge of kitchen staff

Ann Norton—nursery maid at Highland

Gordon McTavish—steward at Highland

Donald Miller—age fifteen; boy taken in by Kate and Jon Foster

Jack Hartman—age fourteen; boy taken in by the Fosters; brother of Rose and Susan

Tom Perkins—age twelve; boy taken in by the Fosters

Lucy Wallingford—age fifteen; girl taken in by the Fosters

Edna Snook—age eleven; girl taken in by the Fosters

Rose Hartman—age ten; girl taken in by the Fosters; sister to Jack and Susan

Susan Hartman—age six; girl taken in by the Fosters; sister to Rose and Jack

Irene Jotham—age four; girl taken in by the Fosters

Emily Chambers—age three; Helen's daughter

Winifred Tremont—mother of Alex and Lindy; wife of Roger

Roger Tremont—stepfather of Alex and Lindy; husband of Winifred

Lindy Goodwin—sister of Alex

Marius Ritter—born in Germany; lived in London; prisoner in the internment camp; farm laborer

Siegfried Schultz—born in Germany; lived in London; prisoner in the internment camp; farm laborer

Randal Longmore—wing commander of Alex's squadron

George Meddis—RNAS mechanic

Even the youths shall faint and be weary, and the young men shall utterly fall: But they that wait upon the LORD shall renew their strength; they shall mount up with wings as eagles; they shall run, and not be weary; and they shall walk, and not faint.

—ISAIAH 40:30–31

One

April 1915

Waves of khaki-clad British soldiers flowed across the south lawn of the London Zoological Gardens, slowly making their way toward the chairs and benches surrounding the bandstand. Some men leaned on canes or hobbled on crutches. Others wore bandages or sported slings, testifying to the wounds they had received fighting for King and country.

Penelope Ramsey scanned their faces, searching for Theo Anderson, but her fleeting hope quickly faded. She suppressed a groan and turned away.

She must stop being ridiculous. Theo wasn't here. He was in France. And at this very moment, he was probably performing surgery to save the life of some poor wounded soldier fresh from the battlefield.

She shook her head. These wandering thoughts would never do. She was nineteen now, and it was time to put away childish, romantic daydreams—especially those involving Theo.

Last week he'd written to tell her he was engaged to a Frenchwoman who volunteered at the hospital where he was stationed in Rouen, France.

After she read his letter, she fled to her room and cried until her eyes were red and swollen and her pillow was a soggy mess. How could he fall in love with someone else? She'd always imagined their friendship would grow and move toward romance. Though he'd never made that promise, she'd held on to that hope ever since she first danced with him at her sister Kate's debutante ball almost three years ago.

Was there still a chance she would find true and lasting love, or was she a fool to cling to that cherished dream?

Penny lifted her gaze to the sea of soldiers once more. So many men were caught up in the fight. Thousands from her generation had already been lost. Heaven only knew how long this terrible war would last and how many more would perish.

"Penny, can you take this?" Kate Foster, Penny's sister, held out the large wooden tray filled with sandwiches.

"Of course." Penny tucked away her questions and accepted the tray from Kate. Her sister's face was too pale. "Why don't you sit down for a few minutes and rest?"

"It's almost four o'clock. The men will be expecting their tea." Kate's hand slid to her stomach, and she released a weary sigh. Morning sickness had plagued her for weeks. The poor dear could hardly eat anything more than toast and broth. No wonder she looked exhausted.

"Don't worry. We'll be ready on time." Penny glanced toward the volunteers gathered with them in the large tea tent. At least twenty women and girls scurried around the serving tables, setting out sandwiches, scones, and other baked goods for the men to enjoy. "There's plenty of help. You've done more than your share."

"All right." Kate lowered herself into the nearest chair and gently laid her hand over her rounded middle. She was only a little more than three months pregnant, but she looked much further along, causing them all to be curious and a bit concerned.

"Miss Penny is right." Lydia Chambers, Kate's lady's maid, bustled past with two pitchers of lemonade. "There's no need to wear yourself out. We'll take care of things."

"I hope we made enough food." Kate looked toward the serving tables and back at Penny.

"I'm sure we'll have plenty and Jon will be pleased."

Kate smiled at the mention of her husband. "Yes, I believe he will be."

Today's outing for convalescing soldiers had been Jon's idea. As a member of the staff in the military unit at St. George's Hospital, he tended to the men's battle wounds, but they needed more than medical attention to boost their morale.

Penny and Kate, along with several other volunteers, had pulled together today's program

15

and entertainment, collected donations to pay for the food, and then assembled a team of volunteers to serve.

They hoped to give the men a few hours to relax and enjoy themselves before they returned to the battlefield or traveled home to a very different life.

It was a good cause, and Penny was glad to take part, even if being with so many soldiers did remind her of Theo and make her heart ache a bit more.

She carried the tray across the tent and placed it with the others. Glancing down the serving table, she checked to see what else might be needed, but everything seemed ready for tea.

A strand of hair fluttered across her cheek. She brushed it away with a frustrated huff, then tucked it behind her ear. Her auburn curls were forever coming loose, no matter how many pins she and Lydia used to try to tame them.

She stepped out from under the tent and lifted her gaze to the clear blue sky. It was unusually warm for late April. A light breeze ruffled the scalloped edge of the tent's white canopy. The Union Jack flapped from the flagpole nearby, and red, white, and blue bunting swayed on the bandstand railing. Daffodils bobbed in the flower bed on the far side of the tent, their silver-sword leaves flickering in the breeze.

Across the lawn, the band struck up a lively

march. The soldiers responded with applause and a few loud whistles.

Penny's spirits lifted as she listened to the music. They might be at war, facing a terrible enemy, but a huge wave of patriotism had swept through the kingdom, pulling everyone together. Men of all ranks and occupations had signed up to join the fight. And women bravely stepped forward to carry on the men's duties and keep their homes and businesses running.

Penny felt that patriotic stirring as well. She had considered training to become a nurse or Red Cross worker, but with Jon working long hours at St. George's Hospital and Kate pregnant and trying to oversee things at home, coming to London to help her sister seemed the most practical idea.

So she'd packed her trunks, said good-bye to everyone at Highland Hall, and boarded the train for London, ready for a new adventure. Kate had been terribly relieved when Penny arrived, especially when she promised to stay and help as long as she was needed, even after the baby was born. As for it being an adventure . . . that was yet to be seen.

Music filled the air, and Penny hummed along as she strolled back and joined Kate.

"Well, there's my favorite girl." Kate's husband, Dr. Jonathan Foster, stepped into the tent and leaned down to kiss his wife's cheek. "How's everything coming along?"

Kate smiled up at him. "Very well, thanks to Penny and Lydia. But I'm afraid I haven't been much help."

"Nonsense. Just having you here brightens my day." Jon's eyes glowed as he laid his hand on his wife's shoulder.

A soldier with dark-brown hair stepped into the shady tent with Jon. He looked to be in his early twenties and wore a neatly pressed uniform. The sling around his neck cradled his left arm to his chest, but the injury didn't seem to slow him down too much. He glanced at Penny and sent her a smile.

Her cheeks warmed, and she focused on Jon again.

He motioned toward the soldier. "I'd like you to meet my friend, Lieutenant Alexander Goodwin. We met in India when we were boys. Alex, this is my wife, Katherine Foster."

Kate held out her hand. "Were your parents also missionaries in Kanakapura, Lieutenant Goodwin?"

Alex took her hand and bowed slightly. "No. My father was a chief engineer in charge of constructing the railway between Bangalore and Madgaon." Pride in his father's accomplishments warmed his voice. "He oversaw the building of seven lines through some very rough territory."

Kate nodded. "That sounds quite impressive. He must be a very skilled and diligent man."

"He was, and I hope to honor his memory by being as dedicated to my own pursuits."

Jon motioned toward Penny. "And this is my wife's sister, Miss Penelope Ramsey."

Penny extended her hand to Alex. He took it and bowed again. "Miss Ramsey. It's a pleasure to meet you." He looked at her with a confident smile and dark, glowing eyes that held a hint of amusement.

A delightful shiver traveled up her arm. "Thank you. I'm happy to make your acquaintance." *Good heavens.* Did she sound a bit breathless?

She slipped her hand away, trying to shake off her response. The charming officer was simply being courteous.

"It's wonderful to meet one of Jon's friends from India. You must call me Kate, and I'm sure my sister would be glad for you to call her Penny."

Alex glanced at Penny and lifted one eyebrow.

Penny nodded. "Of course."

"Very well." Alex grinned. "We shall consider ourselves friends on the best of terms, and you may call me Alex."

Jon chuckled. "You can imagine how happy I was to find Alex at St. George's. Not that I was glad he needed medical attention, but I was happy to see him after all these years."

Penny glanced at Alex's sling. "Were you injured on the battlefield in France?"

"No. I'm taking pilot training with the Royal

Naval Air Service. And I had a bit of an accident in one of the airplanes."

"Oh, dear, what happened?"

Kate flashed a warning glance at Penny.

Alex tipped his head and pressed his lips together. "I'm afraid the ground came up a bit too fast on my last landing practice."

Penny pulled in a sharp breath. "You crashed your airplane?"

His face turned ruddy. "Yes . . . that would be correct."

"I'm sorry." Penny swallowed, wishing she hadn't put him in a position of having to admit he was at fault for the mishap.

"Not as sorry as my flight instructor or the men who had to put the airplane back together." His mellow voice and a twitch at the corner of his mouth let her know he wasn't offended.

Relief coursed through her. "I hope your injury is not too serious."

"Just a broken collarbone and dislocated shoulder—nothing that will keep me down for long." He lifted his dark eyebrows and turned to Jon. "Right, Doctor?"

"You should be able to return to training in four or five weeks, as long as you follow my orders and get some rest until then."

Alex saluted Jon with his good arm, his teasing smile back in place. "Yes, sir."

Penny studied Alex, her admiration growing.

She'd never met a pilot before. "Flying sounds terribly exciting. How are airplanes used in the war effort?"

"We fly in cooperation with the Navy, providing defense for Britain and the area around the coast to prevent sea and air attack. Mainly observation and reconnaissance missions—spotting U-boats and enemy aircraft, that sort of thing. We also hope to keep the Zeppelins from doing any more harm."

A chill traveled down Penny's back. In the last few months, those monstrous German airships had dropped bombs on the eastern coast, killing innocent men, women, and children while they slept in their beds. Now blackouts were the rule across the land, and searchlights scanned the sky each night, but there seemed little they could do to protect themselves from the bombing raids. The Zeppelins hadn't reached London yet, but they were coming closer with each attack, putting everyone on edge.

Kate glanced at her watch, then looked up at Jon. "It's almost four. Would you and Alex like to help yourselves to some refreshments before the men come through? I imagine things will be very busy as soon as the concert ends and they announce it's time for tea."

"That sounds like an excellent idea." Jon turned to Alex. "Shall we?"

"I hoped coming with you would put me at an

advantage." Alex grinned and winked at Penny.

Her cheeks grew warm, and she returned his smile. Alex's sense of humor was a good balance to his confident personality.

Jon turned to Kate. "Will you ladies join us?"

"I suppose it would be all right. Our work is done." Kate rose and slipped her arm through Jon's, and they set off together. Penny stood, and she and Alex followed them across the tent.

Penny scanned the serving tables with a pleased smile, then placed a lemon square and a small berry tart on her plate.

Alex chose two sandwiches and added a tart to his plate. He leaned toward her with a smile. "I haven't seen treats like these in quite a while."

She met his gaze, taking in his handsome features. "We've been baking nonstop for two days."

He took a lemon scone. "It all looks delicious."

"Thank you." She picked up a cup of tea and followed Jon and Kate to a round table in the center of the tent. Alex sat down across from her.

While the band music continued in the background, the men discussed the latest news from France. Penny sipped her tea and listened to their conversation. Alex seemed well informed and showed an impressive ability to assess the situation and suggest what might happen next.

Kate looked over at Alex. "I hope you'll come to

dinner one evening before you return to your training."

His eyes lit up, but then he gave his head a slight shake. "That's very kind, but I wouldn't want to trouble you."

"It wouldn't be any trouble at all." She darted a glance at her husband, then looked back at Alex. "We'd love to have you join us, wouldn't we, Jon?"

"Yes, that's a splendid idea." Jon set his teacup on the table. "I'm sorry I didn't extend the invitation myself."

Penny leaned forward. "Oh, I do hope you'll come. I'd love to hear more about your life in India. It must have been thrilling to grow up in such an exotic place."

Kate sent her a surprised look.

Cheeks warming, Penny added, "I know the children would be delighted to meet a real pilot." She paused for a moment, thinking of the lively conversations they had around their busy dinner table. "I'm afraid the children will ask you so many questions you may not have time to eat your meal."

Alex turned to Kate. "How many children do you have?"

"Eight," Kate said with a slight smile.

Alex blinked, and his mouth dropped open. "Eight?"

"Yes, five girls and three boys. Their ages are

four to fifteen." Kate's eyes twinkled with a merry light as she reported those facts.

Penny ducked her head to hide her smile.

"Come on, now." Jon lifted his hand. "We shouldn't tease Alex with only half the story."

"And why not?" Kate's dimples danced. "He seems to enjoy it."

Alex laughed, and they all joined in. "I do like a good joke or a challenging riddle, but I must confess this one has me stumped. You two seem much too young to be the parents of eight children."

"The truth is, Kate and I are expecting our first child in early October, but for the last two years we've opened our home to children who have no family to care for them."

"So the children are orphans?"

Jon nodded. "Most are, but some were abandoned by their parents and ended up living on the street."

Alex's dark brows dipped, his shadowed gaze fixed on Jon.

"We're connected with a ministry in the East End called Daystar Clinic and Children's Center. I started working at the clinic during my last year of medical school. We took in our first child just a few months after we were married." Jon nodded toward a girl standing behind the serving table. "Lucy is fifteen now, and she's growing into a fine young woman. After Lucy, we took in three orphaned siblings we met through our work at the clinic. Jack is fourteen, Rose is ten, and Susan is six. The other children came over the next year, and now we have eight."

Alex sent Kate an appreciative look. "That sounds like quite an undertaking, managing eight children and running your household."

Kate laid her napkin on the table, her smile revealing her pleasure with his compliment. "I don't do it alone. We have two women who live in, as well as a very competent cook. But with Jon working such long hours at the hospital, I needed more help." She reached over and laid her hand on Penny's. "So I wrote to my sister and asked her to come to London. She's wonderful with the children. I don't know how I ever managed without her."

Penny glanced down, a bit embarrassed by her sister's praise. "You and Jon have done a remarkable job. I've been very glad to help."

Alex shifted his focus to Penny. "Where is your home?"

"Highland Hall, near Fulton, in Berkshire." Her throat tightened as memories of her family's country estate flashed through her mind. Both her parents had passed away, and her cousin William and his wife, Julia, oversaw Highland now, but she would always consider it home.

"I've never been to Berkshire, but I hear it's quite nice."

"Oh, it is. Rolling hills, quaint villages, lovely countryside." She sighed and glanced across the lawn, the vision of Highland Hall fading.

"It sounds like you're missing home." His voice softened.

Penny glanced back at Alex. "I do miss my family and friends there, but I'm glad to be in London to help Jon and Kate."

The distant church bell chimed the four o'clock hour.

Kate sent a hesitant glance toward the serving tables. "I should go see if there's anything else I can do to help."

Penny rose and reached for her plate. "There's no need. I'll go."

"Are you sure?"

"Yes. Stay and enjoy your tea." She glanced at Alex, and his twinkling eyes made her feel a bit daring. "And perhaps you can convince Lieutenant Goodwin to accept our invitation to dinner."

Alex's smile spread wider. "It's Alex, remember?"

"Yes, of course."

"And I'd be very happy to join you." His gaze remained on Penny as he replied.

Penny's stomach fluttered, and she shifted her gaze to his empty plate. "Can I get you anything else? More lemonade or sandwiches?"

"Thank you, but I think I've had more than my share."

"All right, then. It was very nice to meet you." Penny turned and started across the tent. Was he watching her? Had she made a good impression?

The memory of her disappointment with Theo came flooding back, sending a warning to her heart. It wouldn't be wise to let her imagination run away with her, to make too much of her encounter with Alex. He was a handsome, charming man who might join the family for dinner one night, but he was on his way to war— and she might never see him after that.

Still, she couldn't help looking over her shoulder and sending him one last smile.

Alex's gaze followed Penny as she crossed the tent and joined the other women preparing to serve the soldiers. He couldn't help admiring her shining blue eyes, wavy auburn hair, and warm smile. Those faint freckles dusting her nose reminded him of cinnamon sprinkled over an apple tart—sweet and delicious.

He looked away. *Hang on, old man. Best take charge of your thoughts.* It was all right to appreciate Penny's beauty and sweetness, but that was as far as he should let it go. A pilot in training with the RNAS had to stay focused. His life depended on it. Getting involved with a woman at this point in his career, even one as appealing as Penny Ramsey, could be a dangerous distraction.

Besides, he had other reasons to put off romance. His jaw tensed and he looked away, trying to banish thoughts of his parents' failed marriage and the painful path their choices had forced him to walk.

He would not make those same mistakes.

But as the soldiers filed past the serving tables, filling their plates, he glanced at Penny again. She stood behind the table, offering each man a smile as she handed him a glass of lemonade or a cup of tea.

Some day he would think about winning a young woman's heart and finding a place to call home. He gave his head a bit of a shake, then he shifted his gaze away from Penny. A sweetheart, a home, and a family . . . such dreams had to wait. First he must earn his wings and do his part to win this war.

Jon finished his last sandwich and pushed his plate aside. "So, Alex, what happens after you finish your training?"

"I may be stationed on the coast, but I hope they'll send me to France. That's where I'd see the most action."

Kate rubbed her arms as though trying to banish a chill. "You're certainly brave to want to fly in France."

Alex grinned again. "Brave or foolish."

Jon's expression sobered, and he leaned back in his chair. "I've treated a few pilots and heard their stories. Flying with the RNAS sounds like a rather risky assignment."

"It can be, but the country that rules the air will be the one that wins the war. I want to do all I can to see Britain come out on top."

A shadow seemed to touch Kate's eyes.

Alex laid his napkin on the table and considered his words. He didn't want to upset Kate, especially in her condition. This was not the time to tell Jon the gruesome stories relayed by his flight instructor or that the life expectancy of pilots on active duty with the RNAS was only three to six weeks.

But his flight instructor said he was a natural aviator. With a few more weeks' practice, he would be a skilled pilot, ready to use everything he'd learned in his training at Upavon, and in India at his father's side, to beat the Germans and keep Britain safe and secure. Then he'd come home and carve out a life for himself—one that would honor his father's memory.

Jon's tone grew more serious. "I know you'll do your duty, but I hope you'll be sensible and not take any unnecessary risks."

Stories Alex had read in the newspaper and heard from the officers at Upavon flashed through his mind. "If we're going to win this war, it will take brave men who are willing to go above and beyond their duty to defeat the Germans."

"Of course, and I've no doubt you are one of the bravest . . . Just don't do anything foolhardy. You have your whole life ahead of you."

"Don't worry. I'll be fine. I intend to beat the odds and come home in one piece." He picked up his glass of lemonade as a slight tremor reached his fingers.

He wasn't afraid to go into battle. He'd always been known for his nerve and daring. But he would be a fool not to realize the danger that awaited him.

Soft, feminine laughter rang out from the other side of the tent. Alex looked up and spotted Penny as she engaged one of the soldiers in conversation. Her dancing eyes and carefree smile stirred a longing in his heart.

He swallowed hard and looked away. He had a duty to perform and a promise to keep. And he wouldn't let anything stand in his way . . . even his own traitorous heart.

Lydia Chambers released a weary sigh and carried two heavy bags of soiled tablecloths up the front walk of the Fosters' home in Kensington. Dr. Jon walked ahead of her with his wife, Mrs. Kate. Miss Penny lifted her skirt a few inches and followed them up the front steps.

It had been a long day at the zoo. Lydia's shoulders ached and her feet were sore, but that was a small price to pay to show those wounded soldiers how grateful everyone was for their brave sacrifices.

Fifteen-year-old Lucy Wallingford walked beside Lydia, lugging a similar load of tablecloths. "I didn't think we'd be out this late."

Lydia glanced up at the fading sunset. "Cleaning up the tea tent took longer than we expected."

Lucy climbed the front steps. "I hope Mrs. Murdock saved us some dinner."

"Oh, I'm sure she did."

Jon opened the front door and stood back. "After you, ladies." He smiled, but even he looked a bit weary from their outing. And it was no wonder. He kept long hours at the hospital, doing rounds, performing surgeries—trying to put wounded men back together. Then he had to watch over his wife, who was expecting their first baby, and keep an eye on all the children they'd taken into their home. It was a good thing he was a God-fearing man, or she wasn't sure how he'd find the strength to do it all.

They stepped into the cool entry hall, and Kate turned to Lydia. "Would you let Mrs. Murdock know we're home and tell her we'll be ready for dinner in twenty minutes."

Lydia shifted the weight of the bags. "Yes, ma'am."

Jon frowned slightly and glanced at the bags. "Would you like me to take those down to the laundry room for you?"

"No, sir. It's fine." Lydia tightened her grip on the handles and glanced at Lucy.

Lucy nodded. "I can manage. I'll just take these down and be back up in a jiffy."

Kate sent them a tired smile. "Thank you, both. I appreciate your help so much." She turned and slipped her arm through Penny's. "It's been quite a day, hasn't it?"

"Yes, it has." Penny patted Kate's arm. "The men enjoyed themselves, and I think all the volunteers did as well."

The sisters' conversation faded as Lydia made her way down the stone stairs to the servants' quarters. She and Lucy dropped off the bags in the laundry room. Thank goodness Mable came in twice a week to help them tackle that job.

"See you later." Lucy hurried back upstairs.

Lydia walked into the servants' hall and found her sister, Helen, seated at the long wooden table with her daughter, three-year-old Emily, and little Irene, who was four and the youngest of the orphan children at the house. The other seven children would have dinner upstairs with the Fosters.

When she and Helen came to work here, the doctor and Kate had invited them to eat upstairs, but it didn't seem right. Kate might call them her assistants, but they were still servants. And servants did *not* eat with the family. Lydia and Helen took their meals downstairs with Mrs.

Murdock, the cook, and Henry, the gardener-chauffeur.

"How did it go?" Helen asked as she wiped Emily's face with a damp cloth.

"Very well." Lydia shifted her gaze to Irene and gently touched the girl's shoulder. "How are you, little miss?"

Irene looked up. "Very well, thank you." She took another bite of potatoes, looking pleased with herself. Irene's curly blond hair, blue eyes, and plump cheeks made her look like a little cherub. Lydia smiled. She shouldn't have favorites, but she couldn't help loving this sweet little one a bit more than the others.

Helen untied Emily's bib. "Did the soldiers enjoy their day at the zoo?"

"Oh, yes. You could tell they were glad for the outing."

"And did you have enough food for everyone?"

Lydia nodded as she sank down on the bench beside Helen. "You should have seen them. They swarmed that tea tent like ants at a picnic and ate every last bite."

Helen laughed. "I'd have liked to have seen that." Emily joined in, though Lydia didn't think she knew why she was laughing.

"It made for a very busy afternoon." Lydia's smile faded as the images of the wounded men rose in her mind. "But it wasn't easy seeing so many soldiers with frightful scars and missing

33

arms and legs." She shook her head. "Those poor men . . . Their lives will never be the same."

Helen sighed. "So many have given so much."

"Yes, they have, and it was good to give a little back today." Lydia rubbed her shoulder, trying to ease her sore muscles. "How was your day?"

Helen clicked her tongue. "Those boys are going to give me gray hair before I turn thirty!"

"Oh, no, what happened this time?"

"I sent Donald and Jack out to the front garden to work off some steam, and they ended up throwing rocks at each other and breaking one of the library windows."

Lydia gasped. They'd been in tussles before, but they'd never broken a window.

"You'd think that would make them settle down and behave themselves, but not a half hour later, Donald got into a fight with Tom. And they nearly knocked me down when I tried to separate them."

"Oh, those dreadful boys!" Lydia shook her head. "Shame on them."

Helen rubbed her forehead. "I hate to think what Dr. Jon will say when he sees that window. I must go up and tell him before he finds it himself."

"He's a good man. It'll be all right." Still, how long would his patience last if the boys continued to stir up mischief every day?

"I don't want him to think I can't manage the children on my own."

"Oh, I'm sure he won't think that."

"What if he does and sends me packing?"

"He won't. He knows the boys are a handful." Lydia shook her head and stared toward the fireplace. "We should've taken the boys with us today. Maybe seeing those wounded men would've sobered them up and made them think about doing what they should, instead of breaking windows and getting into fights."

The Fosters were good people. They took children off the streets and gave them a home and an education. But most of these children had never received the love and discipline every child needed. Getting them on the right path and teaching them how to behave wasn't easy, especially when it came to the older ones.

Mrs. Murdock entered the room. "I thought I heard your voice, Lydia."

Lydia gasped and darted a glance at the clock on the wall. "Dr. Jon and Mrs. Kate want dinner served in"—she calculated the time—"ten minutes."

Mrs. Murdock planted her hands on her hips. "Well now, I wondered when they'd be coming home. I've been keeping dinner warm for over an hour, but it will take me more than ten minutes to get it all upstairs."

Lydia rose from the bench. "I'll wash up and lend a hand." Dr. Jon was a stickler about cleanliness, especially when serving food.

"I'd help you, but I have to put these two to

bed." Helen pushed back from the table. "Then I have to tell Dr. Jon about the window."

Mrs. Murdock pursed her lips. "I wouldn't like to be the one to give him that news. But don't worry about dinner. Lydia and I can serve." The cook bustled down the hall toward the kitchen. Lydia followed.

Thoughts swirled through Lydia's mind as she soaped her hands and rinsed them under warm water. When she first came to London three years ago, as Miss Kate's lady's maid, all she did was dress Miss Kate, fix her hair, and care for all her clothing. There'd been a bit of sewing and repairing hats and undergarments, but that was the extent of her duties.

But now that Mrs. Kate and the doctor had turned their home into a refuge for orphans, Lydia's days were full. She tended the children from sunup until every last one was tucked in bed and fast asleep. Even then there were often tasks she needed to finish.

She loved children, even the unruly ones who had come right off the street. Seeing how a little kindness and a good home could help them change made her happy . . . but it also made her long for a family of her own.

Last month she'd turned twenty-three. The days were slipping away. With the war and all she had to do, how would she ever find a husband?

Would she ever have children of her own to care for and love?

"If your hands aren't clean by now, then there's no hope for them," Mrs. Murdock called.

Lydia turned and grabbed a towel. "Sorry. I'm coming."

"Bring the peas and potatoes." Mrs. Murdock lifted the platter of ham and started toward the door.

Lydia sighed. "I'm right behind you."

Two

Alex climbed the steps that led to his mother's front door, then set his duffel bag by his feet. At least he hoped this was his mother's front door. It had been almost two years since she'd replied to one of his letters. Had she moved since then? He glanced at the number above the door and fingered the folded envelope in his pocket—her last letter.

He pulled in a deep breath and straightened his shoulders. A painful twinge shot across his upper chest, catching him by surprise. He had been released from the hospital and given permission to return to training, but he still had some healing to do—and he'd be wise to remember that. He lifted his good arm, preparing to knock, then pulled his hand back.

What made him think showing up after all this time was a good idea? He should've written to let his mother know he'd been injured and was in town being treated at St. George's. He hadn't even told her he had enlisted, let alone crashed during training. She probably thought he was still at sea, working on the steamship *Mina Brea* . . . if she thought of him at all.

Now he had a three-day leave before he returned to Upavon . . . but nowhere to stay. Would she invite him in, or would she turn him away as she had when he was thirteen?

He clenched his jaw and tried to hold back those painful memories, but they came flooding in and filled his mind.

He and his father had loved their life in India, but his mother had never been happy there. Shortly after Alex turned eleven, she decided to flee her unhappy marriage and return to England, taking his sister, Lindy, with her. His mother said she wanted to take Alex too, but his father didn't like the idea.

His mother hadn't even put up a fight.

Her departure and the divorce that followed stole his father's will to live. Two years later he died a broken man, and Alex had been sent back to England to live with his mother. But she had remarried by that time, and her new husband, Roger Tremont, wanted nothing to do with the active, untamed son of Charles Goodwin.

After a week of stormy confrontations, Tremont shuttled Alex off to live with his father's parents. Grandmother Goodwin had been kind and welcomed him, but his stern grandfather seemed to dislike Alex from the moment he walked through the door. Alex supposed it was because he looked so much like his father, and his grandfather and father had been estranged for years.

He'd only seen his mother once or twice a year after that. When he turned seventeen, he'd gone to sea, and almost five years had passed since his last short, uncomfortable visit with his mother, his sister, and Roger Tremont.

He shook his head, disgusted with his tense stomach and burning throat. He was a grown man, ready to head into battle and fight the enemy. Surely he could face his mother and her husband and say a proper good-bye.

Maybe it would be better to leave things as they were and not try to push back into their lives. He leaned down and reached for his bag—just as the door swung open. He dropped the bag and looked up.

A slender young woman with dark-brown hair and wide brown eyes looked out at him. "May I help you?"

Recognition flashed through Alex. "Hello, Lindy."

Her brow creased. "I'm sorry. Do I know you?"

His appearance had changed quite a bit in the

last few years, but it was still a bit of a blow that she didn't recognize him. He swallowed and forced a smile. "I'm Alex, your brother."

She gasped. "Oh, my goodness! Alex, I'm so sorry. You've grown so much, and with that uniform, I didn't recognize you. Please come in." She stepped back and pulled the door open wider.

There was no going back now. He lifted his bag and stepped inside. "Thank you." He looked around the large entryway. "Is Mother home?"

"Yes. She's upstairs. I'll go and tell her you're here."

She turned to leave, but he reached for her arm. "Is your stepfather here?"

Some unexplained emotion flashed in her eyes, then quickly faded. "No, he's at the club. He won't be home until this evening."

Alex released the breath he had been holding and nodded.

"Please, have a seat in the parlor." She motioned toward the open doorway to the left. "I'll be right back."

Alex walked into the parlor. Should he put his bag down? Perhaps that would make his mother think he expected her to invite him to stay. Maybe he should just hold on to it. No, that would be awkward. He deposited the bag by a chair near the door, but out of view, then glanced around the room.

Heavy, dark-green drapes had been pulled back

to let in some sunlight. Several flowering plants sat on wooden stands in front of the windows. An elaborately carved grand piano filled one corner of the room. Memories stirred and rose to the surface. His mother had a beautiful voice, and she had often played the piano when he was young. After she left he'd tried to learn to play, but with no one to teach him, he'd given up.

He turned and scanned the other side of the room.

Bookshelves lined the wall on both sides of the fireplace, and chairs and sofas were grouped together in the center of the room. A large landscape of the English countryside hung over the fireplace. It was an attractive room, yet there was a stiffness and formality about it that made Alex uncomfortable.

He crossed to take a closer look at the photographs lining the fireplace mantel. His mother and stepfather's wedding portrait sat on the far left, then two photographs of Lindy, and finally one of Lindy, his mother, and Roger Tremont.

He clenched his jaw and glanced at the bookshelves and then the end tables. There were no photographs of him, though his grandparents had taken him to a photographer twice and sent those portraits to his mother.

It shouldn't hurt so much after all these years, but it did.

"Alex." His mother swept into the room wearing a silky blue dressing gown, followed by Lindy. "My, this is a surprise."

The years had been kind to her. She still looked almost as young and lovely as she did in the wedding photograph taken years ago.

"Hello, Mother." He hesitated. How, exactly, should he greet her?

She stretched out her hand, answering his unspoken question. He took it and bowed slightly.

"Aren't you going to kiss me? I am your mother." She lifted her thin eyebrows, a hint of disappointment in her eyes. Or was that embarrassment?

"Yes, of course." He leaned toward her cheek and kissed her, breathing in the soft scent of roses.

"Well, let me look at you." She stepped back and sized him up. "I didn't realize you had enlisted."

"Yes, that's one reason I wanted to see you before I go back to Upavon."

A slight line creased the area between his mother's eyebrows. "Upavon?"

"Yes, I'm taking pilot training with the Royal Naval Air Service. As soon as I get my wings, I hope to be stationed in France."

Lindy's eyes widened. "You're going to be flying an airplane . . . in France?"

"Yes. That's what RNAS pilots do."

She gave an embarrassed laugh. "Of course, but it sounds rather dangerous."

He pondered his answer for a moment. "There are some risks, but I want to do my part to win this war. Certainly soaring through the clouds sounds much more exciting than slogging through muddy trenches."

His mother sniffed. "You sound just like your father." Her voice took on a cold edge. "He never could pass up an opportunity for *excitement.*"

Heat flashed up Alex's neck. How could she still be bitter toward his father after all these years, especially when she was the one who had sought the divorce, quickly remarried, and then settled into a new life that conveniently excluded Alex and his father?

Sympathy shone in Lindy's eyes. "How soon do you have to return to your base?"

Alex steeled himself for his mother's response. "Not until Monday morning."

His mother's eyes widened for a split second, then she schooled her expression. "Roger should be home by six, and we'll be eating at seven. Would you like to stay for dinner?"

So, that was all she would offer—a stiff, formal dinner with his stepfather seated at the head of the table, issuing orders and making Alex and everyone else sorry that he'd come. Still . . . if crumbs were all she would give, he was hungry enough to accept them.

"Yes, thank you."

An uncomfortable silence hung in the air between them. Alex shifted his weight to the other foot and glanced at his sister.

Lindy turned to their mother. "Shall I ask Mrs. Peterson to bring us some tea?"

"Yes." His mother motioned toward the closest chair. "Have a seat, Alex. Tell me how you've been."

Alex sat down and gave her a brief summary of his last few months at sea, ending by telling her about his grandfather's death in November.

"I'm sorry. I didn't realize your grandfather had passed away. No one informed me." She sent him a pointed look.

He would not let her make him feel guilty. "I didn't hear the news myself until we returned to port. By then I'd missed the funeral. Grandmother sold the house here. She's living in Glasgow now, with her daughter, Ethel."

His mother frowned and glanced toward the window. Surely she realized he had no other family in London and nowhere else to stay for the next few days unless he paid for a hotel room.

Lindy walked back into the parlor. "The tea will be here shortly." She sat down across from Alex and asked about his training. He relayed a few details, careful to avoid anything that might make her or their mother worry about his safety.

A door opened and closed. Footsteps crossed the

entryway. Alex looked up, expecting the house-keeper to bring in the tea, but Roger Tremont walked into the parlor.

Alex tensed and met Tremont's surprised look head-on.

Tremont's steps stalled, and he shot a glance at his wife.

She rose and greeted him with a kiss on the cheek, but her movements looked stiff and forced. "Alex is in town, and he stopped by for a visit."

Alex rose and held out his hand. "Mr. Tremont."

Tremont shook Alex's hand, but his grip was cool and loose. He looked him over with a slight frown. "So, I see you've signed up to join the fight."

"Yes, sir. I have."

"Alex is training to be a pilot." Lindy's eyes shone, and she sent him a warm smile.

"Is he?" Tremont's eyebrows rose and took on a haughty slant. "That sounds like something you'd choose."

Alex bristled. "Why do you say that?"

"There's no need to take offense. I simply meant you've always been a rather daring young man. It's probably due to your years in India and your lack of exposure to the gentler influences of English society."

Alex shot his stepfather a dark look. What made the man think he knew him well enough to make that kind of judgment? Was he repeating something Alex's mother had said, or had he come to his own conclusion?

Tremont's expression hardened. "You've grown up to be very much like your father."

Alex straightened and met Tremont's gaze. "I take that as a compliment."

"Take it any way you like."

Alex clenched his jaw, barely able to hold back the sharp reply rising in his throat.

"Your father was a cool-hearted adventurer, a risk taker, but it's unfortunate he didn't consider how those risks would impact others." Tremont glanced toward Lindy and their mother.

Fire flashed through Alex. "You didn't know my father. You've no right to criticize him."

"I may not have known him personally, but I've heard enough to understand he was self-absorbed and cared very little about his wife and daughter."

Alex's mother stifled a gasp, and Lindy's eyes widened.

Alex stepped toward Tremont. "My father was a brave, honorable man, and I won't allow you to discredit his memory."

Tremont's eyes flashed a warning.

"Please, Alex, sit down." His mother reached out her hand. "I'm sure Roger didn't mean to upset you." His mother's face had gone deathly pale. Clearly, everything Tremont knew about Alex's father had come directly from her, and guilty pain filled her eyes.

Alex clenched his jaw and lowered himself into the chair. He must stay calm for his sister's and his mother's sake.

"Of course. Your mother is right. I meant no offense." Tremont took off his hat and laid it on the end table, then sat in a chair across from Alex. "What brings you to London?"

Alex forced his voice to remain calm. "I've been in town for a few weeks, recovering from an injury. I thought I should visit before I return to my base."

His mother shifted in her chair. "What kind of injury?"

"Just a broken collarbone and dislocated shoulder, but the doctor says I'm fine now. He released me to finish my training."

Her expression turned wary. "How did it happen?"

He'd hoped to avoid disclosing those details, but there didn't seem any way around it. "I had a bit of a rough landing. Nothing to worry about."

Tremont laughed. "See, that's what I mean."

"Roger, please."

Tremont lifted his hand. "I'm sorry. It's just so typical. I could've told you how he was injured, even before he admitted it."

Alex clenched his hands and glared at the vile man.

"The boy's as wild and reckless as his father. I'll be surprised if he doesn't kill himself before he—"

Alex sprang from his chair. "This was a mistake. I shouldn't have come." He strode across the room and nearly collided with the housekeeper as she walked through the doorway with the tea tray.

The teacups clattered together, and Alex reached out to steady her.

"I'm sorry, sir." She looked up at him with wide eyes.

"No, it was my fault. I apologize."

The housekeeper stepped around him and placed the tray on the low table in front of the sofa.

"Thank you, Mrs. Peterson." His mother's low voice sounded strained. "That will be all."

"Very good, ma'am." She nodded to his mother and turned to go, sending him a questioning look as she passed.

Alex grabbed his duffel bag, ready to follow her out.

His mother stood and clasped her hands. "Alex, please, won't you at least stay for tea?"

"No. I think it's best if I leave now." He turned away and walked out of the parlor.

"Alex, wait." Lindy caught up to him just as he reached the front door. "I'm so sorry." She glanced over her shoulder toward the open parlor door.

"It's all right. It's not your fault." He kept his voice low, hoping to keep the conversation between just the two of them.

She sent him a sad smile. "I'm glad you came.

48

I've wondered how you were and when we might see you again."

"It seems you're the only one." He couldn't prevent bitterness from tingeing his words.

Lindy reached for his arm. "You must forgive Mother. Life has not been easy for her."

He glanced around at the fine house, doubts stirring his anger again.

She leaned closer and lowered her voice. "My stepfather is difficult most days, and painfully unpleasant others."

Alex stilled, his stomach tensing. He searched his sister's face, and a shocking question formed in his mind. "He hasn't hurt you, has he?"

"No, he's never lifted a hand toward me . . . or Mother, as far as I know."

Alex glared toward the parlor. "He better not, or he will have to answer to me."

A smile lit Lindy's eyes for just a moment, then quickly faded. "I'm afraid he uses other methods to get his way."

"What do you mean?"

"He trades in cutting remarks and a volatile temper. But I've learned to shield my heart from him." She reached for his hand, then waited until Alex met her gaze. "He's not my father, and he never will be."

Their father's image rose in his mind's eye. Alex's throat tightened, and he nodded as the silent bond between them tightened.

"I know you and Mother haven't been close, but it might help if you would write."

Alex pulled back. "I do write, maybe not as often as I should, but at least three or four times in the last year."

Lindy cocked her head. "Really? She told me she hasn't heard from you for several years."

Alex glanced toward the parlor. How was that possible? He had mailed most of his letters from distant ports, but his grandmother had received his letters and responded. What had happened to the letters he had written to his mother? Had Tremont confiscated them? Or had his mother lied to Lindy and simply refused to answer Alex?

He shook off those questions. He might never know the truth, but that wouldn't stop him from staying in touch with his sister. "I don't know what happened to my letters, but I promise you, I have written."

She tightened her grip on his hand. "I believe you."

He glanced toward the door. "I should go."

Still, she held on to his hand.

"I'll write to you, Lindy, but it might be best if I send the letters through a friend. Then there's no chance anyone will keep them from you."

"Yes, of course." She hurried to the table in the corner, pulled open the drawer, and took out a small card and pencil. "I'll give you Elizabeth Hamilton's address." She quickly jotted it on the card and handed it to Alex. "I'm sure she'll receive mail for me."

He slipped the card into his jacket pocket and studied his sister's face, memorizing her features. Would this be the last time he saw her this side of heaven? He reached for her hand again. "Take care, Lindy. Say a prayer for me."

"I will. I promise." She stood on tiptoe and placed a feather-light kiss on his cheek. "Stay safe, Alex."

His throat tightened so much that he could not reply. So he nodded to her, turned, and walked out the door.

The clock in the entrance hall chimed seven as Penny hurried down the stairs. She didn't want to be late for dinner. Jon and Kate liked her to set a good example for the children, and she truly wanted to, but more often than not, she got caught up reading a novel and lost track of time.

A strand of her hair fell and waved before her eyes. Ah, what a bother! She pulled out a pin, tucked the strand back in place, and poked the pin in again.

Just as she reached the bottom step, the front doorbell rang.

Who could that be? They weren't expecting guests this evening, but the unexpected often happened at her sister's home. Whoever was at the door, Jon and Kate would probably welcome them in and invite them to stay for dinner. She crossed to the front door and pulled it open.

Lieutenant Alex Goodwin stood in the doorway, silhouetted against the fading evening light. He looked quite handsome wearing his visor cap and double-breasted uniform jacket with gold buttons.

A ripple of pleasure flowed through her. "Lieutenant Goodwin, hello."

He smiled. "Good evening . . . and it's Alex, remember?"

"Yes, of course, Alex. Please, come in." She stepped back and pulled the door open wider.

"Thank you." He walked inside carrying a military duffel bag. "I was hoping I might speak to Jon. Is he at home?"

"Yes, he is." She glanced at the duffel bag, questions stirring in her heart.

Jon walked out of the dining room, followed by Kate. "Alex, welcome! It's good to see you." He reached out and shook Alex's hand. "We're just sitting down for dinner. Won't you join us?"

Alex's face turned ruddy. "I'm sorry. I know your invitation was for Sunday."

"We're glad to have you any day, aren't we, Kate?"

Kate smiled. "Of course. Please stay for dinner."

Alex hesitated a moment. "All right. Thank you."

"Let me take your bag." Jon reached for Alex's

duffel, placed it by the foot of the staircase, then led Alex into the dining room.

Penny and Kate exchanged smiles and followed the men in. The children stood behind their chairs at the long table, waiting for prayer and the invitation to be seated. Mrs. Murdock and Lydia stood beside the buffet, ready to help serve the meal. All eyes turned toward Alex as he entered the room.

"Children, I'd like to introduce Lieutenant Alex Goodwin. He'll be joining us for dinner this evening."

Alex lifted his hand and glanced around the table. "Hello, everyone."

A chorus of greetings rose from the children. Mrs. Murdock lifted her eyebrows and glanced at Lydia. An extra guest wasn't unusual, but Penny supposed Mrs. Murdock wondered if the meal would stretch to feed one more. The government had urged thrift and great care in preparing meals to avoid waste, in the hope they would not have to enforce rationing. Mrs. Murdock usually calculated the servings very carefully. Penny decided that she would take a smaller amount to make sure there was enough for Alex.

"Please take this seat." Kate motioned toward the empty chair at the end of the table.

Six-year-old Susan's brow creased. "But that's Jesus's place."

Alex's steps stalled, and he shot a questioning look at Kate.

"It's all right." Kate sent Alex a reassuring glance, then turned to Susan. "We set that extra place to remind us Jesus is the unseen guest at every meal, but I know He'd be happy to offer it to Lieutenant Goodwin this evening."

"Yes, I'm sure He would." Jon moved to stand behind his place in the center on the right side, across from Kate. The seven children would be seated between the adults, alternating boys and girls to help keep order at mealtime.

Alex stood behind his chair at the end of the table. Penny slipped into her place between Susan and Tom. They all looked toward Jon.

"Let's close our eyes and bow our heads for prayer." Jon waited while everyone settled and bowed their heads. "Father, thank You for this day and all You have given us. We are grateful for our home, our friends, our family, and the food You have provided. Please guide our conversation and keep us mindful of Your love and presence. In Christ's name, we pray. Amen." Jon looked up. "You may be seated."

The children pulled out their chairs, then took their seats amid shuffling and bits of conversation.

Mrs. Murdock and Lydia carried serving dishes around the table, helping the children but allowing the adults to serve themselves. Soon the simple meal of potatoes, carrots, peas, roasted chicken, and bread filled everyone's plates.

Jon placed his napkin on his lap. "So, Alex, how is your shoulder feeling?"

"Thanks to the excellent staff at St. George's, I'd say I'm almost as good as new." He moved his arm, demonstrating the range of motion.

"I'm glad to hear it."

"I'm sorry I wasn't the best patient. Some men might like to put their feet up to relax, but I'm eager to get back to my training."

Jon chuckled. "Yes, you never did like to sit still."

"That's true. I've always loved being on the move, especially outdoors."

Penny turned to Alex. "Did you develop your love for the outdoors when you lived in India?"

"Yes, I suppose I did. My father had quite a sense of adventure, and he often took me along when he went hunting or when he scouted out the route for a new railway."

"That sounds so exciting." Penny set down her fork. "How long did you live in India?"

"I was born there and stayed until I was thirteen."

"Did your family return to England then?" Penny asked.

Jon shot Penny a warning glance, but she caught it too late.

Alex's expression faltered. "When I was eleven,

my mother left India and returned to England. My parents divorced. I stayed with my father for the next two years, but after he passed away, I was sent back to London to live with . . . my grandparents."

She'd done it again. Put the poor man in an awkward place. Would she never learn to hold her tongue? "I'm sorry."

"It's all right. It was a long time ago." Alex glanced away, but not before she saw the ruddy tint of his face and the sheen in his eyes.

Penny shifted in her seat. "Is your mother still in London?"

"Yes, but she remarried. I don't see her often." He looked down at his plate, obviously uncomfortable.

Oh, she was just making it worse and worse. She pressed her lips together, determined not to say anything else about his family. It was obviously a painful topic for him.

"Children, I think you'll be interested to know Lieutenant Goodwin is training to be a pilot. Very soon he'll be flying for the Royal Naval Air Service." Kate's smile looked a bit forced, but at least her sister had steered the conversation to safer ground.

Fifteen-year-old Donald leaned forward, eyes wide. "A real pilot?"

"Yes." The lines in Alex's forehead eased.

"Did you fly airplanes in India?" Though Tom

was only twelve and the youngest of the three boys, he was not about to be left out of the conversation.

Alex grinned, his good humor returning. "No, airplanes are not common in India, and they've only been flown in England for the last five years."

That set off a round of questions, which Alex answered with good cheer. The boys seemed especially impressed.

"Will you be bombing the Germans?" Jack asked, his expression eager.

"The RNAS focuses on defense. We try to stop Germans airplanes and Zeppelins before they cross the Channel."

Donald's eyes lit up. "I'd blast those Huns to kingdom come if I were a pilot!"

Jon cleared his throat. "Donald, we do what's necessary to defend our country, but we don't rejoice over our enemy's destruction."

"Aww." Donald crossed his arms and sat back with a huff.

Alex sent Jon a questioning glance.

Jon said, "I believe it's important for the children to understand what's happening in the war, but balancing our response to it is a constant topic in my prayers and in my conversations with others who have a like-minded faith."

Alex straightened. "If we don't take a stand against evil, who will?"

Jon nodded. "We must defend ourselves and do what we can to help those who are being oppressed."

"Exactly. Look at what's happened in Belgium. The country has been completely overrun, and the Germans won't stop until they control all of Europe—unless we stop them."

Susan's eyes widened. "Do you think the Germans are coming *here?*"

"Not if I can help it." Alex's voice rang with conviction.

Kate shot a concerned glance at Jon. "Perhaps we should discuss something else. I don't want to upset the children."

"We can't hide the fact we're at war, my dear, not when we're faced with blackouts each night, soldiers on every corner, and newspapers filled with stories of battles and bombings."

A shadow crossed Kate's face as she looked around the table at the children. "No, I don't suppose we can."

"But we can and should prepare our hearts." Jon shifted his gaze to Susan. "When we feel anxious and fearful about the war, or anything else, what are we to do?"

Susan scrunched her shoulders and her brow furrowed.

"We're to pray." Lucy sent Susan a kind smile.

"That's right." Jon nodded. "God understands our fears and concerns. And when we bring those to Him in prayer, He exchanges them for His peace, even in the most difficult and trying times."

Donald gripped the edge of the table, his gaze intense. "Praying is fine, but blasting the German planes out of the sky and sinking a few U-boats sounds like a better idea to me."

Alex met the boy's gaze. "Dr. Foster is right, Donald. Prayer is important. I wouldn't climb aboard an airplane without it."

Tom studied Alex with a skeptical look. "Really? You pray before you fly?"

"I'd be a fool not to. We're in a battle. We need God's help and protection more than ever."

"I'm glad to hear you're a man of prayer," Jon added, his eyes shining.

Alex shook his head. "I have miles to go on my faith journey. But my grandmother taught me prayer is a great source of strength. I doubt I'd be alive today if it hadn't been for my grandmother's prayers. I always try to remember that, especially when I'm flying."

A smile rose from Penny's heart. Alex Goodwin sounded like a man with genuine faith and courage. Surely God would watch over him and protect him when he flew off to face the enemy.

Alex stared into the fire, mesmerized by the leaping flames and their soothing crackle and hiss. How he'd missed this when he was away at sea— this time by the fireside with the family gathered around. Of course Jon, Kate, and Penny weren't his family, but they'd invited him in and given him the same comforting welcome he'd received from his grandmother those few years he'd lived with her and his grandfather in London.

Even though he'd never gained his grandfather's full approval, his grandmother had been an anchor in the storm. If only he had time to travel to Scotland and see her before he left, but that trip would have to wait until he had a longer leave— or the war was over.

He glanced at Jon and Kate, seated close together across from him. Jon was a lucky man. He had a beautiful wife, a comfortable home, and a meaningful occupation. Of course, he carried an extra load of responsibilities with all the children they'd taken in, but he seemed to handle it well. Much better than Alex ever could.

The children were certainly a lively lot, especially the three boys. Penny had encouraged all the children to sing a song for him after dinner. He'd enjoyed that and been touched by their promises to pray for him. The boys each shook his hand and the girls gave him sweet smiles before they said good night and went up to bed.

He glanced at Penny, seated on his left, closest to the fire. She'd been especially kind to him tonight, offering him an extra serving of pudding and making sure he had a comfortable seat in the library. Her eyes had sparkled as she listened to his stories of growing up in India and his time at sea. With her warm smiles and thoughtful questions, she made him feel as though his experiences were worth repeating. She was the kind of girl who would make coming home something to look forward to.

He pulled his gaze away and glanced at the clock. It was past time to take his leave. He rose from his chair. "It's been a wonderful evening, but it's getting late. I should go and let you all get some sleep."

Jon stood. "Can we give you lift? Where are you staying?"

Alex's face warmed. Here it was. The moment of truth. "I'm . . . not sure."

Surprise flashed in Penny's eyes, then they softened with sympathy.

He looked away. She must find it pathetic that he had no family or friends who had invited him to spend his last few days in London with them.

"You're welcome to stay with us." Jon glanced at Kate, and she nodded. "We have plenty of room."

"That's kind of you, but I don't want impose."

"You wouldn't be imposing, not at all." Jon continued, "We have a guest room ready. Stay with us until you go back to—"

A loud explosion cut off Jon's words and shook the house. Alex's heart lurched. Penny pulled in a sharp breath as Kate reached for her husband. Jon and Alex exchanged wary glances. A series of booms, as loud as cannon fire, rattled the windows.

Jon and Alex strode across the room toward the front windows. "Turn off the lights," Jon called.

Kate hurried over and flipped the switch, dousing the room in darkness except for the faint glow from the fireplace. Jon raised the blackout shade and peered outside. Alex looked over his shoulder and scanned the sky. Searchlight beams fanned out over London, highlighting a few breaks in the low clouds.

Kate and Penny joined them at the window.

"What is it?" Kate reached for Jon's arm. "What's happening?"

"It sounds like the guns at Woolwich. They've probably spotted a Zeppelin."

Alex gripped the windowsill. "That first explosion was too loud to be antiaircraft guns."

Penny looked up at Alex. "Do you think it was a bomb?"

"It could have been."

Resounding booms from the guns filled the air again. Shells burst in the sky, looking like fireworks as the lurid red lights flickered and fell to the ground.

"Look. Over there!" Jon pointed to a bright glow above the buildings and trees to the east.

Penny leaned closer to the window, her shoulder touching Alex's. "It looks like a fire."

"Yes, it must be. Listen." The fire brigade's

sirens rose and wailed in the distance, while the guns continued firing.

Another explosion, louder than the first, shook the house again. Penny gasped, and Alex reached out to steady her.

"That one was closer." Moonlight illuminated her face as she looked up at him, anxious questions reflected in her eyes.

An urge to protect her swept through him. He wanted to say everything would be all right, but no one could make that promise. Not now. The German Zeppelins had finally reached London. Who knew how much damage they would do before they flew away into the night?

Hurried footsteps sounded on the floor above, and children's voices called out. "Dr. Foster! Mrs. Foster!"

Jon pulled down the blackout shade. "We must take the children downstairs." He led Kate away from the window.

Alex guided Penny through the darkened library and into the entrance hall.

Lucy hurried down the stairs, holding Susan's hand. "What's happening? Is it an air raid?"

"Are the Germans coming?" Susan bit her lip and searched the adults' faces.

The other children rushed down the stairs behind them.

"Are they bombing us?" Tom hustled past the others.

As Tom reached the bottom step, Donald pushed him from behind. "Sure they are. What else could it be?"

Eleven-year-old Edna burst into tears, and Rose let loose a pitiful wail.

"Please, children, you must calm down and listen to me." Jon's voice cut through the confusion. The little ones quieted, but the booming guns continued their frightening volley.

"We all know what to do in case of an air raid. We've practiced many times."

"But I'm scared." Rose sniffed and clasped her hands in front of her mouth. "I don't want to go down in the cellar."

Jon stepped toward Rose and laid his hand on her shoulder. "We're just going down to the servants' hall. You've had tea there with Mrs. Murdock. It's nothing to be frightened about." Jon's confident tone seemed to reassure the children enough for them to follow his directions.

Penny took Rose's hand, and she and Kate guided the children toward the doorway to the servants' stairs.

Three other women dressed in their nightclothes hurried down the main staircase. Alex recognized the two women who had served at dinner, and he supposed the third was also a servant. She carried a little child in her arms as she and the others followed Penny, Kate, and the children down the servants' stairs.

Jon and Alex waited until everyone else had filed out of the entrance hall, then Alex closed the door and started down the steps after Jon.

Amid sniffing and a few more tears, Kate, Penny, and the other women comforted the children and helped them settle on the benches around a wooden table.

Alex surveyed the room. There were two small windows near the ceiling, both covered with blackout shades. In the corner, a door leading outside could provide an escape route, if needed. It seemed a relatively safe place to wait out the bombing, though he wasn't sure it would offer much protection if a bomb landed directly on the house. A chill shot down his back, and he prayed no bombs would fall on them tonight, for the children's sake.

"How long must we stay down here?" Rose tucked her dark-brown hair behind her ear and looked up at Jon.

"I'm not sure." Jon glanced around at the children. "We'll have to wait and see."

Young Tom looked at Alex. "Do you think they'll shoot down the Zeppelin?"

Alex tensed. Oh, to be able to give a different answer, but shooting down a Zeppelin from the ground was practically impossible. German air-ships could fly two miles high, far beyond the reach of even the largest antiaircraft guns. "The only way to stop a Zeppelin is to attack it from the air."

Tom's face brightened. "That's what our pilots do, right?"

Alex didn't want to dampen the boy's hopes, but he wouldn't mislead him. "We haven't knocked one down yet, but we will."

Tom's eyes clouded, and he sank down on the bench. Guns boomed in the distance, then another loud explosion vibrated the walls and rattled the dishes on the shelves.

Alex looked down the row of frightened women and children and clenched his jaw. It wasn't right. Women and children shouldn't be pulled from their beds and forced to hide in a cellar, fearing for their lives.

In the distance he heard the drone of the Zeppelin moving closer. What cowards! Flying above a city, dropping bombs on helpless—

"Where's Irene?" Lucy jumped up and looked around the room. "Edna, wasn't she with you?"

Edna shook her head. "I saw her get out of bed, but . . ."

Alex tensed and darted a glance at Jon.

His friend circled the table, looking into each child's face. "Did anyone see Irene in the hall or on the stairs?" They all shook their heads, and a wave of panic crossed their faces as they realized the youngest of their charges was missing.

"I'll go up and find her." Jon started toward the door.

A sudden loud blast vibrated the walls, followed

by the sound of breaking glass upstairs. Some of the children cried out, others cringed and hunched closer together. Kate sent Jon a fearful glance.

Alex strode across the room to meet his friend. "Stay with your family. I'll go up and find the girl."

"But you don't know your way around the house."

"Just tell me where her room is." Alex shot a glance at Penny, Kate, and the children. "Your family needs you here."

As though to emphasize his words, the guns sounded again, and the ground shuddered beneath their feet.

Jon met his gaze and nodded. "All right."

Penny pulled open a drawer in the cabinet. She took out a handheld torch and joined Alex and Jon by the door. "Irene's room is upstairs on the first floor." She passed him the torch. "Turn left at the top of the stairs. It's the third door on the right."

One of the younger servants, the one who had served them at dinner, looked up at Alex. "Irene's a sweet child, but she's only four and sometimes fearful."

"I'll keep that in mind." Alex tested the torch, sliding the switch on and off.

Penny laid her hand on his arm.

He stopped and looked up.

"Please, be careful." Her voice was soft, and it held an urgency he hadn't expected.

The warmth of her hand spread through his arm. His mouth tugged up at one corner, and he gave her a slight nod. "Of course. I'll be back as soon as I find her."

He strode out of the servants' hall and took the stone stairs two at a time. His gut clenched and he hurried on, intent on finding the frightened little girl and returning her to her family as soon as he could.

As he reached the main floor, an explosion rocked the house. He grabbed the banister and held on, steeling himself in case the roof came crashing in. The roof stayed in place, but the lights flickered and went out. He turned on the torch and hustled up the stairs. "Irene? Where are you?"

The only reply was the wailing siren in the distance and another round from the booming guns.

"Everyone's gone down to the cellar," he called as he reached the top of the stairs. "Tell me where you are, and I'll take you to Dr. and Mrs. Foster." He fanned the light around the upper hallway, but it was empty. He hurried to the third door and pushed it open. "Irene? Are you in here?"

He scanned the room with the torch beam, spotting three empty beds with their sheets and blankets tossed aside. A pair of shoes, a book, and a doll lay on the rug between the beds. But no little girl.

He frowned and turned around, shining the light

in the corners of the room. She *had* to be here somewhere. He bent down and looked under the first bed, but all he saw was a dirty sock and what looked like a broken shoelace.

He checked under the other two beds and in the wardrobe. Nothing. He looked behind the curtains and lifted the window seat, but Irene wasn't there. Pushing the blackout shade aside, he checked the window, but it was locked and there was no balcony or way for her to climb down. With all the frightening noise outside, he doubted she would try.

But she couldn't just disappear.

He returned to the hall and checked the other bedrooms, calling her name as he opened each door, then shone the light around the room. At the end of the hall, he opened the door to find it led to another set of narrow stairs leading up to the next floor, as well as down. More than likely, the servants used these back stairs.

"Irene, are you up there?" He waited, but there was no reply, so he ran up to check the next floor.

A dry, dusty smell greeted him as he opened the door to the upper hallway. There were no blackout curtains on the windows, which led him to believe these rooms were not used by Jon's family or servants. They didn't have a large staff, so perhaps these rooms weren't needed.

He made a quick check of the six empty bedrooms, but Irene wasn't there. He descended the stairs, walked past Irene's room once more, then continued down to the main floor. Where would a little girl hide to feel safe?

He checked the dining room and drawing room, but there was no sign of her. Finally, he strode into the library. His eyes had adjusted to the darkness, and the glow of the fireplace shed light on a good portion of the room. "Irene, are you in here?"

A sniffle sounded off to his left.

He swung around and shone the torchlight in that direction. A little girl with blond curly hair peeked out from behind the settee. Her eyes looked red from crying, and her chin wobbled as she sucked on two fingers, but she seemed to be all right.

He blew out a deep breath and stepped toward her. "I'm so glad I found you."

She pulled back, obviously frightened by seeing a man she didn't know.

He slowed and knelt in front of her. "It's all right. Dr. and Mrs. Foster sent me to look for you. They're down in the cellar." He held out his hand.

She pulled out her fingers and hiccupped. "I want Lydia."

He wasn't sure who Lydia was, but everyone in the house was in the servants' hall. "Come on, let's go find her."

Irene slowly reached out and took his hand. She wrapped her warm little fingers around his, and his heart melted like butter over a flame. Thankfulness flooded through him.

With the torchlight beam shining on their path, they walked out of the library.

"I found her!" Alex called as he carried Irene down the servants' stairs.

Jon stepped out of the servants' hall and held a lantern high. Kate, Penny, and the children rushed out to the hallway. Penny sent him a warm smile, admiration shining in her eyes.

"Irene!" The younger servant with the cheerful, round face hurried forward and scooped the child out of his arms and into a tight hug. "I've been so worried about you."

Irene flung her arms around the woman's neck.

So . . . this must be Lydia.

The maid pulled back and looked the girl over. "Are you all right?"

Irene sniffed and nodded. "The big mirror fell off the wall and broke."

"Did it hurt you?" Lydia asked.

Irene shook her head.

"Come with me." Lydia carried Irene into the servants' hall.

Penny moved to Alex's side. "You were gone so long. I was worried."

He searched her upturned face, and pleasant warmth flowed through him.

"Where did you find her?"

"In the library." He gave a little chuckle and

shook his head. "I searched her room and the upper floors first, but she wasn't there. I finally found her, peeking out from behind the settee. She looked like a little fairy with her blond curls and rosy cheeks."

Penny laid her hand on his arm. "Thank you, Alex. I'm grateful. We all are."

His chest swelled as he soaked in her words . . . like a thirsty soul who'd finally been given a drink of water after a long hike through the desert.

The guns at Woolwich boomed in the distance once more, and they both turned toward the sound.

There was greater danger ahead than a lost child. They faced a strong and skillful enemy who was determined to destroy them. It would take tremendous effort and sacrifice on all their parts to defend their country and win this war.

He looked at Penny, and determination rose in his heart. He would protect her and all those who were counting on him . . .

No matter the cost.

Three

The next morning Penny stifled a yawn as she spread strawberry jam on her toast. Looking around the table, she noted the children's sagging shoulders and pale faces. They hadn't gone back to bed until three o'clock, when the sounds of the air raid had finally faded and calm returned to London.

She looked toward the end of the table where Alex sat, and a small smile lifted the corners of her mouth. He'd been terribly brave last night, going up to search for Irene while they all stayed in the relative safety of the servants' hall. Seeing him walk down the stairs tenderly carrying that little girl in his arms had touched her deeply.

"Where's Dr. Foster?" Donald laid his knife across the edge of his plate and looked across at Kate.

"He . . . had some things he needed to attend to this morning. I'm sure he'll be back soon." Kate looked away from Donald's curious gaze.

Penny shifted in her seat and glanced at Kate. Jon always ate breakfast with them, then read the Bible and prayed for the family before he left for the hospital and the older children left for school. But today was Saturday, and Jon was not scheduled to work at the hospital. Where had he gone?

Rose leaned forward in her chair. "Are we going to the park this morning?" They usually went each Saturday if the weather was agreeable, and they all looked forward to the outing.

Kate hesitated. "Let's wait until Dr. Foster returns to make our plans. But there's no reason we can't enjoy ourselves at home this morning."

At Kate's forced cheerfulness, the older children exchanged questioning glances.

What was going on?

"Good morning, everyone." Jon walked into the dining room.

Relief flashed across Kate's face. She rose and greeted him with a kiss on the cheek. "I'm glad you're home."

"What did you learn?" Alex's expression grew taut.

Jon looked at his friend, and Penny thought she saw some kind of message in his eyes. Then he glanced around the table. "I'm sorry I'm late for breakfast. I see you're all nearly done." He walked to the buffet and helped himself to eggs, toast, mushrooms, and a broiled tomato.

A frown creased Alex's brows, and he glanced at Penny. She returned the question with her eyes. Apparently, Jon didn't want to discuss where he'd been or what he'd learned in front of the children.

Jon carried his plate to the table, took a seat, and bowed his head for a silent prayer. When he lifted his head, the children's conversation returned to normal while they finished their meal.

Finally, Jon looked around the table. "All right, children. You may be excused. Let's gather in the library at ten. Until then, please find something to read or play quietly indoors."

Jack frowned. "Can't we go out to the garden?"

"Not this morning."

"But Donald and I—"

"Jack, please don't argue." Jon's voice was much more stern than usual, and the boys all straightened. "I need you all to do as I ask, and I'll explain more when we gather at ten."

"All right." Jack quietly laid his napkin on the table.

The children rose and filed out of the dining room.

"Close the door, Lucy," Jon called.

The girl's lips pressed into a worried line as she pulled the dining room door shut.

"What is it, Jon?" Kate lowered her voice. "What did you learn?"

"The damage from the bombing is much worse than I'd imagined. They're still searching through the debris, looking for those who are injured or missing. But we know this much: almost a hundred bombs were dropped. At least seven people were killed."

Penny pulled in a sharp breath and lifted her hand to her mouth. *How terrible!*

"The destruction to homes and business is . . . unbelievable."

Alex's face turned ruddy and his dark eyebrows drew together.

Jon continued, "I'll be going to the hospital as soon as things are settled here."

Kate's face paled. "Of course. It sounds like they'll need every doctor on hand."

Penny's heart clenched as she thought of the families who'd lost loved ones. "What can we do to help?"

Jon turned his sober gaze toward her. "I want you to pack your trunks and return to Highland as soon as possible."

Penny blinked and stared at him. "What?"

Jon's gaze shifted to Kate. "It's not safe for you and the children to stay in London. The risks are too great. I've telegraphed William and explained what has happened. I've asked him to allow you to stay with them until it's safe for you to return."

"But what about you?" Kate's gaze locked on Jon.

"I must stay. The Army requires my services at St. George's. And even if they didn't, I wouldn't feel right fleeing to the countryside when so many wounded men are in need of medical care."

"Yes, but what about the children? How will I manage without you?"

"I know it will be difficult, Kate, but you'll have Penny, and I hope Lydia and Helen will go with you. Perhaps Mrs. Murdock might even agree to move to Highland to help with the extra cooking."

Tears flooded Kate's eyes. "But I don't want to be separated from you."

Jon's serious expression eased. "Please, darling, I must be sure you're safe. That's what is most important."

Penny's throat tightened. It would be very hard

on Kate to leave Jon here, knowing he would be in danger.

"But what if William doesn't want us to come?" Penny asked, though she couldn't imagine William and Julia turning family members away, especially not in wartime.

"Then I'll make some other arrangements." His gaze remained steady. "You can't stay in London."

Kate tried to blink back her tears, but it did no good. She rose and hurried out of the dining room.

Jon closed his eyes and sagged back against his chair.

"She'll be all right," Penny said softly. "Just give her a little time to adjust to the idea."

"I hate to upset her, but this is the only sensible plan. It's not as though we won't see each other. I can take the train out for a visit when I have a day off."

Alex had watched the interaction between husband and wife with respectful silence. Now he laid his napkin on the table and turned to Jon. "Can you tell us any more about what you saw this morning?"

Jon met Alex's gaze. "All right, but prepare yourself."

Alex nodded. "Go on."

"I took a taxi across town to Woolwich. Much of the area is blocked off, but I told them I was a doctor, and they let me through. Police and teams of soldiers were everywhere, trying to restore order and help those whose homes were damaged. People were frantic, searching for missing loved ones or trying to salvage a few items out of their homes. It was heartbreaking. I attended one young man who had suffered terrible burns from the fire. I had to send him on to St. George's for further treatment."

Penny's stomach lurched, and she pushed her plate away. *Oh, Father, help that young man.* And what about the others? What would people do now that their homes had been destroyed? Did they have relatives in the country?

She turned to Jon. "You think the Germans will bomb London again?"

"I'm afraid so."

Penny shifted her gaze to Alex. "And you agree?"

He gave a slight nod. "London has always been their target. Now that they've had a successful run, they'll be back. Sending the family to the countryside is a sensible decision."

Jon sent Penny a direct look. "I know it's asking a lot of William and Julia to take in my whole household, but my parents' cottage is much too small, and I'm not sure whom else to turn to."

Penny clutched the napkin in her lap. "It will be difficult for everyone, but I'm sure they'll agree."

Jon and Kate's cook, Mrs. Murdock, had a very strong personality, and so did Highland's Chef Lagarde. Putting them together in the same kitchen was sure to cause some fireworks. And that wouldn't be the only problem they would face.

The six older children would have to attend a new school, and almost everything about their lives would change. No more visits to Wiltshire Park or the zoo—but most of all, they would miss Jon and his leadership in the family. How would the children react to the move? What would happen when their daily routine was thrown to the wind?

Penny pulled in a calming breath and sent off a silent prayer. Her sister needed her help, now more than ever, and she must not let her down.

Lydia tugged the trunk down the hall toward the top of the stairs. With no footmen in the house, she and Helen would have to carry all the trunks down to the entrance hall. Soon the bags and trunks would be loaded on a truck and taken to the train station, while the family and servants rode there in cars.

Helen huffed as she pushed from the other end. "How many more trunks are there?"

"Three. Then we must get the bags in our room."

"Right. We don't want to leave those behind."

Lydia stopped at the top of the stairs and wiped her forehead. The last twenty-four hours had been a mad scramble, sorting and packing clothing for themselves and all the children. The older ones had helped before they were called down to the kitchen by Mrs. Murdock to carry up hampers of food. No use leaving good food behind, not when there were shortages of so many things.

Thank goodness Kate and Penny had packed their own bags. Lydia wasn't sure she and Helen could've finished the job in one day without their help.

Helen grabbed the leather handle on her end of the trunk. "Ready?"

Lydia nodded and took hold on the other side. They lifted the heavy trunk, then slowly started down the stairs.

Lydia had been surprised to hear they were going back to the country, but she was glad of it. She'd hardly slept a wink since the air raid. And with the threat of more bombs falling on their heads, it wasn't safe to stay in town.

She'd be glad to get back to Highland. With more staff around to help, she might not have to work quite so hard. But bringing the children meant she'd be taking most of her workload with her.

They stopped on the first landing to rest, and she glanced at Helen. How would things go for her sister at Highland? Sir William and his wife, Julia, were good people. They treated their staff well. But Helen was bringing her three-year-old daughter Emily along. She hoped people would understand and not be hard on her.

Kate said their salary and duties would be the

same, but who would be in charge? Would it be Julia, the former governess who had married Sir William and who she must now call Lady Julia, or would it still be Mrs. Kate? And what about Highland's housekeeper, Mrs. Dalton? She'd been in charge when Lydia left Highland to come to London with Kate. Would Lydia be answering to them all?

Just thinking about it made her head spin.

She took hold and lifted the trunk again. It would all be sorted out in time. Everyone had to do their bit to keep things running. That was the only way to show the Germans that the English would not be beaten.

Conversation rose from the entrance hall, and Lydia looked over the banister.

Miss Penny, Lieutenant Goodwin, and Dr. Jon stood together at the bottom of the stairs. Nearby, Donald gave Jack a playful shove, and Jack pushed him back.

"Settle down, boys." Dr. Jon sent them a serious look. "This is neither the time nor the place to roughhouse."

Alex looked up and saw Lydia and Helen. "Wait a minute, ladies." He turned to Donald and Jack. "Come on, lads, let's give them a hand."

Donald scowled. "Do we have to?"

Alex clasped the older boy's shoulder. "Men don't stand by and let ladies carry heavy trunks down the stairs."

Donald grimaced, but he and Jack followed Alex up to meet Lydia and Helen.

Alex reached for the trunk. "We'd be glad to take this down for you, wouldn't we, Donald?"

"Yes, sir." Donald's words didn't sound too convincing, but he took Helen's place and Jack grabbed hold on the corner as well.

"Careful, now. We don't want to drop it." Alex looked over his shoulder and backed down the stairs.

A dreamy smile spread across Helen's face as she watched Alex. "Lieutenant Goodwin is a real nice man, isn't he?" She spoke just above a whisper so only Lydia could hear.

Lydia leaned closer to Helen. "Yes, he is. But he's going off to war, and there's no use getting a broken heart over someone who might never come back."

Helen's brows dipped. "I just said he was nice. You don't have to scold me."

Lydia sent her sister a meaningful look, and Helen had the good sense to blush and look away. The fact that Helen had a daughter and no husband ought to be enough to keep her on the straight and narrow path, but Lydia wasn't sure Helen had learned her lesson, especially when she got all swoony like that.

The lieutenant and the boys deposited the trunk by the front door. "Are there any more that need to come down?"

"Yes, sir." Lydia explained where to find the other trunks in the upstairs hallway. Helen's gaze stayed glued on Lieutenant Goodwin as he and the boys climbed the stairs again.

Lydia tugged her arm. "Come on, Helen."

Her sister huffed. "I don't know why you're scowling at me."

"I'm not scowling. We've got to get our bags and see if Mrs. Kate needs any more help." She started up the steps.

"Well, you do look cross." Helen tromped up the stairs behind her.

Lydia sighed. "I'm just tired and flustered with all that needs to be done."

That was true, but that wasn't all that worried her. Seeing her sister watch Lieutenant Goodwin with such longing stirred up painful memories of the trouble they'd faced three years ago when Helen ran away with Charlie Gibbons.

What a terrible mistake that had been!

Their parents had been crushed, and Helen's situation had gone from bad to worse with Charlie's drinking, lazy ways, and fiery temper. Lydia, Kate, and Jon had searched for Helen in London's East End, hoping to convince her to leave Charlie and get the help she needed to care for herself and her unborn baby. But that search caused such conflict in the Ramsey family that it nearly parted Kate and Jon before their courtship ever began.

Lydia was ever so glad Helen finally got away from Charlie and that Kate and Jon were able to marry. They had a wonderful love story and seemed very happy together. Of course, worries about the war and Kate's pregnancy had put a strain on them of late, but Lydia was sure their love was strong enough to weather any storm.

Lydia glanced at her sister and bit her lip. Helen longed for love, but she seemed determined to find it in the wrong places with the wrong people.

As they reached their bedroom door, she turned to her sister. "You must remember what happened with Charlie and keep hold of your heart."

Helen's eyes flashed and her lower lip trembled. "There's no need to remind me of that man or all the hurt he caused."

"There *is* a need. You have a daughter to think of. The Lord has provided for you both. You must be sensible and not throw it all away."

Helen pushed open the door to their room and walked inside. "You don't know what it's like. You've not been wooed and given away your heart, then seen it tossed aside like so much rubbish."

"No, I haven't, and I'm glad of it. I'm waiting for the right man at the right time." Lydia snatched up her bags and walked out the door, her face flaming and her heart aching.

Penny gripped her handbag and looked across the platform and down the tracks. There was no sign of the train yet, but she was glad for a few minutes to catch her breath before they had to say goodbye to Jon and Alex and start their journey.

William's telegram inviting them to come to Highland Hall had arrived only a few hours after Jon sent his request. They'd spent the last day and a half packing up the house and preparing for their move.

Kate stood next to Penny, her gloved hands clasped tight as she watched Jon and Alex speak to the porter. The stout man touched his cap and nodded, then began tagging their trunks, bags, and hampers. Nearby, Lydia, Helen, and Mrs. Murdock watched over the children. This would be the first train ride for many of them, and their excited chatter made it clear that in spite of the serious issues prompting the trip, they were looking forward to it.

Penny glanced at the crowd gathered on the platform. Soldiers in khaki uniforms seemed to outnumber civilians today. Family and friends surrounded many of the men. A few soldiers held hands with wives or sweethearts while they waited for their train. Some of the women blotted tears from their cheeks, while others wore brave smiles.

She shifted her gaze to Alex again and released a soft sigh. He was leaving today as well, returning to Upavon to finish his training. Her heart clenched. When would she see him again?

He'd stayed at the house with them following the bombing, spending most of his time entertaining the children with card tricks and humorous stories about his childhood in India. He'd done an excellent job keeping them occupied while Kate oversaw the packing and Jon made arrangements to move his family to Highland.

Penny had to admit she'd been as captivated as the children as she listened to his exotic tales.

But there was more to Alex than a quick smile and an adventurous spirit. He was brave and caring, and he'd proved it the night of the bombing. He gave the impression he was strong and confident, ready to face any danger that came his way, yet there was something about him that hinted at a deeper need . . .

And that tugged at Penny's heart.

She glanced around the platform once more. Why hadn't his family come to see him off? Did they know he was leaving today? Did they understand what a dangerous assignment he would face after he finished his training?

She recalled the way Alex had described his late father, but the warmth had faded from his voice when he spoke of his mother. He'd mentioned his sister and said she also lived in London. But neither of them seemed to care enough to meet him at the station today to say good-bye.

Who would write to him and send him packages? Who would pray for his protection and safe return? And who would be here to greet him when the war was over and he finally came home?

Penny's throat burned. No man should go off to battle without knowing someone cared and would be waiting to welcome him safely home again.

Jon approached and smiled at Kate. "Everything's taken care of. The porter will see to the bags."

"Thank you." Kate's voice sounded soft and strained.

Jon took Kate's hand. "Everything will be all right, my dear. I promise."

She nodded, but her eyes glistened. She blinked and looked away.

Alex touched Penny's arm. "Let's give them a moment."

They moved a few paces down the platform, and Penny looked up at him. "What time does your train leave?"

"Four-thirty, if it's on time. Then it's only an hour and a half to Upavon." He adjusted his grip on his duffel bag. "I should be back on base in time for dinner."

Penny looked back at Jon and Kate. "It will be hard on them to be parted."

"Yes, I'm sure it will be."

Penny sighed. "At least Highland's not too far away. Jon can come and visit."

"Yes. He's a lucky man." A wistful look filled Alex's eyes.

Penny stilled, and an ache that matched his wistful expression filled her heart. Though they'd only spent a few days together, she couldn't deny the strong connection she felt to Alex. "I hope you'll come and see us at Highland on your next leave."

"I'm not sure when that will be."

"Well, whenever it is, you're more than welcome. Highland is a huge old place, and there's plenty of room for friends." She forced cheerfulness into her voice.

"Even when you add all these children?"

"Yes, even then."

He cocked his head, and his mouth tugged up at the corner. "You mean it? You want me to come?"

Her face warmed, but she kept her tone bright. "Of course. We'd love to see you."

He looked down. Was he embarrassed or touched by the invitation?

"Thank you." The sudden, husky gratitude in his tone gave her the answer.

And moved her so she could barely respond. "So . . . you'll write and let us know where you're stationed?"

"If you'd like."

"I would, very much." She couldn't believe she'd said that! "And I'm sure the children would love to hear from you as well. We all enjoyed meeting a real-life pilot." That seemed to lift his spirits.

She reached in her purse and took out a calling

card. "The only address you'll need is our name and Highland Hall, Fulton."

He accepted the card and studied it for a moment, looking at a loss for words. Then he slipped the card in his front jacket pocket and patted the spot. "Right next to my heart." He grinned and winked.

She shook her head and laughed. "You are a tease."

He laughed along with her, and the sound warmed her heart.

Just then the bell rang, announcing the approaching train. Penny glanced down the track and bit her lip. Oh, if only they had more time. The breeze blew a strand of her hair loose, and she brushed it away from her face. "I'll be expecting a letter, so you'd better write." She made her voice stern, but it was only to hide her growing emotion.

He frowned at the train, then looked back at her, all the teasing gone from his expression. "I will."

The train's brakes squealed and hissed, sending puffs of steam around them.

She swallowed hard and looked up at him. His dark eyes glittered, and he opened his mouth to say something else—

"Alex! Penny!"

The moment broken, they turned to find Jon waving them over.

"Let's all gather round."

Penny blew out a deep breath. What had Alex been about to say?

Alex glanced at Jon. "We should join them."

Penny nodded, and she and Alex walked across the platform together.

Jon waited until he had everyone's attention, then looked around at each child. "Now, I trust you all to listen to Mrs. Foster and the other adults and follow their instructions on the train and when you reach Highland. I'm counting on you to take care of each other and be brave and obedient. Will you do that for me?"

"Yes, sir," several of the children replied, while the others nodded.

"All aboard!"

At the conductor's call, Jon shook hands with the three boys and gave their shoulders a pat. He kissed the girls' cheeks, then turned to the cook. "Thank you, Mrs. Murdock."

She pulled a handkerchief from her sleeve and wiped her nose. "God bless you, Doctor." Then she turned away and climbed into the train.

"Take care, Lydia. You too, Helen. I'm grateful you're going along." Jon turned to Kate and wrapped her in a tight embrace.

Penny looked away. It hurt too much to watch, and Jon and Kate deserved a private last moment together.

Alex walked toward the train with her, his face somber. "Take care, Penny," he said softly.

She nodded and looked his way. "Good-bye, Alex." Her throat felt so tight she had a hard time pushing out her next words. "Please, be careful."

"I will." His mouth pulled up at one corner, but the smile didn't reach his eyes.

She wanted to say more, but the conductor called again for everyone to board. She scanned his face, hoping to hold that memory in her heart, then followed the children onto the train. With so many in their party, they had to split into two compartments. Penny settled on the bench with Lydia, Helen, and little Emily. She looked out the window and watched Jon give Kate one last kiss before he helped her climb into the next compartment.

Alex waited on the platform, his gaze on Penny. She lifted her hand. "God bless you and keep you safe," she called through the open window.

He waved. "You too."

The whistle blew, and the train pulled away from the station. The last thing she saw was Alex standing tall and alone in the crowd.

Four

Julia Ramsey descended the main staircase at Highland and looked down at the great hall. Beams of sunlight fell across the red carpet from the windows high overhead in the arched ceiling.

She loved this room, with its dark paneling, beautiful paintings, and treasured sculptures. Though the great hall might look large and imposing to others, to her it was the heart of their home. Here they gathered the family and staff for prayer each morning, welcomed guests to their home, decorated a tall Christmas tree each December, and held the annual servants' ball in the early spring.

She and William had hosted their wedding luncheon in Highland's great hall, as well as wedding luncheons for Clark and Sarah, and Jon and Kate. She looked around with a soft smile . . . so many joyful events giving her special memories to treasure.

The hall was quiet this afternoon. Only the ticking of the clock on the marble fireplace mantel and the sound of the maids cleaning in the drawing room broke the silence.

But change was in the air.

Kate and Penny were returning to Highland today, and they were bringing nine children, two maids, and a cook with them.

Julia paused at the foot of the stairs. What would it be like to hear the chatter and laughter of so many young voices echoing through the house? Only two children lived at Highland now— William's ten-year-old daughter, Millie, and Clark Dalton's niece, Abigail, who was also ten. William's fourteen-year-old son, Andrew, was away at school, but he would return in a few weeks to spend the summer holiday at home. Then there would be twelve children—an even dozen.

What a change that would be!

She looked around once more, memories flooding back. When she'd first come to Highland four years ago, it had seemed a dark and gloomy place. She'd just returned from India, where her family had served as missionaries for twelve years. William needed a governess to oversee Millie and Andrew and his young cousins, Kate and Penny. And Julia needed a job so she could help support her parents. She accepted the position—a decision that changed the course of her life.

That God brought her a husband and family here at Highland still amazed her. And now she and William had a new challenge before them. The frightening impact of the war had finally reached Highland, and she prayed they would have the strength and courage to meet the challenges and help the family and staff through this time of testing.

Julia lifted her eyes to the sunlight streaming down from above. *How long, Lord? When will this terrible war end? How much will it cost our country and our hearts?*

A noise below drew her attention. William walked out of the library and glanced at his watch. He looked up at Julia, and even from this distance, she saw the anticipation in his expression. "They should be here any minute."

"Yes." She glanced toward the door. "It's a lovely day. Shall we wait outside?"

He nodded, and she went down the stairs to walk with him through the entrance hall and out the front door. The gravel drive was still damp from an earlier rain shower, and a few shallow puddles reflected the blue sky above. Most of the clouds had cleared, but raindrops still glittered on the wide green lawn beyond the drive.

"I'm glad the weather changed. I'd hate to see them arrive in a downpour." William squinted up at the sun, then turned to her. "Shall we walk?"

Her heart lifted. "Yes. Let's."

He offered her his arm, and she slipped her hand through as they set off down the drive. She matched his steps, enjoying the sound of the gravel crunching underfoot and William's closeness. What a comfort he was. How thankful she was for their life together and the blessings they enjoyed. If only . . .

She bit her lip.

"So, what do you think of having a house full of children?"

His words pierced his heart, and her steps faltered.

He glanced down at her and stopped, his eyes reflecting his regret. "I'm sorry, my dear. That was not how I should've phrased my question."

Julia shook her head. "It's all right." She tried to swallow away the tightness in her throat, but it was useless. It had been almost seven weeks since she'd lost the baby, but her heart still ached. She'd only been twelve weeks along, but she'd let herself hope everything would be all right this time, but it wasn't.

She'd lost their first baby a little over a year ago, only a few days after she'd told William she was pregnant.

He pressed his hand over hers. "I love you, my darling. I wish there was more I could say or do."

She looked down. "I know you do, and I'm grateful."

"Our time will come. I'm sure of it."

Julia's eyes burned. "Are you?" She lifted her gaze and swallowed, trying to hold back her tears. "I hope you're right, but I'm not certain of it anymore."

Compassion filled his eyes. "You are young and healthy, and the doctor says there is no reason we can't try again soon. We must not lose hope."

She nodded, but an ache weighed on her heart. After losing two babies, it was hard to imagine any other outcome. What if God had a different plan for them? What if William's children, Millie and Andrew, were the only ones who would ever call her mother? Could she accept that?

She loved them dearly, but her heart yearned to hold a babe of her own, one born of the love she and William shared . . . a baby with his eyes and her nose or some other feature that stamped the child as their very own.

"Papa!" Millie ran down the gravel drive toward them, and Abigail hurried after her, though she couldn't quite keep up.

Panting and smiling, Millie skidded to a stop beside them, her red curly hair blowing across her face. She brushed it away and looked up at William. "It's almost time, isn't it? Ann said we might come down and ask to wait with you."

William tousled her hair. "So, you're eager to see your cousins?"

"Yes, and the children." Her blue-green eyes glowed as she hooked arms with Abigail. "We think it will be great fun to have more children at Highland. I'm sure we're all going to get along well and become good friends."

Millie was such a cheerful, optimistic child, but her words sent questions thrumming through Julia's mind. The children Jon and Kate had taken into their home came straight off the streets of London's East End, where poverty and crime were the norm. Most had no parents, and they had received little education or training before arriving at Jon and Kate's.

Memories of the young girls she cared for in India rose in her mind. They'd been abandoned by their parents or rescued from a terrible life of slavery in the temples. A shiver raced down her arms as she recalled some of the painful stories the girls had told, describing how they had suffered.

While her experiences in India had prepared her to cope with this new group of children, she wouldn't have her parents on hand to help this time.

A ripple of unease traveled through her, but she told herself not to worry. The main responsibility of caring for the children would fall on Kate, but she would need help from William and Julia, as well as Penny and the rest of the staff. Especially since Jon must stay in London. Handling a dozen children, no matter where they were born or raised, was not an easy task, and it would take teamwork to bring about good results for them and for the children.

Off in the distance, two cars pulled through the main gate and made their way up the drive toward the house. A wagon followed behind, stacked with trunks and bags and carrying a few passengers.

"Here they come!" Millie grabbed Abigail's hand and dashed back toward the front door to greet Kate, Penny, and the children.

"Are you ready, my dear?" William glanced down, a deeper question reflected in his eyes.

Julia pulled in a slow breath, summoning her strength. "Yes." She took her husband's arm again, and they followed the girls back to greet their guests.

• • •

Lydia held tight to the side of the wagon as it passed through Highland's main gate and followed the two cars toward the front entrance. Helen sat beside her on the hard wooden bench, holding fast to her daughter, Emily, who sat on her lap. Mrs. Murdock and Donald rode on the opposite side of the wagon, almost hidden by the trunks and bags stacked in the middle. The wagon seat might be hard, but it gave Lydia a good view. Rolling green hills dotted with sheep, shady forest glades, and spacious parkland spread out around them.

The road curved to the right, opening up a new view. Lydia pointed to the house. "There it is. That's Highland Hall."

Helen turned and gasped. "Why, it looks like a castle!"

"Wait till you see the inside."

Mrs. Murdock, the cook, gave an appreciative nod. "It's a grand place, that's for sure and certain."

Donald stared past Lydia's shoulder, a slight frown dipping his brows. "It looks more like a big school or a government building."

Helen twisted around for a better view. "Oh, no. It's much too nice for that."

Highland Hall was quite a sight—four stories high at the tallest point and built of sand-colored stone. It had scores of arched windows, several chimney stacks, and a tall round tower at one corner. Lydia had loved working here those two years before she moved to London with the Fosters, and it still gave her a thrill to see the great house surrounded by wide green lawns and colorful gardens.

She glanced across at Donald. "Highland Hall is called a manor house."

The boy tipped his head and studied it.

"Mrs. Kate's cousin, Sir William Ramsey, is in charge here," Mrs. Murdock added. She had cooked for Sir William and the family when they came to London for the season, and it seemed she wanted to remind them she was well acquainted with the Ramseys.

Lydia held back her smile. "Mrs. Murdock is right, Donald. Sir William Ramsey is Baronet and master of Highland. But he's a fair and generous man, and you're to show him proper respect."

Donald gave a shrug, trying to look unimpressed, but Lydia could tell he was storing her words away.

She looked toward the house again. Sir William and Lady Julia waited by the front entrance with Miss Millie and Abigail. My, how those little girls had grown! What other changes had happened at Highland since she'd been away?

She looked at Lady Julia again, her heart sinking a bit. She'd overheard Dr. Jon and Mrs. Kate talking about Lady Julia losing a baby recently.

What a heartbreak that must have been, especially when she dearly loved children.

Mr. Lawrence, the Ramseys' butler, stepped outside and joined the family. Patrick, the tall footman, followed him out the door. Mrs. Miranda Dalton, the housekeeper, came next and stood beside Lady Julia. Lydia had worked under Mrs. Dalton for only a few months before Kate and Jon had married. Mrs. Dalton was a kind woman, though she liked things done her way and did not tolerate sloppy work.

The cars ahead of them rolled to a stop. Patrick sprang forward and opened the rear passenger door. Kate, Penny, and several children climbed out. Julia greeted Kate and Penny with a kiss on the cheek.

The wagon rolled to a stop behind the cars. Donald jumped down and joined the other children, looking a bit uncertain. The driver walked around to the back of the wagon and reached out a hand to help Helen climb down, then he lifted little Emily and set her on the ground by Helen. He turned back and helped Mrs. Murdock, and finally Lydia.

Julia opened her arms to them all. "Welcome to Highland."

"Thank you, m'lady." Lydia nodded to her and bobbed a slight curtsy.

Julia looked around the group. "Let's go inside, and we'll help everyone find their way to their rooms." She took Kate's arm, and they walked toward the front door. The children and Penny followed them.

Mrs. Dalton greeted Mrs. Murdock, who set off around the side of the house.

The housekeeper acknowledged Lydia with a nod. "It's good to see you again, Lydia."

"Thank you, ma'am. This is my sister, Helen Chambers, and her daughter, Emily." She glanced at Helen. "This is Mrs. Dalton, the housekeeper."

Helen straightened. "It's good to meet you, ma'am."

Mrs. Dalton nodded, but a question flickered in her eyes as she looked from Helen to Emily. "This is your daughter?"

"Yes, ma'am." Helen shot a quick glance at Lydia and then looked back at the house-keeper.

Mrs. Dalton's mouth turned down as she looked at Emily. "No one told me you were bringing a child."

Helen's face flushed. "Emily's a good girl, no trouble at all. You'll hardly know she's here."

"But how will you do your work when you have a child to look after?"

Helen's eyes flashed. "We managed well enough in London. I'm sure we can do the same here."

"And where do you expect her to sleep?" Mrs. Dalton's tone rose to match Helen's.

"Why, in my room, with me, of course."

101

Mr. Lawrence strode toward them. "Is there a problem?"

Mrs. Dalton turned to him. "Did you know Helen was bringing her *daughter* with her?"

His eyes widened. "Her daughter?"

Helen lifted her chin. "Yes, sir. This is Emily Rose. She's three years old, and she's a sweet child. There's no cause for you or anyone else to be looking down on her."

Mr. Lawrence lowered his dark eyebrows. "I do not appreciate your tone, young woman. This is highly irregular. I will have to discuss it with Sir William and Lady Julia."

"Mrs. Kate is the one you should be talkin' to. She's the one who hired me."

"All the staff in this house work for Sir William, and they are under my direct supervision."

Mrs. Dalton cleared her throat.

Mr. Lawrence inclined his head toward her. "Mine and Mrs. Dalton's."

Helen's face turned a deeper shade of pink.

Lydia bit her lip, praying her sister would hold her tongue and not cause any more trouble.

Helen turned and snatched her bag from the pile Hardy, the chauffeur, and Patrick had stacked on the ground at the back of the wagon. She gripped Emily's hand and started toward the front door.

Lydia pulled in a sharp breath and reached for her sister's arm, but she was too late to stop her.

Mr. Lawrence stepped in front of Helen, his face set like granite. "The *lower* members of the staff enter the house through the doors in the rear courtyard."

Helen glared up at him, then swung around and marched off along the side of the house, tugging poor little Emily with her.

Lydia turned to Mrs. Dalton. "Please, don't think too poorly of Helen. She's never worked in a big house like this. She doesn't know what's expected."

Mr. Lawrence lowered his eyebrows at Lydia, as though she were the one who had broken the rules. "Surely she knows maids do not bring their children along with them."

"Yes, but it's a special arrangement Dr. and Mrs. Foster made for her. They've been very kind, and Helen has worked hard. I hope you'll give her a chance."

Mr. Lawrence and Mrs. Dalton exchanged serious looks. The butler turned to Lydia. "As I said, we will discuss it with Sir William and Lady Julia." Then he turned and walked in the front door.

Mrs. Dalton lifted her chin and followed him inside.

Lydia's heart sank. Would Mrs. Kate speak up for Helen and convince Sir William and Lady Julia to keep her on? Since Mrs. Kate had been suffering with morning sickness, Miss Penny had handled most of the day-to-day routine with the children and servants.

Lydia clicked her tongue, then picked up her bag and headed around the side of the house, hoping and praying it would all work out.

Five

"Good night, Kate." Penny leaned closer and kissed her sister's cheek. She stepped back and searched Kate's face, noting the shadows beneath her sister's eyes and the weary slope of her shoulders. It had been a long, exhausting day for both of them, but poor Kate was still dealing with the difficulties of her pregnancy.

They'd been up since six and had spent most of the morning packing their trunks and closing up the house in London. Jon had decided to take a flat near the hospital rather than rattle around in that big house by himself.

Supervising the excited children on the journey to Highland had been a bit of a challenge, but they'd all arrived safely, just after five-thirty in the evening. Dinner had been served an hour later—a rather hectic affair, especially after Rose spilled her glass of water and Jack called Susan a baby for not liking the food.

Penny sighed and shook her head. Poor little

weary Rose had broken down in tears and run from the table.

Parenting was not for the fainthearted!

The children had gone up to get ready for bed just after eight, and Lydia, Helen, Kate, and Penny made the rounds to hear their prayers and tuck them in.

Now, at last, it was time for Kate and Penny to get some rest.

"I'll see you in the morning," Kate said.

"Yes, bright and early."

Kate gave a soft groan, then opened the door to her childhood bedroom.

"Oh, Kate," Penny called, turning back.

Her sister looked out from the doorway. "Yes?"

"Did you settle things with Mrs. Dalton about Helen and Emily?"

Kate nodded. "She obviously doesn't approve, but once I told her Julia and William were informed and had agreed, she accepted it."

"Good. We need Helen's help, and it would hardly be fair to bring her to Highland and then have Mrs. Dalton turn her away."

Kate yawned. "Yes, you're right. Good night." She slipped into her bedroom.

"Sweet dreams." Penny continued down the hall to her own room, thinking about William's request that they meet at eight to discuss their schedules and responsibilities. With a dozen children in residence at Highland, some things would have to change, though she didn't expect her role would be much different. She planned to continue helping Kate oversee the children, just as she had in London.

They had a comfortable routine there, but without Jon's presence it would be a challenge to maintain the same schedule. Surely William would be as patient and understanding as Jon had been. The children needed a father figure, which meant that role would fall to William . . . if he would accept it.

She walked into her bedroom, and memories came flooding back. This had been her special sanctuary as long as she could remember. The blaze in the fireplace added welcome warmth to the room. Tomorrow would be June 3, but Highland's thick stone walls kept the house cool year round, except perhaps on the south side on the warmest summer afternoon.

Penny crossed toward the window and pushed the drapes aside. She looked down at the padded window seat and smiled. How many books had she read sitting right here, dreaming of the future and taking in the beautiful view out her window?

The sky was dark now, but in the morning she'd see the walled garden with the arched entryway, the long glass greenhouse, and beyond that, flocks of sheep scattered across the emerald-green hills.

She turned and scanned her room once more. When she was sixteen, a fire had gutted it and nearly taken her life. It had burned through almost half the east wing on this floor and the floor above. But expert carpenters had been called in to make repairs and remove all traces of the damage.

Penny sighed and settled on the window seat. Outside, stars glittered overhead and a quarter moon spread silvery light over the parkland and shadowed gardens.

Her thoughts drifted back through the last three days in London, and Alex's image rose in her mind. Had she really seen tenderness in his eyes when they said good-bye? Tenderness . . . for her? Or was he just reflecting the emotions around him as so many people sent their loved ones off to war?

Had he made it safely back to Upavon? Was he looking up at this same moon tonight . . . thinking of her?

She blew out a breath and turned away from the window.

In a few weeks Alex would finish his training and probably fly off to France. She crossed her arms, and a chilly shiver traveled down her back. Just the thought of him in one of those little airplanes flying over the English Channel was enough to frighten her. But flying over those rough waters was nothing compared to the danger he would face when he took to the skies over the front lines in France and Belgium.

She clasped her hands and gazed out at the

stars again. *Father, please watch over Alex. Protect him. Keep him safe, and bring him home again.*

Worrisome questions sent her thoughts swirling away. Why hadn't she said more to him at the station—something encouraging that he could tuck into his heart and recall when times were hard and his spirits were low?

An idea struck, and she rose from the window seat. She might not have his address yet, but there was no reason she couldn't write him a letter tonight. Surely he would keep his word and let her know his address, and when he did she would be ready to mail her reply.

In fact, she could add to her letter each day and fill it with cheerful news, encouraging stories about the children, and descriptions of their life at Highland.

And if his letter was . . . friendly, she might even repeat her invitation to come and spend his leave with them here at Highland. She supposed she ought to ask William and Julia's permission. It might even be better if the invitation came from them. But if she asked him again . . .

Would he come?

Her heartbeat picked up speed. Wouldn't it be wonderful to show him around Highland? He seemed to love the outdoors, and there were so many interesting places they could explore together, walking or riding around the estate.

She crossed to her writing table, pulled open the

drawer, and took out her stationery and a pen. She would start the letter tonight.

And pray for him as she penned each line.

Alex brought his Morane-Saulnier in steep and fast, barely missing the earthwork surrounding the sandy airfield at St. Pol, France. The plane touched down with a nerve-racking jolt. He blew out a deep breath and taxied toward the hangar, trying to avoid the worst of the bumpy tufts of grass.

Just yesterday, one of the other pilots, James Ross, came in too low, hit the earthwork, and turned turtle, flipping his plane upside down. Ross received only a few cuts and bruises. He was lucky he hadn't killed himself.

Alex turned off the plane's engine and lifted his goggles, thankful one more mission was complete.

Lead mechanic George Meddis ran toward the plane, his face red. "Goodwin, where have you been? You were due back over an hour ago!"

Alex unhooked his restraint, vaulted over the side, then jumped to the ground. "I had a bit of trouble over Ostend."

"What kind of trouble?"

"Ground fire." He wiped his hand down his dusty face.

"I hope you steered a zigzag course and headed out to sea."

Alex glanced away and rubbed the back of his neck. That was what he'd been trained to do, but this was his first coastal reconnaissance flight on his own without an observer, and he didn't want to turn tail and head home at the first sign of trouble. He gave his head a slight shake. "I kept going and made it through to Zeebrugge."

"Well, it shouldn't have taken you this long to fly up to Zeebrugge and back."

Alex gave a slight shrug. "I spotted a German Taube just past Ostend, and I chased him back to his base at De Haan."

Meddis groaned and shook his head. "There can't be more than a pint of petrol left in your tank. You were probably flying on fumes. Did you think about that?"

"I watched the gauge."

The mechanic pointed at the bullet-riddled fuselage. "How'd that happen?"

"The German in the Taube shot at me with his rifle."

Meddis rubbed his forehead and muttered under his breath.

"Don't worry," Alex grinned. "I shot back with my revolver, and his plane looks a lot worse than mine."

The mechanic ran his hand over the bullet holes. "Do you know how long it's going to take me to fix this?" His tone was scolding, but Alex could tell Meddis was concerned about him as well as the plane.

"It's not that bad." He clapped Meddis on the

shoulder. "I'm sure you'll have her repaired and ready to fly in no time."

"It will take me at least two days, if not longer, and that means you'll be grounded until the work is done."

Footsteps crunched on the grass behind Alex. "Goodwin."

Alex pulled in a sharp breath and turned. Wing Commander Randal Longmore stood behind him, frowning at the plane.

Alex whipped his arm up in a quick salute. "Sir."

"At ease." Longmore scanned the plane's fuselage. "What happened?"

"I spotted a German Taube on my way up the coast and gave chase. We exchanged fire, and I forced him back to his base at De Haan."

Longmore clasped his hands behind his back and studied Alex for a few seconds.

Alex's neck warmed, and he shifted his weight to the other foot. Longmore was a strict disciplinarian, a traditional Navy man. He expected his men to stick with the mission and obey orders.

When Alex arrived two weeks ago, Longmore called him into his office and warned him he would be watching him closely. The crash-landing during training was a black mark on his record. His flight instructor at Upavon had written in Alex's file that he was brave and intelligent, but could also be impetuous and reckless. That obviously worried Longmore.

111

Since that talk, Alex had done his best to keep his head down and do as he was told. Had his decision to chase the Taube today destroyed the trust he had tried to build with his commander?

Longmore finally spoke. "I've ordered another Morane. It should arrive by the end of next week."

Alex lifted his eyebrows. "You ordered another plane . . . for me?"

Longmore gave a curt nod. "That way you'll have one to fly while the other is being repaired." He sent him a serious look. "I want to keep you in the air, Goodwin."

Alex's chest expanded. "Thank you, sir."

"Don't thank me, and don't get puffed up about it. Overconfidence and recklessness are a deadly combination." Longmore glanced at the bullet holes. "Taking risks may be necessary, but know your limits. Remember your training. If you do, you might stay in the sky long enough to do some damage to the enemy. If you don't, you won't live long enough to make a difference." Longmore paused, his gaze riveting. "Do you understand, Goodwin?"

Alex straightened. "Yes, sir."

"Keep your wits about you. Take care of yourself and your plane . . . or planes, I should say."

A smile pulled up one side of Alex's mouth. "I'll do my best, sir."

"I'm counting on it. Now, go get something to

eat, then report to my office. I want to hear exactly what happened on your flight today." The commander turned and strode back across the airfield without waiting for his reply.

Meddis turned to Alex. "You don't see that often."

"What?"

"Longmore handing out compliments. Or ordering extra planes."

"That's true." Alex glanced at the Morane again. She could be temperamental, but she was quick and light at the controls, and that suited Alex just fine. All the other planes in the squadron were biplanes, but the Morane had a single, high wing above the cockpit. That made it ideal for artillery spotting and aerial photography. The wood-framed fuselage was 22 feet long and the wingspan was 36 feet, giving her good stability in the air. She had an 80-horsepower Gnome engine that accounted for more than a third of her total weight. She was a real beauty . . . and now she'd have a sister.

He'd never have to be grounded.

"Longmore makes you think he's all about rules and regulations," Meddis continued. "But he knows it's going to take some fancy flying to beat the Huns. And I suppose he thinks you're one of our top pilots."

Alex grinned and slapped the mechanic's shoulder again. "Thanks, Meddis."

"You can thank me by staying out of trouble up

there." He pointed his thumb toward the sky.

Alex's smile spread wider. "I will. I promise."

Meddis growled and waved him off. "I'll believe that when I see it!"

Alex chuckled, then turned and set off across the field. He passed the hangars, then walked toward the long wooden building that served as the squadron's dining hall and briefing room.

Just before he reached the door, Sublieutenant Fletcher hustled toward him carrying a large canvas bag. "Mail just arrived."

Alex's pulse jumped, but he pushed down his hopes and held the door open for Fletcher.

The other man tossed the bag on the closest table and pulled open the drawstring. Several men gathered around while Fletcher reached in, pulled out a stack of letters, then began calling names. "Reynolds, Peterson, Harvey, St. Charles . . ."

The men strode forward and accepted their mail, most with a smile and look of anticipation on their faces.

Alex's shoulders tensed. Would he receive a letter today? He'd written to Lindy, Jon, and Penny shortly after he arrived at St. Pol, but letters took at least a week to be delivered and then another week to receive a reply.

"Wilson, Lundmere, Miller, James . . ."

Alex swallowed and glanced at the clock on the wall. Why was he standing here waiting for something that wasn't coming? Lindy, Jon, and

Penny all had busy lives and plenty of friends and family back at home. Even if they had received his letters, he doubted they'd write back, especially not this soon.

Fletcher handed out the last letter, and a groan passed through the group. Alex clenched his jaw and berated himself for hoping someone cared enough to write.

Fletcher lifted his hand. "Wait, there's more." He reached in the bag and pulled out two packages.

Alex's breath snagged in his chest. A package would be even better than a letter, but he was a fool to hope for one. His empty stomach growled and he turned away.

"Goodwin."

A jolt shot through Alex at Fletcher's call. He turned and stared at the package in the man's hand.

Fletcher's eyebrows rose. "Well, do you want it or not?"

"Yes." Alex stepped forward and took the package wrapped in brown paper and tied with red string. It was about a foot square and about eight or nine inches deep—a fine-looking package, and it had his name on it.

He scanned the wrapping to see who had sent it. There was no return address, only a small pen-and-ink drawing of a wild rose in the corner signed *From H. H.* He didn't recall knowing anyone with the initials *H. H.* Who had sent it?

All thoughts of eating a meal vanished as he strode toward the far end of the room, his package in hand. He sank onto a bench, pulled out his pocketknife, cut the string, then carefully unwrapped the paper and pulled off the lid. A child's drawing of an airplane flying over a house lay on top. It said, "To Lieutenant Goodwin, Our Favorite Pilot, from Rose." He smiled, then gave a little chuckle. So this package was from Penny and the children at Highland Hall. Ah, that explained the *H. H.*

He sorted through six other drawings and below them found a pair of hand-knit brown socks, a packet of loose tea, a tin of hard candies, a bar of chocolate, and a small eagle carved of dark wood. Tucked in next to the eagle was an envelope with his name written on the outside.

He set the box aside and tore open the envelope. Inside were three sheets of ivory stationery covered with fine, feminine handwriting. He pulled them out, turned over the last sheet, and saw Penny's signature at the bottom. Pleasant warmth spread across his chest.

June 2, 1915

Dear Alex,

Today we arrived at Highland, and it has been a whirlwind of activity since we walked through the door. We received a warm welcome and had dinner together with only a few incidents. The children are all settled in bed, and I finally have a few moments to myself. I hope you arrived safely at your base and are doing well. I'm looking forward to your letter and will write more soon.

He stopped and smiled. She'd started the letter the day they arrived at Highland Hall? The very day they'd last seen each other in London? Why, that was almost a month ago!

June 9
   You would not believe how busy we have been. Keeping the children occupied and out of mischief is much more challenging than I could've imagined. They are not used to living in such a large house, especially one filled with so many antiques and expensive furnishings. I must continually remind them to slow down and not run through the halls or slide down the banisters.
   It is an adjustment for all of us, but it is so good to be home. I am grateful for the comfort of familiar places and being with the people I love, especially in the face of the uncertainty of the war.
   Since the school term is so close to the end, we've decided not to enroll the children, but

we will continue with some light studies at home. Julia is helping me with that. The warm weather and new routine make it hard for the children to focus and finish their schoolwork. I'm glad there are only two more weeks, and then we can all enjoy our summer holiday!
I am thinking of you and hoping all is well.

June 22

I was so glad to receive your letter and know you arrived safely at St. Pol, France. I hope this package and our small gifts will remind you of your friends at home in England. Please know we are thinking of you and praying for you each day.

His throat grew tight, and he stopped and looked up. He hadn't realized how much it would mean to know someone remembered him and prayed for him. He swallowed and lowered his gaze to the letter again.

We are officially on summer holiday. Thank goodness the weather is warm, and I can take the children outdoors for walks and games. The older boys are especially restless, and keeping them focused and out of trouble is my daily challenge. Treasure hunts, croquet, badminton, and long walks through the woods and fields take up a good part of each afternoon. The girls have all taken up knitting for the troops. Lucy made these socks for you. I know they're probably not as nice as the ones you usually wear, but they were made with much care, just for you.

He could just see Penny teaching Lucy and the other girls how to knit socks for the troops, guiding their small hands, encouraging them.

Jon visited last Saturday, and Kate was so very happy to have him home even for a short time. He says the hospital is incredibly busy, and he is working much longer hours now that he is not needed at home each day. I hope he doesn't wear himself out with all he is doing for the men at St. George's. We are all praying it won't be long until the war is over, and you, Jon, and all the troops can come home and be reunited with your family and friends.

He released a sigh. News from the front wasn't encouraging. Britain and her enemies were deadlocked. An end to the war was not nearly in sight.

I hope you'll write again and let us know how you are doing. What would you like in your next package? Please ask for whatever you want. We would be happy to send it.

When you're granted your next leave, I hope you will stay with us at Highland for as long as you're able. It would be wonderful to see you again. We could go exploring, and I could show you all my favorite spots. It's beautiful here in the summer. Until then, stay safe and please take very good care of yourself!

With warm thoughts and prayers,
Your friend in Berkshire,
Penny Ramsey

P.S. I thought these verses might encourage you. They are what prompted me to send you the eagle. "The everlasting God, the LORD, the Creator of the ends of the earth, . . . He giveth power to the faint; and to them that have no might he increaseth strength. Even the youths shall faint and be weary, and the young men shall utterly fall: But they that wait upon the LORD shall renew their strength; they shall mount up with wings as eagles; they shall run, and not be weary; and they shall walk, and not faint." ISAIAH 40:28–31

Alex read the letter again, his heart growing stronger as he savored each line.

How had she known just what he needed to hear?

He picked up the eagle and studied the carefully carved wings and curved beak, pondering the verses Penny had added to the closing of her letter.

Looking to the Lord for power and strength . . . waiting on Him and expecting His guidance right there in the cockpit. That's what he would remember the next time he flew off to face the enemy.

Six

Afternoon sun warmed Penny's shoulders as she walked across the broad south lawn at Highland. A slight breeze cooled her face and lifted the green leaves of the nearby oak tree in a shimmering dance. The warm temperature and mostly clear sky made it a pleasant day to bring the children outdoors for a few hours. She hoped it would help them burn off some energy and sleep well tonight.

To her left, Donald hit a birdie across the badminton net to Jack. Tom stood by the center of the grass court, waiting for his turn to challenge the winner of the match.

To her right, Millie and Abigail were teaching Lucy, Edna, Rose, and Susan how to play croquet. Penny smiled as she watched her young cousin, Millie, patiently working with the other girls. Why did girls seem to find it so much easier to get along than boys? It seemed Penny was forever pulling Donald, Jack, and Tom apart and warning them they would lose the privilege of time outdoors if they didn't stop arguing and scuffling with one another.

Lydia, Helen, and Ann sat on a blanket in the shade of the oak tree with little Emily and Irene. Emily rested her head in her mother's lap, looking as though she might fall asleep at any moment. Irene had picked a pile of little white flowers, and Lydia was tying them together to make a daisy chain.

Kate sat nearby on the stone bench, watching the children, her face pale and her gaze somber.

Penny's shoulders tensed as she studied her sister. Kate hadn't been herself since they'd returned to Highland a month ago. No wonder her sister's spirits were low. Jon had only been able to visit twice for a few hours, and Kate's morning sickness rarely seemed to lift.

Penny sighed. She wished she could encourage Kate and help her find a way to climb out of this valley. No solution came to mind, but she sent off a prayer, asking that one would.

She checked her watch. It was almost four o'clock. She lifted her silver whistle on the ribbon around her neck and blew it hard. The whistle's sharp call drew everyone's attention. "We'll be going in for tea in five minutes. Time to finish up your games."

Tom groaned, obviously not happy about missing out on the next badminton match. The girls took the warning in stride and picked up their croquet game.

Julia crossed the wide gravel path, walked down the slope, and approached Penny. "How is it going?"

"Much better today. I've only had to break up one fight and send three children to the stone bench to take a break."

Julia's eyes twinkled and a slight smile lifted her mouth. "I'm sorry, I don't mean to make light of their misbehavior or your having to deal with it, but it seems rather ironic."

"I suppose I deserve it. Kate and I caused you quite a bit of trouble when you first came to Highland."

"Well, it was mainly your sister who objected to having a governess, but you did follow along sometimes."

"Yes, I'm afraid I did." Penny glanced at Kate. "Do you think she's going to be all right?"

Julia studied Kate for a moment, some unspoken emotion flickering in her eyes. "The longer she carries the baby, the better chance she has."

Surprise rippled through Penny. "I was thinking of how much she misses Jon and how sad she seems."

"Oh, yes, of course. I know it must be very hard for her to be separated from Jon, especially since she's feeling unwell with her pregnancy."

Penny nodded, pondering Julia's response. Did

she suspect something was wrong with Kate or her baby? Julia had knowledge of medical issues since she'd worked with her father at the clinic in India for twelve years. They were all a bit concerned that Kate seemed larger than her due date would suggest. Was that what worried Julia?

Julia shifted her gaze back to Penny. "It's wonderful the way you've stepped up to help with the children. I know that's a great comfort to Kate."

"I enjoy it, though the boys seem to challenge my authority every day."

"Yes, they are quite . . . energetic. They remind me of Andrew." A line creased the area between Julia's eyebrows.

"Is something wrong?"

Julia bit her lip and glanced toward the house. "William received a telegram this morning from St. Alban's. Andrew is being sent home tomorrow."

Penny pulled in a sharp breath. "What happened?"

"They didn't explain, but they said he'll bring a letter with him when he comes home. William is concerned, but we won't know what we're dealing with until Andrew arrives and we read that letter."

"I'm surprised they're sending him home so close to the end of the term." She didn't want to say it, but that probably meant he hadn't just broken a minor rule. It had to be a serious infraction.

"Yes, we're both disappointed." Julia crossed her arms and watched Donald swat the birdie to Jack. "William has such high hopes for Andrew. As do I."

"He's only fourteen. There's certainly time to help him get him back on the right path."

Julia looked at Penny. "I hope you're right. All of this will be his one day." She gestured across the open parkland. "He'll need an education, as well as wisdom, to manage it properly."

The chatter of girls' voices filled the air as Lydia walked down Highland's terrace steps and past the front lawn and gardens. Lady Julia had asked her and Miss Penny to take the six older girls outdoors after lunch and keep them occupied for at least an hour, so they had decided to take a walk to the stream and sheep pens.

Helen and Ann stayed behind to take the two younger girls upstairs for a nap. The three boys had been sent to help Clark Dalton in the kitchen garden, though they had put up a fuss about it.

Millie and Abigail strolled along, hand in hand, beside Lydia and Miss Penny. Lucy, Edna, Rose, and Susan followed behind.

Lydia scanned the gray sky, then pulled her sweater a bit tighter around her. "I hope the rain holds off a little longer."

"I'm sure we'll be fine." Miss Penny sounded

confident, but when she looked up at the heavy, gray clouds, she bit her lip.

It was odd Lady Julia had sent them outside when a storm seemed to be brewing. Then Lydia recalled what she'd heard in the servants' hall after breakfast—Master Andrew had been dismissed from school for stirring up trouble. What kind of trouble, no one seemed to know, but it must have been something serious for him to be sent home before the end of the term.

She wished she knew more, but she didn't dare mention it or ask the family any questions. It was not her place to discuss their private matters. Still, she couldn't help wondering what Sir William would do.

Andrew always had been a headstrong boy, but he should've outgrown his wild behavior by now, especially since he was going to be master of Highland Hall one day. Still, her own brothers had been dreadful when they were fourteen, and they'd grown into fine young men. That gave her hope for Andrew.

"What are those men doing?" Millie pointed to the large open area that had been tilled and planted. A dozen or so men worked in the field with hoes and spades.

Miss Penny looked up. "It appears they're tending potatoes."

Millie cocked her head. "We've never grown potatoes in the parkland before."

"That's true, but we've never been involved in a war like the one we're fighting now."

"Are we growing potatoes to feed the soldiers?" Abigail asked.

"I believe these potatoes will be eaten by people here in Berkshire, but some may be sent to France for the men who are stationed there." A wistful look filled Penny's eyes, and she shifted her gaze to the east.

Was she thinking of someone off fighting in France? Perhaps that handsome Lieutenant Goodwin? She seemed to enjoy his company in London. Whether she was thinking of him or not, they all knew men who had joined up. It was hard knowing they were so far away from home, living in trenches, and facing gas attacks and machine-gun fire. She shivered, then took charge of her thoughts and turned them into a prayer for the safe return of the troops and an end to this terrible war.

As they approached the potato field, she glanced at the two men working closest to the lane. The taller one raked his hoe across the ground with strong strokes, like an experienced farmer. He wore brown work pants and a light-blue shirt with the sleeves rolled up, revealing strong, tanned arms. A straw hat shaded his face and light-blond hair.

The other man wore black pants, a faded red shirt, and a gray cap over his curly brown locks. He lifted his head and looked at Lydia, then he stepped toward the blond man and spoke in rough, guttural words Lydia couldn't understand.

The blond man darted a glance at Lydia. His eyes were a striking blue, like the summer sky.

She pulled in a sharp breath and looked away.

Lucy leaned toward Miss Penny. "What language is that man speaking?

"I believe it's . . . German."

Lucy's eyes grew round. "Like the Germans who bombed London?"

"Yes, but these men are not soldiers," Miss Penny added. "They're just men of German descent who were living in Britain when war was declared. The government decided to . . . move them to internment camps, and now they work on the farms and estates to help replace men who've gone off to fight in the war."

Lydia looked at the men in the field, and a ripple of unease traveled through her. Everyone talked about the danger of German spies. Those loyal to the Crown had been warned to watch out for anyone who looked suspicious and report them. Was that why the government put these men in the camps? Had they been reported?

Lucy touched Miss Penny's arm. "Isn't it dangerous, having Germans working at Highland?"

"The guards keep an eye on them." Miss Penny nodded down the lane to the two soldiers who stood off to the side under a large tree, their gazes focused on the men in the field.

As Lydia, Penny, and the girls continued down the lane, they came closer to the men.

The German with the curly brown hair stopped and leaned on his hoe. "Hello, pretty ladies." He lifted his eyebrows and grinned. "Where are you going?"

Miss Penny's cheeks turned pink, and she quickened her step. "Come along, girls."

"Wait, don't run away." He started down the row to keep up with them. "Come over and talk to us. We're lonely."

Lydia's face grew hot, but she couldn't help feeling a bit of sympathy. She knew what it was like to be away from home and family and feel alone.

Miss Penny slipped her arm through Lydia's. "Don't speak to them. Just keep walking."

The brown-haired man chuckled and continued to keep pace. "Don't listen to her. You're a smart girl. You know what you want."

"That's enough!" The tall blond man strode down the row toward the other man, his expression stern. "Leave them alone."

The first man laughed. "What's wrong, Marius? Don't you want to talk to the pretty ladies?"

Marius ignored the comment. He doffed his hat, giving Lydia a clear view of his pale blond hair, sky-blue eyes, and handsome face. "Please, don't think we're all as ill-mannered as Siegfried."

Surprised by his polite words, she sent Marius a

slight smile. He responded with a nod and smile of his own. Lydia looked away. What was she thinking, smiling at a German?

"What's going on here?" One of the guards marched toward them, his rifle in hand. "Are these men bothering you?"

"No, sir." Miss Penny faced the guard. "They were just saying hello."

"Well, they ought not to be saying anything to anyone." The guard glared at the men. "You know the rules. Get back to work, or I'll have to report you."

Marius straightened, and a muscle in his jaw flickered. He looked at Lydia and back at the guard, then turned away and shoved his hoe into the dirt.

Siegfried glared at the guard, as though daring him to follow through on his threat.

"I mean it. Get to work!" The guard's rough voice sent goose bumps racing along Lydia's arms. He lowered his rifle and looked Lydia over with a slow, suggestive smile. "You live here at Highland?"

A warning flashed through her. She shoved her hands in her sweater pockets and started down the lane with Miss Penny and the girls.

The guard chuckled. "You don't have to be afraid of me. I'm here to protect you."

Lydia strode on, glad to get away from the guard and that first man who'd called out to them. But the tall blond man, the one called Marius . . . he had been kind and respectful.

She glanced over her shoulder. Marius looked up. His gaze connected with hers, as though asking for understanding—but also reflecting his pride and determination. She pulled in a quick breath. How could he communicate so much in one look?

Who was this man? Why had he been sent to the camp?

William stood by the library fireplace and stared at the letter in his hands. The condemning words reporting his son's behavior burned into his eyes. He looked at Andrew. "How could you cheat on an exam? What were you thinking?"

Andrew shifted his sullen gaze away.

Julia stood on Andrew's left, in front of the settee, her face pale and her gaze filled with a plea for compassion. But how could William excuse his son's dishonesty?

"Andrew, look at me when I'm speaking to you."

His son slowly turned back, but his stance remained unyielding.

"I want an explanation. Why did you do it?"

"I wanted to pass."

"Then why not study hard and learn the material, rather than—"

The boy's eyes flashed. "I *do* study!"

William pulled in a breath, trying to rein in his temper. "If you did, there would be no need to copy the answers from another student's paper."

Andrew huffed and shook his head. "You don't understand. Teddy hates me. He just wanted to get me in trouble and have me sent home."

William clenched his jaw. "Did you copy his answers?"

Andrew shifted his weight to the other foot, his face growing a deeper shade of red under his freckles. "A few, but I knew most of the answers."

"If that's true, then it would've been better to do your own work, even it if meant receiving a lower mark."

"Really?" Andrew narrowed his eyes at William. "Wouldn't that just set you off and put me in line for another lecture about not working up to my potential?"

Heat flashed up William's neck and into his face. How did his son always know exactly what to say to send his blood pressure soaring? "I want you to apply yourself and do your best. But what's more important is that you choose to do what's right and become a man of honor who is worthy of the title of Baronet of Highland Hall."

Andrew's chin quivered and his eyes flooded. "I do try! I study hard, but it's no use. I'll never be good enough to please you!"

"What pleases me is honest effort rather than

wasting your time, frittering away your opportunities—"

"No! You don't understand. The other boys read the material once and have it all memorized. I pore over my books every day, but it doesn't stick."

"I don't believe that's true. You're simply giving up too soon because your schoolwork is challenging." He stepped toward Andrew. "But you're my son. And I know you can do better than this." He thrust out the letter.

Pain flashed in Andrew's eyes. He blinked, as though trying to hold back his tears, but they spilled over and ran down his cheeks. He spun away and dashed out of the room.

William shuddered out a breath and lowered himself into the desk chair.

Julia walked over and laid her hand on William's shoulder. "I'm sorry. I know this is a painful disappointment for you."

"Yes, very painful. But I don't know whom I am more disappointed in—Andrew or myself." He looked up at Julia and shook his head, ashamed at the way he'd struggled with his temper. "I have no idea what to do now."

She looked toward the window for a few moments. Finally, she shifted her gaze back to William. "He shouldn't have copied those answers, but I can understand his struggle. Andrew has always had a difficult time settling down to focus on his studies. Remember how he used to pace across the day nursery between solving his mathematics problems?"

William nodded. It was true. It had been almost impossible for his son to sit in a chair and finish his lessons. William had hoped the strict routine at school would help the boy overcome his weaknesses.

Julia's soft voice soothed William's aching heart. "When he was studying at home, I tried several techniques to help him stay focused. The best solution seemed to be allowing him to get up and move around while he was thinking through a problem, but I don't believe they allow that at St. Alban's."

"No, I'm sure they don't."

She sighed. "He must learn how to manage himself and complete his studies."

"Do you think he has the potential to succeed at St. Alban's?" Then another disturbing thought followed. "If they'll even allow him to return."

"I believe he does, but he must develop the character needed to compensate for the challenges he faces. He will have to learn to work harder than the other boys. But most of all, he must develop the courage to stand strong in the face of temptation."

Yes, that was what he needed—moral courage. "But how do we teach him that?"

Julia studied William for a moment, compassion

reflected in her eyes. "Andrew needs to develop honesty and diligence, and those qualities must be cultivated in the heart before they will be seen in his actions."

"Exactly." He drummed his fingers on the desk. He wanted to punish his son, force him to change, but his wife's words reminded him there was another path. A better one.

"Somehow, we must give him hope and a vision for improving his character," she continued. "He must see the value in it and believe it's a real possibility for him to change and be successful."

"The principle sounds correct, but we need the practical."

She pressed her lips together, then glanced toward the bookshelves. "What if we found biographies of men who were guided by those qualities and we all read them and discussed them together?"

William rubbed his chin. "That might help, though Andrew has never been a strong reader."

"We could read them aloud to all the children. I'm sure they'd benefit. And there are several men in the Bible with admirable character. We could have Andrew look for those qualities and discuss them with him."

The weight William had felt pressing down on him since they'd received the telegram from St. Alban's began to lift just a bit. Perhaps Julia was right. It might not be too late to help Andrew change his ways. "I like that idea. School assignments ought not to stop just because he has been sent home."

"I also think he needs some real work to do, hard work, something that will challenge him."

"Yes, maybe we could think of a project that would occupy his time and give him a sense of accomplishment."

Julia thought for a moment. "Could he build something . . . maybe a bench in the garden?"

"Too tame. He needs something more demanding."

Julia's eyes lit up. "Didn't Mr. McTavish say he wanted to buy a horse?"

"Yes, his brother in Devon has some ponies for sale. He thought he could use a strong little horse to do some the jobs around the estate, especially with the fuel shortage. But what does that have to do with Andrew?"

"Most of Mr. McTavish's men have gone off to fight. Won't he need someone to help him train and care for the pony?"

Memories of the riding accident that had taken his wife's life sent a chill through him. He paced toward the window. "I'm not sure I want Andrew involved with horses."

Julia crossed to stand beside him. "What is it, William?"

He steeled himself. "Did I ever tell you how Amelia died?"

He heard her soft intake of breath. "I believe you said it was a riding accident."

"Yes. She was up in Yorkshire. When she tried to jump her horse over a stream, she was thrown off and hit her head on a rock." He clenched his jaw, trying to push away the memories. He hadn't been with her, but her friend had written a detailed account of the accident. "I haven't ridden since, and I didn't want to encourage Millie or Andrew to ride either."

"Training a pony to work around the estate doesn't sound too dangerous, and you might want to consider letting Andrew ride again."

William stared out the window, the view of the parkland blurring before his eyes. Horses were an important part of English country life. Maybe it was time he put those fears to rest. He turned back to Julia. "I suppose if someone was there to supervise, it would be all right."

Julia's face brightened. "If he had a schedule and was accountable to you, then you would have an opportunity to strengthen your relationship with him."

William cocked his head, surprised by the direction she was taking the conversation. "You want me spending part of each day in the stable?"

"It might be good for you both." Affection shone in her eyes. "And if it would help steer Andrew back toward the right path, then it would be worth the time and effort."

William pondered that for a moment, then leaned toward Julia and kissed her forehead. "I believe you're right, my dear."

What had he ever done to deserve the blessing of this woman in his life? Whatever it was, he thanked God with all his heart.

At half past three, Penny followed Lydia and the girls through the front door. They had decided to return from their walk to the sheep pens by a different route to avoid passing the Germans, and that had taken a bit longer than she expected.

Thinking of their earlier encounter with the prisoners left Penny feeling unsettled. Why William allowed those prisoners to work at Highland at all was beyond her, whether there was a shortage of farm laborers or not.

Enough. She'd thought about it entirely too much. She turned to the girls. "Please go upstairs, wash your hands and faces, and tidy up for tea."

Before the girls could answer, the library door flew open. Andrew ran into the great hall. Tears traced wet lines down his flushed, freckled face.

Millie froze, and her eyes widened. "Andrew, when did you come home?"

"Never mind!" He rushed past Millie and the other girls and ran up the stairs.

The girls all fell silent and stared after him.

Lucy looked at Millie. "Is that your brother?"

"Yes, it is."

Penny moved to the bottom of the steps. "I'm sure he'll be all right. Please go upstairs with Lydia and get ready for tea as I asked."

The girls exchanged questioning looks, then mounted the steps with only a few whispered comments between then.

Lawrence entered the great hall through the doorway at the end, carrying a small silver tray.

Penny crossed to meet him. "Has Lady Julia called for tea?"

"Not yet, Miss. I believe she and Sir William are in the library"—he lifted his dark eyebrows—"with Master Andrew."

Penny hesitated. "Master Andrew just went upstairs."

Lawrence gave a nod and held out the silver tray. "A letter arrived for you in the afternoon post, miss."

"Thank you." She took the envelope and noted the strong, masculine script, and her heartbeat sped up.

"Will there be anything else, miss?"

She thought for a moment, pondering the troubling encounter with Andrew. "I think it would be best for the children to take their tea upstairs today."

"Very good, miss." Lawrence turned and exited through the doorway leading down to the kitchen and servants' hall.

Penny turned over the letter and read Alex's name on the back, and her heart lifted. It hadn't been long since she'd mailed the package. He must have replied right away.

The sound of voices in the library broke through her happy thoughts. She walked past the open door, not wanting to disturb William and Julia. Bits of conversation drifted past—they were still discussing Andrew. She sighed. Her young cousin was forever getting into one kind of scrape or another.

She continued down the great hall and slipped into the drawing room. Maybe she'd have time to read her letter in private.

Bright afternoon light flooded the room, highlighting the soft, peach silk wall covering and giving the room a pleasing warmth. On her left, the white marble fireplace was decorated with china figurines and photographs of her family. It was a pretty, feminine room and one of Penny's favorites.

She sat in a comfortable chair by the fireplace and tore open the letter.

June 30, 1915

Dear Penny,

Thank you for your package and letter. They were a wonderful surprise. Please tell the children I enjoyed their drawings, and I put

140

them up on the wall by my bed. The children are quite talented artists. Also, please thank Lucy for the hand-knit socks. They will be warm and comfortable when I'm flying, as it gets very cool at higher altitudes. The tea, candies, and chocolate were a fine treat. I shared some with my friend George Meddis. He is the mechanic who keeps my airplane in top shape, so I thought he should share the bounty.

We are doing well here at St. Pol. I'm not allowed to tell you the details of our missions, but know that your prayers have helped carry me through some challenging times and we are making good progress.

Penny smiled. How wonderful to hear he was safe and well and that he appreciated her prayers!

I plan to secure the eagle you sent to the control panel of my plane, so he will be flying with me on each mission as a reminder of your prayers and God's care. The verses you sent were perfect. I hope to commit them to memory. He has renewed my strength many times when it seemed impossible to go on. Please keep praying. I believe He has used your prayers to pull me through some very difficult situations, and I am deeply grateful.

Penny's throat tightened, and she had to blink before she could continue reading. She knew his work was dangerous, but seeing those words written by his own hand made it even more real and frightening.

You asked what you might send in your next package. That's kind of you to ask. We are well supplied here, but news from home and perhaps a photograph of you would be most welcome.

Penny's heart fluttered, and she read the last few lines again. He wanted her photograph . . . goodness . . . that sounded hopeful.

Thank you for your kind invitation to visit you at Highland Hall. I would like that very much, but I'm not sure when it will be. None of the other pilots here have had enough leave to return to England, so I doubt it will be any time soon. But if there is any way I can get back, I will come and see you. There's nothing I'd enjoy more than that.

She lifted her hand to her heart. *Oh, if only he could come.*

Until then, take good care of yourself, and say hello to all the children and the family there at Highland. I enjoyed hearing how you and the children are spending your days, and I will look forward to your next letter.

With a grateful heart,
Alex

Penny carefully folded Alex's letter, slipped it back in the envelope, and smoothed out a wrinkle on the flap. Almost a week had passed since he'd written—was he still safe and well? A tremor traveled down her arm, and she pushed her worries away.

He might not be able to come to Highland soon, but she could write to him, encourage him, and assure him of her friendship and continued prayers. And . . .

A smile touched her lips.

She could grant his request and send her photograph.

Seven

A tangy, salt-laden breeze blew through the open window of the briefing room and past Alex's shoulder. He pulled in a deep breath, and memories of his time at sea came flooding back. He'd been at St. Pol almost a month, but he'd lived aboard ships for years. The work was hard and the days were long, but he loved being out on the ocean, sailing off on a new adventure every few weeks.

Commander Longmore's voice broke through his thoughts, and he focused up front again. The commander's briefings were usually short and to the point, but he'd kept the men longer this morning. Alex could hear a heightened sense of urgency in his voice.

"There was another bombing raid in England last night."

Alex tensed, and his sister's face flashed through his mind, then Jon's image and the wounded men at St. George's Hospital. He clenched his jaw, thankful Penny, Kate, and the children were safely away at Highland.

"A Zeppelin dropped more than fifty bombs on the eastern shore. There is no word on the number of casualties yet, but the damage is more extensive than the raid earlier this month. The Admiralty is requesting additional reconnaissance flights along the coast today." Longmore scanned across the group. "Wilson, I'm tapping you and St. Charles for that mission."

"Yes, sir," they both replied.

Longmore's gaze narrowed. "The rules of the game are inflexible. If you hear a machine gun other than your own, do not wait to see who the target is. It's undoubtedly you. Stalk your quarry. Fly high, out of sight, into the clouds or the sun. As you move in, stay in his blind spot, behind him and beneath his tail. Get as close to him as possible before you fire. Then shoot in short blasts."

The gazes of all twenty-two men were riveted on their commander.

"Don't waste fuel or time." Longmore continued, "Your goal is to complete your mission and return to base in one piece. Do I make myself clear?"

"Yes, sir." The response rippled across the room.

Alex looked around at the other pilots' somber faces. No doubt they were all thinking of Dwight Harvey. He had taken off yesterday morning to photograph a German submarine base, but he'd never returned.

Had he been shot down, or had he crashed into the sea? It was possible he had engine trouble and made a safe landing in some field behind enemy lines. If that were the case, he would most likely have been taken prisoner by now, but they wouldn't hear about it for weeks.

The muscles in Alex's shoulders knotted. Spending the rest of the war in a German prisoner-of-war camp would be a miserable fate, but he supposed it was preferable to being shot out of the sky. He forced away such chilling thoughts, then focused on Longmore again.

"I expect you to carry out your duty to King and country." His intense gaze eased, and a steady light glowed in his dark eyes. "All right, men, you have your orders. You are dismissed."

Alex rose from his chair.

"Goodwin," Longmore called. "I want you and Meddis to stay behind."

Alex walked forward. His name had not been on the list for a flight today. What did Longmore have in mind?

The commander grabbed his clipboard from the desk, then turned to face Alex. "Meddis tells me he's designed a new bomb rack for your planes."

"Yes, sir. They carry six bombs, with a wire and toggle for release."

Longmore nodded. "I want you to test it out today. I'm sending you to attack one of the German airship sheds."

Energy surged through Alex, alerting all his senses. Destroying an airship shed, with perhaps even a Zeppelin housed inside, could prevent some bombing raids in England and save countless lives. "Where is it located, sir?"

"Near Düsseldorf."

Alex's breath hitched in his chest. Düsseldorf was in northwestern Germany, far behind enemy lines and hours away.

A deep frown slashed Meddis's face, and he shook his head. "That's too far, sir. He won't have enough fuel."

"Yes, it's too far from here, which is why I'm sending you to a forward airfield near Antwerp."

Alex's mind spun. "I thought the Germans controlled Antwerp."

146

"They do, but we have access to an airfield outside the city where you can touch down and refuel before you head east into Germany."

Meddis rubbed his chin. "That sounds risky, sir."

"It is, but that's the only way we can reach Düsseldorf." Longmore fixed his gaze on Meddis. "I want you to go with him."

Surprise rippled through Alex. The Morane was a two-seater, but a single pilot could fly it from the rear cockpit, and that was what Alex had done since his second week at St. Pol.

The mechanic stared at the commander. "You want me to fly with him to Antwerp?"

"Not just Antwerp. I want you to fly with him to Düsseldorf and back."

Meddis's eyes widened. "Sir?"

"He'll need someone to help with observation while he focuses on navigation and staying out of sight of enemy aircraft."

Meddis gave a slow nod, but he didn't look convinced it was a good idea. "The extra weight will burn more fuel."

"True, but he may need a mechanic as well as a copilot."

Meddis glanced at Alex, his brow still creased. Alex returned a confident nod, hoping his friend would see the wisdom in Longmore's plan.

"I think you two are the right men for the mission. Are you willing to go?"

Alex studied the commander. He wasn't usually given a choice to accept or decline a mission. He supposed the danger of flying so far behind enemy lines had prompted Longmore to give them a choice today.

Alex didn't even have to think twice. He straightened his shoulders and looked his commander in the eye. "If there's a chance to destroy a Zeppelin, I'll do it in a heartbeat."

Longmore's eyes lit up. He gave an appreciative nod, then turned to Meddis.

The mechanic's face reddened, and he looked away. Finally, he huffed out a breath. "All right."

"Good. Sir Winston Churchill will be pleased."

Alex blinked and stared at Longmore. "He's the First Lord of the Admiralty, right?"

"Yes. This mission is his idea. I'm confident he'll be eager to hear your report when you return."

Alex couldn't hold back a grin. He'd been given a mission by the First Lord of the Admiralty himself! "We'll give him a good report. You can be sure of that."

Longmore sobered. "Don't get cocky, Goodwin. This is serious business. I'm counting on you to stay focused and do your best flying."

"I will, sir."

Longmore took a map from his desk and opened it. "I've marked the airfield, here, northeast of Antwerp, just past the canal, and this is the location of the airship shed at Düsseldorf." He

148

looked up at Alex. "Study the map carefully and plot your course." He turned to Meddis. "Prepare the plane. I'd like you and Goodwin to take off for Antwerp as soon as possible."

"Yes, sir." Meddis's nod was decidedly grim. Well, Alex couldn't blame him. This would be a dangerous mission. But if they were successful, they'd be saving countless lives.

Alex accepted the map, then saluted and turned to go.

Meddis followed Alex out the door, then gripped his arm. "This has got to be the craziest idea I've ever heard! Refueling in Antwerp, behind enemy lines, and then flying over Germany!"

"Aw, come on. It's brilliant. No one has tried anything like it. We'll take them totally by surprise, destroy the shed, then fly out of there before they know what hit them."

"That, I would like to see."

Alex chuckled and slapped him on the shoulder. "And you will, my friend. You will."

Halfway into their mission they refueled at the small airstrip north of Antwerp with no problem. Then Alex flew east toward Düsseldorf, with Meddis riding in the front cockpit. One hour into the flight they changed course and headed slightly northeast, looking for the Rhine River.

Everything was going according to plan, and they hadn't run into any trouble, but Alex's shoulders remained tense as he scanned the sky. He was used to flying missions up and down the coasts of France and Belgium where he had daily encounters with enemy aircraft. Maybe that was why the stillness unnerved him. But most of the German airfields were farther south, closer to the front. That could be why they hadn't run into any enemy aircraft today.

He checked his instruments again, then surveyed the countryside below. The fields looked like a patchwork quilt from this height, with only a few winding roads and small villages scattered across the landscape.

Meddis looked over his shoulder at Alex and pointed to the left. "There it is!"

Alex strained to hear him over the roar of the motor, then looked in the direction Meddis had pointed. In the distance, the Rhine River came into view. From this height it looked like a deep-blue ribbon, curving back and forth through the fields and forests.

Alex banked to the right and brought his plane around to follow the river south toward Düsseldorf. He pictured the map in his mind, thinking through the landmarks that would lead them to the air sheds just outside the city.

Ten minutes later, Meddis pointed to the cluster of buildings just visible to the south. "Düsseldorf!"

Alex pulled in a deep breath and set a straight

course for the city. The Rhine curved around on the west in the shape of an ear. When he reached the bottom curve of the river, he banked and flew due east. Checking his watch and gauges, he calculated the time it would take to fly the last few miles to the air shed.

He ran his left hand across his goggles to clear away the dust, then scanned the ground, looking for the railroad tracks that would lead him to the target. With any luck, he might even see one of the giant airships tied down nearby to confirm the location.

Patchy clouds drifted toward them, blocking his view. Alex's stomach contracted. He needed to see the railroad tracks to find his way, but descending below the clouds would put him in the range of artillery fire. He might be able to get through without being spotted . . . but his engine was loud, so it wasn't likely.

The same thought must have struck Meddis, because he turned and looked back at Alex as they headed toward the cloud bank.

Alex pointed down with a firm nod. He had no choice. He'd have to fly below the clouds or risk missing the air shed. Diving down quickly wouldn't be a problem, but gaining height again would take time, and if the Germans caught sight of them, he'd have to do some fancy flying to avoid being shot out of the sky.

He gripped the controls and glanced at the

wooden eagle Penny had sent. He'd read those verses so many times in the last few weeks they were permanently etched into his mind. If there was ever a time he needed the Lord's help to mount up on wings like eagles, it was today.

Watch over us, Lord. Help me find my way. He gripped the stick and dove down into the clouds.

A few seconds later, the white, misty veil parted, and the view of the city opened up before him. "Look for the tracks!"

Meddis gave a thumbs-up and leaned to the left, searching the ground. Alex looked to the right, scanning the area below.

Without warning, shells exploded around them. Meddis yelped and ducked. Alex clamped his jaw, made a hard left turn, then nosed the plane higher toward the clouds again. He'd have to circle around and come back for another pass. He rose up through the misty clouds and came out the other side. The railroad tracks appeared directly below them. His heart surged. "There they are!"

Meddis looked over the side and whooped. Alex grinned, then followed the tracks heading east. If his calculations were correct, they should see the air shed in the next five minutes.

With narrowed eyes, he scanned the pathway below. Buildings were scattered along the tracks, but none were large enough to house the giant Zeppelin. Finally, a long building three or four times the size of the hangar at St. Pol came into view. Military trucks were parked alongside, and a high fence surrounded the property. Large sliding doors stood open at one end, and the gray-green nose of a Zeppelin poked out onto the tarmac.

Triumph surged through Alex. "That's it!"

Meddis turned and gave him the thumbs-up again.

Alex passed by, then circled around, rising higher. Penny's image flashed into his mind, then the frightened faces of the children as they hid in the servants' hall while bombs fell on London. He set his jaw, determined to do everything in his power to protect them and make sure the Zeppelin below never threatened his friends and family again.

When he reached five thousand feet, he shouted to Meddis, "Hold on!" Then he turned and plunged the plane toward the air shed. The nerves of his arms tingled, and his heartbeat thrummed with the roar of the engine. The timing had to be perfect. He held his breath, gripped the toggle wire, and released the first bomb. As soon as he felt it drop, he released the second.

Gripping the controls, he pulled up and shot past the air shed, releasing the third bomb for good measure.

A huge explosion rocked the plane, quickly followed by a second blast. Alex held on tight and looked over his shoulder. A giant sheet of flames rose from the roof of the shed, and smoke billowed out around it.

Meddis shouted and waved his arms in the air, a victorious smile wreathing his red face. "We *did* it!"

Relief pulsed through Alex. They'd made a direct hit. The fire would most likely destroy the air shed and the Zeppelin inside. He could return to Antwerp and refuel, then head back to St. Pol, the mission complete.

Alex strode across the airfield toward the dining hall. It had been a long day. His shoulders ached, and his breakfast had worn off hours ago. He pushed open the wooden door and walked inside. The conversations of his fellow pilots and mechanics filled the room with a low hum. The scent of roasting meat and baking bread drifted past and made his empty stomach rumble.

He looked toward the kitchen. "Hastings, is there any dinner left?"

The portly man looked up from behind the serving counter. "Yes, sir. I'll have a plate ready in just a minute." Hastings turned away and bustled across the small kitchen at the end of the hall.

"Goodwin, a letter came for you." Fletcher pointed toward the corner where the mailbag lay on a table, with a few envelopes scattered around.

"Thanks." He crossed the room and sorted through the letters until he found one with his name inscribed across the front in fine, feminine handwriting. He turned it over, read Penny's name, and smiled, then he tore it open and settled onto the closest chair.

July 8, 1915

Dear Alex,

Thank you for your letter. It was wonderful to hear you are safe and your missions are going well. I wish you could tell me more, but I understand you aren't allowed to share the details of your flights. I have been reading the newspaper each day to stay up on the latest information about the war. There have been a few articles that mention our wonderfully brave aviators and their exploits. I didn't realize we had two branches of our military taking on missions in the air. Do the Royal Flying Corps and Royal Naval Air Service share airfields? Do you ever see the RFC planes and pilots when you are on a mission? I'm not sure if you can answer those questions, but I'm eager to learn more about your work and the RNAS.

He grinned. Penny was not only thinking of him, she wanted to understand how his work fit into the scheme of things. That pleased him more than he would've expected.

We are doing well here at Highland, though Kate is still not feeling well, so I try to take as much responsibility for the children as she will allow. She just received word that Jon is coming home for two days, and that lifted her spirits. It will be such a relief to have him here, and I know it will be a great comfort to Kate.

Alex lowered the letter. He was glad for Jon. It sounded like his wife needed time with him. His thoughts shifted to his own hope to travel back to England and visit Penny at Highland. But with the limited number of pilots and the needs here at St. Pol, he doubted it would be any time soon. The way things stood now, he might not see Penny until the war was over.

That sent his spirits into a nosedive. He closed his eyes and tried to shake it off. Though he'd only known Penny a short time, he couldn't deny his growing feelings for her. Did she feel the same, or did she write to him only as a friend, hoping to boost his morale? He pushed away that question and looked at the letter again.

It was very kind of you to send your greetings to the children. I passed them along, and they were quite happy to receive them. They ask about you often, and they wanted you to know they continue to pray for you and wish you well.

They are adjusting to life here at Highland, and I must say country life seems to agree with them. They all have rosy cheeks and seem healthy and strong from their time outdoors and the fine meals prepared for them here. We grow much of our own food on the estate, and the shortages are not as evident here in the country.

The boys continue to be a bit of a challenge. It takes a great deal of creative planning to keep them busy. The girls are much easier to oversee. We usually do quiet, indoor activities in the morning. The girls have been knitting scarves and socks for the troops. But there don't seem to be as many practical things the boys can do to contribute to the war effort. If you have any ideas of ways I might keep them busy, please send them along.

He grinned. Keeping boys occupied didn't sound too difficult. They would probably enjoy fishing, hunting, and hikes in the countryside. If he were there, he'd teach them how to take care of themselves in the wilderness, just as his father had taught him. That kind of training helped a boy become a man. But he couldn't very well expect Penny to do that.

Wasn't there a man who could spend some time with the boys and give them the practical guidance they needed?

He supposed most able-bodied men had enlisted, and those still at home were over-burdened, trying to do the work of two or three others. He turned to the second sheet of stationery.

You mentioned you might like a photograph, so I'm sending two along. One is from Jon and Kate's wedding, so you can see the whole family, and the other is from my presentation. That's the most recent photograph I have. Try to ignore the two ostrich feathers in my hair. I know they look a bit silly, but they're required court dress. It's hard to believe that photo was taken only a year and a half ago. Being a debutante and taking part in the season seem so far in the past now.

Alex reached for the envelope and looked inside. He pulled out the two photographs and inspected the first. Jon and Kate stood on a beautifully carved wooden stairway dressed in their wedding attire, surrounded by the bridal party and several family members. The photo-graph must have been taken at Highland Hall on their wedding day. Jon looked proud and handsome, and Kate was a beautiful bride. Penny stood beside Kate, looking as lovely as her sister. It was obviously a happy day for them all.

He glanced at the second photo, and his breath hitched in his chest.

Penny looked out at him, wearing a stunning white gown with a long train draped around her feet. She held a bouquet of flowers and wore long white gloves that reached past her elbows. Her sheer veil, pearl necklace, and earrings made her look like a bride. The fluffy white ostrich feathers tucked in her hair added a regal touch. He studied her expression, unable to tell what she was thinking. There was an air of mystery about her that was very attractive. He carefully laid aside the photos and took up the letter again.

Patriotism is running very high. Everyone is eager to do their part to help the war effort. Several men on our staff and from the village of Fulton have enlisted. William has agreed to allow German prisoners to work on the estate in the fields. It's a bit unsettling, seeing them so close to the house, but there are guards who watch over them.

I only wish there were more I could do, but I am needed here to care for the children and help my sister and Julia. I am trying to be content with that. Please know I pray for you each day and will continue to write. Remember your friends here are very proud of you, thankful for your brave service, and looking forward to having you home again.

With warm thoughts,
Penny

Alex picked up the photograph and studied Penny once more. The sweetness in her expression and the bright hopeful light in her eyes tugged at his heart. Could he win the love of a woman like Penny? Their background and upbringing couldn't be more different. Her family was wealthy and aristocratic, his was middle class and broken by divorce and distance.

But the harsh reality of war made those differences seem less important. He'd overcome every challenge in his training and become a respected pilot in his squadron. Each time he'd faced the enemy, he'd come out on top and made it back to base.

Perhaps it was time he sought a higher prize . . .

The love of a fine woman with a sweet smile and caring heart.

Eight

William leaned his cue stick against the side of the billiard table and reached underneath for the balls. His brother-in-law, Clark Dalton, lifted a cue stick from the rack on the wall and joined William at the table.

"This will have to be a quick game." Jon stepped up next to William. "I don't want to leave Kate on her own too long."

William placed the balls on the table. "I'm

glad you've come. I've been worried about her."

"I had to pull a few strings to get two days off, but I could tell from her letters she's not been herself."

Clark looked Jon's way. "I know she's not been feeling well . . . Is everything all right?"

"As far as we can tell, though the baby seems larger than normal for this stage."

A ripple of unease traveled through William. "Why would that be?"

"We might have estimated the due date incorrectly, or . . . perhaps there's another reason." His somber expression hinted at a more serious issue.

William frowned. He didn't like the thought of his cousin Kate facing a problem with her pregnancy, and he was even more aware of the possibility since he and Julia had lost two babies early on. But Jon was a doctor, and Jon's father, who was also a physician, lived only a short distance from Highland. Kate had the best care possible. He pushed away his concerns and placed the balls on the table. He was probably worrying for nothing. "Jon, why don't you start?"

Jon bent and took aim, then cracked the ball and sent it rolling across the green felt tabletop. It bounced off the end and rolled back, but not far enough to reach the baulk.

Clark stepped forward and took the next shot. His ball bounced and rolled back, landing in the perfect spot, close to the end. He looked up and nodded to William. "Your turn."

William scanned the table, moved to the end, and lined up his shot. He hit the cue ball and sent it down the table, but when it rolled back, it barely made it into the baulk. He was definitely out of practice.

Clark stepped forward and took aim. His cue struck the red ball and sent it into the side pocket. "Three points." He surveyed the table and chose his next shot.

William turned to Jon. "How are things at the hospital?"

"Very busy. The number of injured men coming in from France has almost doubled in the last few months."

"Fighting always seems to increase in warm weather."

"There was another bombing Tuesday on the east coast," Jon added. "Two Zeppelins made it through this time. They dropped more than forty bombs."

William gave a grim nod, memories of the newspaper article he'd read flashing through his mind. "Ghastly business."

"Sixteen killed, fourteen injured. They hit a nursing home for the elderly."

Clark glared at the table as he took the next shot.

William looked toward Jon. "How is the mood in London?"

"You'd think people would be frightened and worried about the next possible air raid, but anger seems a more common response. They want to strike back."

Clark looked up. "It's no wonder, when the Germans sneak in at night and drop bombs on the elderly and women and children asleep in their beds."

William shook his head. "It's hard to believe the King and the Kaiser are first cousins."

"The King is receiving a lot of criticism because of that connection." Jon took his shot.

"His father, Prince Albert, was German, the House of Saxe-Coburg." Clark's tone revealed his feelings about the matter.

"I don't think we can blame the King for that." William took a shot, but his ball missed the pocket.

"No, but anti-German feelings are very strong now."

Jon set up for the next shot. "I never imagined the war would go on this long. Remember how everyone said our troops would be home by Christmas? Now it's been almost a year."

"And the end is not in sight." William watched Jon, but his thoughts were on the discouraging news from the front. "I'm afraid things are only going to get worse."

Clark looked at William, his gaze growing more intense. "The bombings are bad enough, but when the Germans justify sinking a passenger ship, like the *Lusitania*, and killing more than a thousand men, women, and children . . . It's unthinkable."

"We've seen some new types of injuries in the last few months from the chlorine gas the Germans are using." Jon shook his head. "Blindness and burns."

Would this terrible war never end? William released a heavy sigh. "I'm afraid battle tactics have sunk to a dreadful new low."

Clark straightened and his gaze shifted from Jon to William. "So what are we going to do about it?"

William stilled. What was he saying? "We're doing our duty, watching over our families, providing shelter for Kate and the children, growing extra food, and releasing many of our staff so they can volunteer."

"Is that enough?" Clark's face grew ruddy. "I think I might be called to do more."

William straightened. "What do you mean?"

"I'm thinking about enlisting."

William gripped his cue stick. "That would be very hard on Sarah."

"Yes, it would, but if we want to win this war and preserve our freedom, then more men must step forward and take the place of those who have been injured or killed."

William looked away from Clark's intense, sorrowful expression. Clark's younger brother, Martin Dalton, had been killed in France at the

Battle of Ypres last year. He'd served for only two and a half months before his death. It had been a terrible blow to Clark and his mother, Mrs. Dalton, their housekeeper.

Clark focused on William, his expression intense. "Why should I stay behind when so many others have volunteered?"

"You're doing important work here, and now that we're cultivating extra crops in the parkland, you're overseeing that as well."

Clark shook his head. "That's not enough."

"Well, it's enough in my mind."

"I appreciate that, but McTavish and the older tenant farmers could oversee the work on the grounds and care for the crops. And you have German prisoners to replace the farm laborers."

Clark was right, but William hated to admit it, for his sister's sake. "Have you spoken to Sarah about it?"

"Not yet. I thought I'd take the train up to Windermere and talk to her in person."

William looked toward the windows. Clark's decision would be difficult for the family and heartbreaking for Sarah, but how could he discourage his brother-in-law from following his conscience? "So are you asking my permission to enlist?"

Clark straightened. "No, I'm asking for your understanding when I do."

Clark was a fine man—a dependable, hard-working member of his staff—but he was more than that. He was a caring husband to Sarah, and he'd become a close friend. William would hate to see him go, but determination filled Clark's eyes.

He'd already made his decision.

And no doubt his selfless sister would give her consent and even praise him for it. That thought pushed away his hesitation.

William extended his hand. "You have my support and my promise to watch over Sarah always."

Clark's expression eased and his dark eyes brightened. He clasped William's hand. "Thank you."

William nodded and gave Clark's hand a firm shake, but questions stirred in his mind. How would Sarah handle a long separation from her husband? Could McTavish and the other men find the time and energy to care for the grounds and manage the crops in Clark's absence? How many more of his staff, family, and friends would be drawn into the war?

Even more important, how many would return?

Penny glared at her knitting. "Oh, drat, I've dropped another stitch!" She held out the misshapen brown sock toward Lydia.

Lydia leaned forward and inspected the stitches. Lucy, Edna, Rose, and Susan all looked up from their knitting. The two oldest girls exchanged a smile, then ducked their heads.

Penny's cheeks warmed. How embarrassing! She couldn't even knit as well as Lucy and Edna, who were fifteen and eleven, and they had only learned the skill a few weeks ago.

Penny glanced at ten-year-old Rose. She had almost finished her sock, and it looked perfect. Penny sighed and glared at her sorry work.

Lydia sent her a patient smile. "Just unravel the yarn back to that point, then pick up the stitch, and go on from there."

Penny clicked her tongue and sighed. She slipped out the knitting needle and unraveled the yarn. Knitting was not as easy as it looked. It took concentration and patience, two qualities she obviously needed in greater supply. But the troops needed warm socks, so she was determined to master the skill no matter how long it took. She slowed her unraveling, carefully picked up the dropped stitch, and slid the needle back into place.

A slight breeze ruffled the leaves of the oak tree overhead and cooled her warm face. At least if she and the girls had to knit socks, they could do it outside in the shade of this lovely tree. That made the task a bit more bearable.

A few yards away, Donald and Jack played a vigorous game of badminton. Tom stood by the net, keeping score on a small chalkboard and waiting to challenge the winner to the next game.

Helen stood nearby in the sunshine, keeping an eye on Emily as she ran across the grass. Little Irene chased after Emily, making her giggle.

A wagon drove up the lane pulling an open horse trailer carrying a bay pony. Andrew rode up front in the wagon with Mr. McTavish. Donald and Jack stopped their game and watched them pass.

Donald lifted his chin and smirked. "There goes the little prince and his new pony."

Penny pulled in a sharp breath and rose to her feet. "Donald!"

The boy looked her way. His face turned ruddy, but he set his jaw and did not reply.

"Come here, please." Penny stepped out into the sunshine and waited for him.

Donald slowly crossed the grass toward her, his expression sullen.

When he was within a foot of her, he stopped and looked up.

"I don't want to hear you speak about Andrew in that manner again. Do you understand?"

Donald crossed his arms and shifted his gaze away.

"I'd like an answer, please."

The boy turned back, his face set in a scowl. "What's his father thinking—giving him a horse when he got kicked out of school? It doesn't make sense."

Penny didn't quite understand it either, but that

was not the point. "It's not your place to question Sir William's decisions about his son."

Donald narrowed his eyes. "Well, if I had a son who cheated on an exam and got sent home from school, I wouldn't be giving him a horse. I'd put him to work."

"Is that right?" How had Donald learned those details? Penny had only heard them this morning from Julia in a private conversation.

Donald gave a firm nod. "He'd be chopping wood or mucking out stalls until he paid back every shilling spent to send him to that fancy school."

Penny stared at Donald for a moment, trying to think of a reply. "Well, you don't have a son yet, so there's no need for you to worry about it."

Donald huffed and glared toward the stables.

Lucy rose and walked toward them. "Miss Penny, can we go see the new pony?"

Before Penny could answer, Rose popped up. "Oh, yes, please? I love horses!"

Edna and Susan laid aside their knitting and rose as well, hopeful looks on their faces.

Penny glanced toward the stables. Perhaps spending some time with the new pony might help bridge the gap that seemed to exist between Andrew and the other children. And she could definitely use a break from her knitting. "I suppose we could walk up to the stables."

Lydia set down her needles and stood. "Shall we leave our knitting here?"

Penny nodded. "We can pick it up on the way back."

"Not sure I want to go." Donald looked toward the stables with a frown.

Tom and Jack exchanged uncertain looks.

"Might be nice to see that new pony," Tom said.

Donald's expression eased, and he shrugged. "All right. Come on." He tossed his racket on the grass and started off. The other boys hustled to follow him.

"Wait for us!" Penny called, then lifted her hand to her hat and hurried after them. She wasn't sure what Mr. McTavish would say if the boys appeared at the stables without her, and she didn't want to upset the hard-working steward.

Julia looked into her dressing-table mirror and pulled the brush through her long dark hair. It was wonderful having her brother, Jon, here at Highland again, even if it was only for two days. She smiled, remembering how happy Jon and Kate were to be together again after such a long time apart.

It was comforting to have those she loved close by, especially when the news from the front was so disheartening. The Germans had stepped up their campaign in the last few weeks, and British troops remained deadlocked in the trenches.

Jon's brief comments about the injuries caused

by the poison gas now being used on the battle-fields had been so painful to hear.

She sighed, her heart aching. How long would the war last? In their conversation after dinner, the men seemed to think the end was not in sight. Penny had spoken up and voiced her agreement.

Julia paused her hair brushing. Penny's interest in the war was a bit surprising. When Julia had been Penny's governess, Penny had never been interested in international events, but now she pored over the *Times* each day as soon as William was finished with it. Many of Penny's generation were involved in the fight, so Julia supposed it made sense that she would want to understand what was happening.

Was that the only reason?

William walked into the bedroom. "Almost ready for bed?"

She looked up at his reflection in the mirror and smiled. "Yes, almost."

"It's been quite a day, hasn't it?" He pulled his tie loose from around his neck.

"Yes. It was good to have Jon and my parents here for dinner. I can't remember the last time we had so many people around the dinner table."

He nodded, then glanced away. Lines creased his forehead as he looked toward their bedroom fireplace.

"William, is something wrong?"

He looked back and met her gaze. "I have

171

some news, but you should prepare yourself."

Her heart lurched. The faces of the young men on their staff who had gone off to France to fight flashed through her mind. "Have you had a telegram? Has someone been injured or . . ." She couldn't say the word.

He laid his hand on her shoulder. "No. It's not that." He pulled up a chair and sat next to her, his expression solemn. "Clark has decided to enlist."

Julia pulled in a sharp breath. "I didn't expect that."

"Neither did I. But news of the war has been so grim, he feels our freedom and way of life are at stake, and he must respond."

"Is it truly that bad?"

William's eyes clouded. "It is very serious, and I'm afraid things may become much more difficult before it's over."

"When did he tell you?"

"This afternoon. He made quite a convincing case, then asked for my support, and I gave it."

"Does Sarah know?"

"He's taking the train up tomorrow to see her. He thought that would be better, rather than writing a letter."

Julia nodded. "Poor dear. I know it's been difficult for her to be separated from him for so long, and now this." Sarah had gone to Windermere, in the Lake District, three months ago to care for Agatha Dalton, Clark's elderly aunt. She was ill and had no family close by, so Sarah had volunteered to travel north and do what she could to help.

William's brooding frown deepened. "She's been gone too long. And now to have to face this news on top of the burden of nursing Clark's aunt." He shook his head. "It's too much for her to bear."

"Do you think I should go up and stay with her for a week or two? Maybe that would ease the situation."

"No. I think it's time Sarah comes home. She can bring Clark's aunt Agatha here if she must, but we can't have Sarah staying up in the Lake District now that Clark is leaving." He shook his head. "I never would've agreed to this plan if I'd known she'd be away this long."

Julia laid her hand on William's knee. "She's a married woman now, and that decision was one she and Clark made together."

"Yes, but I am still her brother, and I'd like to think I have some influence on their decisions."

She smiled and reached out and touched his cheek. "You are a dear, and you love your sister, but she and Clark must make their own plans and do what they think is best for their family."

"Of course. But bringing Sarah and Clark's aunt back to Highland makes sense. I could go up and escort them, if needed. No matter how ill the aunt is, if she had a private rail car, I'm sure she could make the journey. She'd receive much better care here with your father close by and the staff and family available to look in on her. We could even hire a nurse to give Sarah a chance to rest."

"It's a good plan, if she and Clark will agree to it."

William gave a firm nod. "I'll speak to Clark in the morning before he leaves."

"Good. Then he and Sarah can discuss it when they're together."

He reached for her hand, and his forehead creased again. "There's something else I need to say."

Julia's heartbeat quickened. "What is it?"

"Clark is right. We all have a responsibility to do our duty."

Julia gripped his fingers, and a fearful tremor traveled down her arm. "You're not thinking of enlisting, are you?"

"No, not yet, but I want to do my part."

She released a shaky breath and studied his face.

"I have a great deal of experience in shipping and moving goods from place to place because of my years managing Ramsey Imports. Perhaps that could be helpful in the war effort."

"I thought fear of the German U-boats has shut down most of the shipping lanes, especially since they sank the *Lusitania*."

"That's true. But Britain must find ways to import the food and goods we need if we're going to survive this war." He ran his thumb over the top of her hand. "Perhaps the Lord gave me that time overseeing our family's business so I would gain the knowledge needed to help our country through this crisis."

Julia gave a slow nod. William and his brother David had inherited Ramsey Imports after their father's death. But when William inherited Highland Hall, he'd sold his half interest in the company to his brother. David managed the company for only a little more than a year before he became involved with Dorothea Martindale, the wife of a leading diplomat.

William warned David of dire consequences and urged him to break it off, but David wouldn't listen, and a few days later he was arrested as a suspect in the murder of Dorothea's husband. The scandal had almost destroyed the family's reputation and Ramsey Imports. But the real murderer finally confessed, and David was released from jail. He sold Ramsey Imports, married Dorothea, and moved to America to make a fresh start.

She wasn't sure what had happened to Ramsey Imports in the last year, but she expected the company was suffering terribly since the war started.

She looked at William. "What exactly would you do?"

"I'm not sure. But I thought I'd speak to Fredrick Pontell. We went to Oxford together, and he works in the War Office."

The government urged economy and careful meal preparation, but Highland Hall hadn't been impacted too much. Since William inherited Highland, he had worked to make the estate as self-sustaining as possible. Now they grew most of their own food and ate fish and game from their own land. They had added to the gardens and greenhouses and enlarged the dairy herd. The orchards Clark planted a few years ago were finally bearing fruit. But not everyone was so well prepared.

William rubbed his chin and gazed toward the fireplace. "Perhaps I could take on some sort of advisory role and help manage the supplies that are imported. With careful planning, we might be able to avert shortages and put off rationing."

"Would you have to stay in London?" Thoughts of the bombings that had driven Kate, Penny, and the children to seek refuge at Highland sent an uneasy quiver through her.

"I don't know." He slipped his hand into hers. "But you mustn't worry. It's just an idea that came to me during my conversation with Clark. I'll have to look into it and see if it's even a possibility." His words were comforting, but the look in his eyes made it clear he was determined to do his part. They all were. She just hoped it wouldn't put him in danger or cause them to have to live apart for long.

Her thoughts shifted to Sarah and Clark, and her heart ached. William was only thinking of traveling to London to offer his help for a short time. That was a small sacrifice compared to Clark's decision to enlist. She must keep things in perspective and trust the One who would watch over them all.

Please, Lord, help us through this war. Protect our family and friends. Show us Your will and help us trust You.

Nine

Penny slipped under the arched entrance to the walled garden, carrying her latest letter from Alex. Just knowing he had written made her steps lighter and her heart feel like singing.

She followed the gravel path across the garden and past the boxwood hedge clipped into an arch, then went out the door in the garden wall leading to Eden's Garden. When Penny was just a little girl, her mother chose the plants and flowers here, and Mr. Dalton, Clark's father, planted them all for her.

Curving flower beds full of bright perennials ran along both sides of the grass pathway. Normally, she would stop to enjoy the flowers and cut a bouquet, but today she was eager to find a quiet, private spot to read her letter.

She reached the far end of the garden path and sat on the stone bench in the shade of the tall hedge. To her left, the gate stood open, leading to the shady lane that ended at the stables.

A bird's song floated down from the trees just past the gate, and the children's voices could be heard in the distance. Lydia and Helen had taken them to watch Andrew and Mr. McTavish train the pony. She hoped that would keep them occupied until luncheon.

She slid her finger under the edge of the envelope and tore it open.

July 17, 1915

Dear Penny,

Thank you for your latest letter and the two photographs. There's no need to apologize for the formality or the feathers. You look very pretty and quite regal, in fact. I'm sure everyone who saw you that day was impressed. I appreciate Jon and Kate's wedding photograph as well. They make a handsome couple, and it's nice to see all the family on such a happy occasion. I've set the photographs on a wooden crate by my bed so I can see you and your family each day. It's a good reminder of why I'm here, whom I hope to protect and whom I look forward to seeing when this war is over.

She stopped and smiled. That was very sweet. She'd been unsure about sending the photographs, but now she was glad she had. They seemed to bring him comfort and remind him of her and her family.

Your letter arrived just after I'd returned from a very long and difficult mission. It was a success, but I was never so glad to touch down and turn off my engine. Reading your kind, encouraging words and your promises to pray for me boosted my spirits when I needed it. Thank you for that. It's hard to explain how much your letters have meant to me, but I am very grateful, and I want you to know I think of you often and pray for you as well.

Her heartbeat quickened. He thought of her often and prayed for her? Did he mean his feelings for her were deepening, just from reading her letters?

Memories of Theo and the letters they had exchanged rose in her mind. They had been friendly and informative, but he'd never asked for her photograph or said he was thinking of her or praying for her. The tone of Alex's letters seemed warmer, more personal, and more promising.

A delightful thrill ran through her. Alex was a wonderful man with strong faith and a good heart, and she couldn't help hoping their friendship would continue to grow into something much more. She sighed, then looked down and continued reading.

We've had some beautiful sunny days this week. Yesterday, I hiked to the beach with one of my friends, and we spent some time there, kicking a football around on the wet sand and chasing the seagulls. We were dirty and soaked to the skin in short order, but it was good to get away for a few hours. We had time off because both my planes are down and being repaired. But I should be back in the air tomorrow.

We've had some hard losses this past week. I can't go into detail, but keep our whole squadron in your prayers. Each man here has become like a brother to me, and I want us all to come through this war and make it home again. We all know when we take off we'll face dangerous situations, but we want to do our duty and to see this war through to the end.

I hope you'll not be too worried by what I've just written. I have come through everything well so far, and I expect, with your prayers and God's hand on my shoulder, I will be just fine.

How are you? What kind of adventures are

you having with the children? I enjoyed reading about your plan to help Donald and the other boys become better friends with Andrew. I can imagine the differences in their backgrounds make it a challenge for them to accept each other. I experienced a bit of that when I first enlisted. But putting all ranks and classes together in the military has a way of evening things out. I hope the boys can overcome their differences and learn to appreciate each other. It's worth the effort to keep trying.

How is Kate feeling these days? I received a letter from Jon last week. It was good to hear from him and know that all is well with him and his work at St. George's. I hope you all enjoyed his visit to Highland.

How kind of Alex to ask after Jon and Kate. It was good to hear Jon had written to Alex. She was glad they stayed in touch and could encourage each other.

She smiled, thinking of the series of events that had made it possible for her to meet Alex: his crash-landing during training and shoulder injury . . . his reconnection with Jon at St. George's . . . her decision to help with the outing for wounded soldiers at the London Zoo . . . Alex coming along with Jon that day . . . What wonderful serendipity!

Was it more than that? Was it a special plan

inspired by her heavenly Father? Her heart warmed as growing assurance spread through her.

As I walked back to my room tonight, I looked up at the sky and was struck by the amazing array of stars and the brilliant half moon. The peace and beauty of the moment eased the burden I carried today, and I was grateful. My thoughts turned to you, and I said a prayer, asking God to watch over you, and keep you safe and well. I look forward to your next letter and to hearing that prayer has been answered.

Until then, good night, dear Penny.

Alex

Penny lifted her hand to her heart and gazed out across the garden. *"Good night, dear Penny . . ."*

That definitely sounded romantic.

Perhaps she should ask for his photograph in her next letter. That would let him know her feelings for him were growing as well.

A shout rose beyond the hedge. Penny's heart lurched. More shouting followed. She jumped up and ran out the open gateway toward the stables.

Julia crossed the great hall and walked toward the drawing room with Mrs. Dalton at her side. "Clark, Sarah, and Agatha should arrive just after three." Julia glanced at the tall clock by the fireplace as they passed. They had less than an hour, and there was still much to be done.

Clark's telegram had been delivered only a short while ago, telling them he was boarding the train at Windermere with Sarah and his aunt and to expect them that afternoon. She wished he had given them a bit more notice, but there was nothing to be done about it now. Fortunately the children were occupied outdoors, and she and Mrs. Dalton could discuss the final preparations.

Julia entered the drawing room and turned to Mrs. Dalton. "Are the bedrooms ready?"

"Yes, I've aired out Clark and Sarah's room and readied the Devonshire room, next to theirs, for Agatha."

"Good."

"Agatha doesn't care for flowers." Mrs. Dalton's brow creased. "She says she's allergic. She also doesn't eat beef, mutton, shellfish, or berries. She believes sweets are sin, and children, especially, should never eat them."

Julia's eyebrows rose. "Really?"

The housekeeper gave a firm nod.

A ripple of unease traveled through Julia. It sounded as though Clark's elderly aunt was quite particular. That didn't bode well. "Is there anything else I ought to know about Agatha?"

Mrs. Dalton tipped her head. "I haven't seen her in quite some time. She used to visit at Christmas, but she hasn't come since my husband passed away."

"She never married?"

"No, m'lady. She did not."

William's idea of bringing Agatha to Highland had seemed sensible when he'd suggested it. Now she wasn't so sure. But it meant Sarah could come home, and that was most important. "I've sent a message to my father. He'll be coming by to see Agatha as soon as she's settled."

"I'm not sure she'll welcome a visit from your father on her first day at Highland."

"But Clark said she's unwell. If we're to care for her properly, we'll need a doctor's direction."

Mrs. Dalton gave her head a slight shake. "I don't know if she'll see him."

Julia sighed. "Well, the message has been sent. He's probably already on his way. We'll just have to deal with it when she arrives . . . Let's go over the menu for the week."

"Very good, m'lady." The housekeeper took a small notebook and pencil from her skirt pocket.

A door banged open in the entry hall.

"Both of you, come with me!" Penny's voice rang out.

Mrs. Dalton's eyes widened, and she turned toward the doorway.

Julia hurried across the drawing room and entered the great hall.

Penny marched Andrew and Donald toward

Julia. Her cheeks glowed bright pink, and several strands of her wavy auburn hair had come loose. Dirt smudged both boys' faces. Andrew's pants showed a rip on one knee, and Donald had a bloody cut on the side of his mouth.

Julia pulled in a sharp breath. "My goodness. What happened?"

Penny nodded to Andrew. "Go ahead. Tell her."

Andrew set his jaw and glared toward the staircase.

"Very well. If you don't want to explain, I will." Penny narrowed her eyes at the boys. "These two had a disagreement and decided to settle it with their fists rather than discussing matters like gentlemen."

Donald's stormy gaze raked Andrew. "He might be in line to inherit Highland, but he's no gentleman."

Andrew swung around. "You take that back!"

"I will not! You're no better than we are, but you treat us like trash."

"That's because you've no family and no—"

"That's *enough!*" Julia stepped forward. "Both of you will stop this argument immediately." She looked back and forth between them. "Sir William and I require mutual respect among all the members of this family, and I will not—"

Andrew's eyes blazed. "He's not a member of my family!"

"I wouldn't want to be! Not in a million years!"

185

William hustled down the stairs. "What is all this shouting?"

Julia looked up at William, her heart pounding in her throat. Andrew glared across the hall and turned his face away, while Donald lifted his chin and sent William a fiery glare.

"I'm sorry for the disturbance"—Penny stepped around Andrew—"but I am at my wit's end trying to resolve matters between these two."

"What's the meaning of this?" William focused his brooding frown at Andrew.

The boy's face flamed, and his Adam's apple bobbed in his throat. "Donald is intent on humiliating me in front of the others."

Donald scoffed. "I am not. If you're humiliated by your poor horse-training skills, then that's your problem, not mine."

William lifted his hand to halt Donald's words, then turned to Andrew. "So this is about training the pony?"

"It's about him, mocking me in front of the others."

Donald shook his head, his expression hard and unrepentant.

William studied the boys for a moment, then shifted his gaze. "Penny, tell me what happened."

"Andrew was working with Mr. McTavish, training the pony, and the children were lined up along the fence, watching them. Donald made a remark about Andrew to the other children.

Andrew overhead him, came bolting over the fence, and knocked Donald to the ground. Fists started flying, and Mr. McTavish and I had to pull them apart."

William's frown deepened to a scowl. "This is not the kind of behavior I expect from you, Andrew."

The boy's eyes flashed. "I should've known you would take his side."

"That is not what I said."

"So you think I should just stand there and let him mock me in front of the others?"

"I think you should have the good sense to not let someone's careless words pull you into a fistfight."

"So this is my fault? What about him? He's the one taunting me every day, stirring up trouble."

William turned to Donald. "Is that true?"

Donald jabbed his finger toward Andrew. "He's the one who has an attitude as big as this house. It doesn't matter what I say."

"I think it might be best if we spoke to the boys, one at a time, in private." William stepped toward Donald. "Take a seat here in the hall and wait with Penny, while we speak to Andrew."

Donald smirked and gave a cocky glance at Andrew.

William narrowed his eyes. "Don't think because I'm calling him in first that you are not in trouble. I take this kind of poor behavior very seriously."

Donald's face fell, and he dropped his gaze to the floor.

"Come with me, Andrew." William turned and strode into the library.

Julia released a deep breath and crossed the entrance hall after them. She dismissed Mrs. Dalton, who had stood by and observed it all, then walked into the library.

Undoubtedly, the rest of the staff would soon know the details of the confrontation.

As soon as they entered the library, William motioned for Julia to continue their conversation with his son.

She hoped a calm discussion would help resolve matters. "I'd like you to tell us what you did wrong."

"But what about Donald? He's the one—"

"We'll speak to him, and he'll be required to answer the same questions. But you need to take responsibility for your actions."

Andrew's mouth twisted. "I suppose I lost my temper and I hit Donald."

"Is that all?"

"I cursed him and called him a . . . rotten street urchin."

Julia's heart clenched, but she kept her voice calm. "Why are those things wrong?"

Andrew looked up with a puzzled expression. "Because you don't like fighting or cursing."

"That's true. But it's not only my opinion that matters."

He glanced at William. "You don't like it either."

William gave a solemn nod. "When we're mocked or insulted, the wise response is to ignore it or speak to the person in private and try to resolve your differences."

"Donald wouldn't listen to me."

"You didn't try, so you don't know." Julia softened her tone. "Jesus asks us to turn the other cheek and love our enemies."

"I can't imagine that." Andrew's words were still strong, but his tone was not as heated.

"It is a high standard but one we should all aim for," Julia added.

Andrew's shoulders sagged. "I try to get along, but those boys don't like me."

"That's a different matter, and I'd be glad to give you some ideas about building friendships with Donald and the others, but right now we need to deal with what happened today."

Andrew gave a slight shrug and looked up.

"What will you do the next time you overhear an unkind remark? Because you can be certain it will happen."

Andrew grimaced. "I don't know why you allow those boys free rein at Highland. They've no schooling, no background. In my opinion, they ought to be put to work with the German prisoners in the fields."

William's expression grew stony. "You will listen to Julia and answer her question, or you will stand in the music room by yourself until you are ready to give an answer."

Andrew glanced at the door leading to the music room, the struggle evident on his face. Finally, he straightened his shoulders and looked at his father. "If I overhear a rude remark, I will try to ignore it or I'll ask the person to stop." He lowered his voice and grumbled, "Though I don't think it will make any difference."

William's dark eyebrows rose. "We'll see what happens the next time you have an opportunity to overlook an unkind remark, won't we?"

Andrew gave a slight nod.

William released a breath. "All right, Andrew. You may go, but you can expect us to call you back to apologize to Donald after we finish speaking to him."

Andrew's face reddened again. "Will he be apologizing to me?"

"We'll see."

Andrew and William looked at each other for several seconds. Finally, William motioned toward the door. "Please ask Donald to come in, and I will be watching to see how you do it."

Andrew turned and strode out of the room. William followed him to the doorway, and Julia stepped to the left to have a clear view of Andrew's actions as well. The boy delivered the message to Donald, then took the stairs two at a time and disappeared from view.

Donald walked in, his steps slow and heavy. The earlier bravado he'd shown had melted away while he waited his turn to speak to them. He stopped only a few steps into the room and stared down at the floor.

"Please come here and look at me, Donald."

The boy raised his head, cast a wary glance at William, and took a few steps toward them. He looked as though he expected a scolding, and Julia couldn't help feeling a bit sorry for him.

"You are here at Highland as our guest, but as we told you the first day, we expect you to be respectful of others and thoughtful in your speech and actions."

"Yes, sir."

"Do you understand what you did that caused this fight?"

He nodded.

"Go ahead and tell us. Confession is good for the soul."

"I poked fun at Andrew and said he'd never train that horse."

"Why was that wrong?"

"Because he hit me for it."

"It caused a fight, yes, but I'd like you to think past the results to the offense itself. Why is it wrong to poke fun at Andrew or anyone else?"

"I guess it hurts their feelings and makes them mad."

"Yes, it does. And we live by a higher standard

here, one that says we are to love and honor each other and build one another up."

"But he was doing a poor job. I felt sorry for the horse."

Julia pressed her lips together to hold back her smile, and she could tell William was struggling a bit too.

Her husband nodded. "Yes, I've seen him, and it's true he's just learning how to work with the pony. But when you noticed he was having difficulties, you had a choice to make."

Donald cocked his head.

"You could've kept quiet or offered some encouragement."

"I don't think he'd have liked to hear anything I had to say."

"Perhaps not, but you still had a choice." William waited. "Do you understand?"

Donald gave a slight shrug.

Julia bit her lip. There was a deeper issue causing strife between the boys, and she wished she could help them see it.

"Donald." She waited until he looked her way. "There are some differences between you and Andrew, but I also think you have many things in common."

He sent her a skeptical look. "Me and Andrew?"

"Yes, you're both determined and intelligent, and you're both strong leaders."

The boy's face turned slightly pink, but she

could tell he was pleased with her assessment.

"The other children look up to you. And you can have a great influence for good if you make the right choices."

He watched her with keen interest now.

"What Sir William said is important. We want everyone at Highland to show honor and respect and learn to become peacemakers rather than troublemakers. If you'll remember that, you'll be admired and appreciated by everyone."

Donald gave a slow nod, then looked back and forth between them. "May I go now?"

"Yes, you may."

Julia watched Donald walk out the door. Would he take what they had said to heart? Would it help the boys understand each other and get along better? She certainly hoped so.

Lawrence stepped into the doorway. "Excuse me, sir, but the car is just pulling up the drive."

William nodded to the butler. "Very good, Lawrence. Thank you." He turned to Julia. "My dear."

She took his arm and walked out to meet Sarah, Clark, and Aunt Agatha.

The sun beat down on Lydia's shoulders as she shepherded the children up the lane, toward the house. She swiped her forehead and glanced at Helen. Her sister walked beside her, carrying Emily. The children were unusually quiet, no doubt still a bit stunned by Andrew and Donald's foolish fight at the stable yard.

Rose slowed her pace. "What do you think Sir William will do about Andrew and Donald?"

"I'm not sure, but I wouldn't want to be in their shoes." The memory of Mr. McTavish and Miss Penny pulling the two boys apart made Lydia shake her head.

Rose looked up, eyes anxious. "Do you think Sir William will get rid of the pony?"

"I don't know. We'll have to wait and see."

Rose bit her lip and gave her head a slight shake. "Donald shouldn't have said what he did, but Andrew shouldn't have hit him for it either."

"No, he shouldn't. Both boys let their tempers get the best of them." Lydia sighed. Andrew was a wild one, fighting and cursing like a lowborn field hand. He ought to be ashamed of himself. Would Sir William punish him by selling the pony? That didn't seem right, but it might be the only way Andrew would take the lesson to heart.

"Look, someone's coming." Helen nodded toward the main gate. The Ramseys' dark-blue motorcar drove past the open gateway and up the main drive toward the house.

"That must be Mr. Dalton and his wife and aunt. Lady Julia said she expected them this afternoon." Lydia glanced at the children and clicked her tongue. She should've brought them back earlier so they could wash their hands and look a bit more presentable to greet Clark, Mrs. Sarah, and his aunt, but there was nothing to be done about it now. She hurried to the front of the group. "Come along, quickly now."

Mr. Lawrence stepped out the front door followed by Patrick, the footman, and Mrs. Dalton, the housekeeper. Sir William, Lady Julia, and Miss Penny walked out to join them. The car rolled to a stop, and Hardy, the chauffeur, hopped out and opened the rear passenger door. Patrick stepped forward and opened the other passenger door.

Where were Donald and Andrew? Probably banished to their rooms. Lydia led the children around the car and lined them up next to Mrs. Dalton. She wiped her hands on her apron and straightened Rose's hair ribbon.

Clark stepped out of the car, then he turned and offered his hand to Mrs. Sarah. She climbed out, and Lady Julia greeted her with hug.

Sir William shook Clark's hand, then kissed his sister on the cheek. "Welcome home, Sarah. We've missed you."

"And I've missed all of you as well." Sarah smiled up at Clark and took his hand.

"Well, is anyone going to help me get out?" The elderly woman's voice came from beyond the open door.

Everyone turned toward the motorcar. Lydia

leaned to the right, hoping for a better view. But she couldn't see Clark's aunt.

Sarah shot a concerned look at Clark. He quickly reached inside to help his aunt.

Mrs. Dalton stepped forward. "I can lend a hand."

"Miranda, is that you?" The older woman's head appeared in the doorway of the motorcar.

Mrs. Dalton leaned down and smiled, though it looked a bit forced. "Yes, Agatha, it's me."

"Thank goodness, a familiar face."

"How was your trip?" Mrs. Dalton extended her hand.

"Terrible. The train was hot and dirty. I've been jostled about all day."

Mrs. Dalton eased the older woman out of the car and supported her on one side, while Clark supported her on the other. She wore a long black coat and prim black hat with netting that shadowed her pale, wrinkled face.

Agatha looked around. "My goodness, who are all these people?"

Sarah motioned toward William. "This is my brother, Sir William Ramsey, Baronet of Highland Hall, and this is his wife, Lady Julia Ramsey."

Agatha squinted at them as they greeted her.

"And this is my cousin, Penelope Ramsey," Sarah continued. "My other cousin, Katherine Foster, is expecting a baby. She's resting inside, but you'll meet her soon."

Lady Julia placed her hand on Millie's shoulder.

"This is William's daughter, Millicent, and this is Clark's niece, Abigail, your great-niece." The two girls gave brief curtsies. "You'll meet our son, Andrew, later. The other children are under Katherine and Jonathan's care. They've come from London to stay with us for a time."

Agatha's watery gray eyes widened. "All these children live here at Highland with you?"

Lady Julia's smile melted. "Why . . . yes, they do."

Clark's aunt pressed her lips into a sour line. "I had no idea the house was full of children. I never would've agreed to come if I'd known that." She wrinkled her nose and sniffed. "How do you expect me to rest and recover my strength with a herd of children running through the house, disturbing me night and day?"

Heat flashed in Lydia's face, and she clenched her hands. *How rude!*

Julia stared at Agatha for a moment, obviously restraining herself. Finally, she said, "The children have a structured routine, and the house is quite large. I don't believe they'll prevent you from getting your rest."

Agatha huffed. "Well, I don't want to stand out here all day, discussing it. I'm not feeling well. I want to go inside and lie down."

Lady Julia shot Sir William a heated glance, then motioned toward the front door. "Of course. Please come with me."

Clark and Mrs. Dalton ushered Agatha through the doorway.

Helen leaned toward Lydia. "What a sour old apple," she muttered.

Lydia couldn't agree more.

"Can you imagine," Helen continued, "complaining about the children before she's even stepped into the house?"

Lydia shook her head. "I'm thinking our job just got a lot harder."

The family followed Agatha inside, and Mr. Lawrence instructed Patrick and Hardy to bring in the cases.

Millie and Abigail started for the door, but Lydia held out her hand and stopped them. "Let's wait a minute and give them a chance to take Mr. Dalton's aunt up to her room."

Millie glanced toward the door, doubt shadowing her young eyes. "She doesn't seem very fond of children."

She patted Millie's shoulder. "Never you mind about that." But a slow-creeping vine of worry wrapped around Lydia's heart. Managing the children was hard enough most days. How would she handle pleasing a fussy old woman as well?

Ten

Lydia hurried down the servants' stairs with the message from Mrs. Kate in her pocket. Her mistress finally seemed to have an appetite, and she'd written down her requests for Chef Lagarde and Mrs. Murdock. When she was halfway down the steps, Mr. Lawrence strode around the corner in the lower hallway.

He met Patrick coming out of the kitchen. "Patrick, I need you to go upstairs and collect Sir William's cases and take them out to the motorcar. Then check with Mr. Dalton and see if he requires any assistance." Mr. Lawrence took his watch from his pocket and checked the time. "They need to leave in fifteen minutes if they are going to catch the eleven forty-five train to London."

"Yes, Mr. Lawrence." Patrick hustled up the stairs, sending Lydia a brief smile as he passed.

The butler looked up at her. "Did you need something, Lydia?"

"Oh, no, sir. I'm just on my way to deliver a message to the kitchen."

His dark eyebrows rose. "Is it from Mr. Dalton's aunt?" The woman had complained about every meal she'd been served, and they were all flustered, trying to please her.

"No, sir. It's from Mrs. Kate."

He gave a solemn nod. "Very good."

Mrs. Dalton stepped into the hall wearing her dark-blue coat and hat and started toward them. "Ah, Lydia, I'm glad you're here."

"Yes, ma'am?"

"I've asked Ruby to sit with Agatha, while Sarah and I go to see Clark off at the station, but would you mind looking in on her? You know how timid Ruby can be, but she's the only maid I can spare this morning."

"Of course, ma'am."

"Thank you." Mrs. Dalton reached up and adjusted her small hat. "Well, I should go upstairs and see if everyone is ready to go." Her voice cracked on the last word. She pressed her lips into a firm line and looked away.

Mr. Lawrence's usually stern expression softened. "Don't worry. We'll manage things here."

Lydia's throat tightened. Mrs. Dalton wasn't worried about them managing the house. She was teary eyed because she'd be saying good-bye to her son, Clark, and sending him off to war. She'd already lost one son, and now she might lose another. She could imagine it would be a very painful parting for Mrs. Dalton, and her heart went out to the kind housekeeper. Impulsively, she reached out and laid her hand on Mrs. Dalton's arm. "I'll be thinking of you today, and praying for Clark as well."

Mrs. Dalton blinked as she took a handkerchief

from her coat pocket and dabbed her nose. "Thank you, Lydia. That's good of you to say."

"It's no trouble, ma'am. We're all fond of Clark. He's a fine man. And we're proud of him."

Her eyes grew misty again. "So am I." She pulled in a deep breath, straightened her shoulders, and slipped her handkerchief back in her pocket. Then she nodded to Mr. Lawrence and climbed the stairs.

Mr. Lawrence watched her with a touch of tenderness in his eyes. He could be gruff at times, but underneath he had a good, kind heart.

The scent of roasting chicken and freshly baked bread greeted her as she stepped through the kitchen doorway.

Chef Lagarde stood at the side of a large table in the center of the room, holding out a bunch of leeks to Mrs. Murdock. "I want you to add *zees* to *ze* soup!"

Her cheeks flushed pink, and she placed her hands on her hips. "I never put leeks in my chicken soup, and I don't intend to start now."

"But the flavor of *ze* leeks is better *zan ze* onions."

Lydia had to strain to understand the chef past his strong French accent.

"I don't think so!"

His eyes flashed. "Well, I am *ze* chef and *zees* is my kitchen. If I say we add leeks to *ze* soup, *zen* you will do as I say."

"You may be the chef, but I'm the one making this pot of soup, and I don't need you or anyone else telling me how to change my recipe."

His face turned blotchy red. He lifted his hand and spouted a string of French.

Lydia might not understand the words, but the emotion behind them was as clear as day.

Mrs. Murdock pulled back, her eyes wide. "Don't you use that kind of language around me! I know what you're saying, even if it is French!"

"You will do as I say, or I will speak to Sir William."

"Fine! Go ahead and speak to him. I take orders from Mrs. Kate. She's the one who pays my wages."

The chef whacked the leeks down on the table, spun around, then strode toward the doorway.

Lydia opened her mouth as he passed, then thought better of saying anything. He was in no mood to take a special request from Mrs. Kate. She'd best speak to Mrs. Murdock and give her Mrs. Kate's note.

"Well, don't just stand there with your mouth hanging open." Mrs. Murdock glared at Lydia as though she were the one who caused the argument.

Lydia snapped her mouth closed, then pulled the note from her pocket. "Mrs. Kate is feeling a bit better, and she wanted me to bring down this note." She passed Mrs. Murdock the folded paper.

The cook pushed her wire-framed glasses up her

nose and scanned the note. A smile broke across her face. "Chicken soup!" She lifted her hand to her mouth and chuckled. "She asked for my chicken soup."

Lydia nodded and smiled. "Yes, she did."

"Then that's just what she'll have." She turned back to the stove and looked over her shoulder. "You can tell Mrs. Kate I'll send up a bowl as soon as it's ready.

The two kitchen maids looked up and grinned. Lydia returned the same, then walked out of the kitchen. Mrs. Murdock had a temper, but she didn't let Chef Lagarde or anyone else break her spirit.

As she climbed the stairs, Lydia glanced out the window overlooking the front drive. The motorcar stood waiting by the door, while Patrick secured Sir William's cases on the back. Sir William and Clark Dalton were taking the same train today. Clark would go on to his training camp, and Sir William would be staying in London for some time.

Lydia stopped on the landing and gazed out the window, taking in the scene. Clark and Sarah Dalton stood together by the front entrance, speaking to Sir William and Lady Julia. Mrs. Dalton walked outside and joined them. Even from this distance, Lydia could read the love and concern on Mrs. Dalton's face as she looked up at her son.

A lump rose in Lydia's throat. Clark was a

grown man now, with a wife of his own, but his mother's heart was breaking, thinking of him going off to war to face dangers they couldn't even imagine.

Her heart ached for them all. *Watch over Clark, Father. Guard his steps and bring him back home to his wife and mother. We're all counting on You to keep him safe.*

Her gaze shifted to Julia. She stood close to Sir William, her hand clasped tightly in his. She wore a brave expression, but Lydia could read the strain in the slope of her shoulders and the way she looked up at her husband. Sir William's work in London didn't seem nearly as dangerous as what Clark would face in France or wherever he was sent, but there was the possibility of bombing in London, and time apart from his family would be hard.

Lydia sighed and turned away. Now Lady Julia would have to make all the decisions about the family and run Highland. Mr. Lawrence would manage the staff, and Mr. McTavish would oversee the estate's tenants and property. Mrs. Kate and Miss Penny would help Lady Julia as much as they could, but in the end, it would come down to Lady Julia to keep everything going.

That would be a heavy load for her to bear. Too much for a woman to carry on her own.

Lift her up, Lord. Help her carry this burden, and help us all do our part.

• • •

Alex hiked a quarter mile from the airfield and climbed the high, sandy bluff overlooking the ocean. The day was warm, but a strong wind swept his hair back from his face and whistled around his ears. Below, the gray-green water churned, and waves crashed on the narrow beach.

He stared out across the Channel. On a clear day he might be able to see the low, shadowed coastline of England. But today, gray clouds hovered on the horizon, blocking his view.

Only twenty-five miles separated him from those shores, but it might as well be one hundred. There was no way he could cross the great divide between war and peace.

He pulled in a deep breath. Fresh, salty air filled his lungs, but it couldn't extinguish the ache in his chest or soothe the longing for familiar people and places and most of all . . . for an end to this war.

He'd lost another friend today.

Closing his stinging eyes, he swallowed hard. If only he could erase those images from his mind, but it was impossible.

He and Jackson had flown off this morning just before eight o'clock to patrol the coast to the north. Jackson flew a new Sopwith Tabloid, and Alex piloted his second Morane-Saulnier. The weather was calm, and the first twenty minutes had been uneventful. But just before they reached

Nieuport, Jackson's plane suddenly jerked and tilted to the right.

Alex gripped his own controls and flew as close to Jackson as he could, yelling at him, urging him to take control of the plane. But Alex's shouts were lost in the wind and roar of his engine.

Jackson frantically fought with his controls, but his engine died. Panic flashed across the young pilot's face, and the plane plunged toward the rocky coastline.

Alex clenched his jaw and pounded his fist against his thigh. It wasn't right. It shouldn't have happened. Why didn't Jackson take control, glide down, and bring the plane in safely as they'd been taught? Was it the rough coastal winds, or had his friend lost his nerve and, in his panic, forgotten his training?

Whatever the reason, it had cost Jackson his life . . . and there was nothing Alex could have done to save him.

He sank down on the rough sea grass and lowered his head into his hands. Weary waves of sorrow washed over him, burning his throat and sapping his strength.

Why, God? Jackson was only twenty-three. He has a wife and son back in Yorkshire, waiting for him. What will they do when they hear the news? How will they carry on without a husband and father to provide for them?

If You are so powerful and able to do anything,

why didn't You save him as You've saved me, and so many others, time and time again?

He looked up at the gray sky, searching for an answer to his plea, but the only reply was the low moaning of the wind rushing up the cliff. The mournful sound tore away his reserve and broke through the wall he'd kept around his heart to protect himself from the pain and losses.

Is that all the future holds for me? Will I crash into the ocean or be shot down out of the sky? Do I only have days or weeks left to live? And if I die, has my life mattered at all . . . to anyone? Have I done anything that makes a difference?

He swallowed hard again, but he couldn't hold back the painful cry that rose in his throat and finally broke free.

He laid his head in his arms and wept, for his friend and all the hopes and dreams he would never see fulfilled. For himself and all he feared would never be his.

He wasn't sure how long he sat there, releasing the storm that had been building inside since he'd come to St. Pol. Finally, he lifted his head, weary and spent, and looked across the Channel again toward England.

A slight break in the clouds revealed a small patch of blue sky. From that opening, a brilliant beam of sunlight shone down on the water. The ocean swelled and sparkled in that small circle of light. And a tiny flame of hope flickered to life within him.

He might not understand why God had spared his life and taken his friend, but that didn't give him an excuse to stop fighting for what he believed was right. His father taught him the importance of honor and duty. He'd promised to defend his country and protect those he loved. And that was a promise he would keep, even if it cost him his life.

He pulled in a deep breath, allowing the strength of that commitment to flow through him again. Then he reached in his pocket and pulled out the letter from Penny. He'd picked it up almost an hour ago, but he hadn't been ready to read it until he peeled away this first layer of grief for his lost friend.

He sniffed and tore open the envelope.

July 25, 1915

Dear Alex,

I hope this letter finds you well, and you are enjoying a day as beautiful as the one we are experiencing here at Highland. The warm weather has been a great boon for our crops and gardens, and we are taking full advantage of it. The German prisoners continue working in the fields, bringing in a wonderful harvest. It looks as though we will have enough food to supply the estate and the village of Fulton.

Thank you for your letters. It was good to read about your outing to the beach with your friend. I'm glad you had some time off from flying. I'm sure you need a break now and again. It's wonderful to know you've become good friends with the men in your squadron. I'm sure that's a comfort when you are so far from home. It's an honor to keep you, and all the men there with you, in my prayers.

Alex's eyes grew misty again, and he had to blink a few times before he could continue. If she only knew how much he was counting on those prayers for himself and the other men.

I'm glad the photographs arrived safely and you are enjoying them. Thank you for your kind words. I'm not sure I'll ever dress like that again, but it was a magical day I'll never forget. Do you have a photograph you could send me?

Pleasing warmth spread through Alex's chest as he read that line again. He had a photograph that was taken when he earned his wings at Upavon in June. He'd put it in his next letter.

Much has happened here in the last week. Clark Dalton, who is my cousin Sarah's

209

husband and the head gardener at Highland, has enlisted. He is leaving for training on Thursday. Sarah is trying to be brave, but I know she is terribly worried about him.

My cousin William will be going to London to join an official committee that will be making recommendations to the government about the food supply. They hope to help the country deal with shortages and prepare for rationing, if needed. We're not sure how long he'll have to be away, but that means Julia will have to manage the day-to-day running of Highland. It will be quite a heavy responsibility, but I think she is up to the task, and of course we will do all we can to help her.

William's son, Andrew, was sent home from school because he was caught cheating on an exam, and I'm afraid it's not the first time. Andrew doesn't get along well with the other boys. Yesterday he got into a fistfight with Donald over an unkind remark. I was nearly knocked to the ground when I tried to separate them. Fortunately, Mr. McTavish, our steward, stepped in, and that put an end to it. William spoke to Andrew about it, but I worry what will happen when his father goes to London.

We've added someone else to our household, Clark's aunt Agatha. Her home is in Windermere, in the Lake District. Sarah went up three months ago to stay with her. But now that Clark is enlisting, it was decided Sarah should come home and bring Aunt Agatha with her. She made it clear on her first day here that she is not fond of children. But she usually stays in her room, and I am determined to win her over in time. The children have made cards and picked flowers for her. Unfortunately, we learned too late that she is allergic to most flowers, so we've returned to cards, poems, and pictures. We will succeed!

I know my troubles are nothing compared to the trials you must face each day. I've been keeping up with news about the war, but I'm not sure we hear the full story. William says the War Office wants to keep morale high, and that impacts how much is reported. I'm praying for victory soon and a safe return for you and all our brave men.

Well, it's late here. The house is quiet, and I am sitting in my favorite spot in my room, looking out over the parkland from my window seat. The moon is full, casting soft blue light over the quiet scene. It all looks so peaceful, and that makes it hard to believe only a few hundred miles away there are battles taking place. My hope and prayer is that you are doing well and enjoying a similar peaceful view tonight.

With warm thoughts and ceaseless prayers,
Penny

Alex closed his eyes and took a slow, deep breath, savoring the comfort of Penny's words.

Penny stopped at Kate's open bedroom door and looked inside. She didn't want to disturb her sister if she was sleeping, but she found Kate sitting up in bed with a soft green blanket covering her rounded midsection, legs, and feet.

Kate grimaced at the needlework she held in her hands, then muttered something Penny couldn't hear and plucked at the threads.

"May I come in?"

Kate looked up. "Yes, please. I'm about to go mad from boredom."

Penny smiled and held out an envelope as she crossed the room. "Then here's something to brighten your day, a letter from Jon."

Kate's eyes lit up, and she laid her needlework aside. "Thank goodness. That's just what I need."

Penny passed her Jon's letter, then slipped her hand into her skirt pocket and wrapped her fingers around the letter that had just arrived from Alex. She was eager to read it, but she had decided to deliver her sister's letter first.

Kate looked her way. "Do you mind if I read this now?"

"Not at all. I have a letter too." She hesitated, and her cheeks warmed.

Kate quickly tore open Jon's envelope. "Let's both read our letters, and then we can visit."

Penny bit her lip and pressed down her disappointment. She'd hoped Kate would ask her who had written her. That would make it easier for her to confide in her sister.

She released a soft sigh and sat in the chair next to Kate's bed. She loved her sister, truly she did. Since Kate had fallen in love with Jon and taken all the children into their home, she'd softened and become more thoughtful. But the strain of her difficult pregnancy and the separation from Jon seemed to make her a bit self-focused again.

Penny couldn't blame her. Spending weeks resting in bed would be a trial for anyone, even if it was best for the baby.

Penny opened the envelope from Alex and unfolded his letter. Before she read the first line, her sister gasped, and Penny looked up. "What is it?"

"They want to send Jon to France," Kate whispered, a tremor in her voice.

Penny stared at Kate, hardly able to process her words. "I thought he was needed at St. George's."

Kate looked down at the letter. "He says the number of casualties is much higher than expected, and there's a terrible shortage of doctors in the field clinics and hospitals. They're asking all the younger doctors to take a six-month rotation in France to give our injured men the best opportunity of survival."

"So it's decided? He's going to France?"

"I don't know." Kate continued reading aloud. " 'The single men will be going first, so I hope I will not be called upon until after the baby comes.' " Kate's voice choked off. She lifted her hand to cover her mouth and broke down.

Penny rose and wrapped her arms around her sister, holding her while she cried. "I'm sorry, Kate. I know this is hard, so hard."

Kate clung to Penny, her hot tears wetting Penny's dress at the shoulder. Finally, Kate's tears slowed. Penny released her sister, then passed her a handkerchief from the bedside table.

"Thank you." Kate blotted her cheeks. "At least he doesn't have to go right away."

"Yes. He'll be here when the baby comes. That is what's most important."

Kate sniffed and blinked away a few more tears. "Maybe the war will end soon, and he won't have to go to France at all."

Penny glanced away. From what she'd read in the newspaper and heard in conversations with William and Clark, an early end to the war was unlikely. But she didn't want to steal that hope from Kate. She looked back and sent her a faint smile. "We can pray it does."

Kate's face brightened. "Yes. I've been praying for the troops and for victory, but I'll double those prayers now. If we do win the war in the next six months, then Jon might not have to go and all the troops would be home before Easter."

Penny reached for her sister's hand and gave it a squeeze. "I hope so, but whatever happens, we'll be all right. We have each other and our home here. Nothing is going to change that."

Kate nodded. "If Jon has to go, I'm sure he'll be fine, just fine." Her gaze fell to the letter Penny held in her hand. "Whom is your letter from?"

Warmth rose in Penny's face again, along with a slow smile. "Alex Goodwin."

Kate's eyes widened. "Really?"

Penny nodded, suddenly uncertain what to say.

"I know you and the children sent him that package, but I didn't realize he'd replied."

"This is his third letter." Penny's smile spread wider.

"Well, that sounds promising."

"His letters have been . . . quite friendly."

Kate's eyes danced. "Penny, that's wonderful. Why didn't you tell me?"

"I wasn't sure if I should say anything yet, especially after what happened with Theo. I didn't want you to think I was a hopeless romantic."

"I'd never think that." Kate's expression softened. "I'm sorry about Theo. I know he was fond of you, and we all thought the friendship might develop into something more." She gave her head a slight shake. "I still can't believe he's engaged to a Frenchwoman."

"It's all right." Penny waved away her sister's words and sat in the chair beside Kate's bed.

"I'm sure she's lovely. And the truth is, Theo never made any promises to me. I was the one who had my heart set on romance. I feel foolish now for allowing myself to believe he truly cared."

Sympathy flooded Kate's eyes. "You're not foolish, Penny."

"Maybe not, but I definitely don't want to make a mistake like that again." She glanced at Alex's letter. "I was hoping you might give me some advice about how to handle things with Alex."

"Of course, I'd be happy to." Kate shifted toward Penny, her eyes bright. "Tell me about his letters. Has he given any clear signals he wants to deepen your friendship?"

"He said he thinks of me often, and he asked me to send my photograph."

"Oh, that sounds promising."

"Yes, it does." Penny couldn't help releasing a soft sigh.

Kate's expression grew more serious. "Sweet words are fine, but it's what's in his heart that truly matters." She thought for a moment, then looked back at Penny. "I was impressed by his manners and conversation when he stayed with us in London."

Penny's smile bloomed again. "So was I."

"He was very kind to the children."

"Yes, remember how he went up and searched for Irene during the air raid? And then he stayed on to help us pack up the house before we left."

Kate leaned back against her pillows. "Very admirable. What about his faith? Does it seem genuine?"

"He mentioned memorizing the verses I sent in my letter, and he always asks me to pray for him and the men in his squadron."

"That sounds positive, and I know Jon thinks a great deal of him." Kate smoothed her hand over the blanket, then looked back at Penny. "He sounds like a fine man, but I wouldn't make any promises to him until you spend more time together."

Penny's spirits deflated a bit. "Yes, I suppose you're right."

"Perhaps we could ask William and Julia to invite him to Highland the next time he's in England."

"I already mentioned that idea, and he said he'd like to come, but he doubts he'll have leave any time soon."

"Then you'll just have to keep writing and get to know him that way."

"I suppose so."

"Don't look so glum. This war can't go on forever. Alex will come back, and you'll have more time together."

"I hope so." Penny glanced at his letter again, trying to keep her fears at bay, but it was impossible. She reached for her sister's hand again. "Pray for him, Kate. He said he can't tell

217

me the details, but they've already lost some of the pilots in his squadron."

Kate tightened her hold on Penny's hand. "I will. I promise." She sent her a fleeting smile. "And you'll pray for Jon?"

"Of course. Always." She leaned forward and hugged her sister once more, drawing strength and comfort from their embrace.

Would their prayers be enough to protect Alex and Jon? Could they truly look forward to being reunited with them, or was that only a foolish dream of two women hoping for the safe return of the men they loved?

Penny stilled.

Loved? Did she . . . love Alex?

They might not know each other well, but they shared a special connection, one that could grow into something deeper if they opened their hearts to the possibility . . . and if Alex survived the war.

Eleven

"Wake up, Goodwin!" Someone shook Alex's shoulder.

He rolled over and squinted up at Private McCall. "What is it?"

"Commander Longmore wants to see you in his office—now."

Alex swallowed a groan and rolled out of bed.

Five minutes later, he strode down the dimly lit path at the side of the airfield toward the commander's office. Lights glowed from the three small windows, and he heard voices inside.

He knocked, and the commander called him in. Alex stepped through the doorway. Three other pilots—Wilson, Ross, and Mills—stood around Longmore's desk. They looked his way as he approached.

"You wanted to see me, sir?"

"Yes. Now that you're all here, we can get started. I received a call on our direct line from the Admiralty. They picked up signals from two Zeppelins heading back across the Channel. They believe they're headed toward Evere, just outside of Brussels." Longmore focused on Alex. "I want you and Ross to try to intercept them before they reach the air shed."

Adrenaline pumped through Alex, bringing him fully awake, and he nodded.

Longmore shifted his gaze to Wilson and Mills. "I want you two to fly toward the sheds at Evere. If they get past Goodwin and Ross in the air, you might be able to destroy them on the ground."

Mills nodded, an eager look in his eyes. Wilson frowned and rubbed his chin. He was generally a bit more cautious than the others, but he was a highly skilled pilot.

Alex's shoulders tensed as he considered the mission. Flying at night with limited vision would be more challenging than a daylight mission, but if it meant he had a chance to take down a Zeppelin, it was worth the risk.

Longmore spread out the map on his desk and spent the next few minutes detailing the information he'd learned from the Admiralty and advising them on the best routes for the mission.

"I've already sent word to the mechanics to prepare your airplanes. Gather your gear as quickly as possible. There's no time to lose."

"Yes, sir." Alex saluted and turned toward the door as the other three pilots filed out ahead of him.

"Goodwin," Longmore called.

Alex turned and met the commander's steady gaze.

"You made a name for yourself, blowing up the air shed at Düsseldorf. Churchill asked that you be assigned to this mission."

Surprise rippled through Alex. "Churchill asked for me?"

"That's right. We're counting on you to do what's needed."

Alex's chest swelled and he stood straighter. "Yes, sir. I'll give it my best."

Longmore walked toward Alex. "Stay focused and alert. We want to take down those Zeppelins, but I don't want to lose any more pilots or airplanes in the process."

Alex gave a firm nod. "Yes, sir."

Longmore clamped his hand on Alex's shoulder. "Go on, then. I'll be waiting for a report as soon as you return."

Alex strode out of the office and back toward his room to collect what he needed.

Fifteen minutes later, he climbed aboard his Morane, pulled down his goggles, and tucked the scarf Penny had sent around his neck and into his flight jacket. He touched the eagle wired to his control panel, reminding himself of the verses and saying a quick prayer.

This was an important mission, and he was wise enough to know it would take more than natural skill and good luck to pull it off.

On his left, Ross waved from the cockpit of his plane, then taxied down the airfield and took off into the darkness.

"Take care of yourself, Goodwin," Meddis called from where he stood in front of the plane. Lines creased his face as he swung the propeller. The motor sputtered to life, and the smell of burnt castor oil filled the cockpit.

Alex checked his instruments once more by the dim light on the control panel. He glanced at his watch and noted the time, just after two-thirty in the morning. Lifting his arm, he waved to Meddis to signal readiness for takeoff. The mechanic saluted, and Alex returned the salute, then sent his plane roaring down the bumpy airfield and into the night sky.

The lights of the runway flares flickered then disappeared as he rose through the swirling fog. The cold wind and vibrations from the motor sent a rush of energy through him. The plane lifted past the clouds and into the clear night sky. A three-quarter moon and a thousand distant stars lit the canopy overhead. Alex searched to his right and left, looking for Ross, but he didn't see him. He scanned the sky once more. Had Ross discovered a problem with his plane? Had he turned back to St. Pol?

He swallowed and focused on his instruments again. Only five minutes into his flight and he was already on his own. He tried to shake off his concern. Ross was a good pilot. He would be all right and so would Alex. He was used to flying solo.

That thought brought a few lines from Penny's last letter to mind. *"It's a comfort to remember you don't fly alone. The Lord, the Maker of heaven and earth, flies with you. You are never out of His care. And remember, you are always in my thoughts and prayers."*

His muscles relaxed, and warmth flowed through him, boosting his courage.

He flew tonight for Penny and the children, for his sister Lindy, and for all the others back home in England. And he flew for Someone else as well. *I put myself in Your hands, Lord. Lead me and guide me tonight.*

Calm settled over his sprit. With his mind clear and his prayers said, he could focus on the mission. He checked his instruments and headed north toward Dixmude, passing over the area where he'd successfully knocked out a long-range gun the week before.

Fifteen minutes into his flight, he spotted a pencil-slim, silver shape floating into the clouds far to the north past Ostend. He gripped the controls and leaned forward, squinting and trying to see it more clearly, but it vanished into the mist. His nerves tingled. Was it a Zeppelin or just an oddly shaped cloud?

He pushed up his goggles and rubbed his eyes, then replaced the goggles and searched the sky again. He didn't see anything, but he banked northeast, following the path of the ghostly vision, just in case.

Two minutes later, his breath snagged in his throat. The strange vision appeared again, and this time there was no doubt in his mind. Moonlight glowed off the back of the long, silvery-green airship as it floated across the night sky. It was headed southeast.

Toward Evere.

Energy surged through Alex. This was it—his chance to stop that Zeppelin from ever dropping another bomb on unsuspecting civilians.

He set his course to converge with the Zeppelin's and calculated the time. At this speed it would probably take him about twenty minutes to come close enough to do any damage, but that would give him time to formulate his plan. He watched the airship carefully, losing sight of it in the billowing mist for a few seconds, but then it reappeared. He rose steadily higher, putting himself in position to approach it from the stern.

To the north, the distant lights of Brugge came into view. He flew closer to the hulking airship until only a short distance separated them. Setting his jaw, he prepared for his dive.

Suddenly, lights flashed from the rear of the Zeppelin, and shells whizzed past his plane. Alex gripped the controls. *Blast it all!* He'd come too close and thrown away his best advantage: the element of surprise.

He pulled the stick back and banked the plane steeply out of range. He wasn't giving up, oh, no. He was giving chase—but he'd have to outsmart the gunner and the crew if he was going to do any damage to the Zeppelin.

He rose higher, came around, and swooped down for a second run, trying to bring his plane directly over the back of the airship. But the gunner heard him coming and sprayed the air with machine-gun fire.

Alex swerved, intending to circle around once more, but as he did, the Zeppelin rose several hundred feet higher into the clouds.

Energy pulsed through Alex, and conflicting

thoughts rushed through his mind. He had to get above the Zeppelin before it rose too high. He checked the altimeter. They had already passed ten thousand feet. He could take his plane up another two thousand, but he couldn't risk going much higher, or his engine would stall.

He pulled back to give himself time to think. If he kept pressing the Zeppelin, the airship would simply rise out of range. But if he made the crew think he'd given up, they might drop their guard and give him another chance to take them down.

But how much longer could he play this game of cat and mouse?

He checked his gauge, calculating the fuel needed for his return flight to St. Pol. He was already below a half tank. Time was running out, but he couldn't turn back now, not when he had the Zeppelin in sight. There had to be a way to make them think he'd given up and gone home.

He continued following the Zeppelin, but stayed behind and out of range for several minutes. He'd wait them out, as long as he could.

The Zeppelin gradually turned south, and the nose dipped down a few degrees.

Alex clenched his jaw. This was it. The Zeppelin must be nearing its home base. If he was going to attack, it had to be in the next few minutes. But how could he get close enough? His engine was so loud it would alert the gunner before he could bring the plane into range.

An idea flashed through his mind. If he turned off his engine, he could glide down over the airship without being heard. It was a crazy risk. Once he cut the engine, he couldn't turn it on again while he was in the air. If he survived the attack, he'd have to glide down and find somewhere to land. Even if he could manage that, how would he start the plane on his own?

He cast that last thought aside. It didn't matter. Whatever it took, he was going to knock down that Zeppelin. Or die trying.

He pulled back the stick and climbed to eleven thousand feet, steadily closing the gap between his plane and the airship.

The sky grew lighter as dawn broke. The first pale rays of the sun made it easier for him to navigate, but it would give the gunner on top of the Zeppelin a better view of his plane as well.

He calculated the distance once more and eased the stick forward, then flipped off the engine. The wind whistled past the Morane as Alex dove down at top speed. He swept around toward the stern of the Zeppelin, closer and closer, until the broad back of the gray-green monster lay directly underneath him.

He gripped the controls and held his breath, waiting for the right moment. He flew over the gun platform on top of the airship with only one hundred and fifty feet between him and the giant Zeppelin. He felt like a tiny gnat attacking a giant elephant, but he had powerful weapons no gnat possessed.

He grabbed the toggle wire and jerked, releasing the first bomb, then the second. Nothing happened. He released the last four bombs in quick succession. A second ticked by, then a terrific explosion rocked the plane. Flames shot into the sky, fueled by the gases inside the airship.

Currents of hot air rushed upward, engulfing Alex's plane. He yelled and covered his face with his arm. The plane flipped and rolled over and over, caught in a wild vortex of heat and motion.

The safety harness held Alex in his seat as the plane tumbled and then plunged in a tail-spinning dive.

"Lord!" Alex gripped the controls. He might not have the power of his engine, but he had flaps and a rudder. He pulled back with all his might. The plane shuddered and shook for a few seconds, but finally, just past three thousand feet, he pulled out of the dive.

He leveled off, caught an updraft, and looked over his shoulder in time to see the fabric covering of the Zeppelin curl in on itself as the airship floated down through the sky like a giant flaming cloud. His head buzzed as he stared at the scene, feeling strangely detached from it all. Cool, moist wind rushed past his face, bringing him out of his stunned state.

He heard a dull explosion far off in the distance as the wrecked Zeppelin crashed to the earth. He hoped it landed in an open field and no one on the ground had been hurt, but it would be days before they heard a report. Although the Germans held a tight rein on the news, word would eventually leak out.

He couldn't worry about the Zeppelin now. He had to find his way back to St. Pol. One look at his fuel gauge and his stomach took another dive. His main tank was empty. Had he lost the rest of his fuel when the plane rolled?

How would he make it back to his base now?

Dripping-wet clouds swirled around Alex as his plane glided down through the misty sky. He squinted and brushed the moisture from his goggles. Suddenly, the ground rose up to meet him, and the plane landed with a jolt, lurching and creaking as it rolled to a stop on an incline.

He blew out a shuddering breath and lifted his goggles. The fog was so thick he could barely see past the propeller of his plane. He had landed on a slope, with the nose of his plane pointing down, but he couldn't see much more than that.

He climbed out of the cockpit on stiff, shaky legs and jumped down to the ground. Rough patches of grass covered the hillside. A few birds called in the distance, but after the wild explosions and ear-piercing gunfire he had just endured, the quiet of the Belgian countryside was unsettling.

Shivers raced down his back, and his teeth began to chatter. He quickly realized it wasn't the cool temperature that caused his response, but the stress and shock of all that had happened on his mission.

He closed his eyes and pulled in a few deep breaths, trying to calm himself. He had to regain his focus and check out the plane. His training kicked in, and he started his inspection.

There didn't seem to be too much damage, several bullet holes in the fuselage and wings, but nothing that would prevent him from trying to take off again. If he could get some fuel and start the engine.

If he couldn't, his orders were to destroy the plane by setting it on fire and to burn his papers so they wouldn't fall into enemy hands.

His gut clenched, and determination coursed through him. He was not giving up yet. All the time he'd spent in the hangar with Meddis had taught him how the plane worked and how to make some basic repairs. He walked around to the front and peered at the engine.

A dog barked in the distance. Alex gripped the propeller and froze. The barking continued, but it didn't move closer. He held his breath and waited, his heart pounding in his throat. He heard a sliding squeak, like someone opening a window. A man yelled at the dog in French. The animal whined a few times, then fell silent.

Alex released a breath and turned back to the plane. There was no time to waste. The sun would burn off the early morning fog soon, and his protective curtain would be gone. Even now, the news of the Zeppelin's destruction might prompt the Germans to send out patrols to search the area.

He systematically checked the inner workings of the plane and discovered the line between the pressure and gravity tanks had come apart. He worked as quickly as he could, trying to reconnect it, but his hands fumbled, and he dropped some of the small parts in the long grass. He muttered under his breath and searched until he found all three pieces. Finally, he secured the line, and a triumphant smile broke across his face. That should do the trick.

The main fuel tank might be empty, but he had some fuel left in the reserve tank. Would it be enough to get him back to St. Pol or at least carry him back across the front lines to safety?

There was only one way to find out.

He swung the propeller hard, then ran toward the cockpit, but the engine sputtered out before he could climb aboard. He tried three more times without success. Starting the plane and keeping it going was a two-man job.

Frustration burned in his chest. The sun was rising higher, and the fog was starting to clear.

How much longer did he have before the owner of that dog came outdoors to begin his morning chores?

Off in the distance a horse whinnied, and the sound of several horses trotting through the woods reached him. His heart lurched. He turned and searched across the field—and his breath stopped in his throat.

Not more than a quarter mile away, a squadron of German cavalry rode out of the trees and into the open farmland. One of the men shouted to the others, and the sound of his guttural voice sent a terrifying jolt through Alex.

He had to get his plane off the ground now, before they spotted him, or he would spend the rest of the war in a German prison camp.

Help me, Lord!

He swung around, and an idea rushed through his mind. If he could get the plane rolling downhill, he might be able to keep the engine going long enough to climb aboard. He grabbed hold and started pushing the Morane, then swung the propeller. The engine sputtered and died. What if the sound of the engine alerted the Germans to his presence? He had no choice. He had to try again.

He swung the propeller once more and pushed the plane as hard as he could, and she started rolling downhill. He made a mad leap for the cockpit and pulled open the throttle. She responded beautifully and roared to full speed, racing down the hill.

Shots rang out behind him. He ducked and darted a quick glance over his shoulder.

Germans on horseback raced across the field, shouting and shooting as they rode toward the plane.

Joy surged through Alex as he lifted off into the fading mist. He rose above the Germans as they raced along below. Leaning over the side, he lifted his arm and shouted, "Give my regards to the Kaiser!"

A bullet whizzed past, and he ducked back, laughing and shouting his thanks to the heavens.

Alex flew higher until he cleared the mist. He'd done it—started his plane on his own and escaped capture by a whole troop of angry German cavalrymen.

He glanced at his fuel gauge, and his elation quickly deflated. With the main tank empty, he was flying on what was left in reserve, and he had no idea how far that would take him.

He descended through the light clouds again, looking for landmarks. Should he set a straight course to the west, hoping to find St. Pol? Or head south, praying he made it past the front lines? How was he to decide when all he knew was that he was somewhere between Brugge and Evere?

He mulled that over as he flew on, looking for any clear sign that would help him pinpoint his location. Suddenly, the ocean came into view, shimmering in the morning sunlight. Relief coursed through Alex, and he shot off another quick prayer of thanks. He banked to the left and followed the coast south, back toward St. Pol.

It couldn't be too far now. Searching the coastline, he spotted the jetty and beach north of Dunkirk with rows of seaside cottages. Only a few more minutes, and he would pass over Dunkirk and then, south of that, he'd see the landing field at St. Pol. He'd be home safe and would share the news about the Zeppelin with Commander Longmore and his friends. What a celebration that would be.

Without warning, the engine sputtered and the plane jerked. Alex grabbed hold of the stick. The engine gasped and sputtered again—then died.

Had he run out of fuel?

A strong wind from the ocean caught the plane and sent it tilting at a crazy angle. Alex gripped the controls, scanning the ground, looking for somewhere to put her down.

The beach was too rocky. The roads were narrow and packed with rows of small homes on both sides. Wooded areas filled the land beyond the houses.

Lord, please, I can't bring her down on top of someone's house!

He tried to bank to the left, away from the village, but the plane was not responding. The wind caught him again, tipping the plane and spinning it around. A loud *crack* filled the air. A piece of something broke off and crashed into his propeller. The plane convulsed—

—and plunged toward the ground.

Alex's cry rose up on the wind and echoed out across the morning sky.

Penny rolled over in bed and tugged the thick blanket up to her chin. Opening her eyes, she squinted at the light slipping in around the edge of her bedroom curtains. She checked the clock on her bedroom fireplace mantel and saw it was only ten after six. Why had she woken so early?

She closed her eyes once more and settled down beneath the covers, but hazy images rose in her mind and sent a tremor through her.

In her dream she was back in London, walking down the street with the children. Then she heard a strange roaring sound and looked up. A fleet of huge German Zeppelins approached from the east. Panic shot through her. She must take the children to safety. But when she looked around, the children were gone. Crowds filled the street, pushing past her while she frantically called the children's names.

Where was Alex? He would help her find them. She turned and looked for Alex, but she couldn't see him. Pushing against the crowd, she called for Alex, then begged for help from the passing crowd, but no one seemed to hear her pleas. On and on she ran, struggling against the tide of people, searching for Alex and the children. Bombs fell and exploded around her, rocking the street and knocking her to the ground.

She threw off the blanket and sat up in bed, her heart pounding. She blinked a few times, trying to shake off the hold of the frightening dream. She was not in London. She was safe at Highland. No bombs would fall here. The children were still safely tucked in their beds, and Alex . . .

What about Alex?

A strange sense of foreboding swept through her.

She shook her head. He was all right. He must be. She had just received a letter from him three days ago. But an anxious gnawing clawed at her stomach, stealing away her usual sense of calm and confidence.

She rose from her bed and strode across her room toward the window. Pulling open the drapes, she lifted her face to the soft morning light and looked outside.

Sunshine streamed across the parkland, high-lighting the bright-green grass on the hillsides. She shifted her gaze to the lush flower garden on the east side of the house. Curving stone paths and neatly trimmed hedges crisscrossed the garden.

Taking in the peaceful view usually soothed her spirit, but not this morning.

She sat on her window seat and clasped her hands. It was foolish to give in to anxiety brought on by a dream, but as much as she tried, she couldn't brush those feelings aside. A strong urge to pray flooded through her, and she lowered her head.

Dear Father, please watch over Alex this morning, wherever he is, and keep him safe. I don't know what kind of danger he faces today, but You do.

She closed her stinging eyes. *Help me, Lord. I'm not sure if these fears are simply a result of that crazy dream or if there is some real threat Alex faces today. Either way, help me let go of my fear and put my trust in You.*

She waited a few more minutes, gazing out the window until her emotions settled enough for her to rise and meet the demands of the day. It was almost time to wake the children and help them wash and dress before they all gathered in the great hall for Scripture reading and prayer.

But as soon as they finished breakfast and she had the children settled in a quiet activity, she intended to write to Alex and tell him about the dream. Maybe that would calm her heart and help her shake off this unsettled feeling.

Twelve

Penny gasped at the headline on the front page of the newspaper and quickly scanned the first paragraph of the article.

Julia and Sarah looked across the dining room table at Penny. Several of the children turned her way as well.

"What is it?" Julia asked.

"Listen to this!" She read aloud, " 'British Aviator Bursts Zeppelin in Mile-High Duel. For the first time on record, a Zeppelin in flight has been destroyed by an aviator in an airplane.' " Penny looked up and beamed her smile around the table, bursting to read the next section.

"Alexander James Goodwin, a young lieutenant in the Royal Naval Air Service, who made his first flight only five months ago at Upavon, is the hero of this extraordinary exploit, which was performed aloft over Belgium at six o'clock yesterday morning."

"Hooray for Alex!" Donald shouted, and several of the children applauded.

Andrew glared at Donald. "As if you know him."

"I do. We all do. He came to see us in London and told us about training to be a pilot."

Andrew sent them a skeptical look.

"It's true, isn't it, Miss Penny?" Jack said.

"Yes, Alex was with us during the air raid, before we moved to Highland."

Andrew gave a slight shrug, trying not to look impressed.

Julia turned to Andrew. "Lieutenant Goodwin is an old friend of our family. My brother Jon and I knew him when we lived in India." She looked back to Penny. "What else does the article say?"

Penny continued reading.

"The King has been graciously pleased to grant the Victoria Cross to Lieutenant Goodwin of the Royal Naval Air Service, for the act of bravery specified below:

'For most conspicuous bravery on the Third of August, 1915, when he attacked and, single-handed, completely destroyed a Zeppelin in midair.'

This brilliant achievement was accomplished after chasing the Zeppelin from the coast of Flanders to Ghent, where he succeeded in dropping his bombs on it from a height of only one hundred and fifty feet above the airship. One of these bombs caused a terrific explosion, which set the Zeppelin on fire from end to end, but at the same time overturned his airplane."

Penny's voice faltered, and she stared at those words.

Was Alex all right? She quickly scanned the rest of the article.

Concern lit Julia's eyes. "Is there more?"

Penny nodded, debating if she should read the rest aloud. But she'd come this far. " 'In spite of this, he succeeded in landing safely in hostile territory and after a short time started his engine again. On his return flight, he was forced to make an emergency landing and . . . was injured.' "

Lucy leaned forward. "What happened to him?"

Penny's heart pounded while she scanned the article again. "It doesn't say."

"But he's all right, isn't he?" Donald's usual cocky expression had been replaced by an anxious, searching gaze.

Penny's throat burned. What could she say? She sent Julia a pleading glance.

"I'm sure we'll hear more soon." Julia's voice remained calm, but Penny could read the concern in her eyes. "Until then, I'm sure Lieutenant Goodwin would appreciate our prayers."

Lucy looked around the table. "I think we should pray for him right now."

"That's a wonderful idea." Julia sent her a tender look. "Let's bow our heads, and perhaps two or three of you would like to pray, and then I will close."

Penny clasped her hands and lowered her head.

She wanted to pray aloud, but a dreadful lump had lodged in her throat.

"Dear God, would You please take care of Alex and help him feel better soon." Rose's sweet voice sent a comforting wave through Penny.

After a short pause, Donald added, "Dear God, thank You for Alex. He is a real hero for knocking down that Zeppelin. Would You help him heal up from that crash-landing so he can fly again? Thank You, amen."

Jack and Lucy prayed aloud for Alex, and strength flowed into Penny's heart as she listened. Surely, with such sincere pleas from the children, God would hear and answer.

Finally Julia spoke. "Dear Father, we're grateful for Alex's heroic service, and we ask You to be with him now. Please provide excellent medical care for him, and bring him comfort and speedy healing. We also ask that You help us trust You while we wait for more news. Help us remember that You love Alex and You're constantly caring for him. May those truths calm our hearts and provide an anchor for us all. In Jesus's name we pray, amen."

"Amen," echoed around the table.

Julia looked up. "Thank you, children. You may all be excused. Please go to the library, choose a book to read, and wait for us there."

The children were subdued as they pushed back

their chairs, carried their plates to the sideboard, and walked out of the dining room.

Penny waited until the last one passed through the doorway, then she looked across the table at Sarah and Julia. "I have to find out what happened to Alex."

Julia gave a slight nod. "Jon may be able to help. I'll write to him today."

"What about William?" Sarah asked. "Perhaps he could use his connections at the War Office to find out more details."

"That's a good idea," Julia said. "I believe Alex's mother lives in London. I think she would have been notified about Alex's accident. We could contact her."

Penny bit her lip. Writing letters and waiting for replies would take days or weeks. Where was Alex *now?* What if his injuries were serious? Could they find a way for him to return to London and be treated there? Surely it would be better for him to come to England than to stay in a field hospital in France.

She looked up and met Julia's gaze. "I want to go to London . . . today."

Julia's eyes widened. "What would you do there?"

"I want to make sure Alex receives the best care possible."

"I'm sure his commander and his family will see to that."

Penny gripped her napkin in her lap. "His father is dead, and he's not close to his mother. She didn't even come to see him off when he left for training. We're probably the closest friends he has. We have to do something."

Sarah's eyes flooded with sympathy. "You might find some answers in London, but I don't think it's wise for you to go alone."

"Would you go with me, Sarah?"

She hesitated. "I wish I could, but I don't think I should leave Aunt Agatha. She nearly drove poor Ruby to tears when I went to see Clark off at the station, and I was only gone an hour."

Penny sighed and sat back in her chair. Of course Sarah was right. It wouldn't be wise to leave Aunt Agatha. And even if it took them only one day to find out what happened to Alex, where would they stay? Jon and Kate's home in town had been closed up since they brought the children to Highland.

Still, the sticking point wasn't where she would sleep or even how she would find her way around—the main issue was traveling to London alone.

Julia laid her napkin on the table. "I'll go with you."

Penny sat up. "Thank you, Julia, that would be wonderful."

"I think Lydia, Helen, and Ann can manage the children without our help for a day or two, and

Mr. Lawrence and Mrs. Dalton will see to the house and meals."

The children's daily routine ran through Penny's mind, bringing a ripple of unease. It was a lot to ask of Lydia, Helen, and Ann, but she had to go to London and see what could be done for Alex. "If we give the children a list of activities to do while we're away, that might help. I'm sure they can handle the girls, but we might want to ask Mr. McTavish to watch over the boys."

Sarah laid her napkin on the table. "I have an idea. Mr. McTavish said the cherries in the orchard are ripe and ready for picking. Perhaps that would keep the children busy."

"Yes." Julia smiled. "That's an excellent idea. They could even plan a picnic and give a prize to the child who picks the most cherries."

Relief flowed through Penny. "I'm sure the children would enjoy a contest like that."

Julia pushed her chair back and stood. "Oh, dear, I forgot, my father is coming at ten to check on Kate and Aunt Agatha."

"It's all right." Sarah stood. "Mrs. Dalton and I can meet him and explain your absence."

Julia gave a slight nod, looking distracted. "I wanted to speak with him about something else, but it can wait until his next visit."

"Are you sure?" Penny asked. "We could wait and take a train this afternoon."

"No, I'd like to leave as soon as possible. It

would be best if we could take care of matters by late afternoon and return home tonight."

Penny rose, eager to prepare for their trip. "Thank you so much."

"You're welcome, my dear." Julia came around the table and gave her a hug.

Penny closed her eyes, soaking in the comfort of Julia's warm embrace. With Julia's marriage to William, she had become much more to Penny than her former governess. She had stepped into the role of cousin, guardian, and elder sister, all wrapped into one.

Thanks overflowed from her heart. Surely, with Julia's help, she would be able to find out what had happened to Alex. If his injuries were serious, Julia would help her deal with that news. And if that was the case, she would do everything in her power to bring him back to England and St. George's to recover.

But what if that wasn't possible?

She pushed that thought away. She would not accept defeat. Alex had gone to great lengths to protect his country. Now she would do whatever it took to see that he had the best care possible.

Painful throbbing pounded in Alex's head, stabbing the back of his eyes. It felt like someone was hammering a stubborn nail into solid oak. He moaned and tried to turn his head, but it felt so heavy he could hardly move.

Why couldn't he open his eyes? Where was he?

He parted his lips and pulled in a ragged breath, and pain shot through his jaw. His mouth was so dry . . . his tongue felt like a swollen piece of meat. He tried to swallow the dryness away, but it was no use. He moaned again.

"There now, Lieutenant." The gentle female voice drifted toward him. "Rest easy."

Who was that? He tried to pry open his eyes, but only one opened a slit.

A fuzzy female form bent over him. She wore a gray dress and a white apron with a large red cross stitched on the front. A white cap covered most of her dark-brown hair.

"Who are you?" His voice came out as a hoarse whisper.

"Nurse Johnson."

His mind felt so fuzzy he could barely think how to form his words. "I'm thirsty," he croaked.

"I'll get you a drink." She walked away but returned a moment later, propped him up a little, and held a cup to his lips.

Cool water slid across his parched tongue and down his raw throat. Relief. Blessed relief.

"Slowly now. There's no need to gulp it down."

He took another sip and moistened his lips, then she eased his head and shoulders back on the pillow. He lay there, breathing hard, spent and confused. Just drinking that water had taken all the energy he possessed. He squinted up at Nurse Johnson. "What happened to me?"

"You don't remember?"

He searched his mind, trying to recall how he'd landed in the hospital in such pain.

She laid her hand on his shoulder. "You crash-landed two days ago, just outside Dunkirk. But before that, you brought down a German Zeppelin." She smiled and small lines crinkled at the corners of her eyes. "You're a hero. The King plans to give you the Victoria Cross as soon as you're well enough to travel to England."

Memories rushed back at her words, and his eye drifted closed. He remembered taking off in his Morane, flying up into the darkness . . . heading for Belgium . . . spotting the Zeppelin . . . chasing it through the starlit sky. Then the gunner on top of the airship spotted him, and bullets whizzed past his plane.

Pain pulsed through his head again, clouding his thoughts. He'd taken down the Zeppelin, but he'd crashed his plane before he could return to St. Pol. Yes, he remembered now. Somehow, he'd reported the bare facts of his mission to the men who had rushed to the plane after he'd crashed. Then . . .

He couldn't remember anything after that.

A sudden thought jolted through him, and he forced his eye open. "Nurse?"

She turned back to him. "Yes?"

"What's wrong with me? What are my injuries?"

Her lips parted, and some unnamed emotion flickered in her eyes.

"Tell me. I want to know."

She returned to his bedside and leaned over him. "You have three fractured ribs, a compound fracture of your left arm, and a broken collarbone." She started to say more, then glanced away with a slight frown.

"What else?"

"The doctor will be coming around soon. He'll explain everything to you."

"I want to know now." His voice sounded raspy, demanding.

She sat down beside his bed with a tired sigh. "All right. You've ruptured your spleen. You have a head injury, probably a concussion. You have multiple cuts and bruises to your face, and your right eye is . . . damaged."

His eye? Was that why everything was so fuzzy? Slowly, he lifted his right hand off his chest. Piercing pain shot across his side. He gasped and stifled a shout but kept going until his hand reached his face. Slowly he traced the bandages covering his right eye and the right side of his head.

With a gentle touch, the nurse took his hand and laid it across his chest again. "How's your pain level? I can give you more medication if you need it."

He gave his head a slight shake, but that set off the throbbing pain again. He clenched his jaw and closed his eye. He hurt so bad he could barely think, but he didn't want to take more pain medication, fall asleep, and then miss talking to the doctor. He needed to find out how long it would be until he could fly again.

A wave of nausea hit his stomach and rose in his throat. He tried to swallow it down, but it was no use. "I'm going to be sick."

She reached for a basin and held it out just in time.

When it was over, he shuddered and lay back. Waves of pain crashed through his pounding head, side, arm, shoulder, jaw, ribs. Was there *any* part of his body that did not hurt? "I think I'll take that pain medication."

"Very good. I'll be right back."

"If you see the doctor, tell him I want to speak to him."

She sent him a sympathetic smile. "I will."

"And tell him if I'm asleep to wake me up."

She didn't reply as she hurried off.

He released a slow, deep breath and let his eye drift closed. His mind danced in and around reality, floating from one thought to the next. He shouldn't have tried to make it all the way back to St. Pol. He could've brought the plane down sooner and saved it and himself all this trouble. Was his plane destroyed? He tried to remember, but everything was so fuzzy after the crash.

This was bad . . . but he could've crashed in enemy territory instead. Then he'd be in a German field hospital or, worse, a prison camp. Who knows what they would've done to him if they learned he was the aviator who'd knocked one of their prize Zeppelins right out of the sky?

The King wanted to award him the Victoria Cross? He'd have to go to England for that. Out of his misty thoughts swirled a smiling face . . . Penny.

If he went back to England, he would see Penny. Maybe he could visit her at Highland Hall. That would be wonderful. Then he'd go back to St. Pol and rejoin his squadron. They had a war to win. Yes . . . He'd see Penny, then go back and fly again . . . That's what he'd do.

He drifted off to sleep then and blessed relief.

Lydia looked up through the lush green leaves of the cherry tree to a cluster of fruit hanging over-head. She'd have to climb higher up the ladder if she was going to reach them. She looked down at the ground, and a dizzy feeling washed over her. She clutched the sides of the ladder and closed her eyes tight. *Take a deep breath. Calm down. You'll be all right.*

But it was hard to stamp out the memory of seeing her brother fall out of the hayloft and break both arms when he was only nine years old. It had scared her to death, and ever since then she liked to keep her feet firmly planted on the ground.

"Lydia, look, my basket's full again!" Rose pushed a branch aside and held out the almost overflowing load of cherries.

"Rose, hold on to the ladder!"

"I am holding on."

"Well . . . just be careful when you climb down."

"I will." But Rose scrambled down the ladder almost as fast as she usually ran down the stairs. She hopped to the ground, carried her cherries to the farm wagon, and poured the fruit into one of the wooden crates.

Lydia sighed. It was a wonder Rose or one of the other children hadn't gotten hurt with the way they were all running up and down ladders like it was nothing at all. She glanced at the wagon with the six crates stacked in the back. Three of them were already full of cherries. Thank goodness Mr. McTavish drove the wagon out to the orchard and left it with them to carry the fruit back to the house.

Mrs. Murdock and the kitchen maids would have their hands full, making preserves and baking tarts and puddings. Maybe Chef Lagarde would use some of the cherries in one of his recipes. Just thinking about it made her mouth water. She smiled and popped a sweet, warm cherry in her mouth.

Rose ran back to their tree and scooted her

ladder over to a new section. Lifting her skirt and basket in one hand, she scampered to the top.

Goodness, that girl was as surefooted as a mountain goat.

When Rose was settled and picking again, Lydia turned and scanned the orchard. She had ten children with her today, the three boys and Andrew, and four girls, plus Millie and Abigail. They all seemed to be enjoying the outing and had been working at top speed for the last hour and a half. No doubt the promise of a prize for the one who picked the most cherries was spurring them on.

It wasn't quite fair. The older children with longer arms had an advantage over the young ones. Maybe she should make sure they all got a reward for their work today.

She looked up through the leaves again. There were still plenty of ripe cherries on her side of the tree. It was time she got busy and finished this section. She slowly inched her way up to the next step. *Just don't look down and you'll be fine. Rose is higher than you, and she's not afraid.*

In the distance she heard the sound of tramping feet. She turned to look through the trees. A group of German prisoners walked up the lane toward the orchard, carrying scythes and rakes over their shoulders. A stern-faced guard in a khaki uniform walked behind them, carrying a rifle.

Lydia gripped the sides of the ladder. Why were

they coming this way? She took hold of her half-full basket and carefully started down.

Rose looked at Lydia through the leaves, her lips in a slight pucker. "Are those the German prisoners?"

"I think so." Lydia stepped down into the tall grass. Did they intend to pass through the orchard, or were they planning to work nearby?

"Hey, the Huns are coming!" Donald shouted from a tree to her left.

"What are you talking about?" Andrew called from another tree.

"Look and see for yourself!" Donald swung out from his ladder and pointed to the approaching men.

Lydia gasped. "Donald, be careful!"

The boy sent her a surprised look, but he took hold of the ladder again with both hands.

Lucy, Edna, Abigail, and Millie climbed down their ladders and walked over to join Lydia, while Rose and the boys continued picking.

Lydia brushed her hands on her apron as the prisoners drew near. She glanced at the men, and recognition flashed through her. The two at the head of the line were the same men who had spoken to her the day she and the children passed them working in the field.

The tall blond man, Marius, looked up at Lydia, and a slight smile lifted the corners of his mouth. He nodded to her. "Good morning, miss."

A smile overtook her before she could look away.

"Keep moving," the guard called from the rear of the group.

The shorter man walking beside Marius touched his cap and grinned at Lydia. Then he chuckled and elbowed Marius, saying something in German.

Marius scowled at him, and his ears turned red. "That's enough, Siegfried."

Lydia didn't even want to guess what Siegfried had said.

"Halt!" The guard frowned at Lydia and motioned for her to come over.

She looked around, but there was no one else he could mean, so she took a few steps closer and stopped in the middle of the lane.

"I have orders for the prisoners to cut the grass in the orchard. But we can't very well do that with you here." He shifted his rifle to the other shoulder and sent her a stern look. "Are you about finished?"

Lydia straightened and met the guard's gaze. "No, we planned to pick until noon."

Irritation flashed across the guard's face. He shot a glance at the farm wagon, and his mouth twisted into a surly line. "Looks like you've picked more than enough cherries to me. Take the children and go home."

Who did he think he was, ordering her around

like that? She lifted her chin. "That section is done"—she nodded to the right—"we just have these last few trees to finish. I don't see why you can't start over there."

He pulled back and looked at her as though she was simpleminded. "These are dangerous German prisoners. Aren't you afraid of them?"

She wasn't happy about working near them, but she wasn't about to admit it to this rude guard. "No, I'm not afraid."

The guard huffed. "Well, you ought to be."

She held her tongue, determined to wait him out. Just past the guard's shoulder, she had a clear view of Marius. He watched her, admiration shining in his eyes.

The guard snorted and shook his head. "All right. I warned you. If you won't listen to me, that's your problem."

Lydia clenched her hands. *Arrogant, foolish man!* He had no right to speak to her as if she were a child. If he did his job and kept a good eye on the prisoners, she should have nothing to fear.

"We'll start on that far side. But you better finish picking by the time we reach these trees." The guard directed the men to the opposite side of the orchard, barking orders as he marched them off.

Lucy stepped closer to Lydia. "Are you sure it's all right for us to stay here with those prisoners so close by?"

She swallowed, hoping she hadn't let her pride

get the best of her. "I don't think we have to worry. The most dangerous man among them is probably that awful guard."

"We'll protect you," Andrew shouted from the tree on her left. His laughter rang out, and Donald, Jack, and Tom joined in.

The boys' carefree response seemed to reassure the girls, and they climbed their ladders again and went back to picking.

Lydia watched the prisoners spread out around the trees across the lane. Marius set to work with his scythe, swinging it back and forth in a smooth, easy rhythm. Siegfried worked next to him, but he took shorter strokes, and it didn't look as though he was putting much effort into it.

Lydia turned away and walked back to the farm wagon. She dumped her half load of cherries into the wooden crate, admiring the growing pile of shiny, dark-red fruit.

A startled cry filled the air. Lydia spun around. On the far side of the lane, under one of the largest trees, Marius reached for his leg and fell to the ground. Lydia's hand flew up to her mouth to stifle her cry.

"Marius!" Siegfried tossed his scythe aside.

Marius groaned and writhed in the grass.

The other men ran toward Marius and Siegfried. "He's bleeding!" one man shouted. "It looks bad!" The men crowded around Marius, blocking Lydia's view.

The guard strode toward them, his gun aimed at the group. "Step back! Let me through!"

The prisoners made way for the guard, opening the view for Lydia again. The guard looked down on Marius, his mouth set in a hard line. He shook his head and muttered something Lydia couldn't hear. His lip curled. "What happened?"

"It doesn't matter now!" Siegfried shot a wide-eyed look around the group. "We've got to help him."

The guard glared at the men. "Who did this?" No one replied. "There will be no help for this man until someone tells me exactly what happened."

The group stood silent, their eyes on the ground. Marius lay still on the grass now, his hand wrapped tightly around his leg. If he knew who had done it, he wasn't willing to say.

"He stepped in my path," Siegfried cried. "I couldn't help it."

The guard gave an impatient snort. "I'll have to report you."

"But it's not my fault! I didn't mean to do it! It was an accident!"

Lydia shook her head. What was wrong with these men? Didn't they realize Marius needed help? She tossed her basket into the back of the wagon and strode across the orchard. The men stared and stepped back as she approached.

She dropped down on the grass next to Marius.

His face had gone pale. He clutched his pant leg at the calf, and bright-red blood oozed out around his fingers.

"We've got to stop this bleeding." She whipped off her apron, wrapped it around his leg, then eased his hand away.

"Thank you," he said softly, then winced and closed his eyes as she tied the apron around the wound.

She looked up at the guard. "Have your men carry him to the wagon. I'll take him back to the house."

"No! He can't go there."

Lydia stood and faced the guard. "He needs a doctor, and there's one at the house right now, if we hurry."

The guard studied her through narrowed eyes. "I'd have to get permission from my commander."

"There's no time! He must have help now, unless you want him to bleed to death on your watch."

The guard took a step closer, deep lines cutting across his forehead. "I can't let him go. Not without a guard. And I can't leave these men."

Lydia clenched her hands. She would not stand by and let this hard-hearted, ignorant man have his way. Marius could die if someone didn't tend to his leg. "I insist you load him into the wagon now!"

The guard looked down at Marius and then at

the men. Marius closed his eyes, his face etched with pain.

Siegfried stepped toward the guard. "Let him go! Surely you don't think he'd try to run away, not with his leg cut like that."

The guard gave a dismissive wave. "All right. Carry him to the wagon." He turned to Lydia and pointed his beefy finger at her. "I'm holding you responsible for keeping him at the house until we send someone to bring him back to camp. Do you understand?"

"I understand. Now step aside." She strode past him.

A few men gathered around Marius, lifted him, and carried him to the wagon. Siegfried climbed up in the back with Marius.

"What do you think you're doing?" the guard shouted.

"Someone has to put pressure on that cut, and she'll need my help to carry him into the house."

Lydia opened her mouth to protest, then stopped. Siegfried was right. Putting pressure on the cut would help slow the bleeding.

The guard scowled at Siegfried. "Go on, then. We'll head back to camp and report what happened. Stay with him until someone comes to pick you two up."

Relief flashed across Siegfried's face, and he nodded to the guard.

Lydia climbed up into the driver's seat and

unwrapped the reins. It had been a few years since she'd driven a team of horses on her family's farm, but she was sure she could keep these two tame bays in line for the short drive back to the house.

She called Lucy and Andrew over and asked them to gather all the baskets and bring the children home. They agreed, looking pleased she'd put them in charge.

She glanced over her shoulder at Marius and Siegfried. "Are you ready?"

Siegfried nodded, then reached for the sweater Lucy had left in the back of the wagon. He folded it and slipped it under Marius's head. "You'll be all right, Marius." But his voice betrayed his doubts.

Lydia's arms tingled as she lifted the reins and called out to the horses. The wagon lurched, then rolled down the lane toward Highland Hall.

She tried to guide the horses around the rough spots in the road, but she hit one, and Marius cried out. She bit her lip.

Please, Lord. Help Marius, and don't let the doctor leave before we arrive.

Thirteen

Penny lifted her skirt a few inches and followed Julia up the wide marble stairs inside St. George's Hospital in London. "I hope Jon is not in surgery."

Julia looked over her shoulder as they reached the third floor. "We'll know soon enough."

They set off together, Penny checking the names on the office doors to the right while Julia looked at those on the left. The scent of antiseptic and starched sheets floated in the air.

Searching and not finding seemed to be the theme of the day. They had spent the first two hours in London trying to locate William. They'd gone to the building where the committee usually met, but they were told the committee was not in session today. Next, they stopped by the flat William shared with Jon, but neither of them was home. Finally, they went to William's club and asked for him there.

William came out, surprised and pleased to see them, but women were not allowed past the front reception area, so he suggested they go to a tearoom a short distance away.

Over steaming cups of tea, William listened while Julia explained the reason for their trip to London.

"I saw the article about the Zeppelin's destruction in the paper this morning." William stirred sugar into this tea. "Everyone is talking about it, but I didn't notice the pilot's name. I'm not sure I would've recognized it even if I had."

"I've mentioned Alex to you a few times," Julia said with a gentle smile.

"I'm sure you have, my dear, but I'm afraid I've never been good with names, and I have been a bit distracted lately."

"Of course. I understand. But I hope you'll do what you can to find out what happened to Alex."

William frowned at his teacup. "It won't be easy to get information like that."

Penny had tried to be patient and let Julia lead the conversation, but she felt she would burst if she didn't speak up. "Oh, please, Cousin William. Alex doesn't have close ties to his family, and I'm not sure he has other friends who will step forward to help him."

William studied her more closely. "So this young pilot is special to you?"

She nodded. "We've exchanged a few letters, and I do want to help him if I can."

He lifted one eyebrow and looked at Julia. She gave a slight nod, and he turned back to Penny. "All right. I'll speak to Alfred Cummings at the War Office. He might be able to help." He thought for a moment more. "And Michael Burlingame is with the Red Cross. Perhaps he could look into it."

Penny tried to press down her disappointment. "Thank you. I appreciate your help."

She wanted an answer today. Still, she didn't intend to rest until they discovered Alex's location and condition, and had a clear plan in place to bring him back to England. Which was the reason for their next stop, St. George's Hospital, where they hoped to speak with Jon.

"Here we are." Julia knocked on Jon's office door.

No one answered, and Penny blew out a frustrated breath. "What shall we do now?"

A nurse approached carrying a clipboard. "May I help you?"

Julia turned toward her. "Yes, we're looking for Dr. Jonathan Foster."

"I'm sorry. The doctor is seeing patients this afternoon. But I can give him a message if you'd like."

"I'm his sister, Lady Julia Ramsey, and this is his sister-in-law, Miss Penelope Ramsey. We have a bit of a . . . family emergency, and we need to speak to him."

The nurse motioned toward the door. "Why don't you wait in his office, and I'll see if I can find him and let him know you're here."

"Thank you." Julia reached for the doorknob. "We'd appreciate that very much."

Julia and Penny walked in and took seats on the plain wooden chairs facing Jon's desk. Stacks of file folders and papers covered most of the desktop. Bookshelves, overflowing with medical texts, lined the wall behind the desk. One tall window looked out on the street below.

Penny tapped her foot and checked her watch three times before Jon finally walked through the doorway. He wore a white doctor's coat over his dark pants and white shirt, and a stethoscope hung around his neck.

"Julia, Penny, what a surprise. I didn't know you were coming to town today."

Penny rose from her chair. "Did you hear about Alex?"

Jon walked behind his desk. "No, what's happened?"

"He brought down a Zeppelin over Belgium two days ago, but he was injured on his return flight."

Jon's eyes flashed. "I was in surgery all morning, and I've just finished my afternoon rounds." He sank down in the desk chair and rubbed his eyes.

Julia studied her brother with a slight frown. "Jon, you look exhausted. How long have you been working?"

"I came on last night at seven."

"My goodness, how do they expect you to care for patients after that many hours on your feet?"

Jon slipped off the stethoscope and laid it on the desk. "Don't worry. I'm coming off duty now."

"I should hope so."

"As soon as we finish here, I intend to go

home, have a bite to eat, and then get some sleep."

Penny clasped her hands and leaned toward the desk. "Before you go, is there any way you could find where Alex is and . . . how badly he's injured?"

Jon shook his head. "Not if he's in France. I don't have access to that kind of information."

"But you receive so many wounded men here. There has to be some sort of system for keeping track of the wounded and what's being done for them."

"I'm afraid I don't know how they manage it."

Penny knew he was tired, but she couldn't give up yet. "Isn't there someone on your staff who could find out? And then once we know Alex's condition, perhaps we can make arrangements for him to be transferred to St. George's so he can be cared for here."

"It sounds like you have a plan in mind." Jon sent her a weary smile.

Julia laid her hand on Penny's arm, sending a silent message to let her speak. "We're all concerned about Alex, but he and Penny have been exchanging letters and become . . . good friends. So you can understand why she's so eager to help him."

Jon gave a slow nod. "I see. I'm sorry, Penny. I didn't realize. I don't mean to make light of the situation." He opened one of his desk drawers, searched through it, and pulled out a letter.

"Alex gave me this before he left for France."

Penny straightened and stared at the letter.

"He said if anything happened to him he wanted me to give it to his sister."

She blinked. "His sister?"

"Yes, Lindy Goodwin lives here in town, and Alex wanted me to pass it on if—if it was needed."

Penny gripped the arm of the chair. "Do you think it's that serious?"

"I hope not, but Alex wrote her address on the envelope." He handed it to her. "Copy it down and pay her a visit. If anyone has received word about Alex's condition, it will be Lindy. She's the one he listed as his next of kin."

Finally, a lead that sounded promising. Penny took the letter and copied the name and address in her small notebook, then handed it back to Jon. They thanked him and left the hospital.

Thirty minutes later, their cab rolled to a stop in front of a large, stately home in St. James's Square.

Penny peered out the window, while she waited for the driver to open her door. "My, it's certainly a lovely home. I didn't realize his sister was so wealthy."

"I believe this is his mother and stepfather's home."

"Oh, yes, of course." Penny stepped out of the cab and waited while Julia paid the driver, then they walked up the steps to the front door.

Penny reached for the knocker, then hesitated. "Do you think we should ask to see his mother or Lindy?"

"Alex addressed the letter to his sister, so I suppose she's the one we should speak to."

"That seems a bit odd, but he must have his reasons." Penny knocked, and a few moments later a maid answered the door. They asked if they might see Lindy Goodwin, and the maid showed them inside. They waited in the entrance hall no more than two minutes when a lovely young woman walked down the stairs. Her dark-brown hair was put up in a fashionable style, and it was easy to see her resemblance to Alex in her large brown eyes and the shape of her face.

"Good afternoon, I'm Lindy Goodwin. What can I do for you ladies?"

Julia stepped forward. "Hello, Miss Goodwin. I'm not sure if you remember me, but we met in India when you were quite young. I was Julia Foster then, but now I'm married to Sir William Ramsey." She motioned toward Penny. "This is my husband's cousin, Miss Penelope Ramsey."

Lindy's eyes glowed with genuine warmth. "Why, of course I remember you, Julia. What a nice surprise. How did you find me?"

"My brother, Jon, is a doctor at St. George's. He cared for Alex last spring when Alex injured his shoulder during his training."

"What a coincidence."

"Yes, a happy one for Jon and his wife, Kate. Alex stayed with them at their home here in London for a few days before he left to finish his training. Penny was there at the time as well. He and Penny have continued writing to each other these last few months."

Lindy's eyebrows rose slightly. She turned to Penny and smiled. "How nice."

"So you can imagine how concerned we were when we read the article in the newspaper this morning," Julia said.

A shadow crossed Lindy's face. "Yes, it's wonderful what Alex has done, but it sounds as though it's come at a great cost."

Penny clasped her hands. "Have you heard from Alex? Do you know where he is now?"

"I'm afraid not. Mother and I are both quite concerned."

Penny's heart plunged. "You haven't heard anything?"

"No. We're hoping for a telegram or letter, but we haven't received one yet."

"Oh, I see." Penny pressed her lips tight, fighting to control her emotions. What would they do now? How would they find out what had happened to Alex?

A tall, middle-aged woman walked through the doorway at the end of the hall. Her elegant dress and hairstyle made it clear she was the lady of the house. When she saw Penny and Julia, her steps slowed, and she sent Lindy a questioning glance.

"Ladies, this is my mother, Mrs. Winifred Tremont. Mother, this is Lady Julia Ramsey and Miss Penelope Foster. They've come to see if we have had any news from Alex."

It seemed odd that Lindy didn't mention knowing the Foster family in India. Did she think her mother wouldn't remember Julia or that the connection would bring up unpleasant memories? Alex had told Penny his parents divorced when he was quite young, that his mother had left him and his father and returned to England with Lindy.

"It's kind of you to ask after Alex," Mrs. Tremont said, "but we haven't heard from him for quite some time. He's a dear boy, but he never was one to write many letters." Her words were pleasant enough, but they carried an underlying coolness that made Penny doubt the sentiment behind them.

Penny studied Mrs. Tremont. "We were very concerned when we read the article this morning. We thought you might have received a telegram or some official notification about his injuries."

Mrs. Tremont's dark eyebrows slanted. "You'd think he would contact his family, but we've had no word from him, none at all. We have to read about it in the newspaper, like everyone else. How can they allow a story to go out like that without all the facts? What am I to think? What are we to do? It's all quite upsetting."

Penny swallowed and looked at Julia as an uncomfortable silence stretched out between them.

Lindy forced a smile. "May I offer you ladies some tea?"

"That's very kind of you." Julia smiled at Lindy and then at Mrs. Tremont. "But we need to catch the train back to Berkshire."

"Oh, I didn't realize. I thought you lived in town."

"No, our home is at Highland Hall near Fulton."

"Well, we don't want to delay you." Mrs. Tremont looked toward the front door, obviously ready for them to leave.

Penny reached in her purse. "If you do hear from Alex, would you let us know?" She took out her calling card and held it out to Lindy. "The only address you'll need is Highland Hall, Fulton."

"Of course." Lindy accepted the card with a slight nod. "I'll send word as soon as we hear something."

"Thank you. I'd appreciate it." She should go, but there were a few more things she had to say. "If Alex needs medical care of any kind, St. George's is an excellent hospital with the most modern equipment and treatments available. Jon has cared for hundreds of wounded men, and I know he's eager to help Alex. We'd be happy to put in a word and have Alex moved there if it's possible."

Lindy nodded. "Thank you. I'll remember that."

Julia took Penny's arm. "We should be going. Thank you for seeing us. We'll look forward to hearing from you."

Lindy opened the front door, and Penny walked out into the late afternoon sunlight, her heart heavy and her mind filled with unanswered questions.

Lydia pushed open the door to the lower hallway at Highland, then stepped back so Siegfried and Patrick could carry Marius inside. "There are three steps," she called, then held her breath as Patrick shifted his hold on Marius's wounded leg.

Marius clamped his mouth closed. A bright-red stain spread out on the apron tied around his calf. He looked up at Lydia as he was carried past. She forced a slight smile, but her stomach clenched into a fearful knot.

Siegfried looked over his shoulder and backed down the steps, holding Marius under both arms. He had only carried Marius a short distance from the wagon to the house, but his face was flushed, and he puffed out each breath. Obviously he was not used to carrying a heavy load. He muttered something under his breath and stepped to the side.

"Watch out!" Lydia called, but it was too late. Siegfried banged Marius into the brick wall.

Marius pulled in a sharp breath between clenched teeth.

Siegfried jerked back. "Sorry."

"Take him into the kitchen." Lydia pointed down the hallway.

Mrs. Murdock looked out of the kitchen doorway and placed her hands on her hips. "Who's this?"

"One of the German prisoners." Lydia hurried toward her. "He has a deep cut on his leg. Is Dr. Foster still here?"

"I don't know." Mrs. Murdock scowled, clearly irritated Lydia had brought a wounded prisoner into the house.

"Can you send someone upstairs to look for the doctor?"

The cook pursed her lips, then called one of the maids out of the kitchen and sent her off in search of Dr. Foster.

Lydia glanced at Marius and then Mrs. Murdock. "He'll need somewhere to lie down while the doctor tends his leg."

"Well, I don't want his blood all over my kitchen."

"The servants' hall, then?"

The cook shook her head. "That won't do."

Mrs. Dalton strode down the hallway toward them, the keys to the supply closets jangling from the chain hanging at her waist. She took in the situation and motioned to Patrick. "Bring him into the stillroom, and be quick about it."

Patrick turned and led the way down the hall.

Lydia explained to Mrs. Dalton what had happened as they followed the men into the stillroom. Patrick and Siegfried placed Marius on the wooden table and stood back.

"Dr. Foster is with Agatha." The housekeeper turned to the footman. "Patrick, please go up and—"

"We've already sent Marie up to get the doctor."

Mrs. Dalton lifted her eyebrows at Lydia. "Well, then . . ." She nodded to Patrick. "Make sure the doctor is on his way."

"Yes, ma'am." The footman hurried out of the room, looking relieved he didn't have to stay any longer.

Mrs. Dalton turned to Siegfried. "I suppose you can take a seat and wait with your friend."

Siegfried shuffled over to the corner and sat on a stool. He looked around the room, studying the shelves lined with jars of preserved fruit and containers of flour, sugar, lemon peel, and nuts. The stillroom was used for preparing afternoon tea. Chef Lagarde and Mrs. Murdock cooked the main meals in the kitchen, but Mrs. Dalton did much of the baking here.

Mrs. Dalton turned to Lydia. "I'll stay here until the doctor comes. You may go."

"I'd like to stay."

"Aren't you supposed to be watching the children?"

"They're walking back from the orchard. I left

Lucy and Master Andrew in charge. I'm sure they'll be fine until we're finished."

Mrs. Dalton studied her with a hint of disapproval in her eyes. She glanced at Marius and Siegfried, then turned back to Lydia. "I'll wait with you, then."

Dr. Foster strode through the doorway carrying his medical bag. He nodded to Mrs. Dalton and Lydia. "Ladies." Then he shifted his gaze to Marius and approached the table. "What happened to you, young man?"

"We were working in the orchard"—Marius glanced at Siegfried—"and I got in the path of a scythe."

Lydia stepped up next to the doctor. "I was with the children, picking cherries, when it happened. The cut is quite deep. I tied my apron around his leg, but I'm afraid it's still bleeding."

The doctor nodded and set to work unwrapping Marius's leg. "What's your name?"

"Marius Ritter."

"Where are you from, Marius?"

"I was born in Bonn, Germany, but my family moved to London when I was eight." He had a slight German accent, but it was barely noticeable.

The doctor opened his bag and took out a pair of scissors. "Mrs. Dalton, can you bring me some hot water and towels?"

"Of course, Doctor." She bustled out of the room.

The doctor cut away the fabric of Marius's pant leg below the knee, exposing the bloody gash across the back of his calf.

Lydia clenched her teeth and looked away. Thank goodness the doctor was here to stitch him up. What would've happened to Marius if they'd tried to take him back to the camp?

"Do you have family in London?"

"Yes, my mother and a younger sister live there."

"And your father?"

Marius hesitated. "He passed away three years ago."

"I'm sorry to hear that. It must have been difficult for your family." Kindness shone in the doctor's eyes.

"It was, especially for my mother."

"What was your father's occupation?" The doctor worked quickly, but there was still a gentleness about him that eased Lydia's fears.

"He was a furniture maker, a fine craftsman. He made a fair living, but we had little savings. When he passed away, I had to leave school and go to work to support the family. And now that I can't provide for them . . . It's been very hard . . . on everyone."

Lydia watched Marius with growing sympathy. How terrible to lose his father, then be taken away to an internment camp and separated from his mother and sister.

"So you've lived in England since you were a

boy?" The doctor took a needle and thread from his case, and Lydia tried not to grimace.

"Yes, sir."

"How old are you now?"

"Twenty-four."

Surprise rippled through Lydia. She would've guessed he was older.

The doctor looked up and met Marius's gaze. "It's too bad you never became a British citizen."

"I planned to apply when I finished school, but after my father died I wasn't sure we would be able to stay in England. We thought we might have to go back to Germany and live with my mother's family. But I found work, and we decided to stay."

Siegfried leaned forward. "Citizenship wouldn't have made any difference for Marius or for me. They arrested every man of German descent who was military age, even those who were British citizens."

The doctor raised his eyebrows. "Is that right?"

"Yes. My cousin Heinz has been a citizen for almost five years, and he was arrested along with the rest of us after the riots in London last fall."

"I'm afraid the bombing raids and the sinking of the *Lusitania*, along with the use of poison gas on the battlefield, have hardened people's hearts against people of German descent."

"And you think Britain is innocent?" Siegfried

scowled at the doctor. "They use some of the same tactics against my countrymen."

The doctor straightened and leveled his gaze at Siegfried. "That may be true, but we are defending our nation and the countries Germany invaded. Our goal is peace, not conquest. That is the difference."

Siegfried leaned back and crossed his arms. "That's not the way I see it."

The doctor shifted his gaze to Marius. "And what about you? What do you think?"

"I'm sorry for the conflict between our countries, but I support Britain. I tried to enlist last September, but they wouldn't take me. I was arrested a few weeks later."

"You see? That's what I mean." Siegfried pointed to Marius. "The government doesn't care what you believe or who you support. If you are German, you can't serve in the military. You can't even keep your job or take care of your family. Instead they arrest you and put you in a camp and make you work like a slave."

The doctor cocked his head. "I understood you were paid for your work."

"Well, yes, they give us a pittance, but that doesn't change the fact that we're locked up and treated like spies or criminals."

"It's not the doctor's fault." Marius turned his head and sent Siegfried a stern look. "He is doing me a good a turn, tending to my leg. I'm grateful, and I don't think we should argue with him about the war or anything else."

That comment silenced Siegfried, but resentment still burned in his eyes.

Mrs. Dalton walked through the doorway with a pitcher, basin, and stack of clean towels and bandages. The doctor took them and thanked her, then set to work, washing away the blood. Marius clenched his jaw and fixed his gaze on the ceiling.

"I'm going to stitch it up now. It will be painful. Are you ready?"

Marius tensed. "Yes, sir."

Mrs. Dalton took a step back. "If you don't need anything else, I'll take my leave." She turned and walked out before the doctor even answered.

Lydia moved closer and took hold of Marius's hand. His cool, rough fingers wrapped around hers, and he looked up at her with gratitude flowing from his blue eyes.

The doctor took the first stitch. Marius grimaced and tightened his hold on Lydia's hand.

She had cut her hand last year and remembered how painful it was to have stitches. Perhaps she could distract him as the doctor had with a few questions. "What did you study when you were in school?"

His eyes flashed to hers. "Many subjects, but my focus was botany."

"So you're interested in flowers and plants?"

He gave a slight nod. "And crops. I was studying how to apply modern techniques in agriculture to help farmers increase the quality and quantity of their crops."

She sent him a slight smile. "My father would like that."

"He owns a farm?"

"He's a tenant farmer for Sir William here at Highland."

"What does he grow?"

"Oats, barley, and potatoes mostly. And of course he has sheep and cows."

The doctor took the next stitch. Marius clenched his teeth and pulled in a slow, deep breath. "And you work here with the children?"

"Yes, I work for Dr. and Mrs. Foster."

He glanced at the doctor.

"Not this doctor—his son and his son's wife."

"You are a governess?"

"No, I'm a lady's maid, but I help keep an eye on the children for the Fosters."

"They have a large family."

Lydia smiled. "I suppose you could say that."

He sent her a quizzical look.

"The Fosters have taken in several orphans from London's East End."

"That's very kind."

"Yes, they're good people. They saved those children's lives."

His eyes shone as he looked up at her. "And you're a part of that."

She smiled again. "A small part."

Patrick stepped into the doorway. "There's a Sergeant Thompson and another soldier at the back door, asking to see the prisoners."

"It's fine with me," the doctor said. "Show them in."

Patrick strode off, and a few seconds later, the two uniformed men walked into the stillroom. One was the guard from the orchard, but Lydia had not seen the other man before.

"I'm Sergeant Thompson. We've come to transport these two prisoners back to Everson Internment Camp."

"I'm Dr. Phillip Foster, and as you can see, I'm in the middle of stitching Mr. Ritter's leg."

"How long will that take?"

"I'm almost finished, but this is a serious injury. I wouldn't advise moving Mr. Ritter anytime soon."

The sergeant shot a glance at Siegfried and then Marius. "My orders are to bring these prisoners back to camp as soon as possible."

"That man may go." The doctor nodded at Siegfried. "But I don't want Mr. Ritter moved a great distance until I'm sure the wound is going to stay closed."

"How long will that take?"

The doctor glanced at his watch. "It's almost three o'clock. He ought to rest here at least overnight. I'll can check on him in the morning and see how soon he can be moved."

The sergeant's eyebrows dipped and he motioned toward the guard. "Take Schultz outside to the wagon." He turned to the doctor. "Will you step out into the hall, please?"

The guard took Siegfried's arm. "Come along, Schultz."

Siegfried glared at the guard, but he rose to his feet. He looked at Marius and cocked his eyebrows. "Enjoy your stay." Then he smirked at Lydia as he passed.

Her face flushed and she averted her eyes. The two soldiers took charge of Siegfried and left the stillroom.

Dr. Foster finished the last stitch and stepped back. "I'll speak to Mrs. Dalton about finding a room for Mr. Ritter." He walked out, leaving Lydia and Marius alone.

Marius adjusted his hold on Lydia's hand, but he didn't let go. "I'm sorry about Siegfried. He's an unhappy man, bitter about all he's lost."

"You mean because he has to stay at the camp?"

Marius nodded. "He had a fine job at a bank before the war, and he was planning to get married. But after he was arrested, his fiancée broke it off and became engaged to another man, an Englishman. Siegfried can't get past it."

"No wonder he's hurting."

"Yes, every man at the camp has a story. Each

has loved ones and a life they had to leave behind . . . not because of anything they've done wrong, but simply because of their German heritage."

She looked down at him, her heart aching. "I'm so sorry . . . I don't know what to say. It all sounds terribly unfair."

"It's not your fault. You've been very kind. I'm grateful." His gaze grew more intense as he searched her face. "What is your name?"

Her heartbeat quickened. "Lydia . . . Lydia Chambers."

"That's a fine name and very fitting." His eyes twinkled.

She smiled then, touched by his compliment. A sudden thought struck, and she tightened her hold on his hand. What if she hadn't been in the orchard today? What would've happened to Marius?

Alex sat down and gripped the side of the exam table, fighting off the wave of dizziness and nausea sweeping through him. "All right. I'm ready."

The young doctor reached up and began unwrapping the bandages around Alex's head. "Now I want you to keep your expectations in check. It's only been ten days since the accident. Your vision in your right eye may be blurry, or it may not function at all."

"I understand." But he was sure everything would be all right. He'd prayed and believed his eyesight would be restored. It had to be. That was the only way he could return to his squadron.

The nurse standing next to Alex held out a basin, and the doctor dropped in the used bandages. Finally all that was left was the patch over Alex's eye.

The doctor met his fuzzy gaze. "All right. Let's see how it's healing."

Alex swallowed, anticipation and fear battling for control in his mind. The doctor pulled the tape off and removed the patch. Pain shot through his eye. He squinted and blinked. "It feels like there's broken glass in there." He lifted his hand, but the doctor intercepted it and moved his hand aside.

"Just close both eyes and give it a moment," the doctor said. "I'm going to put in some drops to help with the pain. Tip your head back."

Alex obeyed and struggled to force his injured eye open. The doctor splashed in a drop, but rather than soothing, it burned. He squeezed his eyes closed and pulled in a sharp breath. That was a rotten trick. What was the doctor trying to do?

"Sorry," the doctor said, but his tone didn't convey much sympathy. "Keep your eye closed for a few seconds."

Alex waited, praying the burning sensation would ease.

"All right. Open your eyes and let me take a look."

Alex pried his eyes open, and tears overflowed,

trying to wash away the painful drops. The doctor moved closer and shined a light toward Alex's eyes.

"Can you see the light?"

"Yes." Of course he could see the light. He wasn't totally blind.

"Lift your hand and cover your left eye."

Alex slid his hand over his good eye, and the darkness closed in. His stomach dropped, and he sucked in a sharp breath.

"Can you see the light now?"

He strained and blinked, but he saw nothing. A tremor traveled down his back. What did this mean? Why couldn't he see the light?

"Lieutenant?"

"I don't see anything." His voice came out low and rough.

"Not even a faint glow or a fuzzy image?"

"Nothing."

The doctor sighed. "All right. You may uncover your left eye."

Alex dropped his hand and focused on the doctor again. "How long will it take my right eye to heal?"

The doctor looked away and gave a slight shake of his head. "I'm afraid the damage to your right eye may be permanent."

"What?" Alex's head spun as he tried to take in the doctor's reply.

"I'm sorry. I'll fill out the report and turn it in

to the commander. With this type of injury you'll most likely be invalided out and sent back to England." The doctor started to turn away.

"Wait!" Alex grabbed his arm. "That's all you have to say? You're not going to do anything?"

The doctor's expression remained cool as he looked down at Alex's hand on his arm. Alex dropped his hand, and the doctor met his gaze. "I've done what I can for you."

A cold dread washed over Alex. "But I'm a skilled pilot. I just knocked down a Zeppelin." His voice rose. "We've got to win this war, and that won't happen unless we control the skies!"

"Calm down, Lieutenant."

"Don't tell me to calm down. You don't understand. My squadron is depending on me. I *have* to fly."

The doctor stepped closer. "Lieutenant Goodwin, I know this is difficult to hear, but you won't be flying anymore."

Alex pulled back as if he had been slapped in the face. "No! I won't accept that!"

A hint of pity softened the doctor's expression before he looked away. "Nurse, take him back to his bed." He turned and strode off.

Alex stared after him. Tremors hit his shoulders and rippled down his arms and legs. This couldn't be happening. He couldn't be blind in one eye.

A mind-numbing wave of shock settled over him like a heavy blanket, dousing his every hope.

Fourteen

Penny plumped the pillow and tucked it behind Kate's back. "Are you comfortable?"

"Oh, yes, very comfortable. Thank you." Kate rested on a chaise lounge in the library with her feet up. She looked around the room with a happy sigh. "It feels wonderful to be downstairs again."

"I'm glad the doctor suggested it." Penny sent Dr. Foster a grateful smile. His attentive care meant so much to them. "I'm sure Jon will be thrilled that you're feeling better."

William had sent a telegram that morning announcing he and Jon would be arriving from London on the four-thirty train and would be staying through Sunday. The house had been buzzing with excitement since then. The children painted a Welcome Home sign and hung it outside the front door. Then they picked flowers for the great hall and bedrooms.

The doctor glanced toward the front windows. "I'll stay to greet Jon and William, then be on my way."

Kate shifted to face her father-in-law. "We'd love to have you stay and join us for dinner."

"That's very kind, but Mary is expecting me at home."

"Then perhaps you could both come tomorrow.

I know Jon will want to see you while he's here."

"Thank you. We'd like that."

Penny pictured the usual dinner scene in her mind and suppressed a smile. "It will be a busy time with all the children around the table."

"That's all right. We enjoy them." Smile lines crinkled at the corners of the doctor's eyes. It was wonderful how Jon's and Julia's parents had taken an active interest in the children. Penny sighed. She hoped one day she would share life with a man whose family loved her and her children.

Julia hurried into the library, her cheeks pink and her blue eyes sparkling. "The car is just pulling up the drive."

It was good to see Julia so happy. Though Julia always did her best to encourage others, Penny knew it was terribly difficult for her with William gone. Almost as hard as it had been for Kate to be without Jon.

"Two whole days with Jon." Kate sent Julia a blissful smile. "I can't wait to see him. It's been more than a month since his last visit."

Dr. Foster glanced toward the great hall. "Where are the children?"

"Outside, playing on the lawn," Julia said. "Lydia, Helen, and Ann are supervising."

"Ah, very good. I'm sure they're eager to be the first to greet Jon."

Soon they heard the motorcar's tires on the

gravel drive and the children calling out their greetings. Then footsteps sounded in the great hall, and William and Jon walked into the library wearing happy smiles.

"Welcome home." Julia met William at the doorway, and they embraced.

Jon hurried across the room and knelt on the floor next to Kate. "Hello, my darling, I'm so glad to see you." He leaned toward her and kissed her cheek. "You look wonderful."

William held Julia for a moment, and the reunion was so touching Penny had to look away.

William stepped back and shook hands with his father-in-law, then greeted Penny and Kate.

Jon rose and turned to the doctor. "How are you, Father?"

Dr. Foster clamped his hand on Jon's shoulder. "I'm well and grateful for the good Lord's care and healing." He looked Jon over with a slight crease in his brow. "You look tired. I hope you're taking care of yourself."

"I've been working long hours, but it's necessary right now. The number of men coming through the hospital is unbelievable."

The lines creasing Dr. Foster's forehead deepened. "Perhaps I should reconsider and offer my services there as well."

"Don't even think of it. You're needed here." Jon shifted his gaze to Kate. "How are you feeling?"

"So much better. I think these last two months will be much easier for me."

"I'd still like you to rest as much as possible," Dr. Foster said.

"I agree." Jon turned to his father. "I'm glad you're nearby and able to look in on Kate often."

"Yes, I've been stopping in at Highland at least three days a week. I'm attending Clark's aunt Agatha as well."

"Yes, I've heard," Jon added with a bit of a grin and a glance at Kate.

So, Kate must have written to her husband and told him how challenging it had been to have Agatha join their household. Penny couldn't agree more.

"Did you hear they've opened Northcote Manor as a convalescent hospital for recovering officers?" Dr. Foster asked. "I volunteer there on Mondays, Wednesdays, and Fridays."

Jon's brow creased. "I'm not sure I like the sound of that."

"Don't worry. I pace myself and I enjoy it. Julia sends Hardy over to pick me up at nine-thirty. I stop at Highland and look in on Kate and Agatha, then Hardy takes me to Northcote. Julia sends him back at six in the evening to drive me home. I'm becoming quite spoiled with all the attention."

Julia tucked her arm through her father's. "I'm very glad to do it. You have valuable wisdom and skills that are being put to good use here and at

Northcote. We're grateful, and I'm glad to lend the use of the car and driver."

"All right," Jon said. "I won't object. Just be sure you're getting your rest on those alternate days."

Dr. Foster chuckled. "What a change! My son is now acting as my physician."

Jon sent his father a good-natured smile, then turned to Penny. "I have something for you." He reached in his jacket pocket, pulled out a small envelope, and held it out to her.

Her heartbeat sped up. "What is it?"

"Information about Alex and his address in France."

Joy surged through Penny. "How did you get it?" She took the envelope and tore it open.

"A very kindhearted woman who handles patient records at the hospital heard about our search for Alex and was able to help."

Penny's fingers trembled as she pulled out the paper and skimmed the note.

Lieutenant Alexander James Goodwin, RNAS Squadron Number One, St. Pol, France, is a patient at the Calais, Château Boursot Hospital. His injuries include a broken collarbone, compound fracture of his right arm, three broken ribs, injury to his right eye, concussion, ruptured spleen, and facial cuts and bruises.

Penny's eyes stung and she blinked several times. "I knew it must be serious since I hadn't received a letter, but I didn't think . . ." Knowing Alex was in such pain was almost too much to bear.

Jon laid his hand on Penny's arm. "He's alive. That's what matters. It sounds serious but not life threatening. You may write to him, but he might not receive your letter."

She looked up. "Why not?"

"Because he will be back in England very soon. He's coming to St. George's for more treatment."

Penny gasped and gripped Jon's arm. "Oh, Jon, that's wonderful! How did you manage it?"

"I spoke to Dr. Gleason, the president of the hospital. When he heard the pilot who brought down the Zeppelin was returning to England and in need of medical care, he used his influence to have Alex assigned to St. George's."

A happy, lightheaded feeling swept through Penny. "Thank you. This is such a great answer to prayer."

"I won't be his primary physician, but I'll be able to look in on him and be sure he has what he needs."

"I'm sure that will be a comfort." Penny tried to keep her hopes in check, but now that Alex was coming home to England, and only a short train ride would separate them, nothing seemed impossible.

Of course he was dealing with some very serious injuries and would need time to heal, but she could visit him in London, help him through this difficult time, and make sure he knew how very much she cared.

Lydia sank down on the bench at the long table in the servants' hall and released a heavy sigh. She'd hoped having Sir William and Dr. Jon home from London would lighten her load, but it had been a hectic day.

The children were excited and eager for time with the doctor, but he had focused most of his attention on his wife, as was good and proper. The children didn't understand, and it had taken every last ounce of her patience to keep them busy and out of trouble. Especially the boys.

Usually Miss Penny shared those duties with her, but Miss Penny had not been as much help since she heard Lieutenant Goodwin was on his way home to England. Lydia was glad to hear it too, and she hoped he would recover soon. Maybe then Miss Penny would feel at ease and be able to focus on helping her with the children again.

"Penny for your thoughts." Patrick took a seat next to her on the bench.

"They're worth much more than that, thank you."

"I'm sure they are," he said with a grin.

Lydia placed her elbow on the table and rested

her chin in her hand. "I was just thinking about all that's happened in the last few days."

"You've certainly been busy. We've hardly seen you all week."

"I've been on the go, that's for certain."

He studied her a moment more. "Ever since you brought that German back from the orchard, it seems you've no time for us."

She cocked her head. "Why would you say that?"

"Because you usually sit and talk after a meal, but not lately."

"I've had more than my share of work to do, that's all."

He lifted one eyebrow. "You mean with the German?"

"His *name* is Marius Ritter."

"Oh, so you know his name now, do you?"

Lydia pulled back and clicked her tongue. "Patrick Lambert, are you jealous?"

"No, I'm not jealous!" But his ears turned bright red. "It just seems odd, you being so interested in this German fellow."

"Well, someone had to help him." She sat back, recalling the frightening scene in the orchard. "The poor man was lying on the ground bleeding while the guard and the other prisoners argued about who was to blame. Thank goodness we had the wagon and I could drive him back here to see the doctor."

"Lucky for him."

"Yes, and the doctor was very kind. He was the one who insisted Marius stay until he was certain it was safe to take him back to camp."

Patrick lifted one eyebrow. "So that's what's kept you away, caring for the German?"

"That and Miss Penny's in a dither about"—she glanced around, then lowered her voice—"her sweetheart crashing his plane and then being out of touch for so long. He's on his way back to England now, and she can't seem to think about much else besides that."

"Sweetheart, is it?" Patrick grinned again.

She lifted her finger to her lips. "Shh! Don't tell anyone I called him that."

"I won't." He shifted on the bench. "Her Lieutenant Goodwin will probably get a hero's welcome when he comes back."

"I should hope so. He deserves it."

Patrick narrowed his eyes. "The Germans thought no one could take down their Zeppelins, but he showed them we won't be beaten."

Mr. Lawrence walked through the doorway, and Patrick and Lydia rose to their feet.

"Lydia, a letter arrived for you." Mr. Lawrence held out the envelope.

"Thank you, sir." She took it and glanced at the handwriting, but it didn't look familiar. She turned t over, and surprise shot through her. Marius Ritter's name and Camp Everson's address were written in neat block letters on the back.

Patrick leaned closer and looked over her shoulder. "So, this Marius Ritter is nothing special to you?" His voice carried a teasing note.

Lydia turned and lifted her chin. "Whether he is or isn't should be nothing to you."

His eyes widened, and he took a step back.

She strode out of the servants' hall, clutching the letter. Her steps quickened as she hurried down the corridor and pushed open the door leading to the rear courtyard. Biting her lip, she glanced up at the windows. She should go up and help Ann and Helen with the children, but this was the only way she would be able to read the letter in private.

She tore open the envelope and pulled out the two folded sheets of paper.

Dear Lydia,

I am writing to thank you for your kindness and the help you gave me the day of the accident in the orchard. I am very grateful for the courageous way you stood up to the guard and insisted I be taken to Highland Hall. If you had not been so brave and taken up my cause, the results of my injury could have been much worse.

Lydia's heart lifted. She had never thought of herself as brave. But she did care about people especially those who needed someone to stand up for them. That's what she'd done for her sister, Helen, when Charlie mistreated her, and she supposed that was what she'd done for Marius as well. Still, it didn't seem brave. It was just the right thing to do.

I'm sorry I did not find out the address of the doctor who attended me. I thanked him before he left, but would you tell him again how grateful I am for his excellent care? I was a stranger, but he treated me as though he had known me all my life, with skill and compassion.

My leg is healing, though not as quickly as I would like. I have been allowed to stay in camp and rest for now. And I'm thankful, since I know that is what is needed for my leg to heal completely, but the days are long and quiet when all the other men go off to work.

It may seem odd to you, but I am eager to go back to work in the fields and orchards. You see, I feel alive and free when I am outdoors, surrounded by God's great creation. He is a wonderful designer, and I never tire of observing all He has made. The changing seasons, the growth of flowers and trees, the work carried on by the birds, insects, and wild creatures are all such a wonder. They feed my soul and give me the strength to carry on.

Lydia reread that paragraph again. A man who loved nature and gave God credit as designer was a rare thing.

I also enjoy reading, hiking, woodcarving, and fishing, although I'm not allowed to do any of those, except reading, while I am here. But we have very few books in camp. When one of the men receives a book, we pass it around to be read over and over by everyone.

Perhaps she could ask Sir William if he had a few books she might send to Marius. But would Sir William approve of giving books to a German prisoner? It might be better for her to go to Fulton, visit the bookshop, and choose a book or two there. Yes, that way no one would scold her for it. A prickle of unease traveled through her, but she pushed it away.

I have a few friends here who have a good outlook and can be trusted, and I am glad for that. I try to encourage others to make the most of each day and trust God for the future. Some men scoff and call me a fool, but I don't mind. My faith in God keeps me strong and helps me look ahead with hope.

Warmth rose and flowed through Lydia. He not only believed in God, he let his faith guide him through hard times. That was rare indeed.

My mother and sister write to me some-times, but those are the only letters I have received since I've been here. I would welcome a letter from you, if you would be inclined to write. I can tell you have a good heart, and I would like to know you more. If you are engaged or prefer not to write, I will understand and not think less of you. But if you would like to correspond with me, my address is below. May God bless you for your kindness and give you strength for each day.

Your friend,
Marius Ritter

Lydia stared at the last few lines. Should she follow through on her idea and send him a book or two along with a letter? Her stomach fluttered. Should she accept his offer of friendship . . . and open her heart to the possibility of something more?

Jon strode down the second-floor hallway at St. George's Hospital and stopped at the nurses' station. "Where will I find Lieutenant Alexander Goodwin? I believe he arrived late yesterday afternoon."

The gray-haired nurse took a clipboard from the desk and scanned the list. "He's in Ward B, bed number eight."

Jon thanked her and set off down the hall. Dr.

Gleason was Alex's attending physician, but Jon wouldn't let that hinder him from visiting his friend and making sure all was well.

He reached in his jacket pocket and touched the letter Penny had given him last weekend at Highland. She'd made him promise he would put it in Alex's hand as soon as he arrived at St. George's. And the sweet, sincere look in her eyes made him understand how important it was to her.

But the last time he introduced Penny to one of his friends . . .

He gave his head a little shake. Theo's choice had certainly been a surprise to Jon and Kate and quite a letdown for Penny. But Kate told Jon not to worry. Penny would bounce back. And she had. Still, he didn't want to encourage his sister-in-law to pursue another ill-fated romance.

Perhaps he should speak to Alex and try to discern his intentions before Penny became too attached . . .

Remembering the look on Penny's face when she found out Alex was coming home told Jon it might be too late for that.

He walked into Ward B and scanned the room. Men with bandaged arms, legs, and heads filled the beds. Some slept, while others read books or played cards. A quiet hum of conversation floated across the room as nurses and female volunteers stopped at the men's bedsides, adjusting pillows and delivering medications, newspapers, and words of encouragement.

A curtain was partially drawn around Alex's bed. Jon stepped closer and looked around the side. A young female volunteer stood opposite Jon, holding out a tray of food. Alex lay on the bed propped up by several pillows, one arm in a sling, and a black patch covering his right eye.

Jon's chest tightened. A jagged red scar ran from the center of Alex's forehead, behind the patch, and across his cheekbone.

"I'm not hungry. Take it away." Alex's gruff voice surprised Jon.

"Hungry or not, you should be thankful for your food and eat your meal." The young volunteer moved the tray closer to Alex.

"I said, take it away!"

The girl's face flushed and she straightened. "You have to eat so you can regain your strength."

His mouth twisted. "Just give it to someone else."

"I can't very well do that. Not once it's been delivered to you."

Alex turned his head away but not before Jon saw the glitter of moisture in his one good eye.

Jon pulled in a deep breath to steady his own emotions. He saw hundreds of wounded men every week, but this was his friend, and the broken look on Alex's face cut him to the heart. He stepped past the curtain on Alex's right, but Alex didn't see him.

The young woman looked up, and her eyes widened. "Doctor."

"It's all right, miss. Take away the tray."

Alex turned toward Jon, and recognition flashed across his face.

As the young woman slipped out past the curtain, Jon walked around to the left side of the bed, pulled up a chair, and sat down. "I'm glad to see you, Alex, though I'm sorry your need to recover is what brings you back to St. George's."

"So am I." Alex lay back on his pillows and stared at the ceiling.

Not a promising response.

Jon studied Alex more closely. The purple and green bruises around his scar contrasted sharply with his pale skin. His cheeks were sunken, and his face had a pain-filled, haggard look.

It seemed his friend needed encouragement as well as physical healing. "We're all very proud of you for taking down that Zeppelin. You lifted everyone's spirits. In fact, I'd say you've given the whole country a reason to hope for victory."

He huffed. "Really?"

"Yes, it was quite daring the way you turned off your engine and outsmarted that Zeppelin crew."

"Too bad I wasn't smart enough to shoot it down somewhere else." Alex's tone was raw, his words clipped. "Did you hear? It crashed into a convent. Three nuns and seven children died."

Jon gave a slow nod. He'd read the report in the

newspaper a few days ago and wondered if Alex knew where it had crashed. "It's not your fault, Alex. Everyone knows that was not your intention. The Germans are responsible for that, not you."

"If I'd known it was going to crash there, I—" Alex clenched his jaw and he looked away.

"You were assigned a mission, and you carried it out. At great cost to yourself."

He shook his head. "It's not that simple."

"It won't help to second-guess your actions now. You can't change the past. You have to focus on the future and on getting back on your feet."

"Why *should* I?" Alex jabbed his finger toward his eye patch. "You know as well as I do that this takes me out. I'll never fly again."

Jon swallowed, trying to push past the pain he felt for his friend. "I'm sorry, Alex. I know it's a hard blow. But you still have two legs, two arms, and a sound mind. You're not out of the game yet."

"This is not a game. We're fighting a war. We need pilots."

"Yes, we do. But flying is not the only way to win the war. You can still do your part."

"Right." He waved his good hand toward the window. "The King wants to award me the Victoria Cross and parade me around town so he can raise morale and enlist more troops."

"Receiving the Victoria Cross is an honor. You should be proud to accept it."

He shook his head. "I'm not going to do it. I don't want people staring at me, pitying me."

"No one will pity you unless you pity yourself and give up the fight."

Alex leaned forward, his one-eyed gaze intense. "Look at me, Jon. Can you honestly say this won't make a difference in how people see me?"

Jon studied Alex's scarred face. "I won't lie to you. It might . . . put people off at first. But it won't matter to those who know you and truly care."

"And who would that be?"

"Me for one." Jon reached in his pocket and took out the envelope. "And Penny Ramsey, for another."

Alex stared at the missive in Jon's hand, and a muscle flickered in his jaw. "Send it back." He turned his face away.

"Why would I do that?"

"Because once she sees this face, she won't want anything to do with me."

"Don't be ridiculous. Penny is not that shallow. She knows outward scars have nothing to do with the man you are inside."

"Return the letter. I don't want to see her. I mean it, Jon!"

Frustration coursed through Jon. "This is no time to make a decision like that. You're not thinking clearly."

"Why should I keep writing? What could I offer

her? I'm blind in one eye, and I only have one good arm."

"I read your chart. Dr. Gleason believes they can repair your arm with surgery. He wants to schedule it as soon as possible."

"With my luck, it won't make any difference. I'll probably be crippled for life and have to live off charity."

There had to be some way to break through his friend's dark mood and offer him hope. Jon leaned toward Alex. "Listen, I know you're hurting and discouraged. That's a natural response to what's happened. But in time I believe you will see things differently."

Alex stared at the wall, pain glittering in his eye.

"Even though you can't see it right now, I believe God is at work, healing and restoring you. He has a plan and purpose for your life, and these injuries don't have to prevent you from finding it."

"I don't see how I'll be much good for anything now."

"That kind of thinking isn't going to get you anywhere."

Alex shook his head and closed his eye, looking more miserable than before.

Jon's throat tightened. *Please, God, give me the right words. You know what Alex needs to hear.* Within moments, a calming Presence filled him. "I won't lie to you. You're facing a difficult challenge."

Alex raised his good arm across his chest and grabbed his injured shoulder, as though trying to shield himself from Jon's words.

"You have a choice to make, Alex. You can either let your losses destroy you, or you can take hold of courage and, with God's help, forge a new future . . . It's up to you."

Alex's gaze drifted back to Jon. A tremor shook his chin. He blinked and looked away.

Jon rested his hand on his friend's shoulder. "You're not alone. There are many people who want to help, and Penny is one of them. I hope you won't close the door on a trusted friend." He placed her letter on Alex's bedside table.

"She's probably just writing because she feels sorry for me."

Jon stood and looked down at Alex. "She cares about you. And if I were you, I'd do whatever it takes to convince her you're still a man worthy of her trust and admiration."

Alex's mouth twisted, and he started to reply, but Jon held up his hand.

"I think we've both said enough for now. I'll come back and see you tomorrow. If you have a reply for Penny, I'll make sure it's delivered." He turned and strode out of the ward, his heart thumping hard in his chest.

Had he done the right thing . . . or had he just doubled the pain of a wounded hero and destroyed his bond with one of his oldest friends?

Fifteen

Alex clenched his jaw, fighting back the surge of anger rushing through him. He didn't deserve a lecture from Jon or anyone else.

His so-called friend had no idea how he had struggled to stay sane and keep flying after losing so many friends in his squadron. Nor did Jon understand the pain and shock he'd gone through since the accident.

Should he have told Jon he woke up in a cold sweat two or three times a night, trying to escape terrifying nightmares? Or that he started each morning in pain, confused and exhausted and dreading nightfall, when he would have to fight his way through those same nightmares again?

What would Jon say then?

Alex closed his eyes, trying to push away the wave of hopelessness washing over him. The agony of his injuries was hard enough, but knowing he had caused the death of innocent nuns and children . . .

He choked back a sob. It was almost more than he could bear. There was no way to make that right. And to know he would never fly again?

Alex flung an arm across his eyes. Who *was* he now? What good was his life?

But Jon expected him to shrug it all off and press on.

How was he supposed to do that? He couldn't just pretend the crash and the last few weeks had never happened. His world had turned upside down, and he didn't know if it would ever come right again.

He looked at the letter from Penny on the bedside table. A painful ache rose in his chest. He longed to tear it open, soak in her kind words, and let them ease the pain of his guilt and losses. But what was the use? His life, as he had known it, was over.

There was no hope for a future with her now. He might as well accept that truth and let her go, along with every other hope he'd had for his life after the war.

He clenched his jaw, fighting a tug of war with his conscience.

If he were truly brave and honorable, he'd read that letter, then write to her one last time and end their friendship.

He reached for the letter with his good arm, and pain shot across his upper chest and shoulder. He grimaced and lowered the envelope, then pinched it between the fingers on his broken arm and slowly tore it open with his good hand.

The letter slipped out and fell between his sheet and blanket. He slowly fished it out, then struggled to unfold it with one hand.

Squinting, he tried to decipher the small, neat handwriting. The doctor in France said in a few weeks his left eye would adjust to doing the work of two eyes, then they could test his vision and prescribe glasses. Until then, he had to make do. He lifted the letter closer, and the words slowly came into focus.

Dear Alex,

I am so very relieved to know you're on your way back to England and will soon be at St. George's, where you can receive the very best care possible. The children and all the family send their greetings and wishes for a speedy recovery.

How very pleased and proud we were to read about your brave and daring actions to destroy the Zeppelin. I've clipped all the articles from the newspaper and saved them for you, but how I long to see you and hear you tell the story yourself.

His throat tightened and burned. If she knew what he looked like now—the scarred face and patched eye—she wouldn't long to see him. He shook his head and dropped his gaze to the letter again.

The first article we read in the newspaper said that you had crashed after taking down the Zeppelin, but there was no information about your condition. I was so concerned I convinced Julia to go with me to London to see if we could learn what had happened to you. We met with William and Jon and asked them to find out what they could. Then we visited your mother and sister to see if they had heard any news, but all to no avail.

She had visited his mother and Lindy? How had she found them? He didn't remember giving her their names.

I feel a little foolish now for being so des-perate for news of you . . . but I do care, and I felt such a strong urgency to see what I could do to help. Finally, Jon brought us the news we longed to hear, and I wrote this letter and sent it with him to be hand delivered to you.

Please let me know how you are doing as soon as you're able. I understand you have a broken arm, so writing may not be possible, but perhaps you could dictate a letter to one of the nurses or volunteers, or you could send a message through Jon. We are all so eager to hear from you and be reassured that you are improving and feeling stronger each day.

What could he tell her? Would she be satisfied with a list of his injuries, or should he be totally honest and give her a painfully clear report of his dismal future? He stifled a groan and looked down at the letter again.

Our invitation to come to Highland still stands, and we would welcome you here if you need a place to rest and recover after your time at St. George's.

I hope to come to town and see you soon. Until then, you are in my every thought and prayer.

With fond affection,

Penny

He lowered the letter and closed his eyes. That settled it. He would write to her and put an end to it before she tried to come to London to see him.

But his head throbbed and his chest ached so much he could barely think straight. He couldn't do it today. Soon . . .

But not today.

Lydia placed the books she had chosen on the counter and looked across at Mr. Dickson, owner of the Fulton Book Shop. "I'd like to buy these two, please."

It had taken her almost half an hour to make her selection, but she had finally chosen *Treasure Island* by Robert Louis Stevenson and *A Pocket Guide to British Birds*.

"Very good choices, miss." Mr. Dickson smiled, making his gray moustache twitch. He totaled the sale and told her the amount.

She took the money from her purse and handed it to him. "Could you please wrap them together in brown paper? I want to mail them to . . . a friend."

"Of course, miss. I'd be glad to." The old man's eyes twinkled. "That will just be an extra pound."

Lydia pulled in a sharp breath. "A pound?"

He chuckled. "Not really. I'm teasing. There's no charge for the wrapping paper."

Lydia's cheeks warmed, and she returned a slight smile. She should've guessed he was making a joke, but she was so anxious to finish her purchase and leave the shop that it had gone right over her head.

Mr. Dickson pulled a piece of brown paper from the roll behind the counter and tore it off. "I'll weigh these and let you know how much the postage will be." He placed a small pad of paper and a pencil on the counter. "Just write down the address where you want them sent, and I'll take it to the post office for you."

Lydia froze, her mind racing. "That's kind of you, but there's no need. I'll take care of it."

"Are you sure, miss?" He cocked his head and studied her.

"Yes, I'm certain."

"I have a few other packages to mail today. I

wouldn't mind taking yours." He swiftly wrapped the books. "No charge."

"I'm headed that way now. I'll take them." Lydia reached for the books, then stepped away from the counter. "Thank you." She turned and hurried out the door before he could ask her any more questions.

The bell overhead jingled as she pulled the door closed behind her. That was close. She'd almost had to confess she was mailing books to a prisoner at the camp. It wasn't that she was ashamed of writing to Marius or sending him the books, but she wasn't sure Mr. Dickson would understand. And she certainly didn't want to make trouble for herself or Marius.

She set off down the street toward the post office, dodging puddles and trying to keep her shoes and skirt hem dry. She had a letter for Marius in her pocket, and she wanted to add it to the package before she sent it off. But if she unwrapped the books and tucked the letter inside, how would she seal it up again?

She rushed around the corner and ran smack into a woman. The package tumbled out of her arms and landed in a puddle with a splash. "Oh, no!" Lydia bent and tried to snatch it up, but she only managed to pull off the brown paper.

"Lydia?"

She looked up and stifled a gasp. "Miss Penny!"

"Are you all right? I'm terribly sorry. I should've

been paying more attention." Penny reached for one of the books, pulled it out of the puddle, and wiped the cover with her gloved hand.

"Oh, don't dirty your glove, miss." Lydia grabbed the other book out of the water and shook it off.

"It's all right. If we wipe them quickly, there might not be too much damage." Penny brushed off the book again, then held it out to Lydia. "I'd hate to think I've spoiled *Treasure Island* for you. It's a wonderful story."

"Mr. Dickson said it's one of his favorites."

Penny's eyes widened. "You just bought these at the bookshop?"

"Yes, miss."

"You know Sir William is happy to loan any book you'd like to read from his library. You just sign them out and then check them back in when you've finished."

"Yes, that's very kind of him."

Penny tilted her head, obviously waiting for an explanation.

"These aren't for me, miss. They're a gift for . . . someone."

"I'm so sorry." Penny glanced down the street toward the bookshop. "You must let me take you back to the bookshop and replace them."

"Oh, no, miss. You don't have to do that."

"I'd be glad to. Are they a birthday gift for someone in your family?"

Lydia's face flamed, and she shook her head. "Please, don't worry. I'm sure a little water stain won't matter to him."

Penny's eyebrows rose. "Him?"

Lydia lifted her hand to her mouth. Now she'd done it.

Penny's eyes flickered with understanding, and she laid her hand on Lydia's arm. "Don't worry. Your secret is safe with me."

"My secret?" A tremor shook Lydia's voice.

Penny leaned closer. "I know Mr. Lawrence and Mrs. Dalton don't approve of young men coming around to see the maids, but that seems so unfair. Everyone ought to have a chance to find love and someday marry and have a family."

Lydia's face burned. She didn't know what to say to that.

"Is he a kind, respectable man?"

"I believe so."

"I see he's a nature lover." Penny motioned toward the *Pocket Guide to British Birds* in Lydia's hands. "That speaks well of him."

Lydia nodded and tried to smile, but she was sure it looked false.

"Did you meet him here in Fulton?"

Lydia bit her lip, trying to think of an answer. She couldn't lie, not to Miss Penny. "No, miss. I met him at Highland."

Penny's eyes shone, and she leaned closer. "So he's someone on the staff?"

Emotion swelled in Lydia's throat. If only that were true, it would be so much easier. She shook her head.

"Is he one of the tradesmen who makes deliveries?"

Lydia shot a glance around, but there didn't seem to be any way out of telling Miss Penny the truth. "His name is Marius Ritter." As soon as she said those words, she couldn't hold the rest back any longer. "He's one of the German prisoners from the camp, but he's not really German. He's lived in England for years, ever since he was a boy. He tried to volunteer for the Army, but they wouldn't take him. And then they arrested him and put him in the internment camp, when he was the only man left in his family to care for his mother and sister. Don't you think that's unfair?"

Penny blinked and stared at her. "You're sending books to one of the prisoners at the camp?"

She swallowed and nodded. "He's the one who stayed at Highland after he got that terrible cut on his leg. I think you were away in London when that happened. I was in the orchard with the children when he was injured, and I brought him back to the house. Dr. Foster sewed up his leg, and I helped take care of him."

Penny's eyes clouded. "And that's when he asked you to send him books?"

"No, he wrote to me after, to thank me for helping him, and he mentioned he likes to read, but they don't have many books at the camp, so I thought it might lift his spirits if I sent him these." She looked down at the two soiled books. Not much of a gift now.

"It's kind of you to want to help him, but I'm not sure it's wise."

Lydia looked up. "Why not?"

"Well, you wouldn't want him to think he could just ask for whatever he wants and you'll send it."

"Oh, no, miss. Marius isn't like that. He is a kind, God-fearing man. He hasn't asked for anything." He had asked her to write, but that wasn't what Miss Penny meant, was it?

The look of concern in Penny's eyes eased a bit. "I suppose it's all right to send the books, but I hope you'll be cautious about future gifts."

"I will, miss. I promise."

Penny gave a slight nod. "All right then. I won't say any more about it to anyone."

Lydia sent her a tremulous smile. "Thank you, miss." She said good-bye and hurried off. As she rounded the corner, she glanced over her shoulder, but Miss Penny had disappeared into one of the shops.

Was it a mistake for her to write to Marius and send him the books? It seemed like a small way to help someone in need. And didn't the Bible say she ought to remember prisoners and do what she could for them? That's all she was doing—just a small kindness to encourage him.

She shook off her questions. Her letter was written, and the books were purchased. She might as well send them.

How could that cause any trouble?

Lawrence held open the drawing room door, and Julia stepped outside to the veranda followed by Kate, Sarah, and Agatha.

"Why don't you sit here, Aunt Agatha?" Sarah took the older woman's arm and guided her toward a wicker chair with a thick cushion. "I think you should be comfortable here."

Agatha wrinkled her nose. "I don't know why I let you talk me into coming outdoors."

"It's a lovely day." Julia exchanged a smile with Sarah. "And we thought you'd enjoy some fresh air and sunshine."

Agatha sat down with a thump. "I'll probably catch a chill and be sent back to bed for a month by that doctor . . . What is his name?"

"Dr. Foster," Sarah supplied.

Kate turned her head and rolled her eyes, then slowly lowered herself to the wicker settee. Her dress was styled for maternity, but it pulled tight across her rounded midsection, making her look as though her delivery date was imminent, rather than six weeks away.

Julia swallowed and looked away. Would she ever know the joy of carrying and holding a babe of her own? *Please, Lord, help me trust You.*

Pulling in a deep breath, she turned back to Kate. "Would you like a footstool?"

"Yes, that would be wonderful. Thank you."

"How are your ankles today?" Julia slid the stool over in front of Kate.

"Much better." She put her feet up. "The swelling has gone down."

"That's good to hear."

"Aren't you going to offer *me* a stool?" Aunt Agatha lifted her silver eyebrows.

"I'll get you one." Sarah rose and brought over a stool for Agatha. The older woman put up her feet and adjusted her skirt so as to not expose any more than the toes of her shoes.

Julia took a seat next to Kate and settled back in her chair. She lifted her hand to shade her eyes and look across the terraces and south lawn. The children laughed and called out to each other as they dashed across the grass, playing a game of tag. Penny stood close by, watching over them, while Lydia, Ann, and Helen sat on a blanket in the shade of a nearby cedar tree, entertaining the youngest three children. A smile rose to Julia's lips. It was good to see them all so carefree, enjoying the day.

Her gaze shifted to the left, and she spotted Andrew, sitting off by himself, wearing a bored scowl. He hacked at the grass with a broken stick, looking up every few seconds to shoot glares at the other children.

Julia's heart sank as she watched him. Poor boy. He looked so miserable. What had happened to the happy, energetic boy they'd sent off to school two years ago? She knew he missed his father, but he had been struggling long before William left for London to help with the war effort.

Father, please help me understand what is at the bottom of all this and find a way to help Andrew bounce back. And could You please give me an extra measure of wisdom, patience, and love . . . I really need it.

Penny strode across the grass toward the house, where Julia, Kate, Sarah, and Aunt Agatha sat on wicker chairs in the shade on the veranda. "Hello, ladies. How nice to see you all outdoors."

Julia smiled at Penny. "We thought we'd take our tea outside since it's such a lovely afternoon."

"That's a splendid idea. I'm sure the children will enjoy it."

Agatha frowned at Julia. "We're having tea outdoors, with the children?"

Sarah looked from Agatha to Julia, her eyes wide.

Julia didn't hesitate. "Yes, I asked Lawrence to serve us all out on the veranda today."

Agatha sniffed and pulled a handkerchief from her sleeve. "I can't imagine that being enjoyable."

Heat flashed through Penny, and she had to bite her tongue to hold back a reply. Didn't Agatha

318

realize how hurtful her comments were? Thank goodness the children were out of earshot. Why couldn't the woman at least tolerate the children without complaining—especially after all she and the others did to keep them quiet and occupied so she wasn't disturbed?

Lawrence stepped through the doorway carrying a small silver tray with several letters. Penny's heartbeat picked up speed. Would she finally receive a reply from Alex? Surely Jon had delivered her letter to him by now.

"These arrived in the afternoon post, m'lady." Lawrence held the tray out to Julia.

"Thank you, Lawrence." All the women watched eagerly as she sorted through the pile. "Sarah, this one is for you." Julia held out the envelope.

Sarah took it and glanced at the sender's name. A smile broke across her face. "It's from Clark."

All the women responded with relieved smiles. Clark's unit had arrived in France a short time ago, and his last letter had been disheartening for them all as he described daily life in the trenches.

Julia handed the next letter to Kate. She eagerly tore open the envelope—it was most likely from Jon.

Julia glanced at the last envelope and looked up at Penny. "This one is from William." She spoke softly, a hint of apology in her eyes.

Penny's heart sank. She nodded and looked away. Why didn't Alex write? She knew he had a broken arm, but surely there was someone he could ask to transcribe a short note.

"Penny"—Kate looked up from her letter—"Jon wanted me to read this part to you."

Penny stilled. Had Alex relayed a message to her through Jon? Oh, she hoped so!

Kate began reading. " 'Please tell Penny I delivered her letter to Alex soon after he arrived. The break in his right arm was a compound fracture, and it was not healing properly. He had surgery the next day and is still recovering.' "

Penny released a deep breath. So that was why he hadn't written.

" 'It took some extra persuasion,' " Kate continued, " 'but we've made arrangements for Alex to be transferred to Northcote when he is ready for the next phase of his recovery.' "

Penny's heart surged. Alex was coming to Berkshire! Northcote was only six miles away, close enough for her to see him often, and perhaps even take the children to visit him.

Kate continued reading, " 'Dr. Gleason wanted him to stay at a convalescent hospital in London, but I thought he would recover more quickly in the country, and he would have the advantage of being near Highland. I've written to my father and let him know Alex is coming. I'm sure he'll do all he can for him.' "

Kate looked up and smiled at Penny. "Isn't Jon wonderful? He thinks of everything."

"Yes, it sounds like a good plan." Alex was sure to recover quickly with Dr. Foster overseeing his care.

" 'But you must warn Penny . . .' " Kate's voice trailed off, and her forehead creased as she continued reading silently.

Penny tensed. "Must warn me about what?"

Kate glanced up, then quickly lowered her gaze and continued reading. " 'You must warn Penny that Alex's injuries are quite severe. He has lost the vision in his right eye, and his face is badly scarred.' " Kate's voice faltered. She had to clear her throat before she could continue. " 'He wears a patch over his eye, and his appearance is greatly altered. We hope he will regain the use of his right arm in time, but that is not certain.' "

Penny stared at Kate, trying to take it in. She'd read the list of injuries days ago, but Jon made it sound much worse. Poor Alex! The sooner he arrived at Northcote and could continue healing, the better.

"There's more."

Penny swallowed at Kate's soft words and nodded to her sister. "Go on."

" 'Alex's spirits are quite low,' " Kate read. " 'He doesn't want to see anyone, and he barely tolerates short visits with me. Yesterday he turned away his sister, Lindy, which made me quite sad and concerned for him. Please keep him in your prayers. We expect his transfer to Northcote to take place Friday.' "

Penny pulled in a breath and tried to steady her churning emotions, but tears pricked her eyes. Alex was suffering terribly, and it tore at her heart.

Kate read the rest aloud. " 'I hope to be home for a visit in a few weeks. Until then, all my love to you and the children, Jon.' "

Julia rose from her chair and met Penny at the bottom of the steps. She slipped her arm through Penny's. "Let's take a walk."

Penny nodded, unable to force any words past her tight throat.

When they'd gone a short distance, Julia tightened her hold on Penny's arm. "He'll be all right. He just needs time to adjust and heal."

Penny sniffed. "Jon makes his condition sound so dreadful."

"Jon is a doctor. He must report the facts. I'm sure he thinks preparing you will ease the situation when you see Alex."

"But he doesn't want to see me." A tear escaped and slipped down her cheek. She quickly brushed it away.

"I know that's hurtful, but I'm sure you want to do what's best for Alex."

"Why wouldn't it be best for me to see him now? I'm sure I could cheer him."

Julia smiled. "I'm sure you would try . . . but it sounds as though Alex needs more than cheering.

His life has changed dramatically, and he needs time to come to terms with that."

Penny chewed her bottom lip. "There has to be something I can do for Alex."

"It sounds like the best way to help him is to be patient and give God time to work in his heart."

"But you're the one who always says we are the hands and feet of God on earth, and when there is a need, we should try to meet it. How can we expect Alex to adjust and heal unless someone comes alongside and encourages him?"

Julia inclined her head. "It's true, meeting needs is important, and sometimes God wants us to step up and do our part. Other times He asks us to wait and trust Him. But there's never a need to worry. He's not limited by our small efforts or by the lack of them. All the power and resources in heaven and on earth are at His command."

"I don't know if I can just stand back and wait to see what will happen with Alex."

Julia sent her a tender smile. "It takes faith to put those we love in God's hands and trust Him for the unknown future. But it's easier when we remember He loves them even more than we do."

Penny sighed. Could she trust God like that? She wanted to, but it seemed so hard, especially when it concerned someone who was so special to her and had such a great need.

Julia squeezed her arm. "Let's pray about it while we walk. That will ease our minds."

"All right." Penny tried to calm her heart and focus her thoughts into a prayer, but before she could speak the first words, shouts broke out behind them.

Oh, not again! Penny spun around, tugging Julia with her.

Andrew wrestled Tom to the grass, grunting and cursing. The other boys circled around, urging them on, while the girls shrank back.

Julia lifted her hand to her forehead. "Oh, dear, I feel quite dizzy."

Penny looked from Julia to the wrestling match. What should she do?

"I'm sure I'll be fine." But Julia's face had gone terribly pale. "Go put a stop to the fight."

Penny nodded, then raced across the grass. "Boys! That's enough!" But they wrestled on, as though they hadn't even heard her.

Oh, Lord, help me with these boys!

Marius stood in line with the other men, waiting for breakfast. Many complained of the tiresome daily routine, but Marius wouldn't let it spoil his day. The sun was shining, the medic had finally given him permission to return to the work detail, and he was eager to be off.

Leaning to the left, he glanced around the line toward the serving window connected to the kitchen.

"Don't bother looking. I'm sure it's porridge

again." Siegfried shuffled along next to him.

"There might be bacon or bread today."

"Don't count on it." Siegfried turned his glare toward the guard standing watch by the kitchen doorway. "I can't believe they expect us to work all day with only a tasteless bowl of porridge for breakfast." He tugged up his pants at the waist. "I had to pull my belt in another notch this morning."

Marius turned his face away to hide a smile. Siegfried had lost an inch or two around his waist, but he was probably healthier for it.

"If they don't give us more to eat," Siegfried said, "soon we'll be too weak to carry a rake or shovel. Then who will be left to work like slaves in their fields?"

"We aren't slaves. We're paid for our work. And we've no call to complain about the food. It may be plain, but it's sufficient."

Siegfried snorted. "Not for me." He narrowed his eyes and looked toward the kitchen. "What I wouldn't give for a plate of eggs and sausage with some toast and marmalade."

The thought of sweet-tart marmalade made Marius's mouth water. They'd had some last Christmas but none since. He dismissed the thought and turned to Siegfried. "We can't expect to eat like we did before the war. Think of the troops in France, living in the trenches. I'm sure they wish they had a hot breakfast like this."

"You can bet they eat better than we do, and

most of them get packages from home with extra food to go along with their regular meals." Siegfried reached the head of the line, and when the balding, muscular man behind the counter held out a steaming bowl of porridge, Siegfried grimaced. "Why do we have to eat the same thing every day?"

The server's eyebrows drew down in a V. "No one says you have to eat it."

Siegfried huffed, took the bowl, and moved down the line.

Marius stepped forward and accepted the next bowl. "Thank you."

The man behind the counter gave a slight nod and continued scooping porridge.

Marius took a slice of dark bread from the tray and laid it on top of his bowl. He picked up a cup of coffee, then turned to search for an open spot at one of the tables. Siegfried motioned him over. Marius crossed the room and sat down next to his friend. Siegfried leaned over his bowl and dug into his porridge, but Marius lowered his head and closed his eyes to say a silent prayer.

"I don't know how you can thank God for this slop."

Irritation sparked, and Marcus lifted his head. "This *slop* keeps me going. I'm grateful to God for it."

"If God had anything to do with it, or with us, He'd see that we had something decent to eat."

Marius clenched his jaw. He'd had about all the negative talk he could stomach from Siegfried. "If you don't want yours, pass it to me." His voice came out harsher than he intended.

Siegfried pulled back. "You don't have to get mad." He glanced around, then leaned closer and lowered his voice. "I've got an idea."

Marius blew out a breath. Not again. Siegfried was forever coming up with plans for escape. Thankfully, he had never tried to follow through on any of them. Marius didn't want to encourage him so he took a spoonful of porridge and pretended he hadn't heard.

"If I can get assigned to kitchen detail," Siegfried whispered, "I bet I could slip away in one of the delivery trucks."

"Don't waste your time thinking about it."

"Why not? I'm sick of being treated like a criminal."

"It's a foolish idea, and the sooner you forget about it, the better."

"I could make it work. I'm sure of it."

"And what then? Even if you got out of camp, you wouldn't get very far before they'd arrest you and put you in a real prison where you'd never see the light of day."

Siegfried gulped down a swig coffee and pulled a sour face. "This tastes like mud."

Marius shook his head. Nothing was ever good enough.

The whistle blew. "Five minutes! Finish up!" the head guard shouted.

Siegfried grumbled under his breath and shoveled in his porridge.

The whistle sounded again. "The following prisoners come forward for mail."

Marius stilled and looked up. It had been more than a week since he'd written to Lydia. Each time they announced mail, he hoped he might receive a reply, but it hadn't come. He looked down and focused on his half-empty bowl, trying to pretend he didn't long for a letter.

The guard called several names. Marius tensed and strained to hear, then he scoffed at himself. He was the foolish one now. Why would a sweet and caring woman like Lydia Chambers want to write to a scorned German prisoner? Better not to hope, then he wouldn't be disappointed.

"Hans Huber, Miles Kauffman, Heinrich Renke, Siegfried Schultz, come forward."

Siegfried grinned and elbowed Marius, then sprang off the bench and sauntered up to accept his letter.

Marius's spirit sank. He must put his hope aside. Lydia would not write.

The guard reached in the large canvas mailbag and pulled out a package wrapped in brown paper. "Marius Ritter, come forward."

Marius pulled in a sharp breath and rose to his feet. Had his mother sacrificed her own needs to buy something for him? He hoped not. She needed every shilling she earned from taking in laundry and ironing to support herself and his sister, Jenny. He strode forward.

The guard cut the string around the package and peeled away the brown paper. Marius clenched his jaw. All packages had to be opened in the presence of a guard and inspected. It was the usual routine. Still, it seemed unfair.

The guard scowled. "Books." He flipped open the covers and shook them. An envelope slipped out and fell to the floor.

Marius reached down and snatched it up. He read the name on the back—*Lydia Chambers, Highland Hall*—and his heart swelled.

"Go ahead." The guard waved him away. "Take them."

"Thank you." Marius grabbed the two books and strode back to the table. Lydia had written and she'd sent him books. He glanced at the titles, surprised and pleased with her choices. How did she know just what he would enjoy? He supposed he had mentioned he liked being outdoors in nature and looked forward to returning to the work crew. And from that comment she had chosen *A Pocket Guide to British Birds* and *Treasure Island*. They looked new, not used. How much had they cost?

Siegfried frowned at the books. "Your mother sent those?"

Marius shook his head, unwilling to say who had sent them.

"Who, then?"

Marius laid the books on the table. "We'd best finish our breakfast."

"Why won't you tell me who sent the books?" Siegfried tipped his head to read the titles. Suddenly, his eyes lit up, and he snatched the envelope sticking out of the top book.

"Hey!" Marius reached for it, but Siegfried pulled back.

Siegfried scanned the back of the envelope and grinned. "So, you've made a friend at Highland Hall."

"Give me the letter! Now!"

Several men turned and stared at them.

"Take it easy." Siegfried tossed the letter on the table. "I was just teasing."

Marius snatched up the letter, shoved it in his shirt pocket, and rose from the table. He could not listen to Siegfried one more minute, or there would be no accounting for what he would say or do. He grabbed his bowl, tucked the books under his arm, and strode away from the table.

"Marius, you don't have to go off in a huff," Siegfried called.

But he didn't turn around or answer. Better to stay silent than show Siegfried and everyone else that he most certainly *did* need to leave.

Before they both regretted him staying.

Sixteen

Julia sank down on the stool of her dressing table and stared at her father. "Pregnant? Are you sure?" She couldn't deny she'd considered the possibility, but she'd made excuses for each sign, not daring to hope it might be true.

Her father's eyes glowed with happy light. "Quite sure."

She shook her head, feeling dazed. "But with William away . . . I didn't think . . ."

"I'd say you're almost four months along."

"Really?" Happy tears came to her eyes. "Then I'm past the time when I lost the other babies."

Her father's smile faded, and compassion softened his expression. "Yes, but you still need to be cautious. I'd advise you to avoid strenuous activities. And you must eat well and rest as much as possible."

Julia gave a quick nod. "Of course." She would do whatever she could to protect the precious life growing within her. But her thoughts clouded, and she looked up at her father. "There is so much that needs to be done with William and Clark away."

"Do what you must, but let the staff and family take on the rest." He thought for a moment. "Perhaps your mother and I could lend a hand. We may not know much about managing an estate, but we learned some practical lessons from our time overseeing the mission station in Kanakapura."

"I'd welcome your help." How pleased her mother would be to know there was a second grandchild on the way. And now Kate and Jon's baby would have a little cousin who was only a few months younger, if everything progressed as it should.

She looked up at her father again. "Do you think the baby will be all right?"

"There's no reason not to hope for the best." He placed his hand on her shoulder. "Try to rest in the Lord and have a positive outlook."

"I will." A new surge of hopeful possibilities rose and filled her heart and mind. "Thank you, Father." She stood and reached for his hand. "Will you keep this to yourself for now? William is coming home this weekend, and I'd like him to be the first to know."

His blue-gray eyes twinkled. "I'll have a hard time keeping it from your mother."

"Oh, it's all right to tell her. I know she can keep a secret."

He grinned. "Yes, she's quite good at that."

Julia stepped forward and embraced her father. "What a comfort it is to have you here with me."

He gave a soft sigh. "Yes, we're blessed, and I'm grateful to God for His kindness and faithfulness to our family."

Julia stepped back and ran her hand gently

across her abdomen. What a wonder. She couldn't feel any difference, yet there was a tiny life growing inside. A thrill ran through her, and a prayer rose from her heart. *Please, Lord, bring this dear little baby safely into the world. And may he or she be a joy and delight to all the family and give us another reason to hope for a brighter future.*

Her father sent her a warm smile. "I should be going. I'm headed to Northcote this morning." He took his medical bag from the table by the bed. "I believe our friend, Lieutenant Alex Goodwin, is expected to arrive today."

"Yes, Jon mentioned that in his last letter to Kate."

Her father's brow creased. "Did Jon tell you he's quite concerned about him?"

Julia nodded, her shoulders tensing at the memory of Jon's letter.

"He asked me to look in on him to see what I can do to help."

Her father would be a wonderful blessing to Alex. "I'm glad. We've all been praying for him."

"Yes, that's what he needs, the Lord's strength and healing."

"Did you know Alex and Penny have been writing to each other? They met in London at Jon and Kate's before he left for France."

"Yes, Jon confided that to me."

"From what Penny says, they've grown quite

close, but he hasn't been in touch with her since he was injured. You can imagine how upset she's been, waiting for news, and then to hear from Jon that Alex didn't want to see her." Julia shook her head. "She was quite hurt."

Her father paused at the door. "Recovery can be very difficult. Some have lost arms or legs and gone through unimaginable pain, waiting for treatment on the battlefield and in the field dressing stations. For many the course of their lives is permanently altered by their injuries." He looked up and caught her gaze. "And sadly, some of their sweethearts can't accept the changes and they break things off."

"I can't speak to the depth of Penny's commitment to Alex, but I believe she has the strength of character to look past his injuries and be a great support."

Her father gave a slow nod. "Don't say anything to her yet, but I'll see what I can do."

Julia settled back in her chair. If anyone could get through to Alex, it was her father. She only prayed it happened soon.

Before Penny lost all hope.

Alex stepped outside and slowly made his way across the gravel walkway toward the chairs set up on the lawn at Northcote. Each step took more effort than he would have thought possible. Amazing how weak a man could become after two surgeries and weeks lying in a hospital bed. Finally, he reached the nearest chair and lowered himself into it with a stifled groan.

The day was warm with only a few clouds overhead. He let his blurry gaze travel across parkland to the fields beyond. Several sheep grazed on the hillside to his right, while a few others lay in the shade of one of the large trees. Low rock walls and thick hedgerows crossed the fields, keeping the sheep from wandering too far. To his left, the lawn dipped down to a small stream, and past that stood a thick forest of trees.

He sniffed the air. Fresh-mowed grass and honeysuckle filled his senses. Quite a change from the dense, stuffy air in London. He should be grateful he was no longer stuck in St. George's Hospital, but somehow he couldn't drum up the appropriate emotion. He grimaced and turned his face away from the view.

Why couldn't he shake off the dark cloud hovering over him?

Before he left St. George's, Jon encouraged him to take a more optimistic view and think of all the reasons he had to be thankful. Well, he could at least give Jon's advice a try.

He frowned, struggling to come up with something for which he was thankful. He was back on his feet . . . but he had to use a cane to get around, and his legs were so weak he felt as shaky as a newborn calf—

335

He drummed his fingers on the arm of the chair, replaying all that had happened since the crash. Each memory tore at him, until he finally shook them away.

What was the use of looking back? That was only more depressing than the present.

He gave a disgusted grunt and shifted in his chair. There was the problem. No matter which way he turned his thoughts, he always came to the same condemning conclusion. He had no one else to blame for his trouble but himself. He'd been in that cockpit and made the decision to try and make it back to St. Pol. One foolish choice had destroyed his future.

"Lieutenant Goodwin?"

Alex looked over his shoulder. A tall, distinguished man in a brown tweed suit crossed the lawn toward him. He had silver hair with a beard and moustache, and he carried a small black bag. As he came closer his face came into focus, and recognition flashed through Alex. "Dr. Foster?"

The older man smiled. "Yes. You have a good memory."

"Jon mentioned you worked here."

"Volunteer, actually. I'm just here three days a week. I'd like to do more, but my wife is not in favor of it, and we must keep her happy." He smiled. "You remember Mrs. Foster, don't you?"

"Yes, sir. She was always very kind to me when I was a boy."

Dr. Foster nodded. "That's Mary, for sure."

Now that they'd finished their greetings, Alex looked away, uncertain what else to say.

"How are they treating you so far?"

Alex gave a slight shrug. "Fine, I suppose. I just arrived this morning."

"Has Dr. Addison been by to see you yet?"

Alex shook his head. "No, sir."

"So they haven't set up your treatment plan yet?"

Alex sighed. "I'm blind in one eye. There's no treatment that's going to cure that."

Dr. Foster studied him a moment. "What about the other eye? How is it functioning?"

It seemed the doctor would not leave him alone until he answered all his questions. He turned back and looked up at the man. "My distance vision is blurry but not too bad. I have more trouble reading or seeing anything up close."

"Not to worry. They'll do a vision test soon and prescribe glasses. That should help a great deal."

He'd heard that before, but glasses wouldn't hide the ugly scar cutting through his face or keep people from staring at him everywhere he went. He sighed again and looked away.

"Mind if I sit down?"

Alex hesitated. He couldn't very well turn away Jon's father, though that was exactly what he wanted to do. He motioned toward the chair next to him.

"How are your ribs healing?"

Apparently the doctor had seen a list of his injuries. "They're still sore, but the pain is not too bad."

"And your arm? How is it healing since the surgery?"

"Fine, I suppose." He still wore the sling and went out of his way to keep anyone from bumping into him.

"May I take a look at it?"

Irritation flashed through him. What did Dr. Foster hope to achieve?

The doctor looked as though he could read Alex's thoughts. "I'd like to make sure there's no infection. A nurse or doctor should check it every day." He waited, apparently unruffled by Alex's irritation. "May I?" He gestured toward Alex's sling.

"All right." The doctor stood and untied the sling from around his neck, then he lifted his sleeve and unwrapped the bandage from Alex's arm.

Dr. Foster pushed his glasses up his nose and leaned closer to see the wound at the site of the surgery.

Alex glanced down at the stitches and pressed his mouth closed. He'd seen several men who'd lost an arm or leg, and he certainly didn't want to add a similar loss to his list. "How is it doing?"

"Very well. No sign of swelling or infection." The doctor rewrapped his arm.

Alex released a deep breath. At least he would have the use of two arms when he eventually left Northcote. That was something he could be thankful for.

"So, Jon tells me you wouldn't see your sister when she came for a visit last week."

Alex stilled, then lifted his gaze to meet the doctor's. "I don't know why that should be any of your concern."

"My role here at Northcote is visiting physician, counselor, and mentor. I like to take a personal interest in some of the men, help them through their time here and as they transition to the next phase of life. In order to do that, I have to take into account all aspects of their condition—physical, emotional, social, and spiritual. Then I can see what's needed and how I might help."

That certainly seemed beyond the call of duty.

"I'd like to do that for you, Alex, if you will let me." His tone was gentle, and unmistakable kindness filled his eyes.

Alex's throat tightened and he turned his face away. He had to swallow twice before he could answer. "Don't waste your time on me. There are plenty of other men who will make a complete recovery and be fit to fight again."

"That's true, but I've been praying about it, and I believe the Lord wants me to help you."

Shock waves rippled through Alex. Why would this doctor care? Why would God care, for that matter? "I don't know what to say."

"There's no need to say anything now." Dr. Foster stepped closer and laid his hand on Alex's shoulder. "Just think about it. I'll be back on Monday, and we can talk again." He started to walk away, then turned back. "Oh, I was at Highland Hall this morning."

Alex's head jerked up, and he searched the doctor's face.

"There is a young lady there who is quite concerned about you and would very much like to pay you a visit."

Did he mean his daughter, Julia—or had Penny told him about the letters they had exchanged? Either way, there was no point to it.

"I'm speaking of Miss Penny Ramsey."

His heart lurched. "I don't want her to see me, not like this."

The doctor watched him with a calm, non-judgmental expression. "All right. It's your choice, but I'm not sure it's the right one." With those words hanging between them, he walked back toward the house.

Alex stared at the doctor's fading image.

Call him back. It's not too late. Tell him you want to see her.

He clenched his jaw and looked across the parkland. He'd seen the shock and pity in the eyes of the nurses who tended him, and he couldn't bear the thought of Penny looking at him like that. No, it was better this way. If he kept her and everyone else away, he wouldn't have to worry about how they would respond.

Or about any more pain and loss.

Lydia trotted down the stairs and hurried into Highland's warm, steamy kitchen. Chef Lagarde stood at the worktable in the center, instructing one of the kitchen maids about the proper way to debone a duck. Mrs. Murdock stirred a tall pot on the stove, while she conversed with a second kitchen maid.

"Mrs. Murdock!" Lydia hurried toward her.

The cook turned. "Goodness gracious, what's the matter?"

"Sorry." Lydia stopped and tried to catch her breath. "Miss Penny asked me to come down and deliver a message."

Mrs. Murdock's eyebrow rose. "Well?"

"Today is Mrs. Kate's birthday, and Miss Penny would like you to make a special pudding to be served after dinner."

"A special pudding?" Mrs. Murdock set aside her spoon. "How am I to do that when sugar is so scarce?"

Chef Lagarde leaned to the right and looked around the kitchen maid. "We have plenty of Highland's own honey."

Mrs. Murdock crossed her arms over her chest. "It's not the same."

He lifted his gaze toward the ceiling and turned back to his task.

"I suppose I could make Cherries Jubilee and use the cherries we preserved. Those are already sweetened."

Lydia gave an eager nod. A special pudding was just what they needed to lift everyone's spirits. "Mrs. Kate loves cherries. I'm sure she'd enjoy whatever you'd make with them."

Mrs. Murdock lifted her hand to her forehead. "Oh, law, I forgot Sir William and Dr. Jon are home from London. That'll be eighteen for dinner, counting all the children."

"Don't forget, Lady Julia's parents are coming for dinner too," Lydia added.

"Blimey! I'll have to triple the recipe!" Mrs. Murdock shook her head. "I know I don't have enough sugar for that."

Chef Lagarde strode across the kitchen toward them, his face ruddy. "If you do not know how to make *ze* substitution with honey, I will show you."

Mrs. Murdock's face flared pink. "I know how to make Cherries Jubilee."

"But to replace sugar with honey, *zees* requires a special touch."

"My touch is just fine, thank you very much!"

He pulled a sour face. "Why are you so stubborn?"

"Ha! You're the one set in stone."

He growled under his breath. "If you would listen to me, you would learn some valuable lessons!"

"I don't need to learn anything from you! I know what I'm doing."

The chef's nostrils flared as he narrowed his eyes. "We shall see!"

Mrs. Murdock lifted her chin, taking an equally stubborn stance. "Yes, we shall!"

Lydia stepped back, hoping not to get caught in the middle of verbal battles between the French chef and the Scottish cook. The conflict between them had been brewing since Mrs. Murdock's arrival at Highland, and it didn't look like it would be settled anytime soon.

Helen looked in the kitchen doorway. "Lydia, it's time to go. Everyone is waiting."

She bit her lip and looked from Chef Lagarde to Mrs. Murdock. "What shall I tell Miss Penny?"

Chef Lagarde and Mrs. Murdock turned toward her, their faces lined in surprisingly similar scowls.

"You can tell her I'll be making a Cherries Jubilee, and Mrs. Kate's birthday will be celebrated in style!" Mrs. Murdock waved her off. "Go on, then! There's no need to stand around and clutter up my kitchen."

"*Your* kitchen?" Chef Lagarde huffed. "*Non*, Madame. I think not."

Mrs. Murdock's eyes widened and she sputtered, but the chef strode away before the cook could reply.

Lydia scurried out of the kitchen.

Helen met her in the hallway. "What was that all about?"

"Not to worry." She grinned. "Just the same old tug of war."

Helen chuckled, and they started up the stairs together.

Penny looked down the long, dining room table. All the children seemed to be on their best behavior tonight, and so far, there hadn't been any spilled water or quarrelling. That gave everyone an opportunity to relax and enjoy Kate's birthday dinner. The meal had been delicious, but Penny could hardly wait for the dishes to be cleared so they could move ahead with their surprise.

Mr. Lawrence stepped up behind her. "Are you finished, miss?"

She nodded, and he reached down and whisked away her dessert plate.

She glanced at the children's empty dessert plates. It looked as though they had enjoyed their Cherries Jubilee as much as she had.

Julia laid her napkin beside her plate. "Ladies and children, shall we pass through?"

Penny popped up. "The children have prepared

344

a special surprise, and we hope you'll join us in the great hall in five minutes."

Murmurs and smiles traveled around the table. Even Aunt Agatha lifted her eyebrows in interest.

"We'd be delighted." Jon nodded to Penny and then the children. "You may be excused, and we'll see you in a few minutes."

The children grinned and exchanged secretive glances as they rose from the table and hurried out of the dining room. Penny followed them into the great hall.

Helen, Lydia, and Ann were arranging chairs for the adults in a semicircle facing the large marble fireplace. They looked up and greeted Penny and the children as they joined them.

"All right, children. Take your places." Penny crossed to the piano and sat on the bench. The piano had been moved to the left of the fireplace and turned at an angle so she could play and see the children's faces.

The older children—Donald, Jack, Tom, Lucy, and Edna—took their places in the back row, a few feet out from the hearth. All but Andrew, who stood to the side, his shoulders slouched and a frown lining his face.

Would that boy ever grow up? "Andrew, please take your place next to Donald."

He gave a bored sigh. "I'd rather not."

Did he mean he didn't want to stand beside Donald or that he didn't want to take part in their songs? Either way, she was not going to let him spoil their presentation for Kate and the rest of the family. She rose from the piano bench.

His eyes widened for a split second, then he quickly resumed his bored, unhappy expression.

Penny crossed the room, leaned toward him, and lowered her voice. "Andrew, we've practiced these songs for days. What is the problem?"

"I'm not a child. I don't want to sing with them."

She pulled in a breath, determined not to lose her temper. "You're right. You're a young man, and it's time you put aside childish ways and thought about doing what is best for others."

He glared at her. "I'm not one of them. I'm the future master of Highland, and I ought not be required to sing with them."

Penny clenched her hands, determined to keep her temper under control. "Keep your voice down."

"This is my home, and I will say what I want, however loudly I'd like to say it."

"That's quite enough! You will either join the others and sing with us, or you may go upstairs to your room right now." A nervous tremor traveled through Penny, but she kept her gaze steady. What on earth would she do if he refused? No matter, as she couldn't back down now. "Well? What is your decision?"

He glared toward the group gathered by the fireplace. "Oh, all right. But I'm only doing it so

I don't have to endure another lecture from my father." He walked across the hall and stood at the end of the row of children, leaving a gap between himself and Donald.

Penny motioned him to move closer. He responded by taking a small step toward Donald, but there was still a noticeable gap. Well. It would have to do. She returned to the piano.

Lydia helped Rose, Susan, Irene, Abigail, and Millie find their places in front of the older children.

Helen took her daughter, Emily, by the hand and brought her forward. "Now stand here nicely by Miss Millie."

Emily stuck her fingers in her mouth, looking a bit confused, but she seemed willing to stay with the others. Millie laid her hand on Emily's shoulder and smiled down at her. The little girl dropped her fingers from her mouth and grinned up at Millie.

Penny released a soft sigh. At least one of the Ramsey children had a tender heart toward others. Millie didn't care that the children had been born on London's East End. She was kind to everyone. Why couldn't her brother be more like her?

Julia peeked out the dining room door. "Are you ready for us?"

Penny turned. "Yes. Please come in."

The adults entered the great hall and took their

seats facing the children. Mr. Lawrence, Mrs. Dalton, Patrick, Ann, and Mrs. Murdock stood behind the chairs with several other members of the staff.

Penny nodded to Millie, and she stepped forward.

"Tonight we would like to sing three songs to honor Cousin Kate on her birthday and also to welcome Cousin Jon and Father home to Highland." She stepped back with a beaming smile.

Penny played the introduction to their first song and nodded to the children. They sang a bit timidly at first, but soon their voices warmed and grew stronger, and the sweet sound filled the great hall. After the final note, the adults clapped and Dr. Foster called, "Encore."

Happy smiles wreathed the children's faces, and even Andrew looked pleased at the response. They sang two more songs, and the adults clapped after each one, obviously enjoying the children's performance.

When the final song ended, Donald stepped around Andrew. "Mrs. Foster, we hope you enjoyed our songs, and we all want to wish you a very happy birthday."

Kate smiled. "Thank you very much. The songs were lovely."

Donald nodded to Rose, and she took a basket from the hearth and brought it to Kate.

"What is this?" Kate asked.

"Birthday cards. We made them for you." Rose's eyes shone as she handed the basket to Kate.

"Why, that's very kind. Thank you." She looked up. "This has been the nicest birthday I've had in many years."

"I want to add my thanks as well," Jon said. "Mrs. Foster and I are very proud of you children. We're pleased by your good behavior at dinner and the report given to us by Miss Penny."

William rose and held out his hand to Julia. She stood up next to him, her cheeks and eyes glowing. "Before we end this happy gathering, Julia and I have an announcement we would like to make."

William smiled at Julia, then looked around the group. "We are expecting an addition to our family this winter."

Happy gasps and smiles flashed across several faces.

"An addition?" Rose asked, looking confused.

"A baby! They're going to have a baby!" Millie exclaimed, then she ran to Julia and her father and gave them hugs.

Tears misted Penny's eyes as she rose from the piano. What happy news! William and Julia had hoped for a child for so long, and now that dream would finally be fulfilled. Their child would be born only a few months after Jon and Kate's. They would grow up together and bring the family even closer.

Jon and Kate spoke to each of the children, thanking them for their cards and performance. The children said good night to everyone and went upstairs to prepare for bed. The rest of the family gathered in small groups to congratulate Julia and William and to wish Kate a happy birthday.

Julia's father approached Penny. "Might I have a word with you?"

"Of course." She stepped to the side of the room, and he followed.

"That was a fine performance. You've done wonders with the children."

"Thank you. They keep me on my toes, but I enjoy them so very much."

"That's clear for anyone to see. You have a gift, and I believe you are making good use of it."

She lifted her hand to her chest. "Thank you. That's very kind."

He stroked his silver beard for a moment. "I have an idea I wanted to propose."

Penny tipped her head and waited.

"Might you bring the children to sing at Northcote?"

Her heartbeat surged. "Northcote?"

"Yes, we have about twenty-five men there, all recovering from injuries. I think they'd enjoy hearing the children."

"What a wonderful idea! Of course we'll come."

He smiled. "I believe you know one of the

young men there, Lieutenant Alex Goodwin?"

Her face warmed and she gave a slight nod. "Yes, I know him."

His expression softened, and an understanding light filled his eyes. "Jon wrote to me about Alex and asked me to look in on him and see what I could do to help."

Oh, how she longed to hear some news about Alex. "Have you seen him? How is he doing?"

Dr. Foster rubbed his moustache. "He is improving physically, walking with the help of a cane and building up his strength. His arm is healing well since the second surgery, but I'm afraid his spirits are quite low."

Penny gave a slight nod. "I've written to him, but he hasn't replied."

"Yes, he told me."

She couldn't restrain her surprise. "He mentioned my letters?"

"Julia told me you had been corresponding with him and wanted to visit. I thought that might help, so I asked him if I could arrange it."

"What did he say?" But even as she asked, she was afraid she knew the answer.

He looked down, then lifted his eyes to meet her gaze. "He said he doesn't want you to see him as he looks now."

Penny's throat tightened. "I don't care how he looks. That's not important to me."

A slight smile touched his lips. "I thought you

351

might say that. And I think after you see him the first time, the physical changes will fade from your mind."

"I can't stand the thought of him being there by himself with no family or friends coming to visit."

"I agree. It's not healthy. But if you brought the children to sing for the men, then your visit wouldn't be specially to see Alex. That might break the ice and give you a way to reconnect."

Penny's heart lifted. "Yes, it's a brilliant idea. When can we come?"

"I'll speak to the people in charge on Monday and see when we can arrange it. Perhaps Wednesday?"

Hope rose, and she struggled to contain her growing excitement. "Yes, Wednesday would be fine. Thank you."

The doctor excused himself and returned to his wife's side. Penny nearly floated across the room as she rejoined the others. Only a few more days and she would see Alex!

But what if he turned her away as he had his sister?

No. She wouldn't even consider that possibility. She had prayed and waited, and now the door was opening for her to visit Alex. She would trust and hope for the best.

Seventeen

Alex pushed open the door of his bedroom at Northcote and stepped into the upper hallway. The sound of children singing drifted up the stairs. He looked over the banister, but he couldn't see them. They must be in the drawing room, where most of the programs and meetings were held.

One of the nurses told him there was a group coming this afternoon, but he hadn't expected them to be children. He stopped at the top of the stairs . . . Should he go down or head back to his room?

It was one thing to face doctors, nurses, and other patients—they were used to seeing men who were wounded and disfigured by war—but walking into a room full of impressionable children? One look at him and they would probably run for the door.

The song ended, the men clapped, and a woman spoke in a soft voice. He strained to hear what she said, but he couldn't quite make out her words. Still, something about her voice made him pause and want to hear more.

The pianist played the introduction to the next song, and the children's voices rang out again in a cheerful, rousing tune. The men began to clap and sing along.

Well, it couldn't hurt to go down and look in on them. No one would notice him if he stayed in the back and didn't sit down with the others. Leaning on his cane, he slowly descended the stairs and crossed the lower hall.

He stopped at the doorway to the drawing room and looked inside. A group of children stood together at the opposite end of the room. He squinted . . . if only he could see their faces more clearly, but that was hopeless. The doctor had examined his eyes and glasses had been ordered, but they weren't expected to arrive for another week.

Patients in chairs and wheelchairs filled the rest of the room, enjoying the program. A few of the nurses and orderlies stood at the back.

He slipped into the room and found a spot near the corner, in the shadow of a tall, potted palm.

Clapping wasn't an option for Alex, but soon he was tapping his foot in time to the music. The song lasted several more minutes, with a rousing chorus the men obviously enjoyed. As soon as it ended, they broke out in applause.

The woman seated at the piano rose and turned toward the audience. She motioned toward the children, and they bowed. "Thank you very much."

Alex stared and blinked, trying to clear his vision. The young woman had wavy auburn hair and looked about the same height as Penny, but from this distance he couldn't see her clearly.

"And now the children would like to express their gratitude for your sacrifice and service by giving each of you a small gift they made." The woman signaled to the children, and they hurried toward a basket on the floor by the piano. Alex's heartbeat picked up speed, and he looked around. He should leave now, before anyone noticed him. But his gaze darted back to the woman at the front.

Dr. Foster said Highland Hall was only a few miles away. What if it was Penny? He leaned to the right and strained to peer around the men who had risen from their seats to greet the children and receive a gift.

Suddenly, the woman stepped from the group and turned toward him. She looked his way and stilled, then her smile spread wider, and she walked straight toward him.

Her face came into focus, and all doubt vanished. Penny Ramsey, beautiful, fresh, and full of life.

"Hello, Alex." The sweetness of her smile and the kindness in her eyes nearly knocked him to his knees.

He gripped his cane to steady himself and gave a slight nod. "Penny." One word. It was all he could push past his tight throat.

"I looked for you earlier, but I didn't see you." Her gaze remained on his face, her expression open and accepting.

"I was here, in the back. I . . . I didn't know you were coming."

Her cheeks turned a pretty shade of pink. "Yes, we wanted it to be a surprise, but when you weren't sitting with the others, I was afraid that was a mistake."

He had to force out his words. "No, it was a good idea." If he had known, he wouldn't have come down, but now that he'd seen her and spoken to her, well, he couldn't seem to make himself look away.

How many nights when he was in France had he dreamed of her? Her letters and the thought of seeing her again gave him a reason to hold on to hope and keep flying. But since he'd come back to England, he'd tried to push thoughts of her from his mind, and he had almost succeeded.

Seeing her now was like a vision come to life, and he could hardly wrap his mind around it.

"May I pin this on?" She held up a red, white, and blue ribbon tied in a small bow with a little wood disk hanging from it. The word *Courageous* had been painted on the disk in slightly shaky red letters.

He clenched his jaw, trying to bring his emotions under control.

Penny glanced at the ribbon. "I think Rose made this one." She looked up at him again. "The children chose different words like *Brave, Strong, Determined, Kind, Good.*" She smiled

"They wanted them to look like real medals."

He shook his head. "I don't deserve that."

Her gaze softened. "It's not so much for what you've done in the past, but for what you will do in the days ahead."

Her words washed over him like a gentle wave. He looked down at the inscription on the disk, and his eyes burned. He had not been courageous since the crash. He'd given in to guilt, pain, and hopelessness and had nearly given up the fight altogether.

"May I?" Her voice was as soft as a caress.

He looked up and met her beautiful blue-eyed gaze. How could he say no to such kindness? "All right."

Dimples creased both her cheeks as she pinned the ribbon to the lapel of his shirt. "There, that looks perfect." She stilled and looked up at him. "Alex, I want you to know that I—"

"Lieutenant Goodwin!" One of the girls rushed toward him, bringing another woman. As they came closer, Alex realized it was Lucy, the oldest girl who had been taken in by the Fosters. The other woman was one of the servants he'd met at the Fosters' home in London.

Penny glanced at them, then looked back at Alex. "You remember Lucy and Helen?"

Lucy smiled at him expectantly, while Helen stared at the scars on his face with slightly widened eyes.

He stiffened. "Ladies."

Lucy clasped her hands. "We were so excited when we read the story in the newspaper about the way you bombed that Zeppelin, but then we heard you were injured. We were all so worried."

Alex blinked. What should he say to that?

Helen seemed to have recovered from the initial shock of seeing his face. She fluttered her eyelashes and smiled up at him. "Yes, we all thought you were very brave."

Heat infused his face and he looked away. The last thing he wanted was to talk about his final mission.

"Did you like our songs?" Before he could answer Lucy, she rushed on. "Oh, I'm *so* glad to see you and know you're all right."

He was alive, that was true, but he wasn't sure if he would ever be "all right" again.

"How long will you be staying at Northcote?" Helen fluttered her eyelashes again. Did she have some sort of eye problem?

"I'm not sure." He glanced around the room. There had to be some way to tactfully escape the conversation, but that would mean stepping away from Penny as well.

"It's wonderful luck you're staying so close to Highland," Helen said. "Maybe we can visit you again soon."

Lucy's eyes brightened. "Oh, that's a good idea."

Penny laid her hand on Helen's arm. "Could you and Lucy check on the other children? We want to make sure every man receives a ribbon. We don't want to leave anyone out."

Helen gave a quick nod. "You can count on us. Come on, Lucy." She turned away, then looked over her shoulder. "Take care, Lieutenant."

"And don't worry," Lucy added. "We'll come back to see you just as soon as we can." She slipped her arm through Helen's, and they walked off together.

"I'm sorry," Penny said softly. "I think they're both quite fond of you, possibly even a bit awe-struck."

He frowned. "I'm not sure why."

She tipped her head and smiled. "You're a hero in their eyes."

That might be the impression people got from reading the articles in the newspaper, but did they know the rest of the story? "I don't deserve that title."

"Of course you do. You've done something remarkable and given us all a reason to believe we can win this war."

He shook his head, doubt deflating him again.

She stepped closer. "It's true, Alex. Before you took down that Zeppelin, everyone thought there was no way to prevent the bombings. Even the Germans believed their airships were unstoppable. But you proved we can protect our country and gain the victory. People have hope now, and that's priceless."

Frowning, he sifted through her words. He wanted to believe what she said was true, but did she realize the cost? What about the innocent children and nuns who had died when the Zeppelin crashed on their convent? How many more lives would be lost until they could finally be victorious or at least end the war?

"Alex, the King awarded you the Victoria Cross. He wants to pin it on you himself as soon as you're well enough to receive it."

Heat flashed through him. "They just want to use me to boost morale and convince more men to enlist." Her face paled, and he immediately regretted his harsh tone. "I don't want to be singled out or called a hero. There are plenty of men buried in France who deserve that title, not me."

She looked up at him, her gaze steady. A hint of sorrow clouded her eyes, but there was strength there as well. "I'm sorry, Alex. I didn't mean to upset you. I only wanted you to know we're proud of you. And whether you want to believe it or not, you are a hero, worthy of our thanks and much more."

He closed his eyes, struck to the heart by her sincere words. He didn't want to hurt her or appear ungrateful for her kindness. There had to be some way he could turn the conversation around and take their friendship back to the way it was when they first met in London. And what about all the letters they'd exchanged? He'd let her believe he cared for her. He grimaced and shook his head.

What was he thinking?

He pulled in a shaky breath and opened his eyes. "I know you mean well, but you don't understand."

"You're right. I don't. But I'd like to."

He clenched his jaw, trying to steel himself and harness his runaway emotions. "This changes everything." He lifted his good hand toward his eye patch. "There's no future for me or for us, and I don't want to give you any false hope."

Moisture filled her eyes, and her chin quivered.

"Forget about me, Penny. Find someone who has something more to offer you."

She straightened and met his gaze. "I hear what you're saying, but my offer of friendship still stands. You may choose to accept it or not." With that, she turned and walked away.

An arrow pierced his heart. Was he being a fool? Should he call her back?

No.

He clamped his mouth closed. It was time to show some true courage and do the one thing in his power: let Penny go. Let her find a man who could love her, provide for her, and give her the kind of future she deserved.

A future he could never supply.

• • •

Penny strode out of the drawing room and into Northcote's entrance hall. The fierce burning in her eyes made it nearly impossible to see. She blinked hard and took a deep breath, trying to calm her pounding heart. She longed to turn around, run back to Alex, and plead with him to open his heart to her again. But that wouldn't be right.

She wasn't sure if it was foolish pride or the voice of wisdom telling her she must walk away and let Alex decide. But she couldn't . . . she *wouldn't* sink to begging or manipulation.

If Alex wanted her in his life, he must make that choice, and if not, then he must bear the responsibility. But she never imagined it would be so painful to see him again, then have to walk away.

Dr. Foster looked out through the drawing room doorway and crossed toward her. "That was a wonderful program, Penny. Thank you for coming. I know the men enjoyed it."

"Not all the men."

Understanding flickered in his eyes. "You spoke to Alex?"

"Yes. He seemed glad to see me at first, but when I tried to tell him I was proud of him and that everyone thought he was a hero, he didn't want to hear it. He acted like I'd insulted him."

The doctor rubbed his forehead. "I'm sorry. It

seems my idea, or at least the timing, was not the best."

"It's all right. It's not your fault."

"But I encouraged you to come."

That was true, but she was the one holding on to the foolish hope that Alex cared for her. "I thought my visit would lift his spirits, but I'm afraid I've done just the opposite."

"I don't believe that's true. Alex needs the support of his friends."

"But he doesn't want my support or friendship. He told me I should . . . forget about him."

The doctor's brows knit. "You must give Alex time to accept the changes these injuries have forced on him."

"But he's alive. Why isn't that enough, especially when he knows there are thousands of men whose lives have been blotted out, leaving behind heartbroken friends and family?"

"I'm afraid that's part of the problem."

Penny stilled. What was the doctor trying to tell her? "I don't understand."

"I think Alex feels guilty for living when so many of his fellow pilots have died."

How could that be? How could he not see what a gift it was that he was alive?

"He's on his way to recovery," the doctor continued. "He can rebuild his life and never have to face the enemy again, while the rest of the men in his squadron risk their lives every day. He can never rejoin them, and I think he's struggling with that as well."

Understanding dawned in her aching heart, and she gave a slight nod. No wonder he was confused and weighed down with regret. His whole life had changed course. He not only had to heal, he would also have to find a new purpose and direction—and a way past feeling as though he'd let down his fellow pilots.

"I hope you won't give up on him."

Penny straightened. "No, of course not."

"He'll be here for another week, possibly two."

"Where will he go then?"

"I'm not sure, but as soon as he can function on his own, he'll have to leave."

A dizzy, lightheaded feeling swept through her. If Alex left Northcote as things stood between them now, she might never see him again.

"Most men go home to their families to continue their recovery."

His family? Considering his mother's cool reception when Penny met her, and the things Alex had said about her and his stepfather, she doubted he'd want to go there. "Alex is not close to his mother and stepfather. He has a sister, but she lives with his mother."

"Do you know if there are any other family members who might take him in?"

"He mentioned a grandmother in Scotland, but

she lives with her daughter. I'm not sure they have room for him there."

"Well, we'll have to cross that bridge when we come to it."

Penny nodded, her thoughts darting in several directions at once. Where could he find a place of refuge and healing? Who would take him in and give him the kindness and care he needed to heal his heart and mind as well as his body?

He might not want her help or friendship, but she would *not* let Alex be turned out of Northcote with nowhere to go and no one to care for him.

Lydia crossed the rear courtyard at Highland and started down the path toward the walled kitchen garden. Lady Julia had asked her to bring in some herbs that would be brewed in a special tea to soothe Mrs. Kate. Her mistress was growing so large and uncomfortable she could barely sleep at night. The baby's birth was still a few weeks away, though Mrs. Kate looked like she was ready to deliver any day.

The warm sun on Lydia's shoulders felt wonderful. She blew out a breath, thankful for a break from overseeing the children. She'd grown up with a houseful of siblings, but they'd never demanded as much time and attention as this makeshift family.

Andrew and Donald had been in another tussle this morning. She wasn't sure what started the argument this time, but it didn't end until Miss Penny forced her way between them and was nearly knocked to the ground. She wouldn't be surprised if Miss Penny was sporting a black eye.

Those boys needed a man to box their ears or at least give them a lecture. If only the war would end and Dr. Jon and Sir William could come home. Boys needed men in their lives, and the way things were now, Highland was overrun with women and unruly children.

She rounded the bend and passed under the arched entryway to the garden. To her left stood the long glass greenhouse. Looking to the right, she glanced through the open doorway, into the tool room. Spades, rakes, hoes, and every kind of garden tool you could imagine hung on the wall in neat rows. Wooden crates, holding smaller hand tools, were stacked to one side of a long potting bench. On the opposite end of the room, a short wooden door led to a storage closet holding extra wheelbarrows and fertilizer.

She walked in and took a small pair of clippers from the top crate, then stood on tiptoe and reached for a basket hanging from a hook on the wall. That should do. Carrying her basket and clippers, she walked out of the tool room and entered the garden.

It looked lush and full this late summer afternoon. Vegetables and herbs grew in neat rows within the four large squares, and gravel pathways gave access to each area. A few climbing roses clung to the brick walls, and colorful blooms filled the flower beds closest to the walls. Clark Dalton had expanded the kitchen gardens over the last few years, and it was a good thing too. Now that the war was on and food supplies were strained, they had enough fresh vegetables to feed the family and staff a good part of the year.

She started down the path, reading the small signs tucked in by the herbs. Finding the first on her list, she knelt, clipped a few bunches of mint, then laid them carefully in the basket.

Men's voices sounded in the distance. The wooden door at the far side of the garden wall opened. Lydia looked up and five men walked through. She blinked and stared.

One of them was Marius.

"Come this way. I'll show you where we keep the tools." Mr. McTavish strode ahead of the men. A guard followed them in, then closed and latched the door.

Lydia rose, her heart pounding out a fierce rhythm. She never expected to see Marius today, but she supposed it made sense. The men from the camp worked in the fields and orchard, and it seemed now a few would work in the kitchen garden as well.

Marius looked her way, and his eyes flashed. He quickly subdued his response and glanced at the guard, but the man didn't seem to notice. He was listening to something Mr. McTavish said.

When the men were only a few yards away, one of them called, "Hello, pretty lady."

She turned and recognition flashed through her. Marius's friend, Siegfried, nodded to her.

"Move along." The guard scowled at Siegfried, then shifted his gaze to Lydia. He lifted his eyebrows and sent her a suggestive smile.

Irritation slashed through her. He was the same guard she'd faced in the orchard, the one who would've let Marius bleed to death if she hadn't insisted on taking him back to the house.

She clenched her hands. *Help me, Lord. I don't want to hate him.* She shifted her focus to Marius, watching him as he walked under the archway and entered the tool room. It looked as though his leg had healed. He didn't even walk with a limp now.

They had exchanged several letters since she'd sent him the books, and he had revealed a bit more about himself in each one. He wrote about his life at the camp, but he also shared his dream of owning a farm someday and using all he'd learned to improve crops and raise income for himself and other farmers. He'd asked her questions about her family and work at Highland. She'd answered carefully, opening her heart to him a little more each time she had written.

She smiled, thinking of all the sweet, caring things he'd said. Perhaps if she kept busy in the garden for a few minutes, she might be able to speak to him while he worked. She glanced at the guard standing by the tool room door, and her stomach tensed. She'd have to wait until he was distracted.

Mr. McTavish led the men back out into the garden and assigned them their duties. Marius went to work hoeing around the tall bean trellis. Every so often he looked up and glanced her way. She continued clipping herbs, pretending not to care that Marius was working only a few yards away.

The guard walked to the far side of the garden and took up his post in the shade of the wall by the door leading to Eden's Garden. Mr. McTavish finished assigning duties to the other two men, then crossed to meet the guard. They spoke for a few moments, then Mr. McTavish opened the door and stepped out of sight. As soon as he left, the guard took a seat on the bench, stood his rifle on the ground beside him, and leaned his head back against the wall.

This was her chance. She clipped a few more herbs, then walked down the path toward the bean trellis. Marius looked up as she approached.

"I'll wait in the tool room," she whispered.

His eyes widened and he gave a quick nod.

She continued on at an unhurried pace, then slipped into the tool room and shut the door partway.

Her heart pounded in her throat as she wiped the clippers with a rag and placed them back in the crate. She took the herbs from the basket and laid them on the potting bench, then hung the basket on the hook. The door creaked open and Marius slipped inside.

Her heartbeat sped up, and she suddenly felt shy and uncertain.

Marius beamed her a broad smile, looking more handsome than ever with his sky-blue eyes and sun-bleached hair. "I was hoping I would see you today, but I didn't think it was possible."

"Yes, this is a nice surprise." Her voice sounded almost breathless.

"I can only stay a moment." He glanced over his shoulder. "I told the guard the end of my hoe was loose and I had to exchange it for another." He lifted the metal end and wiggled it. "See, it really is broken."

She nodded and sent him a tremulous smile.

"I prayed for an idea. I didn't want to lie."

"No, of course not."

He set the hoe aside and reached for her hand. "I want to thank you for your letters and the books. Each one is a treasure. They give me hope and help me carry on." The sincerity in his blue eyes and the gentle touch of his hand made her feel like melting.

"How is your leg?"

"Much better, but it would be hard for me to work in the fields, so that's why they sent me here to the garden." He lifted his eyes toward heaven.

"That is God's gift as well. He knows how much I wanted to see you."

She smiled up at him, dizzy happiness flooding her.

"Ah *ha!*" Siegfried stepped into the tool room and shut the door. "I wondered if I'd find you together in here."

Lydia tried to slip her hand away from Marius, but he held on tight.

"It's all right." He turned to Siegfried. "What do you want?"

The strength of his voice surprised Lydia but at the same time made her feel safe and protected.

"No need to be angry. I just came for some clippers." Siegfried grinned, then sauntered across the room and rummaged around in one of the wooden crates.

Lydia looked up at Marius, fear coiling in her stomach. Would Siegfried tell the guard he'd seen them here? Would he use this against Marius?

Siegfried turned to them. "Don't worry. Your secret is safe with me."

Marius lifted his chin. "We've done nothing wrong."

"Not yet. But if you want me to keep the guard busy so you can . . ." He lifted his eyebrows.

Lydia gasped and dropped Marius's hand.

Anger flashed in Marius's eyes. "Why, you—"

Siegfried lifted his hands. "Hey, I was just offering to help."

"We don't need that kind of help." He turned his back on Siegfried, blocking Lydia's view of the man, and took her hand again. "I'm sorry. I'd better go."

She nodded, clasping his hand tightly. "Take care."

"I will." He lifted one hand and tenderly touched her cheek. "And I will pray for you."

"And I, you."

Then he turned and walked toward the door. Siegfried grinned and slapped Marius on the shoulder. But Marius strode past without slowing or saying a word.

Eighteen

Penny took one last look in the mirror and shook her head. It was hopeless. No amount of powder would cover the purple bruises around her left eye. She looked like she'd been in a street brawl—and, in fact, that was close to the truth.

Yesterday she struggled to break up the fistfight between Andrew and Donald and received a punch in the eye as a result. She shouldn't be surprised. Andrew and Donald were both taller than she, and they outweighed her.

Blowing out a frustrated breath, she pulled open her bedroom door and stepped into the hall. She must find a way to teach those boys to keep their tempers under control.

As she pulled her bedroom door closed, she saw Julia and Dr. Foster walk out of Kate's room.

Julia linked arms with her father. "This is such happy news. I can't wait to hear Jon's response."

"I'll go into Fulton and send him a telegram after I see Agatha."

"I'm sure he'll be pleased but also a bit chagrined he didn't discover it himself."

Dr. Foster gave a thoughtful nod. "I've suspected it for a time, but I didn't want to say anything until I was certain."

Penny crossed to meet them. "What's the news?"

Julia glanced at her father and then at Penny. "I'm sure it's all right to tell you, but I don't think we should say anything to the children until we receive a reply from Jon."

"What is it?"

"Kate is having twins!"

Penny gasped. "Twins?"

"Yes." Julia beamed. "Isn't it wonderful?"

Happiness swirled up from Penny's heart. "I can't believe it."

"It's true. We clearly heard two heartbeats today," Julia continued, "and that's the perfect explanation for her showing early and for how large she is now."

Dr. Foster stroked his silver moustache. "Twins

often come early. We should prepare for them to arrive well before their due date." He glanced toward the window, then looked back at Julia. "It might be wise for your mother and me to stay here at Highland for the next few weeks so that one or both of us will be here when the time comes."

Julia clasped her father's hand. "Oh, that would be such a comfort. I'd feel so much more at ease having you here."

"Do you think Jon will be able to come home to be with Kate?" Penny asked.

Dr. Foster's brow creased. "I'm not sure they can spare him at St. George's, and we don't really know when the babies will arrive."

Penny's stomach tensed. "But Kate will want him here with her."

"We can send a telegram when labor begins. With first babies, that's often a long process, even with twins. That may give him time to travel home for the birth."

"Oh, I hope so." She couldn't imagine Jon missing the birth, especially now that they knew Kate was expecting twins.

"Thank you." Julia leaned in and kissed her father's cheek. "I'll speak to Sarah and tell her the news while you check on Aunt Agatha." She hurried off, and the doctor walked down the hall toward Agatha's room.

"Dr. Foster, may I speak to you a moment?" Penny called.

He turned back. "Of course." As he drew closer, he studied her face. "What happened to your eye?"

Penny explained how she had broken up the fight between Andrew and Donald.

Dr. Foster shook his head. "I'm sorry to hear it. I hope they received some sort of discipline for their poor behavior."

Penny sighed. "I sent them both to their rooms, but I don't know how much that helped."

"Step into the light, and let me take a look at your eye." They moved a few feet down the dim hallway to the window, and he gently turned her chin toward the sunlight. "There doesn't seem to be too much swelling. Have you had a headache or any dizziness?"

"No, just a bit of discomfort."

He nodded. "I'm sure it's not pleasant, having a black eye, but I don't believe there will be any permanent damage. The color should fade in a few days."

"Thank you."

He stepped back. "I should be going. I want to send that telegram before I head out to Northcote."

Pain stabbed her heart. "How is Alex?"

The doctor pondered her question a moment. 'About the same."

She sighed. "Do you know how much longer ıe'll be there?"

"His glasses arrived, and he's making progress with the therapy for his arm, so not much longer, I'm afraid." His face clouded and he glanced toward the window. Suddenly, he looked up, and a slight smile twitched at the corners of his mouth. "Why don't you come with me to Northcote?"

Penny stilled, considering the doctor's request. As much as she longed to see Alex, she didn't want to upset him or face another rejection. "He doesn't want to see me."

"He's had a few days to think about that, and I have an idea that might make him change his mind."

"What kind of idea?"

Dr. Foster draped his arm around her shoulder. "Let me tell you what I'm thinking."

Alex squinted across the room, then took off his new glasses and rubbed the bridge of his nose. "I don't think the prescription is right. I can't see any better with them than without."

Dr. Harding gave a slight nod. "It will take time for your eye to adjust."

If he had a pound for every time some doctor or nurse told him "It will take time," he'd be a wealthy man.

The problem was, he didn't *have* time.

Mrs. Abington, Northcote's head matron, had told him he should begin making plans to leave in a few days. But he had no idea where he would go. The thought of asking his mother and stepfather if he could stay with them in London turned his stomach. Even with Lindy there to help ease the tension, he couldn't imagine it being anything short of a disaster.

He could write to his grandmother and aunt in Glasgow, but the house was small, and his aunt and uncle had four children.

He'd have to come up with a plan later. The doctor was waiting. "How long until I can see clearly?"

The doctor glanced down at his clipboard. "I'm not sure. Wear the glasses a few more days. Then we'll test your vision again and see where we go from there."

"What about the headaches?"

"Those should fade, if they're due to the glasses."

Alex replaced the glasses and frowned. The blurry view made his head swim.

"You have to be patient, Lieutenant. Your brain must relearn how to interpret your world with the help of only one eye, and that—"

Alex held up his hand. "I know—that will take time."

The doctor gave a slight smile. "Yes, it will." He touched Alex's shoulder. "I know your recovery has been difficult, but I hope you'll look around and see that others are dealing with losses as great or greater than yours. You have one good eye, and

I believe your vision will improve in time. Focus on that, and count your blessings."

He gave a slight nod. Of course, the doctor was right. He should be grateful. Many of the other men had lost limbs or were horribly disfigured. He'd only lost an eye. His arm would heal, and the scars on his face would eventually fade a bit.

"I'll be back to check on you early next week," the doctor said. "We'll see how you're doing then."

Alex forced out a thank-you, though he felt anything but thankful. Dr. Harding crossed the terrace and walked back inside.

Alex turned and looked out across Northcote's parkland. The day was warm, with only a few clouds in the sky. He blinked, trying to bring things into focus. But the strain of trying to see clearly made his eye burn and water. He sighed and closed his eye, weary to the bone and so tired of the fight.

God, I know I should think about what I still have rather than what I've lost, but it's hard . . . I feel like I'm walking through a dark tunnel, and I can't even see a pinprick of light at the end. Would You help me? Would You pull me up out of this gloomy pit and help me find my way back to the light?

"Alex." The soft, feminine voice floated toward him from a distance.

He stilled, certain he must have imagined it.

"Alex." The voice was closer now.

He opened his eye and looked up.

Penny stood beside his chair. She wore a light-blue dress and large straw hat with netting that shaded the top half of her face, but he could see her hesitant smile. "I know you said you didn't want to see me, but there's something important I have to ask."

He blinked. Was this real? Was she truly standing there next to him? He never thought she'd come back, not after everything he'd said on her last visit. A wave of guilt washed over him, quickly followed by a splash of wonder. Why had she come now, just as he finished praying? Was it a coincidence, or was her arrival part of the answer to his plea?

He swallowed and looked up at her. "It's good to see you, Penny." His nose tingled, and he had to blink hard to clear the moisture from his eye.

Her smile returned. "I have an idea. Well, actually it was Dr. Foster's idea, but I think it has promise, and I hope you'll agree."

He motioned toward the chair next to him. "Please, sit down."

She took a seat and turned to face him. It was only then that the sunlight fully illuminated her face and he could see her more clearly. His gut clenched. "What happened to your eye?"

She lifted her hand to her bruised cheek. "Oh, this?"

"Yes, that."

Her cheeks grew pink. "I stepped between Andrew and Donald, and I didn't duck in time."

He gripped the arm of his chair. How could they have hit Penny in the face? "Those boys ought to be ashamed of themselves."

"Yes, well . . . *those boys* are the reason I came today."

"What do you mean?"

"You see, Andrew is going through a difficult time. He's been sent home from school for cheating on an exam. He won't be allowed to return until January. And with William and Jon away in London, that means Julia and I must oversee all the children. Lydia and Helen have been a wonderful help with the girls, but the boys . . ." She shook her head. "They need a man to take charge of them."

He gave a slight nod. What they really needed was a kick in the pants and a few hours cleaning horse stalls.

She stopped and clasped her hands in her lap. "I'd like to offer you the position."

He stared at her. "You want me to be a . . . tutor?"

"I was thinking you would be more like a mentor, someone who could organize activities for them. You could draw on your military training and time at sea and teach them the skills boys need to learn."

He pondered that a moment. "I've never thought of myself as a teacher."

"What they need is a leader, someone to guide them and show them by example how to become physically strong, mentally alert, responsible, and hard working. You could do that."

He rubbed his chin. "It sounds like you want me to be a nanny."

"No, not at all. The four boys are in their teens. They need a man, not a governess."

He'd trained crewmen that age on his last ship, the *Mina Brea*. It had been a challenge, but in the end he and his captain had been pleased with the results. Still . . . did he really want to take on a group of young boys?

"They love to play football and badminton, and Andrew is especially good at cricket," Penny continued, "but I'd like them to go fishing, camping, and hiking, learn how to build a fire and find their way through a forest. But most of all, I want them to develop strong character and become wise and disciplined young men."

He had learned many of those skills as a boy at his father's side in India.

A pang shot through his heart. It had been twelve years since he'd lost his father, but not a day went by that he didn't think of him and wish they'd had more time together. If he could step in and give those boys even half the life lessons his

381

father had given him, then he'd be doing something worthwhile.

When he didn't answer, she went on. "It would be such a tremendous help to us if you'd come. You see, my sister, Kate, just learned she's having twins. They're due to arrive sometime in the next two weeks. And on top of that, Julia learned she's also expecting a baby. Then we've taken in the elderly aunt of our head gardener who is married to William's sister."

He squinted, confused by the list of names. "The gardener is married to . . . whom?"

She laughed, and it was a wonderful sound, filled with sunshine and warmth. He found himself smiling back at her.

"What I mean is . . . we're all terribly busy, taking care of those who need us, but we don't want to neglect the children, especially the boys. They need a man's guiding hand and encouragement." She looked at him with hopeful light in her eyes. "So, will you come to Highland and help us?"

His chest swelled and his eyes burned again. Blast, he'd better get hold of his emotions or she would think he wasn't fit to help anyone. He cleared his throat. "I'm not sure how much help I'll be, but I'll come and do what I can."

Her smile spread wide, and those two delightful dimples creased her cheeks. "Thank you, Alex. That means the world to me."

How he loved seeing her smile like that—especially knowing he was the one who'd made her happy. He nodded to her, unable to push a reply past the large lump in his throat.

He might not be able to follow through on his hopes for a future with Penny, but at least he could go to Highland, take on those boys, and teach them how to behave themselves.

It might be difficult seeing Penny each day, knowing he had to keep his distance, but somehow he would manage it. He had to. She deserved someone whole, someone who could provide for her and protect her, and he was not that man anymore.

No matter how much he wished he were.

Marius scrunched up his thin pillow and lay back on his cot. Early evening light drifted in through the open flap of his tent. The sound of birds in the nearby trees and a few muted conversations from other tents floated toward him. He shifted to his side, trying to find a way to ease his throbbing leg and the ache in his lower back. He'd spent the last two days working in the kitchen garden at Highland. It had been easier than working in the fields, but it made him realize he needed time to rebuild his strength after being off his feet so long while his leg healed.

He placed his hands behind his head, closed his eyes, and replayed his meeting with Lydia. What a surprise to see her again. How his heart leaped when she'd told him she would wait for him in the tool room. Those few stolen moments together seemed like a dream now.

If only Siegfried hadn't followed them.

Heat climbed up his neck and into his face as he remembered what Siegfried had said and how it had embarrassed Lydia. He'd wanted to thrash the man.

Siegfried knew Marius wasn't like that. Besides, Marius truly cared for Lydia and would never take advantage of her.

Why did Siegfried have to be so crude? Hadn't anyone ever taught him women should be treated with kindness and respect, not teased and made the butt of lewd jokes?

A more important question was, why did *he* continue to put up with Siegfried? He should just tell him off and end their friendship. Maybe that would teach the cocky man to change his ways.

Guilt hit his heart. *I know, Lord, I must turn the other cheek and go the second mile. But Siegfried doesn't deserve it.*

"No one does. But I continue to offer My friendship and forgiveness to you and anyone who will accept it. You must do the same for Siegfried."

Marius released a deep breath. *Yes, Lord, I hear You. I want to forgive him, but You'll have to help me.*

He wrestled with his irritation for a few more minutes, then chose to let it go. God would supply the patience and strength he needed to deal with Siegfried. All he had to do was ask.

With that issue settled in his mind, he slipped his hand under his thin blanket and pulled out his letters from Lydia. The envelopes were wrinkled and bent from being opened so many times and from staying hidden under his blanket, but that was the only safe place to keep them.

He took her latest letter from the envelope and read her sweet words again, savoring each line. How kind she was, how thoughtful, always asking him about his situation and promising her prayers and friendship.

He finished reading, then closed his eyes, picturing the gentle curve of her face, her soft brown eyes, pink cheeks, and upturned nose. Others might not call her a beauty, but to him, she was a lovely treasure.

If only the war would end and he could find a way for them to be together. If he asked her, would she leave Highland and come with him to London? She could stay with his mother and sister for a time, while he found work and saved enough money for them to be married. That thought sent a thrill through him.

Siegfried pushed the tent flap aside and walked in. "You left before mail call. You got a letter." He tossed it across the tent, and Marius caught it.

"Thank you." He glanced at the writing and recognized his mother's script. Letters from home were always welcome, but sometimes, reading about the way his mother struggled to provide for herself and his sister, Jenny, weighed him down.

Siegfried sat on his cot opposite Marius and tore open a light-blue envelope.

"Who is yours from?" Marius asked as he opened his mother's letter.

"Ada Mason. Remember her?"

"The one who worked at the bookshop with . . ." Marius stopped and looked down, sorry he'd even hinted at Lilly's name.

"Yes, the one who worked with Lilly." Bitterness tinged Siegfried's voice at the mention of his former fiancée. She had broken things off soon after he was arrested and become engaged to someone else. She hadn't written to him since, but her friend Ada kept Siegfried informed about Lilly and a few other friends in London.

Marius turned away to read his mother's letter and give them both some privacy.

Dear Son,

I hope your leg is healing and you are staying well. I haven't written for a few days because I didn't want you to worry, but now I feel I must.

Marius's stomach tensed and he read on.

Your sister is not well. She came down with a fever last week on Thursday. Now she has a terrible cough, and she doesn't even want to get out of bed. Her breathing is labored and has a terrible wheezing sound. She has no interest in food, and I can barely get her to take some broth and a little tea.

I've tried all the usual remedies, but nothing seems to help. She has grown so weak that it frightens me. She needs to see a doctor, but I have no money to pay for a visit and no way to take her there even if I did. And what if they want her to go to the hospital . . . How could I afford that?

I'm sorry to burden you with this sad news and add to your troubles, but I thought I should ask you to pray for Jenny, and I wanted to prepare you in case the worst happens.

Marius stared at the last line. The worst? Did his mother actually think his sister was going to die? He pulled in a ragged breath. "Dear God . . . please, no."

Siegfried looked up. "What's wrong?"

"My sister is . . . very ill, and my mother has no money for a doctor."

Siegfried scowled and cursed under his breath, then rose from his cot and paced to the end of the tent.

Marius's hand dropped to his lap, and the letter

fell to the floor. What was he going to do? He couldn't let his sister die.

Siegfried turned and strode back. "We have to get out of here."

Marius looked up. "What?"

"If we escape and go back to London, you can help your mother and sister, and I can take care of *this*." Siegfried held out the letter from Ada.

"What are you talking about?"

"Read it." Siegfried's eyes bulged as he continued to hold the letter in front of Marius's face.

He took it and glanced at the writing, but he was so upset the words just swam before his eyes. He shook his head and held it out to Siegfried. "What does she say?"

"Lilly broke her engagement to James. This is my chance to win her back. All I have to do is get to London."

Marius squinted up at Siegfried. "Are you crazy? You can't escape, and even if you did, London is miles away. How would you get there?"

"I've got a plan. I know it will work."

Marius shook his head, pain throbbing through his chest. He had no patience for escape plans, not now when he was so worried about Jenny.

"Listen to me!" Siegfried squatted down and leaned toward Marius, his expression intense. "Your mother and sister need you. Come with me Tonight!"

"We'd never get past the gate."

"Sure we will. I've been watching the schedule. I know the routine. We can sneak out in one of the delivery trucks. And in a few hours, we'll be back in London. Tomorrow morning you could take your sister to the doctor."

"No! They would catch us, then we'd be arrested and put in a place much worse than this. How would that help my mother? At least here I earn a little money I can send to her."

"It's not enough! Your sister needs to see a doctor now. If you don't take care of them, who will?"

"There must be charities or someone who could help. I'll write to my mother tonight. She must not give up."

"It won't do any good. No one will help them. They're German."

"Not Jenny. She was born in England."

"It doesn't matter. Your mother is German and so was your father. That's why you're in this cursed camp! Don't you see? We are the enemy. No one will help us. We must take care of ourselves and our own."

Marius stared at Siegfried, his heart pounding out a frantic rhythm. Was Siegfried right? Was escape the only way he could save his sister?

Nineteen

Lydia settled on the bench in the servants' hall and poured herself a cup of tea. She'd already been up for two hours, helping Miss Penny dress and then checking on Mrs. Kate before she went in to see that the children were up and dressing for the day. It was past time for a break and a bite to eat.

Helen walked in and sat down beside her. "Listen to that rain. It sounds like Noah's flood."

Lydia glanced toward the rain-spattered windows. She'd been so busy she hadn't even noticed the stormy weather. Her heart sank. There'd be no chance to see Marius today. Even those hard-hearted guards wouldn't want to stand watch out in this rain.

"Now we'll have to keep the children indoors all day." Helen sighed and poured herself a cup of tea. "How are we going to keep them busy?"

"I guess the girls can work on their knitting, and we can take turns reading aloud."

"I'm not sure the boys will sit still for that." Helen reached for a piece of toast.

"Yes, we'll have to think of something else for them."

"Maybe they can play billiards with Andrew."

"I don't think so. Remember what happened last time?"

Helen bit her lip. "I suppose you're right. That's not a good idea."

Lydia shook her head, remembering it all too clearly. Donald had become bored with the slow-moving billiards game and decided to liven things up by tossing a tennis ball at the stuffed animal heads mounted on the wall. He knocked down a stag's head, and it landed on the billiard table and cut a hole in the green felt tabletop.

Mr. Lawrence was livid. He'd insisted Donald write to Sir William and confess what he'd done. Lady Julia and Mrs. Kate called the boys into the library for a discussion. The boys toned down their rowdy actions for a day or two after that, but it wasn't long before they were back to their tricks.

Lydia took a piece of toast from the platter. "They're not allowed back in the billiard room without an adult to watch them."

Helen rolled her eyes and took a sip of tea. "Those boys!"

Mr. Lawrence walked into the servants' hall, followed by Mrs. Dalton. The staff all rose to their feet.

"Be seated." Mr. Lawrence stood at the head of the table and scanned the group while they settled on the bench again. "We have an important guest arriving today."

Lydia glanced at Helen, and her sister gave the slightest shrug.

"Lieutenant Alexander Goodwin, the Royal Naval Air Service pilot who took down the L42 German Zeppelin, will be arriving this morning."

Helen's eyes lit up.

Patrick glanced at Mr. Lawrence. "How long will he be staying?"

"That is undecided."

Helen squeezed Lydia's hand under the table. Lydia pulled her hand away and sent her sister a warning look. She didn't want her sister flirting with the lieutenant again, especially not when Miss Penny had her heart set on him. That could only lead to trouble.

"Lieutenant Goodwin is still recovering from injuries he received on that important mission, and I want to make sure none of you respond in a way that might make him uncomfortable about his appearance."

Helen leaned forward. "We saw him at North-cote when the children went to sing."

Mr. Lawrence's dark eyebrows rose. Was he surprised they'd seen Lieutenant Goodwin or that Helen was speaking out?

Before Lydia could stop her, Helen spoke again. "He wears an eye patch and a sling, and he has a few scars, but he's just as handsome as ever."

Mrs. Dalton's eyes widened, then she narrowed them at Helen. "I'm sure he is, but that is none of your concern."

Helen's cheeks flushed pink as she leaned back

392

A few of the other servants grinned her way, but Mr. Lawrence sent a stern glance around the table, and that put a quick end to it.

"I expect each of you to treat him with proper respect. He is a war hero, and we are honored to welcome him to Highland. There's to be no gawking or staring at his injuries." He shifted his sharp gaze to Helen. "And there is to be no improper behavior. Do I make myself clear?"

"Yes, sir," they all answered.

"Now finish your breakfast, and carry on with your duties for the day." The butler and housekeeper turned and walked out the doorway.

Lydia leaned toward her sister. "Helen, you *must* watch what you say." She glanced around at the other servants, hoping no one else would hear.

"I don't see why you are always scolding me."

"I'm trying to help you hold on to your job."

Helen lifted her chin and spread marmalade on her toast. "I've done nothing wrong where Lieutenant Goodwin is concerned, and you've no right to punish me for mistakes in the past."

"I'm not trying to punish you. I'm just adding my warning to the others'."

Helen took a bite of toast and turned her face away. The stubborn tilt of her jaw sent a shiver down Lydia's back. Somehow she must make her sister see the importance of sticking to the rules and ignoring her attraction to Lieutenant Goodwin. If she lost this job . . .

Heaven only knew where she and little Emily would go.

Penny glanced at the clock and then tried to focus on her needlework, but it was useless. Alex was due to arrive any moment, and she couldn't seem to untangle her thread or make her fingers follow the intricate pattern. She was definitely not gifted at needlework.

Mr. Lawrence stepped through the drawing room doorway and looked toward Julia. "The car is just coming through the front gate, m'lady."

"Thank you, Lawrence." Julia stood and smiled at Penny. "They're right on time. Shall we go out front to meet them?"

"Yes." Penny rose from the settee, and they walked into the entrance hall. Patrick held open the front door. They passed through the entryway and stepped outside.

The scent of fresh, rain-washed air greeted Penny. Water glistened in a few puddles at the edge of the drive. Hope rose in her heart as the car rolled to a stop in front of the house. Alex had finally arrived at Highland, and now she'd be able to see him every day and help him recover and build a new life.

Mr. Lawrence nodded to Patrick, and he sprang forward to open the rear passenger door. Hardy, the driver, opened the opposite rear door.

Alex climbed out and leaned on his cane, while Dr. Foster came around from the other side of the car. Alex looked up at the house, then he quickly lowered his gaze and met Penny's.

She smiled and rose up on her toes, barely able to keep from running to him.

Julia stepped forward and held out her hand. "Welcome to Highland, Alex."

"Thank you, Julia. It's good to see you again after all these years." His subdued tone didn't quite match his words, and he offered her a stiff smile. "I'm sorry. I should call you Lady Julia now."

"No, please, Julia is fine. We're old friends, and I want you to feel at home with us."

He turned to Penny with a slight nod. "Miss Ramsey."

She held out her hand. "We're so glad you've come."

"Thank you." He touched her fingers lightly, then stepped back and looked away.

Her stomach dropped, and uncertainty swirled through her. Why was he being so cool and formal? Wasn't he happy to see her? She thought their conversation on her last visit to Northcote had finally broken down the wall he'd put up to keep her away.

Perhaps he just didn't want to appear overly friendly in front of Julia, Dr. Foster, and the staff. Yes, that must be it. As soon as they had a moment alone, she was sure he'd warm up and be the same friendly, confident man she remembered from before.

She tried to shake off her unease as she followed him into the house, but her stomach fluttered like it held a captive bird.

Julia motioned toward the staff members waiting at the bottom of the stairs in the great hall. "Let me introduce Mr. Lawrence and Mrs. Dalton. They are in charge of our staff. We couldn't run Highland without them. If there's anything you need, I'm sure they'd be happy to take care of it for you."

Mr. Lawrence nodded to Alex. "We're very pleased to have you with us, sir."

Alex hesitated. "Thank you."

"Shall I show Lieutenant Goodwin to his room?" Mrs. Dalton turned to Julia.

Penny stepped forward. "Oh, I'm sure you have other things to do. I'll show the lieutenant to his room."

Mrs. Dalton lifted her eyebrows.

A hint of surprise flickered in Julia's eyes, but she gave a slight nod. "Thank you, Penny."

Mr. Lawrence and Mrs. Dalton exchanged a look, then turned and left the great hall.

Penny motioned toward the stairs, then glanced at Alex's cane. "It's up one floor. Will that be all right?"

Alex stiffened. "Yes. It's fine." He looked back

toward the door. "I have a case and duffel bag in the car."

"Patrick will bring them up for you."

"I can do it."

"The footman always brings in the luggage."

He frowned and looked up the stairs. "All right."

She led the way up, slowing her normal pace to match his. "We've put you in the Lancashire room. It's the second door on the left in the west wing."

Alex looked up at the huge paintings hanging on the walls of the upper gallery. It was impossible not to notice them. The largest was at least ten feet tall and pictured a gaunt man in a golden robe, gazing up at heaven with a fearful expression.

"That's Saint Julian." Penny glanced at Alex and smiled. "I know, it's dreadful, isn't it? It always frightened me when I was a child. Our nanny used to tell me and Kate we had better be good because Saint Julian was watching." Her blue eyes twinkled as she shared the memory. "I'm glad I've learned the truth about saints and those who've gone on to heaven. No more worries about Saint Julian."

A smile tugged at one side of his mouth, and he followed her down the hall.

They passed one door, then she pushed open the second one they came to. "Here you go." She stood back so he could walk through.

He stepped past her into the spacious bedroom. A green-and-gold oriental carpet covered most of the floor. A tall wardrobe with elaborately carved doors stood against the wall to the left. An equally large mahogany desk and chairs filled the space between the two tall windows. The wide, plush bed, covered by a dark-green spread, filled one corner of the room. A scalloped, green-and-gold canopy gave it a regal look.

"I hope you'll be comfortable here." She watched him with a tentative smile.

"Oh . . . it's very nice, thank you." Much nicer than any room he'd ever stayed in before. Unease prickled through him. What was he doing here?

"This room has a wonderful view." She smiled over her shoulder as she crossed toward the window. "Come and see."

His eyes followed her, admiring the gentle swish of her skirt and the way the flowing peach fabric of her dress outlined her feminine figure. The view of Penny was much more inviting than any landscape ever could be. He suppressed a groan and glanced away.

She leaned toward the window. "You can see the south drive and the corner of the garden, just past those trees."

He stepped up behind her and looked toward the window. A whiff of a sweet, flowery fragrance floated past, and he pulled in a slow, deep breath. Was that her perfume or something she put in her hair? Or was it just her? His gaze shifted from the parkland to Penny.

A wavy strand of her auburn hair had come loose at the back and hung down her neck in a teasing curl. He rubbed his fingers together. How would it feel to touch that soft silky strand?

She turned slightly and looked to the right, giving him an intimate view of her profile. "You can see the roof of the stables and the orchard beyond that."

Her skin looked soft and creamy with a few delightful freckles sprinkled across her nose and pink cheeks. Thick dark eyelashes shaded her blue eyes. His gaze dropped to her full pink lips.

She was lovely, so very lovely, but it was more than her appearance that drew him to her. Her heart radiated kindness and caring, a love for home and family—everything he wanted. But he was a fool to even think he could ever be good enough for her.

Penny turned and looked up at him. Her lips parted, and a sweet invitation filled her eyes.

Every nerve in his body tingled to life. He took a step closer, but she didn't retreat. Slowly, he lowered his head and brushed his lips over hers. Her soft sigh caressed his face as she leaned closer, responding in a way he'd only dreamed possible.

Fire stirred within him, and he pulled her closer, deepening the kiss. Time stopped, painful memories faded, and bliss carried him away.

Voices sounded in the hallway. Alex broke off the kiss and stepped back, pulling in ragged breath. "I'm sorry. I shouldn't have done that."

Penny blinked, confusion clouding those beautiful eyes. A knock sounded at the partially closed door. Her eyes flashed, and she lifted her hand to cover her mouth. Being caught kissing a man in his bedroom could ruin a woman's reputation.

How could he have allowed his feelings to overtake his good judgment? "Forgive me," he said in a hushed voice.

Her chin trembled, and she looked at him with such a bewildered expression it cut him to the heart.

The knock sounded again. "I have your cases, sir."

Alex stepped away from Penny and cleared his throat. "Come in."

The footman entered, carrying Alex's duffel bag and his one scuffed brown suitcase, reminding Alex that was all he owned. A pitiful showing for a man of twenty-three years.

"Shall I unpack these for you now, sir?" The footman shot an uncertain glance at Penny, then looked back at Alex. "Or would you like me to come back later?"

If Alex said later, it might appear that he wanted to be alone with Penny, and that wasn't the kind of rumor he wanted passed among the servants.

"You can unpack them now, or I can just take care of it myself."

"I'm glad to help, sir." The footman glanced at Alex's sling.

"Very well." He turned away from the footman and looked back at Penny.

A deep blush covered her cheeks, and she averted her eyes. She ran her tongue over her lower lip and stepped away. "You may join us in the library, or rest for a time if you'd like. Luncheon will be served at twelve-thirty in the dining room." With that, she swept past him.

His spirits plunged as she disappeared out the door. He'd done it now. Not in the house ten minutes and he'd already broken the first promise he'd made to himself: to keep his distance from Penny.

Twenty

Penny strode across the gallery and fled down the east wing. By the time she reached the end of the hall, her hands were shaking so hard she could barely grip the doorknob. She jerked open her bedroom door, strode inside, and shoved the door closed behind her.

Alex was sorry? Well, so was she. Sorry she'd listened to her heart and given her first kiss to a man who didn't want her!

How could she have been so foolish!

Now she would have to face him every day and remember the way he'd pulled away from that kiss with a painful grimace, as though she tasted like something disgusting.

Moaning, she crossed her room and dropped onto the window seat. Her eyes filled as she stared out the window, but she blinked hard, refusing to give in to her tears.

How could she have let her emotions take over like that? She thought she'd outgrown her hopeless-romantic stage, but it seemed she was just as immature and fond of fantasy as she'd been at sixteen when she danced with Theo Anderson at Kate's debutante ball.

What was wrong with her? Why was she so desperate to win a man's love?

A shameful burning washed over her again. She closed her eyes, trying to sort out her feelings.

All her life she'd longed to feel loved and cherished. But her mother had died when she was young, and her father had cared more about his horses and dogs than his daughters. When her father died before she turned sixteen, Cousin William became her guardian. William was a good man, but he was focused on managing the estate and caring for his own wife and children. She respected him, but she'd never felt particularly close to him.

Her thoughts turned back to her father, and

regret washed over her again. He had not been there to dance with her at her debutante ball, and he would never walk her down the aisle at her wedding.

She huffed out a harsh laugh. If she ever found a husband!

Everyone else in the family was married, but she was single and alone, unchosen and unloved.

Enough! She rubbed her hand down her face and turned away from the window. She must take charge of her feelings and stop hoping Alex would grow to love her. If she didn't, she was going to damage her reputation and end up with a broken heart—again!

She would have to stay far away from Alex Goodwin. It wouldn't be easy, but she could learn to be indifferent toward him and treat him the way she would any other acquaintance.

But the memory of his kiss came flooding back, and she lifted her hand to her lips. Closing her eyes, she released a sigh. She might be able to avoid Alex, but pretending he'd never kissed her . . .

That would be impossible.

Marius hoisted two large baskets of vegetables and walked across Highland's kitchen garden toward the arched gateway.

"Be quick about it, now," the guard called. "No lillydallying at the house."

Marius nodded, then walked on and passed out of the garden. Moist, misty air cooled his face, and he looked up at the cloudy sky. What a stroke of luck the rain had stopped, or was it the kind hand of Providence? Either way, he was grateful he'd been assigned to work in the estate garden one last time.

Please, God, let me say good-bye to Lydia.

He grimaced as he strode up the path toward the house. How could he expect God to answer his prayer when he was preparing to break the law and escape from camp? He shook his head and shifted his hold on the baskets.

But this was the only choice. Siegfried was right. His sister could die if he didn't go to London and see that she got the help she needed. Who else would care for a girl with German parents and no money? Somehow God must understand and would forgive him.

He crossed Highland's rear courtyard and knocked at the door, while the tug of war with his conscience raged on. Not long ago he'd been carried through this very door with a bloody leg. He winced, remembering the agony that gash had caused. Though it had been painful and frightening, he'd met Lydia that day, and that had been a great gift.

Something his mother told him many times came rushing back.

"Remember, God specializes in taking some

thing bad and turning it around for good. You watch, you wait, you'll see."

The door swung open, and a young maid in a white apron and cap looked out at him. His spirit deflated. He should've known Lydia wouldn't answer, but still, he'd hoped she might.

"Good day, miss. I was told to bring these vegetables to the kitchen."

"I'll take them." The maid reached for the baskets.

He held on tight and shook his head. "I'll bring them in."

She looked up at him with questioning eyes, but then stepped back and let him pass by. He walked down the steps and into the lower hall. The tantalizing smell of roasting game floated out from the kitchen, along with a fresh citrus scent. The cook must be making something with lemons, maybe lemon curd?

"Scrub this pot again. It's not clean." The woman's voice came from the kitchen.

He rounded the corner and stopped at the kitchen doorway.

A portly, middle-aged woman in brown dress, apron, and cap waved a young maid toward the sink. "Go on, now, and do a better job this time." She looked his way and lifted her eyebrows. "Who are you?"

"Marius Ritter, ma'am. I'm delivering these vegetables from the kitchen garden."

405

She gave a quick glance to the baskets, then looked back at him. Her forehead creased. "You're that German, aren't you? The one who cut his leg in the orchard?"

"Yes, ma'am." He looked around the kitchen. "Where would you like me to put these?"

"Stay where you are." She looked down at his feet, and her lip curled. "I don't want those muddy boots in my kitchen."

A tall man in a white chef's jacket strode down the hall toward Marius. He slowed as he drew closer. "Oh, look at *zees* onions! You bring *zem* from our garden?" Marius had to listen closely to catch each word, muddled as they were by the man's strong French accent.

"Yes, sir."

The chef nodded and lifted one plump, purple onion and sniffed it. Then he took one basket and plunked it down on the big worktable in the center of the room. Bits of soil trickled out on the tabletop.

"Ah, look at that! What a mess!" The cook bustled over to Marius and snatched the second basket from his hands. "Next time rinse them off outside before you bring them in my kitchen."

Marius stared at her. There wouldn't be a next time.

"Well, why are you still standing there looking at me like that? Go on. I've no use for you in here." The cook waved him off.

He turned and strode down the hall, his ears burning. Footsteps sounded on the stone stairs, and he looked up.

A blond maid walked down carrying a tray filled with dishes. He'd never seen her before and had no idea if she would help him, but he had to try.

Her steps slowed when she saw him waiting at the bottom of the steps. She looked around and then back at him.

"Excuse me, miss." He reached in his pocket and took out the envelope. "Would you give this to Lydia Chambers?"

She bit her lip and glanced toward the kitchen. "Who are you?"

"I'm a friend." He lowered his voice. "I mean no harm. Please, it's important."

A slight smile lifted her lips. "All right." She balanced the tray in one hand, took the envelope, and slipped it in her apron pocket. "But you better go, before anyone else sees."

He touched his hat and nodded. "Thank you." Then he turned and hurried down the hall.

Lydia stared at the note from Marius, and a tremor raced down her arms. He was leaving? That didn't make sense. Where could he go?

Ann glanced around the great hall and leaned toward her. "What did he say?"

"Never mind." Lydia shoved the note in her pocket. "I have to go outside."

Ann's eyes widened. "To see him?"

"Yes, but please don't say anything to anyone." Lydia glanced toward the music room where Penny, Helen, and the children practiced a song.

"You better be careful," Ann whispered. "I almost got sacked when they caught me sneaking out to meet Peter."

"It's not like that." Lydia bit her lip. But it was, and if Mrs. Dalton or Mr. Lawrence found out what she was doing, she could lose her position. Still, she couldn't ignore Marius's note. "This is my last chance to see him."

Understanding flooded Ann's eyes. "Go on, then. I'll cover for you."

"Thank you." Lydia turned and hurried down the servants' stairs.

The clatter of pots and pans sounded in the kitchen, followed by Chef Lagarde scolding someone in French. Lydia tiptoed past the kitchen and scurried out the back door.

Was she in time? Would Marius still be waiting for her? She rounded the corner of the house and ran down the gravel path toward the garden.

Suddenly, someone grabbed her arm and pulled her into the bushes. She gasped and started to scream, but a hand pressed over her mouth.

"Shh, it's all right. It's Marius."

She sagged against him, and he lowered his hand. With her heart pounding hard in her chest she turned and faced him.

"I'm sorry. I didn't mean to frighten you."

"Well, you did." Lydia smoothed her hair back in place.

He laid his hand on her arm. "Forgive me. But I couldn't leave without seeing you once more."

"Are they transferring you to another camp?"

He shook his head and looked down.

Her stomach tensed. "Marius?"

A second passed before he lifted his head. His eyes glittered with moisture. "My sister is very ill, and my mother has no money to pay for a doctor or medicine. She's afraid Jenny will die. I have to go to them."

"But how? Will they give you some kind of pass?"

He shook his head.

A fearful trembling started in her legs, and she gripped his arm. "Oh, Marius, you can't escape!"

"I have to. My family needs me."

"But it's so dangerous! If they catch you . . ." She didn't even want to think what they would do to him.

He took her hand. "I must help my mother and my sister. There's no one else."

"I don't believe that." She pulled her hand away. "There has to be someone who will help them."

His eyes flashed, and his face turned ruddy. "We're German. No one will help us."

She crossed her arms, trying to still her trembling, but it was no use. Marius could be shot for trying to escape. They might think he was a spy.

"Please, Lydia, don't be angry with me. I know it's dangerous, but Siegfried has a plan that's sure to work."

"Siegfried?" She shook her head. "Don't listen to him!"

Marius hurried on as though he hadn't heard her warning. "We tried to get away last night, but our timing was off. If the weather holds, we'll try again tonight."

She shuddered and closed her eyes. *Please, God. You have to stop him.*

"I know it's a risk, but I can't let my sister die. She needs to see a doctor."

An idea flashed into Lydia's mind, and she grabbed his hand. "Don't go! I know someone who'll help your sister."

"Who?"

"Dr. and Mrs. Foster."

Marius sent a fearful glance toward the house. "You can't tell them."

"It will be all right. I mean Dr. Jon Foster and his wife, Kate. When he was taking his training in London, he volunteered at a free clinic on the East End called Daystar. They helped my sister, Helen, when she was pregnant. They see lots of patients every day. No one has to pay. I'm sure they'll help your sister."

"But we don't have time to write and wait for a

reply. My sister needs help now. I must go tonight, if I can get away."

"I could send a telegram." She quickly patted her pocket, hoping for a pencil, but only felt Marius's note. "I'll go get pencil and paper."

"Wait." He reached in his shirt pocket and took out a stubby pencil, but doubt still shadowed his eyes. "You're sure they'll help Jenny?"

"Yes! We can trust them. They'll do whatever's needed."

She pulled his note from her pocket and held it out to him. "Here, write down your mother's name and address on the back. I'll send Dr. Jon a telegram today."

The muscles in his jaw rippled as he debated the decision.

She held her breath. *Please, God, let him agree.*

Finally, he gave a slight nod. "All right." He squatted, pressed the note against his knee, and wrote down the address.

Lydia gripped the sides of her apron. "So you'll stay in camp?"

He stood and handed her the note. "Send the telegram and ask for a reply. If I don't hear something soon, I'll have to go."

She wished she could make him promise to forget his escape plans, but how could she? If her sister were ill, she would do everything she could to try and save her—even escape from an internment camp.

She slipped the note in her pocket. "How will I get word to you when I hear back from Dr. Jon?"

He frowned and looked toward the garden. "I hope they'll send me here again, but if not, would you come to the camp?"

She stilled, her heartbeat pounding in her ears.

"There's a big elm tree just inside the fence, at the southwest corner of the camp. I could wait there each night at eight."

Lydia raised her hand to her heart. Would she dare steal away at night and go to the camp?

Marius pulled back and shook his head. "No, it's too far and too dangerous. I should not have suggested that."

She reached for his hand. "It's all right. I'll come."

"Are you sure?"

"Yes."

He tightened his grip, leaned closer, and kissed her forehead. "Thank you, Lydia. Your kindness has saved my life again, and hopefully the life of my sister."

The sweetness of his words and tender kiss eased her fears. She placed a soft kiss on his cheek, then hurried back toward the house.

"Gather round, boys!" Alex waved his good arm to the four lads chasing each other across Highland's south lawn, then lifted his eyes to the brilliant blue sky overhead. In the distance

412

the treetops shimmered in shades of red and gold.

He'd forgotten how beautiful autumn in the country could be, and experiencing it here in Berkshire was a gift.

This was his fourth day at Highland, and after a rather rough start in his role as mentor to the boys, he had come up with a new idea he hoped would build a sense of teamwork rather than spur competition.

Donald set off at a slow jog toward Alex, but he was soon chasing Jack and Tom again. Andrew bent and placed his hands on his knees as though he needed to catch his breath. He looked up at Alex, and even at this distance Alex could tell he was debating if he would respond to the call or not.

Why wouldn't the boy accept Alex's leadership and fall in line like the others? Was it simply because he would one day be master of Highland and felt entitled to do whatever he pleased? Or did he put on that superior attitude because underneath he was afraid he didn't really measure up?

Whatever the reason, Alex was determined to win the boy over and help him move forward in life . . . or at least see that he learned to cooperate and stop causing so much trouble for Penny.

He glanced toward the veranda where the women and girls had gathered to work on their knitting projects. Penny stood by the bottom of the steps speaking to Julia. She wore a light-green dress that highlighted her feminine curves. Sunlight reflected off the copper strands in her hair.

The memory of the kiss they'd shared came flooding back. He clenched his jaw and tried to pull in a deep breath, but the ache in his chest made it almost impossible.

He forced his gaze away and checked on the boys. They'd stopped chasing each other and were gathering up their badminton racquets and birdies. He ran his hand across his ribs and took a slow, shallow breath. They were still healing. That was what caused the ache. It had nothing to do with Penny or the fact he'd hurt her by stealing that kiss.

He closed his eyes and tried to push away the memories. He had to stop thinking about her. He tried to avoid her as much as possible, but that had only made him more miserable and disgusted with himself.

"Lieutenant Goodwin?"

Alex snapped back to the moment.

Donald cocked his head and looked up at him. "Are you all right?"

"Yes, I'm fine."

"You called us?"

"Yes. I've set up a race course." Alex pointed across the lawn to the small white flags he'd stuck in the ground, creating the boundaries of an ova' track. "I want to teach you how to run a relay race."

Donald squinted up at him, then glanced at the other three boys who'd gathered around. "We race all the time. I can beat any of them."

Andrew placed his hands on his hips. "Not likely."

Donald smirked. "Want to bet?"

Alex took a step toward the boys. "In a relay race, you work as a team. Each boy runs one quarter of the way around the track, and he carries a baton that he passes to the next runner at the quarter mark." He picked up the short wooden dowel from the ground and held it out. "This is our baton."

Jack frowned. "How do you know who is the winner?"

"You're racing against the clock as a team, trying to beat your best time." He passed the baton to Jack and pulled a stopwatch from his pocket.

Andrew gave a confident nod. "I've done relay races at my school."

"You mean where you used to go to school," Donald said in a mocking tone.

Andrew scowled. "I'm going back after Christmas, which is much more than you can say."

Alex held up his hand. "Let's not argue, boys." He pointed at the baton again. "First, I'll show you how to make the hand-off. Once you've mastered that, we'll have our first race."

Donald, Jack, and Tom exchanged eager glances, and even Andrew looked ready to join in.

The boys circled around, and Alex took the baton again. "Both runners must do their parts for a smooth hand-off. The first runner must hold out the baton as he approaches the second runner, like this." He demonstrated the proper angle for the hand-off. "The second runner must start running and get up to speed before he looks over his shoulder and puts out his hand to accept the baton, then he must keep running and not slow down while he grabs it."

Alex looked at each boy, his gaze finally resting on Andrew. "Most of all, the runners must work together and trust each other."

Donald nodded and looked around at the others. "We can do that, can't we, boys?"

Their voices rose in hearty agreement, and they looked eager to give it a try. Alex coached them as they practiced the hand-off a few times, then Jack, Donald, and Andrew jogged off and took their positions around the track, while Tom waited at the starting line.

Alex handed Tom the baton and stood to the side. "Ready?" The boy nodded. Alex looked at the other boys. "On your mark, get set, go!"

Tom shot out, running at top speed around the first quarter of the track.

Alex lifted his hand to his mouth. "Go, Jack!"

Jack took off, looked over his shoulder, and reached back for the baton. Tom held it out, and Jack grabbed hold.

Alex whooped. They'd done it! A perfect hand-off!

The women and girls came down from the veranda and joined Alex, cheering the boys on. Penny looked Alex's way and smiled.

His heart soared, and he returned a playful grin. Maybe they could get past this awkwardness and find their way back to a comfortable friendship. He doubted that would ever be enough for him, but anything would be better than the painful, strained experience of the last few days.

"Go, Donald!" Lucy clapped her hands.

Jack made the hand-off to Donald, and the third boy raced around his section of the track. Andrew crouched low, ready to launch off as soon as Donald came closer.

Alex fixed his gaze on Andrew. This was his chance. If he finished the race well, it could draw all the boys closer.

Andrew sprinted off and quickly picked up speed. Donald grimaced as he struggled to catch up. He held out the baton. Andrew looked over his shoulder, reached back, and grabbed for it, but the baton slipped through his fingers and fell to the ground. Andrew slowed, his face red, his gaze darting around.

"Pick it up! Don't just stand there!" Donald yelled. "Finish the race!"

Andrew's eyes flashed. He lunged and grabbed

the baton from the grass, then spun around and threw it at Donald.

"Hey!" Donald ducked just as the baton flew past.

Before Alex could even call out to stop him, Andrew dashed off toward the stables, leaving the other boys panting on the track.

Donald shook his head and jogged across the grass toward Alex.

Julia lifted her hand to shade her eyes and looked toward the stables. "I suppose I should go after him."

"No, I'll go." Alex set off. He wanted to throttle the boy, but he doubted that would do any good. He needed an idea, some way to break through and help Andrew see that he must take charge of himself and make better choices . . . but how to do it?

That was the challenge.

Twenty-One

Lydia shook her head as she watched Lieutenant Goodwin hustle across the lawn and follow Andrew toward the stables.

Oh, that boy! When would he learn to control his temper? Lady Julia and Mrs. Kate had enough on their minds without having to worry about Andrew's outbursts. They all had high hopes that

Lieutenant Goodwin would help the boys settle down and behave. Donald, Tom, and Jack seemed to listen, but there was no sign of change in Andrew. At least not yet.

"I wish Jon and William were here." Kate lowered herself into the chair next to Lydia, then rested her hand on her bulging middle and put her feet up on the stool. "It doesn't seem right to push our trouble with Andrew off on Lieutenant Goodwin."

"I wouldn't worry. He seems up to the task, but it may take some time." Lydia shifted in her seat, moving closer to Kate, and lowered her voice. "Have you heard any news from Dr. Jon?" She glanced around, hoping no one else had heard. She didn't want to explain her connection to Marius to anyone else, not yet.

"You mean about Mrs. Ritter and her daughter?" Kate spoke in an equally low tone.

Lydia bit her lip and nodded.

"No. There was nothing in the mail today."

"But we sent that telegram three days ago."

Compassion filled Kate's eyes. "I'm sure he'll let us know as soon as he has anything to report."

Lydia nodded, but fear tightened her throat. How long would Marius wait before he tried to break out of camp? What would happen to him if he did? Would he lose his life while he tried to save his sister's? She closed her eyes, trying to calm her fears.

"Lydia." Kate laid her hand on Lydia's arm. "I know it's difficult to wait, but remember how determined Dr. Foster was to help your sister?"

Lydia nodded, and her eyes burned as she recalled the kindness he and Dr. Pittsford had shown Helen as she waited for Emily's birth.

"I'm sure he's putting the same effort into helping Jenny Ritter."

Lydia wanted to believe it was true, but doubt swooped back in. "Things were different then. He worked at Daystar, and there wasn't a war on."

"True, but he is the same man, with the same heart. If there's something he can do for Jenny, he'll do it. Or he'll see that Dr. Pittsford or someone from Daystar Clinic cares for her." Kate squeezed her hand. "Remember, God is in control. Let's trust Him."

Lydia slowly nodded. She wanted to trust God, but she was afraid her trembling hand betrayed her doubts. Kate didn't know Marius's life hung in the balance too . . . and Lydia couldn't tell her.

Alex walked into the stable and scanned the wide central corridor. Stalls lined the walls on both sides, and the floor in the center was swept clean. The scent of hay and horseflesh hung in the air. At the opposite end of the building, the large sliding door stood open, giving him a view to the pasture and parkland beyond. There was no sign of Andrew, though he was certain the boy had come this way.

He walked through the stable, glancing to the right and left, checking each stall. Most were empty, but a few held horses that munched on feed or lifted their heads and gazed out at him as he passed.

When he neared the second-to-the-last stall, someone sniffed, and the horse shuffled his feet. Alex stopped and listened. "Andrew?"

No reply, but the hay rustled, and the horse swished his tail. "I'd like you to come out and talk to me."

"I'm not coming out." Andrew's voice came from the back of the stall.

"All right. I'll come in." Alex pushed open the half door. The horse nickered and stepped to the right.

Andrew sat in the back corner, his knees up to his chest, his shoulders hunched, and his head down. He sniffed again and wiped his nose with his shirtsleeve. "I don't want to talk to you."

"Well, then, I suppose you'll have to listen."

Andrew lifted his head and scowled at Alex through red-rimmed eyes.

A pang shot through Alex's chest. What the boy had done was wrong, but he was upset and hurting. Somehow Alex had to get past his resistance and help him work through the issues.

Alex pulled in a deep breath and sent off a prayer for wisdom. The answer came as a clear impression, and he knew where to start. "You made a mistake out there, Andrew."

The boy rolled his eyes. "I know. I dropped the baton."

"Yes. You did, but the mistake I'm referring to was throwing the baton at Donald and running away."

"Did you hear what he said to me?" Andrew's tone was harsh and mocking.

" 'Pick up the baton and finish the race'?"

The boy's scowl deepened. "He had no right to yell at me."

"He is your teammate, and you—"

"Teammate!" Andrew practically spit out the word.

"Listen, I'm not here to talk about Donald. You can't force people to treat you the way you'd like, but you can learn to take charge of yourself and your actions and to make wise choices."

Andrew's blotchy face turned a deeper shade of red. He shook his head and looked away.

Alex lowered himself to the hay-strewn floor and sat next to the boy. "I know you felt bad that you dropped the baton. But we all make mistakes. That's just part of life." He picked up a piece of straw and twirled it between his fingers, waiting for Andrew's reply.

The boy silently tunneled his hand through th

422

hay on the floor between them, but at least he didn't argue the point.

"When I make a mistake," Alex continued, "I've found the best thing to do is own up to it, see what I can learn from the experience, and then try again."

Andrew slowly lifted his head. "You've made mistakes?"

A grin stole across Alex's face and he nodded. "Yes, quite a few."

"Just small mistakes, or were they big ones?"

Alex rubbed his chin. "When I was just a few weeks into my pilot training, I got cocky during landing practice and crashed my plane."

Andrew's eyes widened. "Really?"

"Yes. I broke my collarbone and was grounded for about six weeks. When I came back, my commander said I should transfer to a ground unit." Alex straightened, remembering the jolt he'd felt that day. "He said I wasn't cut out to be a pilot."

"So what did you do?"

"I wanted to fly. So I asked for another chance, and he gave it to me. Then I climbed back in the cockpit and learned how to handle my plane so well that it felt like we were one when we were in the air." He looked up at the small window at the back of the stall, memories of those exhilarating flights flooding his mind. "That taught me some important lessons."

"Like what?"

"Don't be cocky, for one." He grinned at Andrew, then grew more serious again. "A pilot needs confidence and bravery, but he has to balance those with caution and skill, especially during wartime. There's no place for a careless, overconfident pilot in the RNAS or anywhere else."

Andrew gave a slow nod. "So what happened on that last flight? Did you make a mistake then?"

Alex pulled in a sharp breath. He hadn't expected that question, though the answer had haunted him every day since the accident. He'd replayed his choices hundreds of times, always feeling the same regret. "I made several mistakes on that mission, and I paid a very high price for them."

Andrew's gaze grew intense. "What happened?"

He didn't like to talk about it, but if it would help Andrew, it would be worth the pain of repeating the story. "I was shaken up by that fight with the Zeppelin, and when it blew up, my plane flipped over."

Andrew's eyes widened. "Really?"

Alex nodded. "I went into a nosedive, headed straight for the ground, but somehow I pulled out of it and glided down behind enemy lines. I inspected the plane, but I didn't have much time because a troop of German cavalrymen was headed my way. I lost all the fuel in my main tank when I flipped the plane, so I had to tap into my reserve fuel tank, then restart the engine by myself. It's a miracle I got off the ground before the Germans reached me."

"Holy Moses," Andrew muttered.

"I didn't realize how much the plane was damaged. But that's no excuse. I shouldn't have been so eager to get back to base that I ignored the warning signs and my low fuel gauge."

Alex slowly shook his head. If only he would have done things differently. "I should've landed as soon as I was sure I was out of enemy territory. But I kept going, pushing my luck past the limit, thinking I could make it back to St. Pol."

"So you ran out of fuel? That's how you crashed?"

"I'm not sure. My fuel was almost gone. The engine stalled, and I think part of the wing broke off and hit the propeller. I couldn't get control after that." Alex pulled in a breath, trying to steel himself as the rest of the painful story flashed through his mind.

"I'm sure you did all you could."

He wished that was true, but even more, he wished he could go back and make different choices, choices that would've saved his eyesight and made it possible for him to fly again.

"You knocked down the Zeppelin. That's what's most important." Admiration lit the boy's eyes.

"I did my duty. I only wish I could do more."

Andrew looked up at him, silent understanding strengthening the bond between them.

Alex reached out and rested his hand on the boy's shoulder. "You've got your own mission in life, a path God has laid out for you. And it will take courage and character to travel that path and live your life well." He tightened his hold on Andrew's shoulder. "Learning from your mistakes and trying again is an important part of that journey."

Andrew gave a slow nod.

"All right, then." Alex rose to his feet and reached out his hand to Andrew.

The boy took hold and stood to face him. "Thank you for telling me what happened . . . and for the advice."

Alex slung his arm around Andrew's shoulder, and they walked out of the stable together.

Alex stepped outside and closed the drawing room door behind him. They had just finished a rousing game of charades, and everyone else was busy saying good night to the children and sending them off to bed. He doubted anyone noticed he had slipped away.

Light from the windows spread a soft glow across the veranda and touched the flower beds just beyond. Insects chirped softly, serenading him from the garden.

His thoughts drifted back through the day . . .

his time with the boys and his talk with Andrew in the stable. He supposed he'd call it a successful conversation. Andrew had rejoined the group and run two more races, grabbing the baton each time and finishing strong. He'd even congratulated the other boys when the races were done.

Alex wasn't naive enough to think their talk had solved all the boy's problems, but at least it opened the door for the two of them to keep talking. That was progress.

Why wasn't that small triumph enough to lift his spirits?

He leaned on the stone balustrade and gazed out at the deep-blue shadows cast by the moonlight on the trees. Thoughts of Penny filled his mind, as they did so many times each day. He tried to not let those thoughts linger, but it was hard. The more time they spent together, the more he wished he could find some way to bridge the gap between them and win her heart.

Was he a fool to even consider it?

The door opened behind him, and he turned.

"Oh, here you are." Penny stepped out onto the veranda and crossed to stand beside him. The soft floral scent she wore drifted past on a breeze, stirring his senses. She smiled up at him, tenderness shining in her eyes.

That ache tightened his chest again, and he looked away. Seeing her every day was a struggle, but being so close to her in the moonlight and not being able to take her in his arms was torture.

"I have a confession to make."

At her soft words, he glanced at her. "What's that?"

"I listened in on your conversation with Andrew when you were in the stable."

His spirits sank. She'd heard him admit his mistakes that led to the crash. He set his jaw and stared across the shadowed parkland. "Well, at least now you know the truth."

She turned questioning eyes on him.

"There's no way around it. My poor judgment caused that crash."

"That's not what I heard, not at all."

"Don't try to soften it for me, Penny. I made mistakes, and I'll be paying for them for the rest of my life."

"It's not your fault you ran out of fuel or that your plane broke down."

"Maybe not, but I was trained to weigh the risks and make better choices. And that day, for some crazy reason, I thought I was invincible." He swallowed hard. "I risked it all, and lost everything."

"Everything?" Pain tinged her voice.

He turned to her, and he read the sweet longing in her eyes. But it was no use. He must have been crazy to think he had anything to offer her. "Look at me, Penny. I'm not the same man I was before the war. I have no idea what I'll do when

I leave Highland, how I'll even support myself."

Her lips trembled slightly and she pressed them together.

Regret rolled over him in a crushing blow. "I'm sorry. I shouldn't have come here. I never meant to hurt you."

She lifted her chin. "Well, I'm not sorry."

Her words jolted him.

"The injury to your eye is a great loss. But at least now I know you'll survive this war and you'll have a future."

He shook his head. She didn't understand. "I have to find some kind of work to do, and I have no idea what that will be. Maybe in a few weeks, when I'm done with this sling, I can write to my old captain and see if he'll take me back on the *Mina Brea.*"

"Please, Alex, this is no time to go to sea, not when German U-boats are sinking any ship that flies a British flag."

"Well, I'm not trained for anything else except flying, and that's impossible now."

She was quiet for a few seconds, then she laid her hand on his arm. "If you could do anything, anything at all, what would it be?"

Just for a moment, he let his dreams rise to the surface. There was no way they would ever come to pass now, but what harm would there be in telling Penny and basking in the glow of what could've been?

He glanced her way. "Have you ever heard of an Air Meet?"

"Yes, I read about one that took place before the war. They said it attracted thousands of people."

He nodded. "That's what first stirred my interest in flying, but airplanes can be used for more than crazy stunts or taking people on joyrides."

"What are you thinking?"

"When the war is over, people are going to be even more interested in flying than they are now."

"Yes, I suppose they will be."

"If someone started a commercial flying service, the planes could transport cargo or take people wherever they need to go. There are hundreds of ways planes could be used in business and industry. And when someone does start a service like that, they'll need people who know about airplanes to manage it for them."

A glowing smile lit Penny's face. "I know just the man who could do it."

"Or maybe I could team up with another pilot and teach people how to fly. I could handle the ground training, and he could take students up for practice flights.

"That's a wonderful idea. Or you could set up your own company with a whole flock of airplanes and hire pilots to take people all over the country."

He gazed out across the moonlit parkland

letting his dreams take flight, imagining what life would be like if he started his own company.

But reality quickly swooped in and pulled him back to the ground. He sighed and shook his head. "It would take a lot of money to follow through on any of those ideas."

"Of course, you'd need investors with capital and vision. But with our family connections, and those you'll make when you go to London and accept the Victoria Cross, you could probably put the necessary funds together."

She lifted her gaze to meet his, and hope seemed to vibrate in the air around them. Looking into her eyes, he could almost believe it was possible.

The wind picked up, rustling the leaves in the nearby trees. Clouds scuttled across the moon, darkening his view and whisking away his dreams.

"Those are fine ideas, Penny, but we have no idea how long the war will last or what shape the country will be in when it's finally over."

"All the more reason to make plans now and think of ways we can help rebuild after the war."

That sounded logical, but doubt still weighed him down.

She took his hand. "Remember that first day we met at the zoo in London?"

Warmth flowed through her hand into his. "Yes." How could he ever forget?

"One of the first things you told me was that your father built several railways in India."

He gave a slight nod, though he wasn't sure where she was taking him.

"I think you're a lot like your father. You enjoy a challenge, and you have the skills and determination to see a job through. I'm sure you could accomplish just about anything you set your mind to." She tightened her hold on his hand. "Promise me you won't give up on your dreams."

He looked into her eyes, and his throat tightened. Oh, how he loved her! He swallowed, trying to put words to his feelings. But the door flew open, and Lydia rushed out.

"Miss Penny, come quick!"

Penny dropped his hand and spun around. "What is it?"

"Mrs. Kate says her time's come. The babies are on their way."

Penny gasped, then darted a quick look at Alex. "I have to go."

"Of course."

She stepped toward the door, then looked over her shoulder. "Thank you, Alex."

He frowned slightly. Why was she thanking him?

"For trusting me with your dreams." She sent him the most beautiful, hope-filled smile . . . and his heart took flight again.

Twenty-Two

Lydia pushed open the back door and stepped out into the rear courtyard. A cheerful bird sang from a nearby tree. She lifted her hand to her mouth and stifled a yawn. It had been a long night, waiting for the babies to arrive, and still they hadn't come. Dr. Foster said not to worry, first babies usually took longer, but she couldn't help feeling anxious.

She took the path toward the kitchen garden, praying she'd find Marius there and be able to speak to him. She passed under the archway and entered the garden.

Four men worked among the vegetables and flowers. The lone guard sat on the bench near the far wall. Lydia spotted Marius digging in a row of carrots with a spading fork. His shirtsleeves were rolled up, and his straw hat shaded his face.

She started down the path toward him. He lifted his head and looked her way. Relief flashed across his face.

She offered him a tired smile as she passed, then bent and picked some parsley and rosemary from the rows of herbs. He continued lifting carrots from soil, shaking them off, then placing them in a wooden crate near his feet.

When Lydia had collected a handful of each

herb, she walked past Marius and out under the archway. Then she slipped into the tool room and left the door ajar. If he could get away, he would come. She brushed the dirt from the old wooden potting bench and straightened the tools hanging on the walls, anything to keep herself busy and still the trembling in her hands while she waited.

Footsteps approached, and she turned toward the door.

Marius walked in, his eyes bright. "You have news about Jenny?"

"No, but we should hear something today."

The joy drained from his face, and he shook his head. "I can't put Siegfried off any longer. We leave tonight at midnight."

"No, please, Marius. I'm sure we'll have an answer today. Mrs. Kate is having her babies, and Dr. Jon is on his way from London. He'll be here soon, and I can ask him about Jenny."

Marius lifted his hand and rubbed his forehead. "What if I wait and there is still no answer? It's been more than a week since my mother wrote to tell me Jenny was ill."

"I know. I'm sorry. I'll try to speak to him as soon as I can and bring you word."

Marius moved closer. "I heard Mr. McTavish talking to the guard. We'll be going out to the fields when we finish in the garden."

Lydia nodded. "Don't worry. I'll find you."

"But I won't be able to get away to speak to you when I'm in the field."

"Then I'll come to the camp tonight."

"No! That's too far. It's not safe."

"It will be all right."

Weary lines creased his forehead while he weighed the decision, then he took her hand. "All right. I'll meet you by the tree at eight, but please be careful. And if you have no news, or you can't get away, don't come. I'll understand." His voice broke and he looked away.

"Either way, I'll come."

"Don't risk it. If there's no news, stay home." He tightened his hold on her hand. "This may be the last time we see each other," he whispered.

"Please don't go, Marius."

"I have to, but it's hard for me to leave you."

A tear slipped down her cheek, and he tenderly brushed it away, then kissed her forehead. "Take care, Lydia. Don't forget me."

"You will always be in my prayers." She stood on tiptoe and kissed his cheek, then she hurried back to the house, swallowing her tears.

Penny ushered the children into the great hall after breakfast. Alex and Andrew brought up the rear, continuing their conversation about training the pony.

Helen met them at the bottom of the stairs,

holding Emily and Irene by the hands. "Good morning, miss."

Penny scanned the hall. "Is Lydia coming?"

"I'm not sure, miss." Helen sent an uncomfortable glance toward the doorway to the servants' stairs. "I saw her at breakfast, then she said she had to take care of something."

Penny sighed and rubbed her forehead where a headache was beginning to build. She'd been up until one, waiting for the babies to arrive. When Dr. Foster told them it would still be several more hours, Julia encouraged her to go to bed and get some rest.

Penny had been surprised to wake at sunrise and learn Kate was still in labor. Why did it take so long for babies to be born?

She glanced at Alex as they walked toward the library. He looked rested and as handsome as ever. Apparently, the fact that twins were on their way hadn't kept him awake last night. He took a seat in one of the chairs near the fireplace. Donald and Andrew claimed chairs on either side of him. He certainly seemed to have won those boys' loyalty. The other children settled in around the room without any fuss.

Penny took a copy of *The Secret Garden* from the end table and handed it to Lucy. "Would you read for us?"

Lucy nodded and opened the book.

Penny took a seat next to Rose. "I believ

we're at chapter seven, 'The Key to the Garden.' "

Lucy found the page and began reading. She had a pleasant voice, and soon they were all wrapped up in the story of Mary Lennox, the lonely little girl who had lost all her family and been sent to Yorkshire to live with her uncle at Misselthwaite Manor.

Footsteps sounded in the great hall, and Mr. Lawrence passed the library doorway. The front door opened.

"Am I in time?" Jon's voice rang out. "Have the babies arrived?"

"Not yet, sir," Mr. Lawrence said.

Penny rose from her chair and crossed to the library doorway. Jon charged past and bounded up the stairs.

William took off his hat and handed it to Mr. Lawrence. "Is Lady Julia upstairs?"

"Yes, sir."

"Would you tell her we've arrived?" The butler nodded. "We had to rush off without breakfast. Would you ask Chef Lagarde to prepare some-thing simple for us?"

"Right away, sir." Mr. Lawrence strode off across the great hall.

William turned to Penny. "So, today you'll become an aunt."

"Yes." She looked up the stairs. "I'm just sorry 's taking so long. Poor Kate must be exhausted."

"I think Jon is the only one who is glad about

that." William glanced toward the upper gallery. "It seems strange for a man to be in the room with his wife at a time like that, but he insists it's entirely proper, since he is a doctor."

Penny smiled. "Yes. I'm sure it will be fine."

The door to the servants' stairs opened, and Lydia stepped into the great hall. Her eyes widened when she saw Penny and William. "I'm sorry to be late, miss."

Penny waited a moment, thinking Lydia would give an explanation, but she didn't. "The children are in the library. Lucy is reading aloud. Will you help Helen keep an eye on them?"

"Yes, miss." Lydia hesitated and looked up the stairs. "Have the babies arrived?"

"Not yet, but I think it will be soon."

"Very good, miss." Lydia hurried toward the library.

Alex looked out of the library doorway. "Is everything all right?"

"Yes, please come join us." Penny motioned to William. "This is my cousin, Sir William Ramsey." She turned to Alex. "And this is Lieutenant Alex Goodwin. He's been a wonderful help to us the last few days."

William shook Alex's hand. "Of course, I've heard a great deal about you. We're very happy to have you here at Highland."

"Thank you, sir."

"William!" Julia looked over the railing in the

upper gallery, then quickly started down the stairs. "The babies have arrived. A boy and a girl!"

Penny gasped and lifted her hands to her mouth. How wonderful!

"Thank the Lord!" William exclaimed.

Alex beamed Penny a broad smile. "Congratulations, Aunt Penny."

"Is Kate all right?" William strode across the hall and met Julia halfway up the stairs.

"Yes. She's tired but very happy. Jon arrived just as the second baby, his son, was born." Julia stepped into William's embrace. "I'm so glad you're home."

William held her for a moment, then stepped back and looked at his wife's face. "How are you, my darling? I suppose you've been up all night."

Julia nodded. "I'll be fine. Don't worry about me."

Lydia looked out the library doorway. "Can we go up and see Mrs. Kate and the babies?" Her gaze darted from Julia to William, then she quickly added, "The children are all very eager."

"Let's give them a bit more time," Julia said. "I'll let you know when Kate is ready for visitors."

Lydia's eager expression waned. She bit her lip and looked toward the upper gallery.

"Don't worry, Lydia. I'm sure everything is fine."

Lydia nodded, but she still looked anxious as she slipped back into the library.

That was odd. They were all eager to see the babies, but why was Lydia so disappointed about the wait?

William turned to Julia. "Have you eaten this morning?"

"Not yet."

"Then come with me, and we'll find some breakfast." William took Julia's hand, and they walked into the dining room.

Penny sighed and looked at Alex. "It will be even more of a challenge to keep the children quiet now that they know the babies are here."

"Why don't I take them outside? We could go for a walk down to the stream. That ought to keep them occupied for a while."

"Would you?" Penny lifted her gaze to meet his. "That would be such a great help." Perhaps then she could see Kate and her new niece and nephew without the children crowding around.

"Of course, I'd be happy to. Enjoy some time with your sister and the babies. I'll manage the crew until luncheon."

"Thank you. You are a dear." She stood on tiptoe and kissed his cheek.

His smile spread wider. "I'll have to take them out more often if it will earn me a kiss."

She laughed and touched his arm. "That was just a kiss on the cheek, and quite proper between friends."

He lifted his eyebrows, and a teasing light

glinted in his eyes. "So that's what it was?"

"Yes." She returned his smile. Then she turned and hurried up the stairs, but as she passed the landing, she glanced back at him. "Thank you, Alex."

He looked up at her, admiration—and perhaps more—shining in his eyes.

Penny felt so relieved and happy she almost floated up the stairs. Though the storm clouds of the war still cast a shadow over their family, today there was a break in the clouds, spreading light and hope. Jon had made it home in time to share in the joy of the twins' arrival, and Alex's wounded spirits seemed to be on the mend.

And best of all, his heart seemed to be opening to hers.

An owl hooted in the woods to her left, and shivers raced down Lydia's arms. She wrapped her sweater around her more tightly and hurried down the road toward the camp. The sun had disappeared behind the trees only a short while after she left Highland, and the sky had darkened from dusky purple to deep navy blue. The moon was almost full, and a few tiny stars lit the path before her.

She wouldn't let the night sounds or the darkening sky slow her steps. She had an important message to deliver and no time to waste.

The road rose and curved to the right. At the top of the hill, she stopped and scanned the scene below. Hundreds of tents spread out in the valley. Five long wooden buildings stood in the center of the camp. A few lanterns lit the paths between the tents, and several more hung at the main gate and around the wood-and-barbed-wire fence enclosing the camp.

Her gaze followed the fence line to the southwest corner. She spotted the elm tree Marius had mentioned as their meeting place, but it was surrounded by open fields. Her stomach clenched. What if they were spotted?

She slipped her watch from her pocket and squinted to check the time. She'd left the house just after six, and it had taken her almost an hour to walk here. If she waited another hour to meet Marius, she wouldn't be back at Highland until after nine. Surely someone would miss her by then. What if the doors were locked? How would she get inside?

She swallowed and looked around. *Please, Lord, show me what to do.*

She scanned the camp again. A few men walked along the paths between the tents, and two guards stood on watch at the main gate.

Perhaps the best path was walking in the light. She reached in her pocket, took out the note she'd written to Marius, and walked toward the main gate.

As she approached, the guards stepped forward and lifted their rifles.

"Halt! Who goes there?" the taller guard called.

Lydia's heart hammered in her throat. "My name is Lydia Chambers, and I have a message for Marius Ritter."

The two guards looked at each other, and the taller one chuckled and lowered his rifle. "You can't just walk up to the gate and pass a message. You have to send it in a letter."

"It's urgent! Please, he needs to hear this news tonight."

The shorter guard stepped into the circle of light from the lantern. "What's so important that you couldn't send it in a letter?"

She didn't want to tell him about Marius's private family matters, but if that was the only way to get the message through, she would do it. She walked closer and lowered her voice. "It's about his sister in London. She's been ill. Please, he needs to read this message."

The taller guard scoffed. "His sister? What's this really about? Are you trying to settle a lover's quarrel?"

"No! Here, you can read it yourself." She held out the note and passed it through the slim opening in the gate.

The two guards exchanged skeptical looks, but the taller guard took the note, then opened it and scanned the message. He looked up. "Even if this

443

is the truth, we're not allowed to accept anything for the prisoners."

"Please, he's so worried about her. Couldn't you do it just this one time?"

A slow, sly smile lifted one side of the guard's mouth. "There might be a way I could be convinced."

The hair on the back of her neck prickled, and she gave her head a slight shake. "I can't pay you. I have no money."

He lifted his eyebrows and grinned. "I wasn't thinking of money."

She pulled in a sharp breath. Did he mean what she thought he meant? She quickly stepped back. "No!"

"Are you sure?" He pushed the gate open a few feet, slung his rifle over his shoulder, and stepped toward her. "I could make sure your message gets through."

"Harry, stop!" The other guard shot an anxious glance over his shoulder, then looked back at them. "You're going to get us both in trouble."

"I'm just having a little fun." He focused on Lydia and took a step closer. "I'd say a little kiss would be fair payment for delivering this message." He held up her note and waved it back and forth with a wicked gleam in his eye.

She lunged and tried to snatch the message, but he grabbed her arm. She gasped and tried to pull away.

"Come on, just one little kiss." He tightened his grip.

"Stop! Please!" She turned her face away. "Let me go!"

"Lydia!" Marius ran across the open area toward the gate.

The shorter guard swung around and leveled his rifle at Marius. "Stop!"

The tall guard dropped his hold on Lydia, ripped his rifle from his shoulder, and spun around. "Stay back!"

Marius stopped and lifted his hands, but he kept his eyes on Lydia. "Are you all right?"

"Yes, and so is Jenny! Dr. Jon says she's—"

"Stop!" the shorter guard shouted. "You can't talk to him!"

"What did the doctor say?" Marius kept his hands high, ignoring the guard's glare.

"She was in the hospital three days, but she's home now and on the mend."

The taller guard scowled at Lydia, then walked toward Marius, his rifle aimed at his chest. "Go on! Get back to your tent before I report you to the commander."

Marius shifted his steely glare toward the guard. 'If anyone should be reported, it's you."

"I wouldn't try it." But the tremor in the guard's voice betrayed his fear.

"Come on, Marius." Siegfried moved closer and tugged on Marius's shirt. "Let's go."

Lydia hadn't realized Siegfried was with Marius until he stepped into the light.

Marius slowly lowered his hands, his glare still fixed on the guard. Then he looked at Lydia once more. "God bless you, Lydia."

Tears flooded her eyes, but she sent him a tremulous smile. "And you!"

She turned and hurried down the road away from the camp. It was wonderful she'd been able to see Marius and deliver the message, but knowing he was locked away in that camp tore at her heart.

Please, Lord, strengthen him. Give him peace tonight. Help him trust You.

Fighting off her tears, she prayed all the way back to Highland.

Twenty-Three

A knock sounded at Penny's door. She yawned and turned from her dressing table. "Come in."

Helen entered. "You rang, miss?"

Penny glanced past Helen's shoulder. Lydia usually answered her summons, but she had been disappearing and reappearing at the oddest times lately. "Where is Lydia?"

Helen's face turned slightly pink, and she glanced toward the window. "She . . . had to g deliver a message."

"For Mrs. Kate?"

"Uh . . . no, miss."

"Whom was she delivering a message for?"

Helen bit her lip. "Oh, please, miss, don't make me say."

What a curious response. "Now you must tell me."

Helen's gaze darted around the room for a few seconds. "Oh, she's gone off to that camp to see Marius, the prisoner who cut his leg in the orchard."

"What?" Sensible, honest Lydia?

"Oh, please, miss, don't dismiss her. She's not done anything bad. I'm sure of it. Lydia's not like that."

"Sneaking out at night to meet a man, let alone one of the prisoners, sounds very dangerous. What was she thinking?"

"She had to go and tell him the news about his sister. She's been real sick, but Dr. Jon said she's well now, so he doesn't have to worry."

"Helen, slow down. You're not making sense."

"Mrs. Kate knows about it," Helen rushed on. "She helped Lydia send the telegram to Dr. Jon a few days ago. They asked him to visit Marius's sister, Jenny, in London and help her out if he could. And he did. And then today when the doctor came to see the babies, he told Lydia that Jenny is better, and she had to go tell Marius."

Penny's thoughts flashed back to the day in

Fulton when she'd bumped into Lydia and made her drop her package of books in the muddy street. Lydia said the books were a gift for one of the prisoners. She'd also said they'd exchanged letters, but this sounded much more serious.

"Please, miss. Lydia's a good girl with a kind heart. She's just trying to help."

"I understand what you're saying, but you know what Mrs. Dalton and Mr. Lawrence would say if they found out."

Helen dropped her chin. "Please don't tell them. I didn't mean to get her in trouble. I thought when you heard the story, you'd understand."

Penny sighed. "I do sympathize. It sounds like she has good intentions, but I'll have to speak to her about it."

Helen nodded but kept her eyes focused on the floor.

Penny hated to see anyone feeling so forlorn. "Please, don't worry, Helen. I'm sure we can resolve this. There's no need for you to say anything to Lydia. I'll talk to her tomorrow and set things right."

Helen lifted her gaze. "Thank you, miss. You've always been kind to us."

Penny rose from the dressing-table bench, and Helen helped her out of her dress and corset. The wind rattled the window, making Penny shiver. Lydia was either very brave or very much in love to walk all the way to the camp on a cold windy night like this. Either way, Penny had to warn her not to put herself in danger like this ever again.

Alex walked into the library carrying the book he had borrowed the night before.

"Good morning, Lieutenant." William looked up from his desk in the corner.

Alex turned. He hadn't expected to find anyone here at this hour. "Good morning, sir."

"You're up early."

"Yes, I thought I'd return this book before everyone gathers in the hall." Alex glanced around the room. "You have an excellent library."

"I'm glad you're making use of it."

Alex scanned the shelf, looking for an open spot.

"Julia tells me you and Penny have grown quite close."

Alex's hand stopped halfway to the shelf. He slipped the book in place, then turned to face William. "Yes, sir, we have."

William's somber expression added weight to his words. "I take my role as Penny's guardian quite seriously, but it's difficult for me to watch over her while I'm away in London." He studied Alex for a moment. "I hope I can trust you to treat her in an honorable manner while you're here at Highland."

The memory of the kiss they'd shared the day he

arrived flashed into his mind, and heat rushed up his neck. "Yes, sir."

"She's young but not too young to have her heart broken, and I wouldn't want that to happen."

"Neither would I, sir."

"Good." William gave a firm nod. "From what Jon and Julia tell me, you're a man with good character and strong faith, and your service with the RNAS is certainly commendable."

Alex's chest expanded. "Thank you, sir."

"No thanks needed. I'm impressed by what you've accomplished." William rested his elbows on the arms of his chair and folded his hands. "All that being said, I'd like to know what your intentions are toward Penny."

Alex hadn't expected that question, at least not yet. He knew which way his heart wanted to take things, but he didn't know how William would feel about it. No time like the present to find out. He straightened and met William's gaze. "Penny is an amazing young woman, and spending time with her here at Highland has made me realize how much I care for her, but I'm not sure what the future holds for me now." Alex motioned toward his eye patch. "I'm afraid my injuries raise a rather high barrier between us."

"That sounds more like a problem to solve than a wall that should separate you. That is, if your feelings for Penny are the kind that lead to lifetime commitment."

Alex's heartbeat thrummed in his chest. A lifetime with Penny would be a dream come true.

"Do you love her?"

The answer surged through him. "Yes, sir. I do, very much."

"Does she feel the same way about you?"

The sweet kiss they had shared flashed through his mind again. "I haven't spoken to her directly, but she has given me a reason to hope."

"May I give you some advice?"

"Yes, sir. Please do."

"My first marriage was arranged by my parents to improve our family's business connections. My wife was attractive and accomplished, but we didn't know each other well. And it was only after the wedding that I realized how poorly we were matched. I hoped love would grow, but after a short time we ended up living separate lives. There was a very painful distance between us when she died in a riding accident."

Memories of Alex's childhood came rushing back, shaking him to the core.

Concern lined William's face. "Are you all right?"

"Yes, sir, it's just that your first marriage sounds very similar to my parents' situation."

"In what way?"

Alex cleared his throat. "They met and married in India when my mother was only eighteen. She was never happy there. Finally, she left us, and she returned to England with my sister, Lindy. A few months later she divorced my father."

"I'm very sorry to hear that. It must have been difficult for you."

Alex gave a slight nod. "I've always admired my father, idolized him, in fact. But he was not the best husband." A shudder passed through him. "I don't want to repeat his mistakes."

Compassion filled William's eyes. "You don't have to. Rather, you can learn from those painful experiences and let them guide you toward a better path."

Alex swallowed and nodded, but the memory of his father's failures weighed heavy on his heart.

William leaned forward in his chair. "In my second marriage to Julia, I've discovered the importance of faith and commitment and how those can strengthen the bond that holds a man and wife together through good times and bad."

Alex soaked in William's words, letting them soothe the ache in his chest. Could he take the painful lessons from his parents' failed marriage and turn them around to build a better future with Penny?

William rose and placed his hand on Alex' shoulder. "With God's help and the love of a good woman like Penny, you two could build a fine marriage and strong family."

Alex met William's gaze. "Yes, sir. I believe that's true."

"Good, then you have my permission to move ahead in a courtship with Penny."

Alex's chest swelled, and hope surged through him. "Thank you, sir." William's belief in him and his encouragement meant more than he could say.

"Of course, before you propose, I'd like to be assured you have a way to provide for her, but you have time to work out those details."

"Yes, sir."

"And I think we can dispense with you calling me 'sir.' William is fine."

Alex grinned and held out his hand. "Thank you, William."

William grabbed hold and shook his hand. "You're welcome, Alex."

Lydia knocked softly on Miss Penny's door, then opened it and stepped inside. She quietly crossed the room and pushed the drapes aside. Light poured in around her. "Morning, miss." She glanced over her shoulder and was surprised to see Miss Penny already sitting up in bed.

"Good morning, Lydia." Miss Penny swung her feet over the side of the bed. "Before I dress, there's something I want to ask you."

Lydia's stomach sank, and she turned to face Miss Penny.

"Last night I rang, expecting you, but Helen came instead. Where were you?"

Lydia's mouth went dry. "I . . . had to deliver a message to . . . a friend."

Miss Penny waited a few seconds, and when Lydia didn't offer further explanation, she said, "I know you went to the camp. I was hoping you would be honest and tell me the whole truth."

All the air rushed from Lydia's lungs. Helen must have told Miss Penny where she'd gone. Her sister was the only one who knew. "I'm sorry, miss. I was afraid you wouldn't approve."

"I'm not sure what I think, but I'd like you to tell me the rest of the story."

Lydia clasped together her cool, trembling hands. "Do you remember that day in Fulton when you met me coming out of the bookshop?"

"Yes, I remember."

Lydia poured out the story, explaining how she'd met Marius and what had passed between them in their letters, their meetings in the garden, the news about Jenny Ritter's illness, and finally Siegfried's efforts to convince Marius to join in his plans for escape.

"So you see, I had to get that message to Marius last night. That was the only way to stop him from trying to break out of the camp. And heaven only knows what would've happened if he'd tried that."

Miss Penny stared at Lydia, looking a bit stunned by the story.

"It's not right for the government to take good man like Marius away from his family jus because he's German. He's lived in London since he was a boy. His father is dead, and he was taking care of his mother and sister. They need him. But then it's not right for him to try and escape from the camp either."

"No, of course not."

"So . . . you understand why I had to go?"

"Yes, I suppose so. I'm glad you got the message through, but it was quite a risk."

The weight pressing down on Lydia began to lift.

"I won't say anything to anyone, but if you're ever facing a difficult situation like that again, you must promise to seek my help or Lady Julia's."

Lydia nodded. "I will, miss. I promise."

"Good." Miss Penny's serious expression eased. "You must think a great deal of this Marius Ritter to go to all that trouble."

Lydia's cheeks warmed, and a smile stole across her lips. "I do, miss. He's a fine man, hard working and very thoughtful. Maybe one day, when the war is over, we can be together."

Miss Penny smiled. "If he's truly like you described him, then I hope so too." She rose, crossed the room, and opened her wardrobe. "I think I'd like to wear my coral dress today."

Relief poured through Lydia. The matter was settled. She wouldn't have to worry about a reprimand from Mrs. Dalton or the possibility of losing her position. She followed Penny and took the dress from the wardrobe.

"Are Kate and Jon awake yet?" Penny asked. "I'm longing to see the babies again."

"I don't think so. Mrs. Dalton said to wake you first and let them rest a little longer." Lydia took the dress off the hanger and laid it over the chair.

"It's amazing to think of Kate being the mother of twins."

"Yes, it is." Lydia helped Penny slip her nightgown over her head.

Penny glanced toward the window. "I think I'll go down to the garden and pick a bouquet of flowers for Kate before breakfast."

"I'm sure she'd like that." Lydia helped Penny finish dressing, then fixed her hair in a simple style. "Will there be anything else, miss?"

"No, that's all I need." Penny took her blue shawl from the drawer and followed Lydia out the door.

Lydia glanced at her watch, then continued down the hall at a quick pace. The family and staff would gather in the great hall in less than thirty minutes, and she still had to wake Dr. Jon and Mrs. Kate, then check on the children and make sure they were dressed and ready for the day.

She released a deep breath. It would be a busy morning, but at least her mind was at ease, and there were no more secrets between her and Miss Penny.

Twenty-Four

Misty fog greeted Penny as she stepped out the front door and walked around the side of the house to take the path toward the garden. She would have to hurry if she was going to have enough time to pick a bouquet and take it up to Kate before the family gathered at nine.

It was so good to have William and Jon home with them. It would be comforting to hear William read Scripture and pray for the family and staff. She wasn't sure how long he and Jon could stay, but at least they'd been able to come home to see the babies and spend some time with the family.

She pushed open the door to the garden tool room and crossed to the potting bench. A crate filled with hand tools sat on the floor to the right. She searched through it and took out a pair of clippers.

A scraping sound came from the storage room, followed by a loud *thud.* She turned and listened. Was an animal trapped in there?

She glanced over her shoulder. The outside door to the tool room had been closed when she came in, but what if one of the cats from the stable yard had wandered in when it was open yesterday and been trapped inside overnight with no food or water? Poor thing! She hurried over and pulled the door partly open.

A small window in the far corner shed dim light in the storage room. Sacks of fertilizer were stacked next to several wooden barrels on the right side of the room. Shelves filled with cans and boxes lined the wall on the opposite side. Two old wheelbarrows were parked in front of the shelves, and a broken wooden chair sat beneath the window.

She pushed the door open all the way and stepped inside. "Here, kitty, kitty." She scanned the room but didn't see a cat. Bending low, she looked under the shelf.

Suddenly, someone grabbed her from behind and clamped a rough hand over her mouth.

Panic shot through her, and she tried to wrestle free.

"Settle down, and you won't get hurt!" The man's voice was low and threatening, and he spoke with a slight accent.

She tried to turn her head and force out a scream, but his large hand clamped down tighter, covering her mouth and nose.

"See this knife?" He forced her head down, and the metal flashed as he turned the knife in his hand. "I'll use it if I have to."

Terror raced through her, turning her knees to jelly.

"If you want to live, listen very carefully. I'n

going to lower my hand, and you're going to be very quiet. Do you understand?"

She nodded. He dropped his hand, and she gasped in a breath.

Gripping her arms with both hands, he forced her to turn around and face him.

A shock wave jolted Penny. She'd seen this man before. He was one of the German prisoners who worked in the fields. Lydia's story of the planned prison escape rushed through her mind. "Are you Marius?"

His eyes flashed. "No, that fool wouldn't come with me."

She pulled in a breath, trying to slow her racing heart. This was no time to show fear. If she wanted to gain the upper hand, it would take courage. She lifted her chin. "Who are you?"

"Never mind. I want a horse, and you're going to get one for me."

"No!" She took a step back.

He lunged toward her, grabbed her arm, and flashed the knife. "You'll do as I say!"

She clenched her jaw. Her only chance to get away was to make him believe she intended to cooperate. "All right."

He motioned toward the door with his chin. "Take me to the stables."

Penny's mind spun. How could she distract him? Would anyone hear her if she screamed?

He loosened his hold on her arm as he reached

for the door. This was her chance. She jerked away and banged into a stack of pots, sending them crashing to the floor.

He growled and lunged toward her with the knife. Pain pierced her upper arm, and she cried out. He grabbed hold of her again and shook her shoulder. "See what you've done!"

She wrapped her hand over her wounded arm, and warm, sticky blood coated her fingers. Tremors hit her legs, and her thoughts swirled.

"Let's go!" He pushed her out the door. "Take me to the stables, now!"

Penny's heart sank, and she led her captor down the path and out the wooden door on the far side of the garden.

Alex strolled into the great hall replaying his conversation with William, hope and new possibilities filling his mind. He could hardly wait to see Penny.

He and William walked over and stood in front of the fireplace to wait for the family. Several members of the staff lined up by the stairs. Mr. Lawrence stood at the head of the line with Mrs Dalton beside him. Next came the footman several housemaids, and the kitchen staff.

Chatter and footsteps sounded in the uppe gallery. Julia came down the stairs with Dr. an Mrs. Foster, Sarah, Helen, Lydia, and the whol troop of children. Julia smiled at William an took her place beside him. The other adults and children took their places, forming a line. Lydia and Helen joined the staff across the hall.

The clock chimed nine. William turned to Julia. "Shall we wait for Jon and Penny?"

"Jon is staying upstairs with Kate this morning. I haven't seen Penny." She looked across the hall. "Lydia, did you wake Miss Penny this morning?"

"Yes, m'lady. I helped her dress just after eight." Lydia glanced toward the front door. "She said she was going to the garden and pick some flowers for Mrs. Kate. Maybe she's upstairs with her now."

Julia frowned slightly. "I just checked on Kate before I came down. Penny wasn't with her."

A prickle of unease traveled through Alex. It wasn't like Penny to miss the morning gathering.

"I suppose we'll go ahead, then." William took the Bible from under his arm. "This morning I'll be reading from Psalm Ninety-One." He flipped through the pages, then began reading. " 'He that dwelleth in the secret place of the most High shall abide under the shadow of the Almighty. I will say of the LORD, He is my refuge and my fortress: my God; in him will I trust. Surely he shall deliver thee from the snare of the fowler, and from the noisome pestilence. He shall cover thee with his feathers, and under his wings shalt thou trust.' "

Footsteps sounded on the servants' stairs, and the door opened. Mr. McTavish stepped into the great hall. "Excuse me, sir, but I need to speak to you."

"Come in." William motioned him forward.

"There's been an escape from the prison camp."

Lydia gasped and grabbed Helen's arm. Mrs. Dalton pursed her lips and sent her a stern look.

"Not to worry." Mr. McTavish glanced Lydia's way, then turned back to William. "The prison-camp commander sent out search parties earlier this morning. He asked me to inform you that two guards have been assigned to patrol the estate."

William nodded, concern shadowing his eyes.

"How many men escaped?" Lydia asked in a hushed, trembling voice.

"Just one. Schultz is his name, Siegfried Schultz. He was one of the fellows who worked here in the gardens."

Alex tensed. He didn't like the sound of that. He turned to William. "I want to find Penny and make sure she's all right. I'll go outside and check the gardens."

Andrew stepped forward. "I want to go with Alex."

"So do we!" Donald, Tom, and Jack circled around Alex.

William closed the Bible. "I don't think Alex needs—"

"It's all right, sir. I could use four strong lads right now." With the help of the boys, he could make a thorough search of the gardens.

"Very well." William placed his hand on Andrew's shoulder, then looked at the other boys. "Stay together, and listen to Lieutenant Goodwin. This is no time for games or to wander off on your own. Do you understand?"

"Yes, sir," the boys' answers echoed around the group.

William looked across at the housekeeper. "Mrs. Dalton, will you and the maids search the house for Miss Penny?"

"Yes, sir." The housekeeper and maids scurried off.

"Come with me." Alex led the boys out the front door, and they set off around the side of the house. "Keep your eyes open."

The boys hurried along, scanning the lawns and parkland as they strode down the path with Alex.

Had Penny simply lost track of time, or had something else happened? He set his jaw and quickened his pace, praying he'd find her in the garden and be able to put everyone's mind at ease.

He passed under the archway and followed the gravel path. Brick walls enclosed the garden on three sides, with the greenhouse creating the fourth wall. The plants and flowers were no more than three or four feet high, giving Alex a clear view of the entire area.

One sweeping gaze told him Penny was not here.

"Maybe she's in the greenhouse." Andrew pointed to the long glass building on their left.

"Let's check." Alex hustled down the path, with the boys close behind. They quickly searched the length of the greenhouse, looking under the shelves and out the rear door, but there was no sign of Penny.

Alex stepped out of the greenhouse and scanned the garden once more. All was quiet. Nothing seemed amiss, but he couldn't shake off the feeling that something was wrong.

"Let's look on the terraces and west lawn." Alex followed the path and passed under the archway. He glanced to the right—

A door stood slightly ajar.

He turned to Andrew. "What's in here?"

"Garden tools."

Alex pushed open the door, and his breath hitched in his chest. Several broken pots lay shattered on the floor.

Andrew stepped up behind him. "That's not right."

Alex's gaze darted around the room as he stepped inside. Large tools hung neatly on the wall, and smaller hand tools filled a few crates on the floor. Everything seemed to be in order except for the broken clay pots and a pair of garden clippers left on the potting bench.

"Look!" Donald stepped past Andrew and Alex. He knelt and touched a dark, wet spot on the floor

When he lifted his hand, the end of his finger was stained red.

Fearful questions tumbled through Alex's mind. Had a gardener cut his hand trying to clean up the broken pots, or had something more sinister happened here? "Let's head back to the house."

"But we've got to find Penny." Andrew's wide-eyed gaze darted around the room.

"She's not here. Let's go." Alex ushered the boys out the door and hustled them down the path, trying to make sense of what he'd seen.

Was that Penny's blood on the floor?

He clenched his jaw and kept moving. They rounded the corner of the house, and he spotted Julia and her father standing outside the front door. Alex told the boys to wait by the steps, and he joined Julia and Dr. Foster. "Did you find Penny in the house?"

Julia shook her head, lines creasing her forehead. "No. They've looked everywhere."

"There's no sign of her in the garden or the greenhouse, but we found blood on the floor in the tool room."

"Blood?" Julia's eyes widened, and she darted a glance at her father.

"Not a lot, but it's fresh." Alex kept his voice calm, but his mind and heart raced ahead. "Would anyone else be working in the tool room at this time of morning?"

"I don't believe so. Not yet."

"We need to alert the authorities." Dr. Foster's serious tone matched his expression.

Alex nodded and turned to Julia. "Where is William?"

"He went with Mr. McTavish to search the south parkland." Julia looked in that direction.

Alex followed her gaze, but he didn't see the men. There was no time to waste. No matter whose blood was spilled on the tool room floor, Penny was missing, and there was a dangerous man on the loose. "I'll search the area east of the house and check the stables."

Dr. Foster nodded. "Jon and I can take a look north of the house, and then search west out to the road."

Julia laid her hand on her father's arm. "I'll have Mr. Lawrence send word to the police in Fulton and the camp and ask the other men on staff to join the search."

"I'll get Jon." Dr. Foster hurried inside.

Alex glanced at the boys and then at Julia. "If it's all right with you, I'd like to take the boys."

"Are you sure?"

"Yes, they have better eyesight than I do."

"All right, but please be careful." Julia stepped down and touched Andrew's arm. She looked back at Alex. "I'll be praying."

Alex gave a quick nod, then turned to the boys. "Wait here. I'll be right back." He dashed inside, collected his revolver from his room, and returned to the front entrance, where he met the boys. As they set off down the path, Julia's promise to pray stirred his thoughts. She was right. God's help and guidance were what they needed most.

Please watch over Penny and protect her wherever she is right now. Help us find her and bring her home again.

Twenty-Five

Penny tried to lean as far forward in the saddle as she could, but Siegfried sat directly behind her, his stale breath washing over her cheek and turning her stomach. They'd been riding for at least an hour, and the horse's steady trot jarred her throbbing arm.

The misty fog had lifted. Sunlight filtered through the golden trees shading the old road. They'd left Highland property, passed through the corner of Aunt Louisa's estate, and were now on Carter-Wilson property, not far from Westridge Manor.

She'd ridden down this road many times but had rarely come this far. And with each mile they traveled away from Highland, fear tightened its grip on her heart.

Surely by now someone realized she was missing and had started the search.

Alex's image flashed into her mind, and a powerful ache rose in her chest. If only they'd had more time to talk last night. There was so much more she wanted to say. No matter how he felt about his injuries or his lack of prospects for the future, she believed the best days of his life were still ahead, and she wanted to spend those days with him.

Please, Lord, give me a chance to see him again and tell him how much he means to me.

They came to a dip in the road. Siegfried jerked the horse to the left around a large muddy hole. The horse shied back and almost lost his footing. Siegfried cursed under his breath.

Penny turned her face away. What kind of man treated a horse this way? He'd been so rough, it was a wonder Ebony hadn't thrown them off. "You know you could go much faster if you'd leave me here. You'd be miles away before I ever reached home."

"And have you tell everyone which way I've gone? I don't think so."

She tried to push down her fear and focus her thoughts. If he wasn't going to let her go, then she had to find a way to slow him down and give the searchers time to catch up.

Just then, she heard rushing water in the distance. She searched through the trees as they continued down the road, and a small stream came into view. She lifted her chin and pointed toward it. "Could we stop for a moment? I'm sure the horse would like a drink, and so would I."

Siegfried shifted in the saddle, obviously debating her request, then he tugged on the reins and turned the horse aside. When they'd almost reached the edge of the stream, he dismounted and held his hand up for her.

She hesitated, hating the thought of accepting his help, but with her hands tied, she had no choice. She leaned toward him, and he helped her down. His shoulder bumped her wounded arm as her feet touched the ground. She clamped her jaw, suddenly lightheaded.

She hadn't eaten since last night, and even then, she'd been so excited about the birth of the twins she'd barely touched her dinner. She looked down at her arm and caught her bottom lip between her teeth. Blood stained the sleeve of her dress and shawl. She looked away before it made her head swim even worse.

He scowled. "You ought to wrap something around your arm and stop that bleeding."

If his tone had been kinder, she might have taken some comfort from his words, but he only seemed concerned she might keel over and cause him a bigger problem. "If you would untie my hands, I could."

He narrowed his eyes and studied her a moment, then moved toward her. "Don't try anything." He loosened the knot and untied the rope around her wrists. Taking hold of the reins, he led the horse to the stream.

She rubbed her chafed wrists, walked a few steps away, and leaned against a large rock by the stream. Her shawl was tightly knit, and it would be impossible to tear, but her dress was made of a softly woven coral fabric. She lifted the hem and tore off a long strip.

An idea flashed into her mind, and she carefully ripped a few small pieces from the end of the strip and tucked them up her sleeve. Then she wrapped the strip around her arm and tied it off by pulling one end of the fabric with her teeth. It was not the neatest bandage, but it should stop the bleeding.

"If you want a drink, get it now." Siegfried motioned toward the stream.

She sent him a cool look, then knelt and dipped in her hand. She rinsed off the blood, cupped her fingers, and lifted her hand to her mouth. Cool water soothed her dry throat. She rose and walked back toward the horse.

Siegfried helped her remount, then climbed up behind her, settling in closer than before. He leaned toward her. "You smell nice."

She tensed and tried to lean away, but it was no use.

He chuckled, lifted the reins, and clicked to the horse. "Let's go."

As Siegfried looked to the left, Penny slipped a small piece of coral fabric from her sleeve and dropped it on the muddy road.

Alex and the boys strode into the stable. "Search the stalls. Look for anything out of place or suspicious."

Andrew and Donald started down the left side, while Jack and Tom ducked into the first stall on the right.

The dim light made it difficult for Alex to see much of anything. He glanced toward the far end of the stable. If he opened that big sliding door, it might give him the light he needed. He jogged the length of the stable and pushed it open, thankful he no longer needed the sling and had regained some strength in his arm.

A boy of about sixteen walked up the road toward the stables. Alex had seen him working in the stables before. He wore gray breeches with suspenders over a white shirt and a brown tweed cap. "Can I help you, sir?"

Alex walked out of the stable to meet him. "I'm Lieutenant Goodwin, a guest of the Ramseys'."

"I'm Chester Simms, one of the grooms."

Andrew dashed out of the stable, followed by the other three boys. "Did you hear about the prisoner who escaped from the camp?"

Chester gave an eager nod. "Mr. McTavish came by the farm before breakfast. He said the man—"

Alex lifted his hand. "Hold on, Chester. Have you seen Miss Penny this morning?"

"Yes, sir. She rode out first thing, just as I was coming up the road."

Alex's pulse surged. "Which way did she go?"

Chester pointed over his shoulder. "She took the eastern drive, up through the woods."

Alex scanned the road. Why would Penny take an early morning ride without telling anyone, then skip the family gathering and breakfast? It didn't make sense. He shifted his gaze back to Chester. "Was she alone?"

A slight grin lifted one side of his mouth. "No, sir. She was riding double with her beau."

Alex's stomach clenched. "There was a man with her?"

"Yes, sir. I heard she had a beau, but it's strange . . ." Chester's grin faded. "She usually rides Princess, but this time she took Sir William's horse, Ebony."

Andrew shot a glance at Alex. "That doesn't sound right."

"No, it doesn't." He had no description of the escaped prisoner, and no way of knowing if the man riding with Penny was that man, but it was the only answer that made sense. He focused on Chester again. "You say they came out this way?"

"Yes, sir. I was just coming in when I saw them heading off into the trees."

"Two riders on one horse would make a heavy set of prints." Alex scanned the soft, muddy road.

Andrew took a few steps out and did the same. "Look at these."

Alex knelt and examined the deep set of hoofprints. "That horseshoe must have a ding in the side." He pointed out the indentation on the rear left hoofprint.

Andrew leaned closer. "Yes, I see it."

That was enough for Alex. He stood. "Chester, will you help us saddle some horses?"

"Yes, sir." Chester strode into the stable with Andrew.

Tom kicked the dirt, then looked up at Alex. "I don't know how to ride."

"Me neither," Jack mumbled, his shoulders sagging.

"What about you, Donald?"

He gave a half shrug. "I've ridden a few times."

Alex motioned toward the stables. "Then I want you to come with me."

"Sure." Donald gave an eager nod.

Alex turned to the other boys. "Jack, you and Tom run back to the house. Tell Lady Julia what Chester said and that Andrew, Donald, and I are going to ride out and follow Miss Penny's tracks. Do you understand?"

The boys took off running. Alex would send Chester to the house to confirm the story and urge the other men to follow their trail as soon as the groom finished helping them saddle the horses.

Alex scanned the road leading into the woods

again. The knot that had formed in his stomach twisted tighter. Penny was out there somewhere in the company of a dangerous, desperate man. She had to be frightened and praying someone would discover she was missing and come after her.

He forced his anxious thoughts into submission and strode back into the stable. Many times at St. Pol, he'd taken off knowing he'd face the enemy and possibly his own death. But none of that had frightened him as much as the thought of Penny in danger.

No matter what it took, he would find Penny and make sure she was safe—then he'd wrap her in his arms and never let her go again.

Penny glanced up at the sky. How long had they been riding? The sun was almost directly over-head, so it must have been at least three hours. Her muscles ached from trying to hold herself away from Siegfried yet stay in the saddle, and her arm continued to throb.

Siegfried trotted Ebony over a small wooden bridge that crossed a rocky stream. He glanced to the left, looking at the water.

Penny carefully slipped the last bit of fabric from her sleeve and dropped it to the ground.

Siegfried's gaze flicked her way, and he jerked the horse to a stop. "What are you doing?"

She froze, her heart thumping so loudly she was certain he'd hear it. "Nothing."

"Don't lie to me!" He swung the horse around, jumped down from the saddle, and snatched the piece of fabric from the ground. "How many of these have you dropped?"

She clamped her mouth tight and turned her face away.

"Fine!" He grabbed hold of her arm and pulled her down off the horse.

Pain shot through her arm. She clenched her teeth and blinked away her tears.

"I should've just tied you up and left you back at that stream," he muttered. Then he grabbed the rope from the saddle and tied one end around her wrists and the other to the saddle horn. "Go on!" He waved his hand down the road. "You can walk beside the horse." He climbed back up on Ebony and took the reins.

Penny's face flushed and her empty stomach surged.

They'd only gone a few yards when Siegfried jerked the horse to the left and started down a small trail through the trees.

Panic shot through Penny. "Where are you going?"

"Off this road." He pulled on the rope, tugging her forward.

Penny's hopes plummeted. How would anyone ever find her now? Following their trail on the muddy road wouldn't be too difficult, but this path was covered with moss and dead leaves. She scuffed her feet, trying to leave marks in the moss, but she didn't want to be too obvious and stir Siegfried's anger again. When he turned to look the other way, she broke a small branch and kicked up a piece of moss.

A few minutes later an old stone cottage came into view through the trees. Penny's first thought was that someone might see them and help her, but as they came closer, she saw the two front windows were broken and weeds and vines cluttered the yard around the cottage.

Siegfried's face looked set in stone as he rode around to the back of the cottage. More weeds and broken windows confirmed that the property was deserted. He climbed down and looped Ebony's reins around a low branch, then untied the rope from the saddle.

A terrorizing chill traveled through Penny. Riding out in the open with this man was frightening enough. She didn't even want to consider the possibility of going into that abandoned cottage with him.

"Let's go." He grabbed the rope and started around the cottage.

She planted her feet, and the slack rope tightened

Siegfried spun around. His eyes flashed and he jerked the rope. "You'll do as I say."

"I'm not going in there."

He whipped the knife from his belt and pointed it at her. "Yes, you are!"

• • •

Alex rubbed the small piece of coral fabric between his fingers and searched the road ahead. Surely there was another. Donald spotted the first one at the side of the road about an hour out. Alex thought he remembered Penny wearing a dress that color the day she brought the children to Northcote to sing for the men, and it gave him hope they were on the right trail.

Andrew found the second piece about thirty minutes later, and a surge of gratitude flowed through Alex. Penny was marking the trail and praying someone would follow and find her.

Watch over her, Lord. Lead us on the right path.

He glanced down at the fabric, and his shoulders tensed. "Keep your eyes on those hoofprints," he called, then urged his horse forward at a quick trot.

Donald rode slightly ahead, with Alex following on his left and Andrew on his right, their gazes focused on the ground. Donald slowed and led his horse to the side of the road.

Andrew trotted ahead and then circled back. "The tracks stop here."

Alex reined in his horse and scanned the woods. A breeze ruffled the leaves overhead, and a bird called from the trees on his left. He turned and noticed a small moss-covered path leading off through the woods.

"Let's check that trail." He lifted the reins and

moved ahead, ducking under a low branch. Andrew and Donald fell in line behind him. He searched the thick moss covering the path, but he saw nothing to mark Penny's trail.

"Look up there." Andrew pointed down the path ahead.

Alex rode closer. A clump of moss was turned over, and the dirt beneath it was still moist and dark brown. They all climbed down and examined the chunk of moss and the area around it. A swipe of mud coated the moss just beyond the overturned moss.

"Let's walk a bit and see if we can find anything else."

They continued down the path and found two more clumps of moss turned over and a few broken branches. Could it be a coincidence? They had no other lead to follow, so they pressed on.

About five minutes down the path, an old stone building came into view. It looked like an abandoned hunting lodge or a woodsman's cottage.

Alex held out his hand and motioned the boys to stop. He turned and lowered his voice. "Stay here. Keep the horses quiet." He handed his reins to Andrew.

"We want to go with you," Andrew whispered and Donald added his eager nod.

"Let me check things out. Keep watch here. I'll signal when I want you to come."

Andrew's brow creased, but he gave a reluctant nod. Donald did the same.

Alex crept through the trees, all his senses on alert. He didn't hear any sounds in the lodge, and no smoke rose from the chimney. He circled around, staying about twenty yards out, hidden in the undergrowth. When he reached the far side, his heart lurched. A large black horse stood tied to a tree not far from the back of the lodge. The horse looked up at Alex, then lowered his head and munched on the grass at his feet.

With careful, quiet steps, Alex moved closer to the back of the lodge. A thick tangle of vines climbed the gray stones, partially covering the small window. The pane was broken, and jagged glass still hung from the top. He slipped to the side of the window, then leaned over and looked inside.

His breath choked off, and he gripped the vine.

Penny sat in an old wooden chair, a rope around her waist and wrists and her eyes fixed on the man who stood with his back to the window. Siegfried Schultz. It had to be. Penny's face was pale, and her auburn hair had come loose and flowed down over her shoulders. She watched Schultz with a tense, guarded expression.

The man reached out and fingered a strand of her hair. "I always liked women with red hair."

Boiling anger surged though Alex. He wanted break through that window and choke those words from the man's throat. He blinked hard. *Stay focused!* He couldn't let anger control him. He had to get Penny out of there.

Now.

He pulled his revolver from his belt and dashed around to the front of the house. "Siegfried Schultz! This is Lieutenant Goodwin. You have no way of escape. Surrender Miss Ramsey and come out with your hands in the air!"

A clatter sounded in the house, and a second later Siegfried looked out the broken front window.

Alex aimed toward the window, but Schultz dodged back, shouting curses.

Alex held the revolver steady. A second ticked past, then another. The front door flew open and banged on the wall behind. Schultz stepped out, holding Penny in front of him, a knife to her throat. "Throw down your gun, Lieutenant, unless you want to see me use this knife on her again."

Again? Alex scanned Penny, seeing her torn hem, the red-stained fabric wrapped around her arm. Her wide blue eyes shimmered with a mix of fear and longing that hit him so hard he could barely stand his ground. He clenched his jaw, fighting to stay in control.

"I said, throw down your gun!"

"Let Miss Ramsey go. I won't stop you from leaving."

Schultz barked out a laugh. "You think I'm

480

fool? She's my ticket out of here." He took a step to the side, pulling Penny with him.

"Wait!" Alex stepped forward. "You can have the gun. I'll go with you. Just let Miss Ramsey go."

A fiendish grin slipped across Schultz's face. "Now, why would I want to take you when I have a pretty lady like this?"

A sickening wave rose in Alex's throat. "You'd have the gun, a hostage, and an extra horse."

Schultz narrowed his eyes, studying Alex. "All right. I'll make a trade. Put the gun down on the ground."

Would Schultz truly accept his offer to go with him in exchange for Penny, or was this a trick?

Penny's eyes widened and darted to the side. What had she seen? Was it Andrew or Donald? He didn't dare look or he might alert Schultz that the boys were nearby.

"Let Miss Ramsey go first." Alex turned the gun around and held it out.

"No! You drop the gun now, or I'll give her another taste of this knife."

Alex took two steps forward and lowered the gun to the ground. Schultz loosened his hold on Penny and reached down to pick up the revolver.

This was his chance. Alex shot a swift hard kick toward Schultz's hand and knocked the knife away.

Schultz cried out and stumbled back. Penny

jerked away from the man, and Alex lunged and grabbed the gun off the ground.

Andrew yelled as he ran forward and jumped on Schultz's back. Donald kicked the knife farther away and piled on top of Schultz from the other direction. The boys wrestled him to the ground.

Alex snagged the knife, rushed to Penny, and guided her a few feet away from Schultz and the boys. "Did he hurt you?"

"Just my arm." She trembled as she looked up at him, but strength shone in her beautiful blue eyes.

He untied her wrists, his anger flaring when he saw the red, raw skin beneath.

"Ow! Get these kids off me!"

Alex shifted his gaze from Penny to Schultz and the boys.

Andrew knelt on Schultz's back, wearing a broad grin as he held him down. "Don't worry. We've got him!"

"We sure do." Donald wore a matching grin as he sat on the man's legs.

"Good job, boys. Hold him right there." Alex turned to Penny. "Are you sure you're all right?" He looked her over again.

She sent him a tremulous smile. "I am now."

He slipped his arms around her and pulled her toward him. She melted against him and rested her face against his chest. He held her for moment, relief flooding through him.

She was safe. He hadn't lost her.

It took a moment for his breathing to calm, then he stepped back.

She leaned toward him again and kissed his cheek. "Thank you for coming after me."

Alex's eyes burned and he shook his head, his throat so tight he could barely push out his voice. "You're never going to get rid of me."

She laughed softly, then sniffed and smiled as she slipped her hand into his. "Whatever made you think I'd want to?"

Twenty-Six

Lydia rested her chin on her hand and gazed out the window in the servants' hall. The golden moon was so big it looked like a dinner plate, rising above the dark outline of the trees. What a day this had been. Thank heaven Miss Penny was home and Siegfried Schultz was behind bars.

Helen walked in and sat down on the bench beside her. "Are you writing to Marius?"

Lydia nodded and glanced down at the letter she'd just started. "I want to tell him everything that happened."

Helen sent Lydia a wry smile. "That's going to be a long letter."

"I suppose so, but he needs to know what Siegfried did and how things turned out for him."

Helen shook her head. "That man is in a lot

of trouble. I wouldn't want to be in his shoes."

"Yes, they'll probably lock him up for a long time, at least until the war is over."

A slight frown creased Helen's forehead. "How long do you think that will be?"

"I don't know. It could be months or maybe even years before the fighting ends. But however long it is, I'll be writing to Marius and waiting for him."

Helen laid her hand over Lydia's. "Are you sure about that?"

"Yes, very sure."

"Then I'm happy for you, and I'll pray it won't be long."

"Thank you." Lydia leaned toward Helen and gave her a hug. "It's a comfort having you and Emily here. I know it's not been easy for you . . . but I'm grateful."

"I'm the one who should be thanking you. Without your help, and Dr. Jon's and Mrs. Kate's who knows where Emily and I would be."

Lydia smiled. Thank heaven Helen finally seemed to realize how blessed she was for the kindness the Fosters and Ramseys had shown her. "They've given us both a good place to live and a chance to learn things that will help us step up in the world."

"You think so?" Helen cocked her head.

"Of course. And I'm not just talking about cleaning or caring for children. I'm thinking of t way they love and care for each other. Someday we'll have our own homes and families, and we'll remember that."

"Now that's a fine dream." Helen gazed toward the window with a smile.

The servants' bell rang in the hall, and Lydia started to rise.

Helen laid her hand on Lydia's again. "You stay and finish your letter to Marius. I'll go up."

Warmth rose and filled Lydia's chest. "Thank you, Helen."

"You're a dear sister, and I owe you more than I can say." Helen's eyes glistened, and she sent Lydia a smile, then she walked out to answer the bell.

Lydia watched her sister go, thankfulness filling her heart again. Then she picked up her pen to continue her letter to Marius.

Flames leaped and crackled in the fireplace, casting a cozy glow around the drawing room at Highland. Penny released a soft sigh and leaned back on the settee next to Alex. He'd barely left her side since they'd returned to the house late that afternoon. He'd stayed with her when Dr. Foster treated her injured arm and later held her and when the police arrived and questioned her.

She'd never forget what Alex had done for her today. A powerful wave of love and gratitude flooded her heart, then her gaze traveled around the room, taking in each one gathered there.

They all meant so much to her.

William and Julia sat close together near the fireplace, their hands entwined. Julia wore a peaceful, contented smile as she looked across the room at Jon and Kate and the twins. Her eyes reflected her happiness for them and the hope that she would soon hold a baby of her own. William leaned toward Julia and whispered something to her. Julia smiled and nodded.

Across the room, Jon sat next to Kate, holding their infant son, looking completely at ease, while Kate held their little daughter. Since the arrival of the twins, Jon had been eager to help Kate. He had always been a kind and caring husband and a wonderful father to the children they had taken in. Penny felt certain the twins would grow up surrounded by love and be a wonderful addition to their family.

Penny's gaze traveled to Dr. and Mrs. Foster, seated next to Jon and Kate. They watched their son and daughter-in-law hold the twins, obviously delighted to be grandparents and treasuring these special moments.

Jon looked up. "We've decided on names for the babies." He turned to Kate. "Why don't you tell them, my dear?"

Kate looked down at their daughter with tender expression. "This is Eden Penelope Foster after our mother and my dear sister."

Penny lifted her hand to her heart. "That's wonderful. I'm so pleased."

Alex squeezed her hand, and they exchanged smiles.

"We're so thankful for your safe return," Kate said, "and I know little Eden will enjoy a very special relationship with her aunt Penny."

Penny nodded, her throat too tight to speak.

Kate glanced at the other twin. "We named our son Phillip Jonathan Foster." She looked at her father-in-law, gratitude glowing in her eyes. "We wanted to name him after you, because you mean so much to both of us."

"My goodness . . . I don't know what to say." Dr. Foster smiled and clasped his wife's hand. "Thank you both. That's quite an honor."

"Well, I'm glad you finally named them." Aunt Agatha sniffed and sent the babies a cautious look of interest. "They seem to be quite healthy from all the cries I've heard today."

Sarah lifted her hand to cover her smile. Then she cleared her throat and lowered her hand. "They are wonderfully healthy. We're certainly grateful for that."

Penny's heart felt full to overflowing. What a gift to be part of a family where love and faith bound them together with strong and lasting ties that could not be broken.

She looked toward the other side of the room where Andrew, Donald, and the children sat huddled together. The two older boys shared the piano bench as they took turns retelling the story of following Penny's trail and capturing Siegfried Schultz.

Penny turned toward Alex and lowered her voice. "It looks as though Andrew and Donald's rivalry is finally fading."

Alex studied them a moment. "I think their teaming up today to accomplish something so important was the final step in bridging that gap."

"Do you think it will last?"

"I hope so." He glanced toward the window, then leaned closer until his shoulder touched hers. "There's a beautiful moon out tonight. Would you like to go out on the veranda and take a look?"

A delightful shiver raced along her arms. "That sounds lovely."

He rose and offered her his hand, and they quietly slipped out the side door.

Moonlight bathed the parkland in silvery light, and a thousand stars winked back at them from a blue-velvet sky.

"It's beautiful," she said softly.

He took her hand again, lifted it to his lips, and kissed her fingers. "Yes, beautiful." But his gaze rested on Penny, rather than the night sky.

Her gaze traveled over his face, and the scar and eye patch faded from view. His handsome features were striking and seemed even more s as she contemplated the man he was inside, the man she'd grown to love.

He shifted away and leaned on the balustrade.

"Please don't turn away, Alex."

He gave an embarrassed chuckle, but she could hear the pain behind it. "I know what I look like now."

She leaned closer and looked up at him. "You are the most handsome man in the world to me."

His brow furrowed, and he shook his head. "You don't have to say that."

"It's true. When I see your scars, they remind me of how brave you are and how far you were willing to go to protect and defend those you love . . . including me and my family."

A muscle in his jaw flickered, and he stared across the parkland.

"And today, you proved your bravery again."

"The boys were the ones who tackled Schultz and took him down, not me."

"Yes, but you searched for me until you found me, and you were willing to take my place so I could go free, and that's . . . just the most amazing example of love I've ever seen." Her voice choked off, and she tightened her hold on his hand. "Thank you, Alex."

He turned toward her. The moonlight highlighted his dark eyebrows and strong jaw. "I'd do anything to protect you."

"I know you would, and that's why I love you."

She swallowed and held his gaze. "I know it's not ladylike or proper for me to be the first one to say it, but I do love you, Alex Goodwin, and there is nothing you can say that will talk me out of it."

He stilled, looking into her eyes. "You love me?"

"Yes, so very much! And I can't believe you're making me say it first."

He grinned, a teasing light flickering in his eye. "Well, that's good news."

He was dear to her, so very dear. She reached up and gently ran her finger over the scar crossing his face. "Every time I see this, I'll remember today and the way you rescued me."

His teasing smile faded, and a look of tenderness filled his face. "This morning, when I realized you were missing and Schultz had probably kidnapped you, it nearly killed me." He took both her hands in his. "I don't know what I'd do if anything happened to you."

His sweet words melted her heart.

"I love you, Penny, so very much."

Joyful warmth curled through her.

"You're kind and caring, and you never gave up on me, even when I was at my lowest and pushing everyone away." His smile returned. "You pushed back, and you helped me see my life could still have meaning and purpose. Your faith in God and in me made me believe in a future with hope and possibilities, and there's no one I rather share that future with than you." He stopped and pulled in a deep breath. "Will you . . ." A slight tremor shook his voice. He clasped her hands more tightly. "Would you do me the honor of becoming my wife?"

She pulled in a soft gasp. "Really?"

"Yes." His smile spread wider. "I've spoken to William, and he's in favor of it."

"Oh, Alex! Yes!" Her heart felt like it would burst with joy, and she threw her arms around his neck.

He wrapped her in his embrace, then kissed her tenderly, sealing his words with a promise.

On the twenty-third of October, Alex stood in the doorway to the grand ballroom at Buckingham Palace and glanced over his shoulder. Twenty-seven men lined up behind him, waiting to receive medals at the investiture ceremony.

He brushed his hand down his sleeve. Penny had insisted he order a new uniform so he'd look his best. She'd even helped him with his tie this morning. He smiled at the memory, then glanced down at his jacket to make sure everything was still in order.

The military band marched in, playing the first notes of the British national anthem, "God Save the King." The audience rose to their feet and sang along.

By the time they reached the second verse,

Alex's throat grew tight, but he sang on, lifting the song as a prayer for his country.

"O Lord and God arise,
Scatter his enemies
And make them fall.
Confound their politics,
Frustrate their knavish tricks,
On Thee our hopes we fix.
God save the King."

He looked to the right as he sang the final verse, scanning the rows of guests standing in the ballroom. He'd been allowed to invite only three people, so he'd chosen Penny, Jon, and his sister, Lindy. He spotted them in the front row, near the center aisle.

Penny had encouraged him to contact his mother and stepfather, explain the limit on the number of guests, and ask if he and Penny might visit them after the ceremony. His mother replied, saying she'd welcome their visit. He had no idea if he'd see his stepfather, but having Penny at his side would ease the situation. It was time to let go of the past and rebuild his relationship with his mother and stepfather, as much as possible.

As though Penny sensed his gaze, she looked his way and smiled. He returned the same, proud and grateful she was with him today.

The song ended, the crowd applauded, and a

eyes focused on King George V as he walked forward and faced the audience. The Lord Chamberlain, on the King's right, lifted a note card and glanced toward the door.

That was Alex's signal. He stepped out and strode toward the King.

"Lieutenant Alexander Goodwin of the Royal Naval Air Service, Squadron One, is awarded the Victoria Cross for most conspicuous acts of bravery, valor, and self-sacrifice, as well as extreme devotion to duty in the presence of the enemy." The Lord Chamberlain's voice rang out across the ballroom.

Alex turned and faced the King, then lifted his hand in a brisk salute.

The King studied Alex for a moment, his gaze flicking to the eye patch and scars.

Alex didn't flinch but held his gaze steady.

The King's mouth firmed, and admiration shone in his eyes. "We are grateful for your sacrifice and service, Lieutenant Goodwin, and we are proud to award you the Victoria Cross."

The King took the medal from the attendant at his side and held it up. The center of the bronze cross was emblazoned with a crown and lion. The words *For Valour* formed a semicircle beneath the central crown.

Alex stood taller as the King pinned the medal to his chest. "Thank you, Your Majesty."

The King leaned forward. "I understand we owe

you another debt of gratitude for capturing an escaped German prisoner and rescuing a young woman he held hostage."

Alex hesitated, surprised that news had reached the King. "Yes, Your Majesty, I took part in the rescue, along with two very fine young men."

"Well done, Lieutenant."

Alex smiled. "The woman is my fiancée." He glanced over his shoulder. "She's seated in the front row, fourth from the center on the left of the aisle."

The King looked that way and nodded. "Excellent!"

Alex started to step back.

"One moment, Lieutenant."

Alex stopped and met the King's gaze.

"When you're able, I hope you'll accept a position at Upavon and help train future pilots for the RNAS."

Alex stared at the King for a moment, then quickly recovered. "I'd be honored, Your Majesty."

"Very good." The King nodded, then looked toward the doorway, where the next man waited.

Alex saluted once more and backed away, his heart soaring. The King's invitation meant he would not only be able to do his part to help win the war but also have a way to support a wife and family. Now he and Penny could speak to William and Julia and set a wedding date.

He smiled at Penny as he approached, eager t

tell her the news, but he had to sit in a special section on the side until the ceremony was finished.

She sent him a quizzical smile, obviously eager to speak to him as well.

A half hour later, the band struck up a lively march, and everyone rose to their feet. The program concluded, and Alex made his way through the crowd, searching for Penny. Several people stopped to congratulate him. He appreciated their kind comments and handshakes, but he cut the conversations short and continued making his way across the ballroom.

"Alex!" Penny waved her hand and moved through the crowd toward him. Jon and Lindy followed close behind.

Finally, he clasped her hand and pulled her close to his side.

She smiled up at him, her eyes glowing. "I'm so very proud of you!" She stood on tiptoe and kissed his cheek.

He grinned. "Thank you."

Jon shook his hand. "Congratulations, Alex. It couldn't happen to a finer fellow."

Lindy smiled and took his arm on the other side. "It looked like you and the King had quite a conversation."

"Yes"—Jon sent him a questioning look—"he poke to you much longer than anyone else. What id he say?"

Alex was about to burst with the good news

about the position at Upavon, but he kept it back a moment more. "He heard I helped capture Siegfried Schultz and rescue Penny."

Penny's eyes widened. "He did?"

"Yes, he seemed quite impressed."

Jon grinned. "As he should be."

Alex turned to Penny. "I pointed you out and told him you were my fiancée."

Penny lifted her hand to her chest. "Really?"

"Yes, and he said, 'Excellent!'" Alex did his best imitation of the King's tone and expression.

They all laughed. Then Alex turned to Penny and took her hand. "But the best news is, he asked me to return to Upavon as a flight instructor."

Penny gasped. "Oh, Alex, that's wonderful!"

"Good show!" Jon clapped his hand on Alex's shoulder. "Now we're sure to gain the victory."

Alex gave a firm nod. "You can be sure I'll do everything I can to see that we do."

Lindy glanced around the ballroom. "I think the crowd has cleared enough for us to make our way outside."

"Yes, we should go." Penny slipped her arm through his and looked up at him with a proud, loving gaze.

He was a blessed man. He'd come through one of the most amazing air battles of the war and lived to tell the story. Now he would use those experiences to train others to finish the job he'd started.

But best of all, he fully intended to take the lessons from the past and the wisdom and encouragement of his growing faith and friendships to build a strong and secure future with the woman he loved. With God's help, that's what he would do.

With renewed confidence lifting his spirit, he walked out of the palace with Penny to greet the family and friends who had come to mean so very much to him.

<u>Epilogue</u>

May 1919

Penny clasped Alex's hand and walked up the gravel path toward St. John's Church in the village of Fulton, only a few miles from Highland Hall. The scent of freshly mowed grass drifted past, and beneath the trees at the side of the church, the first bluebells of the spring swayed in a light breeze.

She smiled up at Alex. "What a lovely day for a wedding."

"Yes, it is." He glanced up at the blue sky dotted with only a few white clouds. "Certainly different from our rainy wedding day."

Penny's heart warmed as she remembered their wedding, three years ago in March, right here at St. John's Church. "I didn't mind the rain. I was so happy we could finally be married, I didn't care about the weather."

He chuckled. "Neither did I."

"Papa!" Their two-year-old son, Charles, tugged on Alex's other hand. "Pick me up."

"All right, Charlie." Alex lifted his son into his arms. Penny reached out and smoothed the boy's wavy auburn hair, then patted his dimpled cheek. What a darling boy. She couldn't imagine loving any child more.

They walked under the arched entrance together and stepped inside the church.

Jon and Kate followed them into the narthex, bringing all their children with them. Kate held little Eden's hand. Her daughter's eyes were a striking blue, and Kate had tied a matching ribbon in her curly blond hair. Her twin brother, Phillip, had darker hair, but his eyes were the same handsome shade of blue. The whole family adored the twins, and they never lacked for playmates.

Now that the war was finally over, Kate and the children had been reunited with Jon in London. He'd resigned his position at St. George's Hospital and devoted his time to his family and the Daystar Clinic and Children's Center. Kate seemed wonderfully content in her role as Jon's wife and partner, caring for the children God had entrusted into their care.

Lucy returned for the weekend, taking a break from teachers' training to attend the wedding

Donald was with them as well, though Penny had heard he would soon start an apprenticeship with a printer in London.

Kate stepped toward Penny. "Is the family here?"

"Yes, I think we're the last to arrive." Penny glanced into the sanctuary.

William and Julia were seated on the left, a few rows back from the front. Andrew sat next to William, and Penny was surprised to see he was as tall as his father. But it made sense. He was eighteen now and preparing to start at Oxford next term.

Julia held three-year-old Mary on her lap. With her dark hair and blue-gray eyes, the young girl looked very much like her mother. Millie, who was fifteen, sat next to Julia. She was a kind sister to Mary and was growing lovelier every day.

Sarah and Clark were seated behind William and Julia. Penny smiled, thinking of the happy news they had told the family just two weeks earlier. There would be a baby joining their family this autumn.

Alex turned to Penny. "Shall we go in?"

"Would you take Charlie and find a seat for us? 'd like to wait and speak to the bride."

"All right. We'll save you a place." Alex carried heir son through the side door and took a seat in ne pew behind William and Julia.

Penny glanced around the sanctuary once more. lost of the Highland staff were present and dressed in their finest spring outfits. Mr. Lawrence, Mrs. Dalton, Chef Lagarde, Mrs. Murdock, Patrick, Ann, and the other maids filled two pews halfway back on the left side of the church. Helen was seated near the front.

The side door of the narthex opened, and Lydia stepped in with her father. She wore a shimmering, white silk wedding gown edged with pearls and lace. It was the same gown Sarah had worn on her wedding day, and it looked just as lovely on Lydia. She wore Penny's veil, and carried a small bouquet of pink and white roses grown in Highland's greenhouse and tended by Clark.

Penny crossed to meet her. "Oh, Lydia, you look beautiful."

Lydia's eyes misted as she smiled at Penny. "Thank you." She looked down at her gown. "This doesn't seem real. I feel like a princess."

"It is real, and you look just like royalty. I'm sure Marius will be very pleased."

Lydia's cheeks flushed, and she glanced toward the door to the sanctuary. "Is he here?"

"I'm sure he is." Penny stepped back and looked in the sanctuary once more.

Marius stood up front on the right, looking handsome in his black suit with a white rose pinned to his lapel.

She turned back to Lydia. "He's waiting for you at the altar."

Lydia's eyes shone. She stepped away from her father and reached for Penny's hand. "Thank you for everything, you and your family . . . giving us this wonderful chance at a new life."

"We're very happy for you and Marius, and we know you'll do an excellent job overseeing that farm." Penny looked over her shoulder. All the other guests had been seated. "I better go in." She leaned toward Lydia and kissed her cheek. "I'm praying for you, asking God to bless you and Marius with a long and happy life together."

"Thank you," Lydia whispered through her tears.

"It's time, Lydia." Her father stepped forward.

Lydia nodded and slipped her hand through his arm.

Penny took her handkerchief from her purse and dabbed her cheek and nose, then walked into the sanctuary through the side door.

Alex looked up and smiled as she slid into the pew next to him and Charlie. "Everything all right?"

"Yes, wonderfully so." She took his hand and settled in closer.

The organist began the "Wedding March," and Lydia and her father appeared at the rear door. The congregation stood, and Lydia started up the isle, proudly escorted by her father.

Penny leaned to the right to catch another glimpse of the bride as she walked past. Lydia's face glowed, her gaze fixed on Marius, who watched her with a look of loving amazement.

Penny sniffed and wiped a tear from her cheek. So many blessings had been poured out on them all. She'd seen God work in some amazing ways in the last few years, protecting them through the war, healing and restoring what had been lost, and giving new meaning to all they had endured.

He had been their refuge and strength, proving Himself faithful again and again as they put their trust in Him. She could look back and see it all now, and that helped her trust Him for the future and all that was yet to come.

Alex slipped his hand around Penny's again as they listened to Marius and Lydia repeat their vows, promising to love and cherish each other for a lifetime.

"I'd do it again," Alex whispered and sent her a tender glance.

"So would I," she whispered back, her heart overflowing.

Soon the bells rang out from the church tower, declaring the happy news to the village and surrounding countryside. As Penny listened to the joyful sound, she sensed it not only announced the marriage of one happy couple, but also welcomed in a new season of hopes and dreams fulfilled for the Ramsey and Foster families, and for all those who called Highland Hall their home.

Readers Guide

1. World War I brought stress and many challenges to the Ramsey family and the people of England. List some of those challenges. Which challenges do you think would be most difficult for you to face? Why?

2. Patriotism was very strong in Britain during World War I. Alex and Jon were among the many people willing to make great sacrifices to help in the war effort. Why do you think the country was so united? Have you ever experienced a strong feeling of patriotism? What prompted it?

3. Penny wanted to do her part in the war effort and considered becoming a nurse or Red Cross worker. She decided instead to stay in London to help Kate and Jon with the children they had taken into their home. What do you think of her choice? In what ways do you think it helped (or not) the war effort?

4. Alex was determined to become a pilot with the Royal Naval Air Service. What were some of the challenges he had to overcome to

reach that goal? What made Alex a good pilot? How did those qualities play out in the rest of the story?

5. Penny and Alex's relationship, as well as Lydia and Marius's relationship, grew through the letters they exchanged. Do you think that is a good way for a romance to develop? Discuss a contemporary approach to romance that parallels the way Penny and Alex's relationship developed.

6. Several of the characters struggled because of being separated from those they loved: Penny and Alex, Jon and Kate, Julia and William, Siegfried and his former fiancée, Marius and his mother and sister. How did each one handle the separation? What can you learn from their positive and negative examples?

7. Marius and Siegfried had very different responses to their experiences in the detention camp. Why do you think that was true?

8. Lydia initially kept her relationship with Marius secret from everyone. Do you think that was wise? How did her choice to keep a secret impact others?

9. Alex loved Penny, but after his accident h

pulled away from her. Why did he do this? What helped him work through those issues?

10. Siegfried took great risks to break out of the camp and then kidnap Penny. Why did he think it was worth the risk?

11. Alex initially refused to accept the Victoria Cross, but later he changed his mind and took part in the ceremony. Why did he change his mind?

12. One of the spiritual themes of this story is God's faithfulness and the importance of trusting Him when we go through difficult circumstances. Describe a time in your own life when you were able to trust God to bring you through a challenging period.

Acknowledgments

I am very grateful for all those who gave their support and encouragement and provided information in the process of writing this book. Without your help, it would never have been completed!

I'd like to say thank you to the following people.

My husband, Scott, who provides great feedback and constant encouragement. Your brainstorming efforts gave me a boost and some wonderful ideas for my pilot and heroine. Your love and support allow me to follow my dreams and write the books of my heart. I will be forever grateful.

Cathy Gohlke, fellow author and dear friend, who helped me brainstorm ideas for this book while we toured England and Scotland and visited Tyntesfield, the inspiration for the setting of the Highland Hall series. I love sharing our writing journey together!

Terri Gillespie, fellow author and amazing woman of faith, who continually supports and encourages me and so many other writer friends. You are an inspiration, and I treasure our friendship!

Judy Conroy, who is the best listener and

encourager ever. I am blessed by your friendship!

Steve Laube, my literary agent, for his patience, guidance, and wise counsel. He has been a great advocate who has represented me well. I am blessed to be your client.

Shannon Marchese, Jen Peterson, Karen Ball, Laura Wright, and Rose Decaen, my gifted editors, who helped me shape the story and then polish it so readers will truly enjoy it.

Ruth Moppett of the National Trust staff at Tyntesfield, near Bristol, England, who gave us a special tour and answered all our questions in the most gracious manner. Your work is valuable, and your time with us was a real treat.

Dr. Peter Gray, lead educator for FutureLearn's "World War I: Aviation Comes of Age," an amazing online course that gave me some great information for my story.

Mary Gibson, author of *Warneford, VC*, the inspiring biography of Rex Warneford, the World War I pilot who is the inspiration for Alex Goodwin.

Ethel M. Bilbrough, in association with the Imperial War Museums, the author of *My War Diary 1914–1918*, for the inside scoop on life in London during World War I.

Kristopher Orr, the multitalented designer at WaterBrook Multnomah, and Mike Heath, of Magnus Creative, for the lovely cover design. Thanks for inviting me into the process! I love the way you captured the mood of the story and my heroine—again!

Darna Michie, owner of East Angel Harbor Hats, who created the lovely hat for our cover model to wear for the photo shoot. Your historic hat designs are the best!

Amy Haddock, Jessica Lamb, Lori Addicott, and the entire WaterBrook Multnomah team for their great work with marketing, publicity, production, and sales. You all are the best!

My children, Josh, Melinda, Melissa, Peter, Ben, Galan, Megan, and Lizzy, and my mother-in-law, Shirley, for the way you cheer me on. It's great to have a family who love and appreciate each other—and you do!

Most of all, I thank my Lord and Savior, Jesus Christ, for His wonderful grace and abundant provision in my life. I am thankful for the gifts and talents He has given me, and I hope to always use those in ways that bless Him and bring Him all the glory and honor.

About the Author

CARRIE TURANSKY has loved reading since she first visited the library as a young child and checked out a tall stack of picture books. Her love for writing began when she penned her first novel at age twelve. She is now the award-winning author of fourteen inspirational romance novels and novellas.

Carrie and her husband, Scott, who is a pastor, author, and speaker, have been married for more than thirty-six years and make their home in New Jersey. They often travel together on ministry trips and to visit their five adult children and four grandchildren. Carrie also leads the women's ministry at her church, and when she's not writing, she enjoys spending time working in her flower gardens and cooking healthy meals for friends and family.

She loves to connect with reading friends through her website, www.carrieturansky.com, and through Facebook, Pinterest, and Twitter.

Center Point Large Print
600 Brooks Road / PO Box 1
Thorndike, ME 04986-0001 USA

(207) 568-3717

US & Canada:
1 800 929-9108
www.centerpointlargeprint.com